# The man with the yellow sneakers

## An Australian novel

### (for dog lovers from 15 years)

Marion Birkenbeil

Published in agreement with IngramSpark
https://www.ingramspark.com/

This is a work of fiction. The story is set some time before 2011 and includes actual names of places such as Coolum Beach, Mount Coolum and Noosa. However, the entire plot, all characters and the 'AIRY TOES theme park' are fictional.

Interior Book Layout ©2024 BookDesignTemplates.com

A catalogue record for this book is available from the National Library of Australia

The man with the yellow sneakers / Marion Birkenbeil -- 1st edition
ISBN 9780645981841     (Paperback)
ISBN 9780645981858     (EPUB)

# THE BOOK

Life in Coolum Beach is never boring for the Kuhlmann family. Despite occasional bouts of homesickness, they enjoy living in this Australian coastal town, especially since they have found great new friends among humans and dogs. But they are horrified when somebody discovers the body of a young man in a strange outfit. Why does he have a flipper on his right foot, more than a kilometre away from the nearest beach? The victim was a seventeen-year-old vegan, committed to animal welfare and nature conservation. Why was he killed?

Coming across some creepy people, the Kuhlmanns are starting to feel a bit anxious. And somehow, they become entangled in dangerous events that are connected to the mysterious murder case.

# NOTE TO THE READERS

This book is based on the author's German book 'Der Mann mit den gelben Turnschuhen'. Marion Birkenbeil amended her original story and translated it into English. It is a crime novel about a murder case and some nasty villains, and also a story about family bonds, friendship and new love, foster dogs and other pets.

Further books revolving around the fictive 'Kuhlmanns in Coolum' are available in German and English language.

# Table of Contents

# 1 AIRY TOES

In joyful anticipation, Susan climbed onto the back seat behind Anna's and Sebastian's relatives. She was looking forward to visiting the AIRY TOES theme park that had recently opened on the Sunshine Coast. On their way to Coolum Beach, Aunt Paula was chatting away. She told Susan that the planning of the park had originally sparked some protests. Many locals had been concerned about an existing natural wetland and the native bushland within the proposed development. And indeed, some younger trees and many shrubs had to be removed to make space for new pathways and the 'climbing forest'. However, the wetland had been completely preserved, and further creeks, ponds and a small waterfall had been constructed. As far as she knew, the park should offer something for all age groups. Besides sports activities, one could simply admire the beautiful landscape and subtropical flora, and there was a small restaurant, a botanical garden with a café, a 'Garden of the Seven Senses', and much more. Aunt Paula was keen to see it! And the rather corpulent Uncle Sam seemed to be as excited as Susan, even though he had no interest in climbing at all.

Susan was a slim, sporty and bubbly girl with bright blue eyes and shoulder-length blonde hair. She was thirteen years old, rather small for her age, and lived in in the hinterland of Noosa; in the same village as Paula and Sam, the relatives of her German friends Anna and Sebastian Kuhlmann. The children had met by chance a few years earlier. And Sam had actually saved Susan from drowning once. He'd spotted her as she had been grabbing a tree trunk, holding on for dear life in a wild river during a flooding event. Susan was for ever thankful! And she hadn't hesitated one bit when Paula had invited her to come along to the new theme park in Coolum Beach.

When they arrived at the parking lot, the Kuhlmann family was already waiting for them, studying a map of the extensive park. After cheerful greetings and hugs, they all agreed to start with a hike on a barefoot path which was considered easy. They could have put their shoes in lockers near the entrance, but they packed their flip-flops and sneakers in their own daypacks. Who knows, maybe they wouldn't enjoy walking barefoot all the time?

Aunt Paula moaned softly as she laboriously took off her shoes, and she stepped rather timidly into a long, narrow pool of water that was enriched with a special healing clay. It was lukewarm and calf deep. Suspiciously she peered into the brown coloured water, inwardly worried about some hidden creatures. She hated bloodsucking leeches, for example! Uncle Sam, on the other hand, happily smeared the wet clay all over one of his knees that had caused him considerable pain lately.

The barefoot path was about two hundred metres long and divided into sections with different materials. Alternately, they walked on pebbles, over different kinds of grass, then over bark mulch, loamy soil, and sand. Most of the floors felt very pleasant to the touch, but some of them massaged the soles of their feet quite painfully. Anna squealed as she stepped onto a particularly prickly mulch.

'You are much too sensitive, Anna! Toughen up!' her brother mocked her. He was about the same age as Susan, while Anna was 16 years old. He was fairly small and skinny, with black curly hair; his sister was tall, slender and blonde.

'Foot reflexology is supposed to be very healthy, but I prefer the soft lawn,' Andy said.

Lizzie smiled. 'I'm glad the sand is cool! I once walked barefoot through the dunes in the middle of a hot summer day. Silly me! That was pure torture! I really thought my feet would burn to a crisp in the hot sand!'

Now, she skilfully hopped over a swaying wooden walkway. Aunt Paula didn't dare to check it out and took a side path that had been constructed as an easy detour. So far, they all liked this new park exceptionally well. Individual old trees and entire areas of the original old forest had been preserved, providing shade, and many young trees and shrubs had been planted. Now and then the winding path led through shallow streams and over bridges, and finally they came to the area that was marked with a higher degree of difficulty. Right at the beginning, they had to balance over a thick tree trunk.

'We can do it!' Andy said and winked at his wife.

The path became narrower and steeper and the vegetation much denser. In the distance they heard a thundering waterfall. Next to them was a gurgling creek, and after a while they had to cross it with the help of a thick rope that was attached to high posts on both banks. Uncle Sam anxiously held on to the rope with his thick hands, carefully moving over the slippery stones. A little later the path led back across the creek again, and this time they scrambled over a suspension bridge that was at least thirty meters long. Susan took several photos of the group and was amused by the outraged screaming of the adults when Sebastian deliberately made the rope bridge sway.

'Stop it, you are making us seasick!' Lizzie complained.

Aunt Paula cursed and gave Sebastian a frightening grim look. He had never seen her so angry! Uncle Sam grinned, but he became very queasy when they had to crawl on all fours through a cave that was only dimly lit. Then the light suddenly went out!

At the same moment, a gust of icy air came towards them, giving everyone goosebumps. The light came on again but flickered eerily. And now uncanny sounds came from all sides. They were plaintive and somehow unearthly, like from another world.

'What kind of noise is that?' Anna asked.

'I think the designer of this park had a vivid imagination,' Andy said and joked, 'At least there are no giant spiders or other monsters here!'

But he too breathed a sigh of relief as they strode into bright sunshine again, facing a beautiful pond with water lilies. On one side, there were gnarled paper bark trees, on the other side, tall grasses were blowing in the gentle breeze. Andy was the first to jump over the rocks that were anchored in the pond as stepping stones. Some were large and flat, others small and roundish, and some were underneath the surface of the water.

'There's a crocodile!' Sebastian yelled, and Andy almost fell into the water in shock.

'Nonsense! There are no crocodiles on the Sunshine Coast,' he grumbled annoyed.

'But there is one!' Lizzie cried cheerfully, pointing to a real-looking sculpture.

With its throat open, it was halfway out of the water, staring at them with angry eyes. Soon after, they discovered other sculptures that depicted lifelike, man-sized kangaroos, chubby wombats, cute koalas and possums. Some were fixed in trees; others were sitting in the middle of the lawn. The pathways in this area were wide and easy to access, suitable for people with prams or wheelchairs. There were also lots of seats and benches for visitors to take a rest. But they only paused to put their shoes back on and continued their walk.

Finally they arrived at the playground in the 'Garden of the Seven Senses'. It was pretty busy, full of children of all ages. Some adults rested on nicely curved benches while others explored their senses together with their kids. Gradually, Anna became impatient. She couldn't wait to explore the climbing forest! According to the brochure they'd received at the entrance of the park, they would be allowed to climb around in the trees and on special scaffolding; under the expert guidance of employees. Just like Anna, both Susan and Sebastian looked forward to swinging from tree to tree like Tarzan. It couldn't be far away as they already heard the whooping of young people.

But after another quarter of an hour, they realised that they'd missed a turnoff and gone in the wrong direction. Susan made a grimace, Sebastian's stomach growled audibly, and so Lizzie quickly suggested to take a break. After a snack, they went on. Soon they found a paved path that led in a straight line to the climbing forest. In the meantime, the crowd had increased, and Aunt Paula noticed only too late that it was not her husband but a complete stranger behind her to whom she had been talking eagerly for quite a while.

Uncle Sam was quite tired after the break. He studied his hiking map. Was there no beer garden at all? No, unfortunately not! They were still in the 'Garden of the Seven Senses', where you could see, feel, touch, smell and listen, coordinate movements, and test your balance, gravity and orientation. There were fragrant plants, unusual musical instruments, colourful objects and surfaces to touch, and a maze that seemed like a dense tangle of the aerial roots of pandanus trees. And they found more sculptures along the way. This time, they were not replicas of native animals but abstract stone figures, giant shells and farm animals, made of wood or recycled plastic. A sheep bleated miserably as soon as its horns were stroked, and an artificial chicken constantly laid eggs that rolled noisily down a tiny slide before they disappeared into a small hole with a smacking sound. Susan took many pictures and was completely thrilled.

Sebastian took off his cap and waved some air to himself. Phew, it was once again a hot, sunny day. The sky was blue and cloudless. His gaze wandered to a real bird in a tree and back to another tall sculpture. It was tied to a fence. Should this be a saddled horse? It was half reddish-brown, half blue-turquoise. It had an anti-fly mask and a curly black mane. Sebastian smiled. What a weird horse! And then he froze. What was hanging there from the saddle? Was it a leather glove? Or what could it be? He blinked against the sun. Was his imagination running wild? The horse had been set up a few meters behind the low fence and was surrounded by shrubs and trees.

'Anna, do you see anything strange? Over there!' He pointed to the back of the huge animal.

'What? Where?' At first Anna didn't see anything unusual until she saw a hand that rested on the horse. It was similar in colour to the saddle and therefore not easy to spot. Instantly sensing something dreadful, she croaked, 'Susan, have a look! Is that really a hand up there? Can you take a close-up shot?'

'And there is a flipper under the horse's belly,' Sebastian cried, hardly believing his eyes.

Now the adults caught up with them. Previously they had chatted animatedly with some strangers, amused about an artificial camel that spit water and served as a drinking water dispenser.

'What are you doing?' Lizzie was surprised to see the children staring spellbound at Susan's camera. An elderly man with a walking cane was also looking curiously over Sebastian's shoulder.

'I've found a dead body!' Sebastian burst out.

Andy snorted scornfully. 'Nonsense!'

Uncle Sam laughed. 'Boy, oh boy, you are ...'

Before he could finish his sentence, the senior said hoarsely, 'He's right. There's someone hanging on the horse. On the other side, which you can't see from here. There!'

He raised his walking stick towards the fake horse, accidentally knocking a floppy hat off a young woman's head.

'Sebastian! Stop!' Lizzie shouted. Her son was already starting to climb over the fence. 'Stop it!'

'What's going on here? You're blocking the alley!'

A small man with a commanding voice looked at them questioningly. In the meantime, so many people had gathered in this location that nobody could pass them. Susan held her camera with the enlarged picture section in front of his nose. Incredulous, the man stared at the leather hand. Then he swung himself over the fence with amazing agility and ran behind the huge horse. They heard a choked outcry. Anna felt sick. She had already discovered a corpse once before; together with her friend Barbara in a forest, next to a creek. And now again? In a theme park of all places? Surely that could not be true! Her brother also looked pale, while Susan had red cheeks from excitement. The man returned, facing the crowd. His eyes were wide open and he moved clumsily like an old, bent man. Leaning on a fence post, he croaked, 'There really is a body. It's a dead boy!'

\* \* \*

Very slowly and with the help of the police, the crowd finally dispersed and everyone had to leave the park. The employee who had previously jumped over the fence so light-footedly only managed to climb back with great difficulty and the assistance of two men. He was ashen-faced and had to be treated for shock by a paramedic. The dead boy had been tied to the saddle of the horse with an almost invisible, stable fishing line on his hand, with his face against the sculpture. Strangely enough, he had been dressed with a reddish-brown leather glove and a blue flipper. He had probably been murdered the night before.

# 2 A BLUE FLIPPER

The news was spreading fast. The seventeen-year-old boy named Thomas had been strangled, and a slight swelling on his face indicated that he had been punched. His left hand was in a glove and his right foot in a blue flipper. On the other foot he wore a white tennis sock and a white sneaker, and on his dark, slightly wavy hair he had a beige cap. He wore light brown shorts and a short-sleeved olive-green T-shirt with a picture of a small crocodile on it. Who had killed him? Thomas' family and friends were completely shocked and inconsolable, and none of them could think of a motive for this horrible crime. They called Thomas a good and reliable person, a nature lover and animal friend. His parents were shown on the local channel, asking for help to solve the murder, both in tears and hardly able to speak.

Andy turned off the TV, ashen-faced. 'What a heartbreaking story! Why would anybody kill such a young person who seemed like a nice bloke?' he asked, feeling queasy and vulnerable. When he imagined that something like that could happen to his own children, he got downright sick. Thomas had been just one year older than Anna, still a boy!

'And who'd heave a dead body onto a sculpture? That's insane!' Sebastian replied.

'If you hadn't looked so closely, that poor boy might still be hanging there. Perhaps somebody – maybe a gardener – would have only found him many days later,' Lizzie pointed out.

'The murderer is always the gardener,' Anna giggled.

Her father looked at her sternly for a moment, but then his gaze softened. It had been a terrible experience for all of them, and Aunt Paula, Uncle Sam and Susan had gone home earlier than planned.

Lizzie too was very pale and had dark rings under her eyes.

'Weird that nobody noticed anything, even though some houses are very close to the location of that fake horse.'

'Don't they have security guards or alarm systems in the park?' Sebastian asked.

'No idea! It seems nobody heard a thing. But I'm glad that we only saw the hand. And even that only from a distance … um, although, um … a bit closer on Susan's camera,' Lizzie said with a quiver in her voice.

'Susan also took a photo of that flipper. I'm baffled that she didn't publish the pictures on Facebook straight away,' Sebastian said.

'Maybe she's more careful with her postings on Facebook now,' Anna replied, looking sad. She had been appalled to see a photo of Susan's older brother Scott, Anna's boyfriend at the time, kissing another boy in a disco! As soon as Susan had discovered that photo, she had shared it with Sebastian who had looked at it just when Anna had come into his room. Anna had been dumbfounded! A few weeks later, she still struggled to overcome her anger and disappointment but hoped to remain friends with Scott.

With a tiny smile she now said, 'I already had a chat with Scott this morning. He phoned me as he was worried about us.'

'And how is Susie? No, I didn't mean you, but Scott's sister,' Sebastian laughed and stroked Susi the dog who'd laid her head on his legs, pricking up her ears when she heard her name.

'Scott told me that Susie coped fairly well with it, although she had a nasty nightmare.' Anna petted Sally, their tiny foster dog. Since she bent down to the Mini-Foxie, nobody saw her blushing. She'd dreamed that she and Scott were riding through the forest on a horse, tightly hugging. It had been very romantic until she noticed his reddish-brown leather gloves that rested gently on her belly.

\* \* \*

Later in the week Anna met her friends Barbara and David on the beach, taking the dogs along. David also had a small pet called Teddy. After a short walk, they sat down close to the dunes, and their conversation turned to the grisly murder case.

'Was Thomas actually killed with the fishing line?' David asked, glancing at a fisherman in the distance.

'No, I've heard that someone strangled him with his hands.' Anna swallowed and took off her sunglasses to rub her eyes.

Barbara trembled and David lovingly put an arm around her. She snuggled up to him and watched the dogs playing. Currently, Teddy chased a brown boxer with snow-white paws, while Susi jumped into the waves, followed by a tiny terrier. Sally sniffed extensively at a washed-up tree trunk and took a pee. Barbara sat upright again and straightened her somewhat slipped cap.

'By the way, Freddie knows – uh, I mean, he did know him a bit. Occasionally they went surfing together. Thomas was still a beginner, but he wasn't afraid of high waves. And ...'

'Yuck!' Anna yelled, startling her friends.

Susi shook herself exuberantly, splashing drops of water around her. 'Susi, you are such a pig! Why do you always have to do that right in front of me?'

Barbara and David grinned, although they'd also got wet. Susi lay down beside Anna, and Sally snuggled up to David who stroked her absent-mindedly. Where had Teddy gone?

'Maybe Thomas had gone snorkelling or fishing with some guys and got into a fight?' Anna pondered.

Barbara was aghast. 'You think he knew the murderers? Nah! It's more likely he was robbed by strangers.'

'But that wouldn't explain the flipper and the leather glove.' Anna brushed back her blonde curls.

'Anyway, I hope they catch whoever strangled that poor guy,' David said with a grim expression and stood up. 'Teddy!' he shouted loudly. 'Teddy, come!' He whistled.

Susi jumped up, looking at him expectantly, and Anna laughed. She and Sebastian had trained Susi with the help of a whistle, and she was pretty obedient – at least most of the times. But Teddy was still chasing the boxer, unperturbed by its master's calls. David had to run after him, and it took a while until he returned with the wildly kicking cheeky dog in his arms. Barbara thought she should find out more about Thomas from Freddie, her half-brother. Her parents were divorced, and recently her father had remarried. Although Barbara had initially despised her dad's girlfriend Annika, she now liked her and was quite thrilled to have a 'new brother'.

# 3 ENGLISH CLASS

The face of the English teacher was extremely stern when she reprimanded two of her pupils. 'Sebastian! Jack! What do you think of the story?'

The students smiled, embarrassed. They had eagerly whispered about their upcoming rugby game next weekend, considering swapping one of the players for another. They had no idea what the teacher was talking about.

'If I catch you yakking again, I'll place you away from each other and give you extra homework,' she threatened.

Sebastian had to wipe the grin off his face. Unlike his previous English teacher, Mrs. Mitchell was a nice lady and he didn't think she would fulfill her threat. He winked at Jack.

'Sebastian, please read the second paragraph on page twenty-three aloud!' Mrs. Mitchell ordered. 'And then explain to me what Mr. Bates might intend by his statement.'

Sebastian read the text somewhat hesitantly. Although his English had become quite good, he still had trouble pronouncing everything perfectly. And in this passage, there was a word that he simply could not figure out. He tried it again, stuttered and turned red. Kirsty, a girl in the row in front of him, giggled.

'Kirsty, can you help Sebastian to pronounce this word correctly? Can you form a new sentence with it?' Mrs. Mitchell asked.

Kirsty repeated the word without any problems and explained the meaning in a simple sentence.

'Wonderful!' the teacher praised her. 'And now, Sebastian, please continue reading.'

Sebastian was relieved that he could read the next section of the text fluently and analyse it to the teacher's satisfaction. But he was annoyed with himself, anxious to become like his sister who also blushed very quickly. Was it because Kirsty had watched him attentively when he'd read aloud? She was so pretty! Once again, he was admiring her good figure and gorgeous hair instead of listening to the teacher. Kirsty had thick, long hair that shimmered like light gold or dark amber depending on the light, and her eyes were green and beautiful. She laughed a lot and had a pleasant, deep voice.

As if Kirsty had guessed his thoughts, she turned around and grinned at him again. Sebastian wondered if she liked him. He smiled back briefly and then immediately looked back at the book on his table. However, he kept dreaming and didn't follow the English lesson.

Later he was talking to Jack and two other friends on the school grounds when their classmates Kirsty and Arielle joined them.

Kirsty said to Sebastian, 'Arielle told me that you were the one who discovered the dead boy. That must have been scary!'

Sebastian scratched his head. 'It was! And yet, it seemed unreal at first. When the man shouted that there was a dead boy indeed, I couldn't believe it. I assumed it was a bad joke and someone had put a mannequin on the horse for fun.'

'But you didn't see the body, did you?' Arielle looked at him curiously. Her blue eyes seemed huge.

'Nope, my mother stopped me from climbing over the fence. And then everything was so chaotic! There was a big crowd, all keen to find out what was going on. But some of the park's employees blocked the fence and kept everyone at a distance. And pretty soon, the police and paramedics arrived, and we all had to leave the park.'

Jack frowned. 'Strange that the boy was found on the wrong side of the horse where it was harder to spot him. It would have been much more dramatic if the killer had posed him in front of a big mouth of another sculpture, making it look as if he'd been attacked by an animal.'

'You have quite an imagination,' Kirsty said indignantly. 'You must have watched too many cruel movies.'

Arielle seemed upset. 'I bet Thomas was killed by several men. Or it must have been a guy as strong as an ox who first strangled him and then tied him up on top of the huge sculpture.' Unexpectedly, she burst into heavy sobbing.

Kirsty comfortingly put an arm around her waist. She looked tiny next to her friend who even surpassed Sebastian by almost a head. But he too was quite small. The boys looked distressed. Why was Arielle crying? Everyone remained silent for a while.

'Thomas was Arielle's cousin,' Kirsty said softly.

She also had to blow her nose now, and only with difficulty could she hold back her tears. Sebastian would have loved to hug her. But he didn't dare – especially not in front of his friends.

'Did he have any enemies? Or did he know anything that could've been dangerous to others, a certain secret perhaps?' Toby asked.

Arielle sniffed and looked sadly at her classmates. 'I don't know. He was a great person. I liked him so much!'

Until now, Sebastian had always ignored Arielle, mainly because she was friends with Kate and Fiona, those two silly girls he could not stand. But in the last weeks, Arielle and Kirsty seemed to be quite close, and he wondered if Arielle had fallen out with her former friends. Anyway, he felt very sorry for her and also for her murdered cousin. He didn't pay much attention in the next lesson, although Mr. Smithfield was his favourite teacher and he actually found chemistry very interesting. But he kept thinking about the murder. And as he looked at Kirsty's slender back in front of him, he suddenly felt the desire to protect her. Who were these murderers? Did they even live nearby?

# 4 MOZZIES

In the afternoon Anna and Sebastian were sitting on the patio, their dogs snoozing at their feet. A citronella candle and several incense sticks were burning on the table to ward off the mosquitoes. Much too often, the hungry mozzies came to visit without an invitation. Modern pop music sounded from a neighbouring garden, and somewhere in the distance a lawn mower hummed.

Anna said, 'I've found out that Thomas liked swimming and surfing. And that he was a vegan. So, he was hardly an angler.'

'How do you know?'

'Barbara told me that Freddie knew Thomas.'

Sebastian was confused. 'But why do you think Thomas wasn't an angler?'

'Because vegans don't eat fish and therefore certainly don't go fishing,' Anna explained. 'Some people who don't eat meat, like my friend Audrey, for example, still eat fish occasionally. Well, so Audrey is not a pure vegetarian in the strictest sense. But Thomas never had any meat or fish dishes, and he didn't like eggs or dairy products.'

'And what does a vegan eat?' Sebastian wanted to know.

'Vegans reject all animal products and only eat plants such as veggies, fruit, nuts and so on. I think it's actually good. They surely live in a very healthy way. But I like yoghurt and cheese much too much.'

'And vegans don't? Why? You don't have to butcher animals for yoghurt or cheese.'

'But they're made from milk, so they're animal products.'

'Oh! I never thought of that.' Sebastian was a little embarrassed. In order not to appear quite so stupid, he quickly added, 'Then vegans probably don't eat honey either. And they certainly don't wear leather shoes or leather jackets.'

Now Anna was puzzled. 'You are right! And yet Thomas wore a leather glove on the one hand, around which the fishing line was wrapped.'

'Very mysterious!'

'Maybe his killers wanted to prevent the fishing line from cutting too much into the skin,' Anna pondered, her brow furrowed.

'But Thomas was already dead before he was tied up there. Then it wouldn't have mattered.'

'And why was he wearing a flipper on one foot and a running shoe on the other one?'

'Perhaps the killers were drunk and took pleasure in dressing Thomas up like that.'

Anna was terrified by the imagination. But admittedly there were despicable criminals in the world!

Sebastian told his sister about Arielle now. 'By the way, one of my schoolmates is related to Thomas. She is very upset! Although her cousin was a few years older, they got along splendidly. She still can't believe that he is dead now. She misses him so much, and she had also been looking forward to him teaching her photography. That was his hobby.'

'A terrible story! Thomas was still so young! And very handsome!' Anna had seen a photo of Thomas on television and also in an article in the newspaper, published after the murder. He had been slim and well-built, with finely cut facial features and dreamy blue eyes.

'I wonder if his killers were into snorkelling and fishing.' Sebastian clapped his arm where a cheeky mosquito had settled despite the scents of lemon and cedar wood. 'Bloody beasts!'

Anna smacked her forehead. 'I think the wind is blowing the smoke in the wrong direction.' She stood up and put one of the sticks in a vase on the floor. 'Don't burn your noses,' she admonished the dogs, keeping an eye on them just to be on the safe side. Then she asked, 'Did the flipper actually fit him? Did it belong to Thomas? And was it a fin for diving or for snorkelling?'

'Are you playing detective again?' Lizzie suddenly stood next to them and had apparently overheard Anna's last sentences. 'Dinner is ready. Are you coming in?'

Susi and Sally didn't need to be told twice. Immediately they jumped up and wagged their tails. To their disappointment, they had to wait until their human friends were sitting at the table. Only then (and on a special command) they were allowed to eat their food. Susi, as always, gobbled everything down in no time at all and then tried to run off to eat Sally's dinner too, but was stopped by Lizzie. 'Susi, stay!'

Sebastian spooned up his dessert, vanilla ice cream with fresh mango pieces. 'Delicious! I don't want to become a vegan.'

'What?' his father asked, perplexed.

Now Anna and Sebastian told their parents what they had found out about the dead young man.

Lizzie called out, 'What a coincidence! Today, for the first time ever, I've baked a cake without eggs and without butter as a vegan lady will visit me tomorrow. Her name is Jessica. And I bet you're going to like that cake too, Sebastian!'

The next day Jessica had just left when a couple from Buderim came to have a look at their foster dog. While Susi kept her distance, the little dog ran directly towards the visitors, letting them pat her. Both fell in love with the Mini-Foxie right away and offered to adopt her. They didn't mind that Sally was already nine years old but actually preferred an older dog that didn't do anything stupid; like pulling on the leash like crazy, eating shoes, or jumping up on people. Sally seemed perfect to them! And so they picked her up soon, after filling out some forms and paying the adoption fee to the Moist Nose Rescue Organisation.

Anna and Sebastian were quite sad to see the little dog gone. Susi kept sniffing around the place where Sally's dog basket had been. Andy and Lizzie also missed their foster dog more than they admitted. But the whole family was glad when they received e-mails from the new owners. They absolutely adored Sally, and over the next years, they sent them many photos of the tiny dog who looked very happy and healthy.

On a sunny Saturday morning Anna took Susi along to Barbara's, planning to have a long chat with her best friend. Julie, Barbara's mother, had gone to Noosa to do some shopping with Tom and Lisa, and so Anna could talk undisturbed. She liked Barbara's little siblings very much, but they could be a pain in the butt! And you never knew what they were going to tell others. Anna was still sad about Scott who had been her first and only boyfriend so far, but her grief and her initial shock about his new-found homosexuality had gradually eased. Now, sitting in the shade of a big tree, she told Barbara more about the whole story, feeling relief to get everything off her chest. Barbara was a good listener and only interrupted Anna's monologue with a few questions. Susi lay down to take a nap while a little bird hopped around on the lawn, wagging its tail. Susi lazily opened her eye once more, when this 'Willie Wagtail' pecked at some insects right in front of her nose.

Sighing, Anna said, 'Right now, I still can't imagine to meet Anthony, Scott's boyfriend, but maybe later I won't mind. And I really hope that I can keep Scott as a good friend. Oh, that reminds me: Do you know if Thomas had a girlfriend? She must miss him terribly! At least Scott is still alive, even though I probably won't see him so often anymore.'

'You can't get this murder out of your mind, hey? I feel the same way. And it's totally scary that the killers are still at large, perhaps even in our own town.'

'Are you afraid to walk around by yourself now? Maybe you should get a dog, too.'

'My mother won't have one. She thinks it's too difficult when we want to travel.'

'Yeah, it can be tricky. But there are hotels, apartments and camping grounds where dogs are allowed. And apart from that I could look after your dog during your vacation. Or David? I'm sure he wouldn't mind if his little Teddy had a playmate.'

'Hum, I don't think our mother will give in,' said Barbara. 'Oh, what's wrong with Susi?'

The dog suddenly rushed to the patio for no apparent reason. Anna laughed, looking up into the bright blue sky. 'She's afraid of the parachutists!'

High up, someone was sailing through the air, doing pirouettes. They heard a triumphant cheering, and a second parachute was opening with a soft hissing sound. Soon they could make out the people who looked like little dolls from the distance and heard more shouts of joy. For a while it almost seemed as if they were going to land in their garden, but finally they floated towards the sea and disappeared from their view.

'Good that Susi doesn't live here!' Barbara smiled. 'Otherwise, she would be panic-stricken all the time.'

Almost every day some people jumped – mostly in tandem – out of an airplane over the sea and landed on the beach near Stumers Creek. Unfortunately, Susi – contrary to most other dogs – was terrified by them. She already looked anxiously into the sky when nobody else could even see or hear the parachutes yet. Susi dreaded the sound of this little plane, knowing exactly what it meant: these 'huge monsters' would fly through the air again! Now she remained sitting on the covered patio for a long time until she finally dared to return to Anna.

'You little coward!' Anna stroked her dog tenderly.

Susi put her head on her leg. Now the world was in order again. But not for Anna and Barbara! They wanted to solve the murder case. Was Freddie acquainted with the murderer (or murderers) without knowing it?

# 5 HISTORY LESSON

Not long after Sally's departure, the Kuhlmann family got a new foster dog called Lilly who was about ten months old. It was a shaggy terrier mix with a funny face and an over-bite. The dark brown eyes were almost hidden by the long tufts of hair. Her former life remained a mystery, since she had been found on a street with dirty, matted fur, without a collar and without a microchip. Lilly was a lovely little fellow, and the Kuhlmanns and Susi liked her instantly!

Nevertheless, Sebastian's thoughts still seemed to be occupied with their former foster dog, as he dreamed that two men tried to kidnap his little Sally, and he fought with them desperately until they snatched the dog from him and ran away. Sebastian was devastated! But then three boys appeared out of the blue, offering to help him, and together they managed to get Sally back. In spite of the happy end, Sebastian was rattled by his dream. But he was relieved that Sally was in fact well taken care of by her nice new owners. He went into the kitchen to drink a glass of water when a thought occurred to him. Thomas had certainly not been out in the middle of the night all alone.

Somebody must have known what he had done just before his death! And why hadn't his parents reported him missing earlier? Sebastian decided to ask Arielle about it. Before he fell asleep, his mind turned to Kirsty, and he had a smile on his face when his mother woke him up the next day.

To his disappointment, Arielle wasn't in school and Kirsty seemed to avoid him for some reason. Or was he just imagining it? Mr. Winter, their usual history teacher, was also absent this morning and was replaced by Mrs. Wilder, a small, chubby woman with short black hair.

'What's wrong?' Jack pinched his arm. 'You're looking so glum today.'

Before Sebastian could answer, the relief teacher asked, 'Jack, can you name the first inhabitants of Australia apart from the Aborigines?'

Jack had to admit that he had no idea.

'They were the Torres Strait Islanders,' Mrs. Wilder taught him. 'They came from a group of islands between the northern tip of Queensland and Papua New Guinea. The Aborigines, however, lived on the Australian mainland and in Tasmania. There were over seven hundred different languages and dialects, and the cultures of the Aboriginal people are the oldest of all the cultures still existing in the world. It is estimated to be forty to sixty thousand years old.'

Sebastian was impressed. With the best will in the world he could not imagine such a long period of time. Wasn't it amazing what scientists could find out? Suddenly he had to think of the dinosaurs that were supposedly extinct about sixty-five million years ago. And yet, there was so much information about the different species, not just about their appearance but also about their characteristic behaviour. It was incredible! Sebastian kept dreaming: how would it be to ride an Alamosaurus? Or to fly on a primal bird, hearing the wind mixed with the cries of these creatures? It must be fantastic!

The loud voice of the teacher brought him back to the present.

'Where did the first European settlers come from, Jack?'

'From Britain and Ireland,' Jack replied in a flash.

'And when did the first fleet of ships from England arrive here?'

Now Jack had to think about it. 'In the year 1788.'

'Exactly! A total of eleven ships arrived in Sydney Cove on January 26, and that day is now celebrated as Australia Day.'

Mrs. Wilder briefly ran her hand through her hair, which was already standing on end anyway, and Sebastian had to giggle. Mrs. Wilder bore an astonishing resemblance to 'Mecki', a hedgehog figure he knew from his picture books in Germany. Not only because of her spiky-looking, dark hair, but also because of her pointed nose.

The teacher turned her gaze to him. 'Sebastian, what was the name of the captain of this so-called 'First Fleet'?'

'Philip A... – um, no – ... Arthur Philip.'

'Very good!' Now Mrs. Wilder addressed the whole class again. 'I'm sure you already know that many of the first settlers in Australia were prisoners. Since the prisons in Great Britain were hopelessly overcrowded, it was finally decided in 1786 to transport the convicts to Australia, first to the new colony called New South Wales. Arthur Philip became the first governor there. While he had made sure that there was enough food for everyone on the long, arduous journey by ship, many deaths occurred on further journeys ...'

The teacher continued to tell the students about the history of Australia and the hard life of the first settlers. Sebastian listened only half-heartedly as his thoughts wandered again, this time not to dinosaurs and long-gone times, but to Kirsty in the same classroom, so close to him. Her hair was tied back in a ponytail today, and he admired her delicate ears with the pretty earrings.

'Ouch!' Sebastian glared angrily at Jack who had pinched his arm again.

'It's shocking how people were treated back then,' Jack whispered. 'Many of them weren't bad criminals at all, but had only stolen a piece of bread or something else to eat. And now they were treated like slaves and had to work like oxen. They were flogged for the smallest things.' Jack sounded really indignant. 'And on top of that, they often had to starve.'

As if Mrs. Wilder had heard his last sentence, she now said, 'Life was not easy! Not only the prisoners, but also the free settlers had to work very hard and often suffered from hunger. Even if they owned good farmland, they struggled again and again, trying to overcome disasters like floods, drought and diseases. Many women had to fend for themselves when their husbands died. But out of this difficult time, a special spirit and a feeling of togetherness grew. And we Australians are proud of this.'

'Last night I dreamed that someone kidnapped my foster dog. And a few boys helped me to get Sally back, although I didn't know them at all,' Sebastian told his friend, keeping his voice low.

'I would always help you!' Jack promised a bit too loudly.

Kirsty turned around and grinned, and Sebastian was instantly filled with a warm and fuzzy feeling. Unfortunately, the teacher noticed that some students were not giving her the attention she deserved, and her tone of voice became stricter.

Arielle was back in school on the following day. She looked tired, and her usually shiny dark curls looked stringy. Her school uniform was a little wrinkled in places, her black shoes were dusty, and Sebastian noticed that she was wearing a short white sock on one foot and a longer beige sock on the other. Normally Sebastian would have made a joke about her different socks, but now he felt pity for her. She and her mother certainly suffered greatly from Thomas' death, not bothering about Arielle's appearance. Unlike Lizzie who eyeballed her children every morning before they went to school. And they had to clean their shoes all the time, annoying!

'Sebastian, your fly is undone!' Jack whispered in a conspiratorial tone, grinning all over his face.

That stupid zipper! Sebastian hastily tampered with his trousers, hoping that nobody else had noticed. He glanced furtively at Kirsty who was talking to Ivory, another classmate.

'Have you been studying hard for our math test?' Jack asked.

'Don't worry, we'll be fine.' But Sebastian was also feeling queasy because he hadn't prepared himself well. And the last examination had been quite difficult. Cheating was almost impossible as Mr. Riddles, their math teacher, was very strict. During written exams, he used to sit behind the students in the classroom so that nobody knew in which direction he was looking.

After the math test on this day, Arielle and Kirsty joined Jack and Sebastian in their break.

Kirsty beamed. 'It was so easy!'

'I'm glad we've got it over and done with. I always get a stomach-ache before an exam.' Arielle now had colour in her cheeks again. 'Yesterday I was sick with fear, and therefore I asked my mother to write me an apology so that I could stay at home and get more time to study.'

'And I'd been worried about you,' Sebastian blurted out and blushed a little. Everyone looked at him in surprise.

'Why is that?' Arielle wanted to know.

Sebastian didn't quite know what to reply. 'Hmm, I assumed you were sick because of Thomas.'

Arielle was touched.

Despite his embarrassment, Sebastian quickly continued, 'I'd like to help find out what happened. Do you know if your cousin had been with a friend in the night before he died? Nobody reported him missing, after all.'

Arielle hesitated. 'It's a long story. Would you all like to visit me this afternoon after school? I'll tell you more then.' She gave them her address, and they agreed to meet at 4:00 p.m. Then Sebastian remembered Susi. 'Oh no, I can't come! It's my turn to walk my dog before dinner today.'

'Just bring it along,' Arielle answered spontaneously.

# 6 IN LOVE

As soon as Sebastian knocked on her door, he found out that Arielle had a dog, too. Max was a big short-haired mix with huge paws who galloped joyfully to Susi, trying to play with her. However, Susi growled at him angrily, as she loved small dogs but wasn't so enthusiastic about big puppies.

Arielle smiled apologetically. 'Sorry! Max has to learn that he can't just jump on all dogs like that.'

Max didn't give up so quickly and kept hopping around Susi until he decided to chase Sniff, the cat, through the house. Soon Max and Sniff were woven together in a ball, and Sebastian could hardly believe his eyes how gently the big dog frolicked with the cat. 'They are best pals!' Arielle explained and led her classmates and Susi into her own room. Arielle and Jack plopped down on two armchairs while he and Kirsty sat down on a two-seater couch. Susi got a bit excited seeing the cat, wagging her tail violently for a while; but then she yawned and lay down under the table at Kirsty's feet. In spite of her usual fear of strangers, Susi seemed to love her instantly. Sebastian secretly let his eyes wander. Arielle looked much better now than in the morning. She had washed her hair and was dressed in a light blue T-shirt and shorts that emphasized her athletic figure. Her room was small but cosy, with many pictures of seaside landscapes, musicians and movie stars. Kirsty looked very pretty too, and Sebastian's heart beat a little faster to be so close to her. Her light-coloured T-shirt provided a nice contrast to her tanned, smooth skin.

Arielle's mother brought in a tray of drinks and some home-made biscuits. She greeted them all with a genuine big smile and left them on their own again.

'Your mum seems to be very nice!' Jack took a chocolate cookie without being asked. 'Do you have any brothers or sisters?'

'No, unfortunately not. But Thomas was almost like an older brother to me.' Arielle took a sip of mineral water and they noticed that her hand was shaking. 'He lived near us and we were inseparable as little kids. In the last two years or so we didn't meet that often, though, and I think he was embarrassed to be seen with me, his younger cousin. It got worse when Maryann became his girlfriend. She's a stupid cow I couldn't stand, and they didn't fit together at all. But the relationship didn't last too long.'

Jack took another cookie, this time one with macadamia nuts, and made quite a noise while chewing.

'What did Thomas do in his spare time?' Kirsty asked.

'Thomas was very sporty. He loved to go swimming and snorkelling, and recently he learned how to surf. He also planned to take a diving course in Bundaberg. He had already saved some money for it, and his parents wanted to give him the rest as a present for his birthday.' Arielle was now noisily blowing her nose and Kirsty looked at her pitifully.

'Did he have any enemies?' Sebastian asked.

'Not that I know of! Somebody once complained that he'd talk too much; and it's true that he liked telling stories, but I found that rather positive. In general, he was such a nice person, very generous, open-minded, and quite witty and humerous. And he loved animals and couldn't stand it when somebody mistreated them. He was also a vegan and refused to eat any meat. And some people mocked him because of that.'

Sebastian and Kirsty took a biscuit at the same time and their hands touched for a moment. Sebastian felt as if his skin was electrified. Quickly he pulled his hand away and stroked the back of Susi who immediately turned around to get patted on her stomach. Kirsty also began to scratch her chest, unintentionally touching Sebastian's fingers again. Sebastian blushed. He noticed a tiny smile around the corner of Kirsty's mouth, and her eyes seemed to glow as well. How beautiful she is! he thought. The sun gradually set, casting a warm light on her hair.

'Did you know him too, Kirsty?' Jack asked, already chewing on his third cookie.

'Not really. I only met him once, and that was with Arielle at the Christmas market in Coolum.'

'Hmm, these are yummy!' Sebastian finally ate one of the home-made biscuits.

Arielle said, 'On Friday, the last night before his murder, he'd gone to a party in Mooloolaba and afterwards he'd stayed overnight at a friend's house. Therefore, his parents hadn't missed him straight away.' She started to cry.

Jack jumped up, went to her and put his arm around her shoulder, sitting down on the armrest. At the same time Kirsty and Sebastian took each other's hands under the table. Again, Sebastian felt a tingling sensation. But he didn't know whether it was because of the horror about Thomas' terrible end or because of the happiness about Kirsty. Susi stretched out comfortably.

Arielle took a deep breath and resumed, 'Thomas and his best friends Daniel and John celebrated the eighteenth birthday of another mate and then went to a disco where Thomas got into a fight with a drunk man. This creep punched him right in the face! He overheard Thomas telling his friends a joke that he didn't like, and later they argued about 'Australia Day'. Thomas thought that January 26 shouldn't be celebrated at all, as the arrival of the first fleet of ships in Sydney was the beginning of horrible crimes and unbelievable massacres against the Aborigines. He said the invasion of the Europeans should be seen as a day of mourning. But this drunkard had a completely different opinion and became more and more aggressive.'

'And what happened then?' Jack inquired.

'Well, they should've thrown this mean guy out of the disco. But a big man pulled him away and bought him a beer. And that calmed him down.'

'And Thomas?'

'Thomas and John had already arranged to spend the night at Daniel's in Coolum Beach. His parents were out of town that weekend. The three friends sat together for a short time, and Daniel wrapped a packet of frozen peas in a towel and gave it to Thomas so he could cool his injured cheek with it.' Arielle sniffed, and Jack hugged her briefly.

Sebastian was amazed as he had never noticed before that Jack was interested in her. Or did he just feel sorry for her? Anyway, he himself was in a turmoil of different feelings, hardly believing that he and Kirsty were holding hands.

Arielle jumped up so suddenly that Jack almost fell down. Susi growled softly.

'Max, stop! Give me my sock!' Arielle yelled, trying to catch her dog who quickly ran away with a white sock in his mouth. Arielle had to laugh.

'We really have to train Max better. He always steals my socks, and now and then he chews on the shoes of visitors. Good that you kept your sandals on!'

Jack also smiled now, but as a precaution he sat down on his own chair again. 'Where does Daniel live? Is it close to the AIRY TOES park?'

Arielle nodded. 'Yeah, it would only take a few minutes on foot.'

'Are his friends now suspected of murder?' Sebastian asked.

'No way! They have of course been questioned by the police. John and Daniel can't figure it out. They went to sleep at about 1 a.m., but Thomas wanted to stay up and watch a movie on Daniel's computer. So, the last thing they saw of him was when he was sitting in Daniel's room with headphones on. The next morning, he was gone.' Arielle was close to tears again.

'But why didn't his friends call the police immediately?' Kirsty asked.

'Who would have thought about murder? They assumed he hadn't been able to sleep and had gone home after all.'

'Strange!' Kirsty's eyes gleamed moist.

Susi growled softly again.

'What's the matter, Susi?' Sebastian let go of Kirsty's hand. Everyone looked to the open door, where a man appeared. He was gigantic and almost filled the door frame.

'It's almost time for dinner, Arielle,' her father said in an unexpectedly soft voice. 'And it is already getting dark. Shall I better drive your friends home?'

They gladly accepted the offer, because they did feel a bit scared. What had happened to Thomas that night?

# 7 MOUNT COOLUM

Sebastian helped himself with a second piece of meat and spooned some sauce over it. Lizzie had made a delicious roast with potatoes and red cabbage.

'How was your day with your new girlfriend?' Anna asked him. She had never heard of Arielle before and was curious to find out more.

'She is not my girlfriend! But Jack seems to have a crush on her,' Sebastian said.

'Super!' Anna shouted. 'It couldn't go on much longer that all the schoolgirls fall in love with him and he remains completely unaffected.'

Sebastian had to admit that many girls adored his friend. Jack was very handsome, tall and strong, and one of the best players in the rugby team. However, he'd told Sebastian in confidence one day that he thought his nose was much too big. Sebastian admired him anyway, wishing to be such a muscular boy himself, and not as skinny.

'They would make a beautiful couple,' he said. 'Arielle is much nicer than I thought. And I feel so sorry for her!'

'Why is that?' Andy asked, astonished.

'She is a cousin of Thomas. And they were very close, more like siblings.' Sebastian told his family in detail what he'd found out about the last night of the murdered young man. The story made Lizzie feel upset. She didn't like the fact that her children kept talking about this tragic crime and fervently hoped that the murderers would be arrested soon!

'It's really strange that Thomas left the house without telling his friends,' Andy mused. 'Maybe he wanted to meet someone privately.'

'But the police must have checked Thomas' mobile for any hints!' Lizzie pointed out.

Anna said excitedly, 'He'd possibly planned to see that person before, so that there was no need for a phone call or text message. But who could that have been?'

Lizzie made a grimace. 'I hope you'll never pretend to visit a friend but then meet another person in secret.' She looked sternly at her children. Until now she had been happy and grateful that Anna and Sebastian had a nice circle of friends. After all, teenagers could get in bad company, doing stupid things.

Andy seemed to think the same, saying, 'Thomas might have got involved with bad guys. Did he take any drugs?'

'I don't think so, as Freddy told Barbara that Thomas was very keen on healthy food,' Anna said. 'Even at parties, he seldom drank any booze, not like Freddy who often drinks a beer too much.'

'By the way, your mother is planning to get fitter.' Andy winked at his wife. 'We are going to climb Mount Coolum tomorrow afternoon. Would you like to come along?'

'Sure!' Sebastian called out. 'Why not?' Anna agreed.

* * *

'Oh boy, so many stairs!' Lizzie gasped. 'We should have picked a cooler day.'

Although it was late afternoon, it was very hot and humid. Hungry mosquitoes swarmed around aggressively. Nevertheless, an amazing number of people of all ages were on the way to Mount Coolum. Some even jogged up and down the path, leaving behind a scent of perfume or deodorant, others of insect repellent or sweat. A few tiny children clambered merrily up the stairs that were partly artificially created, partly natural rock stairs made of sandstone and rhyolite. The higher they climbed; the less trees provided shade. The vegetation changed from forest to a heath-like landscape with shrubs and grasses.

'There's a kangaroo!' A little girl was standing on a boulder, pointing into the distance.

Sebastian, Anna and their parents stopped and looked around. They saw forests, buildings and the sea, and just below them was a golf course, a bright green with blue shimmering ponds and golden sand.

'Where?' Sebastian couldn't spot a kangaroo and felt disappointed until he shouted excitedly: 'Yes, now I see it too! Smack in the middle of the golf course!'

They spotted more kangaroos grazing eagerly. It was a pity that they did not have binoculars with them! A man with a baby on his back passed them, smiling broadly at them. They all set off again, and soon they reached the highest point. From there they had wonderful views in all directions, not only of the coastal landscape and the islands in the sea, but also of hills, farmland, residential areas and wetlands. A fresh breeze cooled them down and the sun was not so hot anymore.

Andy addressed his wife, 'We should also hike up Mount Ninderry soon, so that you won't get out of practice, Lieschen.'

Sebastian and Anna grinned. Since they'd moved away from Germany, they hadn't heard that name very often anymore.

On the way back down, Anna suggested, 'There is a climbing spot very close by. Could we have a quick lookie there?'

'Do you think anyone is still climbing there?' Lizzie asked dubiously.

'Never mind, let's go!' Sebastian said.

'All right! I just hope Susi and Lilly don't get into mischief,' Lizzie said, checking her watch. When Lilly got too bored, she sometimes started digging holes in the garden, and Susi helped her enthusiastically, although she had never done anything like that before. The pets had to stay home that afternoon because Mount Coolum was protected as a national park. Dogs were not allowed here, not even on a leash.

After a short hike, the Kuhlmanns arrived at the former quarry. The interestingly shaped cliffs were in the shade and looked gloomy and threatening to Lizzie. The sun was already very low, and some mosquitoes were buzzing around them.

'There are still a few climbers,' Anna said triumphantly.

A young man was trying to climb a difficult overhang, looking for holds for his hands and feet. For a while he hung on with his fingertips, just about to fall off the wall when he found two narrow ledges for his toes. The woman who secured him with a rope supported him with encouraging shouts. He tried all sorts of tricks without success, but finally he hooked his heel on a ledge above his head, and with a skilful turn of his body he lifted himself higher.

'Wow!' Sebastian was utterly impressed.

Lizzie had unconsciously held her breath. She would never dare to climb up such a steep cliff! There was also a lot of loose rubble lying around, and she was afraid a thick stone might fall down on her head at any moment. She was surprised that the climber was not wearing a helmet. A bit further away, a middle-aged man was belaying a woman. Already high up, she too had trouble getting on, and they heard her cursing loudly. But after a short breather, she managed to climb higher. She quickly attached her express set (a sling with two carabiners for safety) to a bolt in the rock face and hooked the rope into it. She then reached for a ledge with her right hand, and her feet were looking for a new foothold when the piece of rock in her hand suddenly broke off. The woman fell down and screamed in shock, but fortunately the rope held her tight. Now she found herself a little below the bolt again, dangling in the air for a while. She gave her arms a rest, dipped her sweaty hands in a small bag of chalk attached to her hip, and then she started climbing again. Everyone watched her spellbound.

'Come on, Conny!' her climbing partner cheered her on.

Contrary to the spectators, he seemed completely relaxed. He continued to expertly regulate his Grigri, a special safety device. Once again, Conny had difficulties to climb higher, but with some groaning and thanks to her strong fingers and skilful climbing technique she made it. Then she moved on quickly and cheered when she reached her goal.

'She climbs like a monkey!' Anna said.

She'd already heard that these cliffs were not suitable for beginners, so there was no point in learning to climb here. But she was keen to try out the climbing forest in the AIRY TOES park, which she had missed during her only visit to the theme park so far. She shivered when she thought about poor Thomas.

In the meantime, Andy had started a chat with a young man who was holding a coiled rope on his arm. Sebastian marvelled at the climber's strong muscles, but then his eyes wandered to a large bag on the ground. In it were various safety devices, a helmet, a figure of eight, carabiners, and slings. And a brown leather glove with a few black stripes! Sebastian was puzzled. Why would you need a glove for climbing?

Impulsively, he interrupted his father in the middle of the conversation, asking the stranger, 'What's the glove for?'

Andy stared at his son somewhat angrily, but the young man replied in a friendly tone, 'It's for abseiling. If you come down too fast, the rope will get hot. And that's why some people wear gloves so they don't burn their hands. I learned that when I went abseiling at Mount Tinbeerwah.'

'I know someone who did an abseiling course there with the entire school class; that must be fun!' Anna said.

'Well, for me it's just a quick way to get down.' The stranger looked at his friends who had just been lowered down by their partners. 'It's getting dark, so it's time to pack it in. We have to go back to Brisbane.'

The Kuhlmanns said goodbye and returned to their car. On the way, Anna contemplated, 'I was thinking of Thomas again. They said he was compassionate about nature and environmental protection. And there was a demonstration against the planned climbing forest in that AIRY TOES park, because they had to clear some vegetation for it. I bet there is a connection! Perhaps Thomas protested too loudly and made enemies who killed him. And they left him in the park as a kind of a secret triumph.'

Sebastian was confused. 'But then the killers could have rather hung Thomas up on a climbing structure.'

'Instead of sitting on a high horse, the poor boy was found in a strange outfit, on the side of an artificial horse! That could really mean something, couldn't it?' Lizzie said.

Andy shook his head. 'I don't know! Well, the enclosure of this horse sculpture was definitely easier to reach than the climbing forest.' Anna got goosebumps. Poor Thomas!

When they came home, they were greeted with overwhelming joy by their four-legged friends. Lizzie didn't discover any holes in the garden, but the dogs had dug up a bromeliad and eaten parts of the leaves. Those rascals!

# 8 FIRST DATE

Kirsty walked to a park near the sea, dreaming away. She had a date with Sebastian! How would it turn out? She had liked him from the start, smitten with his open, honest and infectious laughter, his spontaneity, and his fuzzy black hair. And since they'd held hands in Arielle's room, her thoughts had been circling around him.

Right now, she felt a little queasy about meeting him alone for the first time. Looking at her watch, she realised that she had arrived much too early. She sat down on a covered bench in the park and waited. The light drizzle gradually increased and she was glad that it was still quite warm. A few people walked by with umbrellas, and an elderly woman with a dachshund waved to her friendly. Then she saw a man, completely soaked, sprinting towards a car. After opening the door, he looked around and called impatiently for a dog. But the dog kept sniffing at the base of a tree, totally ignoring him. Even the man's louder and more threatening calls didn't help, and finally he went to the dog and kicked it.

'Leave it alone!' Kirsty jumped up and ran to him, foaming with rage.

The young man looked at her condescendingly. 'What's it to you?' He dragged the dog, a poodle-schnauzer-breed, along by the collar. 'The stupid mutt wouldn't come.'

'No wonder!' Kirsty hissed at him.

The dog was looking very frightened and had its tail between its legs.

'Wait, Steven!' Breathlessly, a young woman came running towards them, holding a little black bag in her hand. 'I had to pick up Sammy's poop.'

'Don't put that stinking stuff in my face!' the man grumbled.

Kirsty was relieved that the dog obviously belonged to the woman. At least she hoped that she treated it better than this guy who was now going back to his car without paying any further attention to Kirsty.

'Kirsty!' Sebastian shouted. He was wearing a raincoat up to his knees and kept Lilly and Susi on leads. 'You're soaking wet!'

Kirsty was still trembling with fury. In her excitement, she had left her umbrella on the bench, and her hair was now straight and snug against her head, and her T-shirt and shorts were sticking to her body. Her green eyes sparkled with anger.

'What's wrong?' Sebastian gave her a light kiss on the lips.

Kirsty took a deep breath to calm herself. Her heart was still pounding. She hated the abuse of animals! And she'd been determined to defend the poor dog in case the bastard would have tried to kick it again. She told Sebastian what had happened, and to his own surprise he tenderly embraced her wet head and kissed her again. Immediately, Susi squeezed herself between them and Sebastian grinned broadly. 'Susi is jealous already.'

Kirsty also smiled and bent down to stroke Susi who now gave her a kiss right on the mouth.

'Bah!' Kirsty laughed and wiped her mouth.

Lilly jumped up on them like a bouncy ball, desperately trying to get attention. Although Kirsty was already quite wet anyway, she opened her umbrella, and together they walked through the park to the beach and let the dogs off-leash. Sebastian took Kirsty's hand. His heart was also beating faster than normal, but not with anger, but with elation. He had kissed her! And seeing how her sour expression turned into a happy smile, he was overwhelmed by his feelings. She was so beautiful and so brave!

'That man looked familiar,' he said. 'I only saw him very briefly when he got into the car, but I'm sure I'd met him before.' He gazed at the gray ocean and the black rocks. They were covered by water at high tide but currently sticking out from the sand, forming interesting patterns. 'Oh yes, now it comes back to me. I saw him once when I thought he was dead.'

Kirsty was stunned. 'Dead?'

'It was at a wedding ceremony at Point Perry. You know, that lookout point at the ocean. It was the wedding of Kevin, Barbara's dad, and his girlfriend Annika. Suddenly, we heard a cry for help from the rocks below. Without thinking, I started to rush down the steep slope to help that person. And for a moment I thought he was dead! It was quite a shock to see a man motionless lying there, with his legs in the water. Later it turned out that it was just a drunk fisherman.' Sebastian scoffed. 'If I'd only known that he was such a nasty bugger, I wouldn't have tried to rescue him.'

'Who knows? You'd probably just follow your instincts.' Kirsty squeezed his hand. 'Anyway, you were very selfless!'

Sebastian wasn't sure whether he blushed from embarrassment or happiness, and butterflies seemed to dance around in his stomach.

The rain subsided, and as it got windier Kirsty closed her umbrella. Lilly barked excitedly and scratched in the sand – and ran away with a sneaker in her mouth, followed by Susi. When she dropped it for a moment, Susi grabbed the prey and both dogs pulled wildly at different ends, growling and snorting. Since Lilly was much smaller and lighter, Susi dragged her over the sand on her belly. Lilly didn't give up, though, but even wedged her teeth more firmly into her new toy.

'Off!' Sebastian commanded.

Susi obediently let go of her end of the shoe, while Lilly dashed away with it in high spirits. Susi looked at Sebastian as if she wanted to ask: 'Now what?' Kirsty started to chase Lilly, but Sebastian stopped her. 'You'll never catch her, she's much too nimble. Let's go back, and she'll follow us.'

Kirsty looked over her shoulder and saw that Lilly ran a little further away. But then she paused, made another turn, stopped again and finally trotted after them. After a while they managed to get the wet sneaker off her.

'And where's the other running shoe?' asked Kirsty.

Sebastian felt a shiver run down his spine.

'It's so scary, Kirsty! Yesterday I saw a right leather glove, today the single sneaker, and everything reminds me of Thomas! It's as if I were bewitched and couldn't find peace until this murder is solved. I am going crazy if I find a blue flipper next!'

'You have a wild imagination, Sebastian!' She glanced at her watch. 'I better go home and take a hot shower. I'm beginning to feel uncomfortable in my wet clothes.'

Sebastian put the sneaker on a wooden post near the dunes, put the dogs back on the leash and accompanied Kirsty home. Until now, they had talked freely and laughed a lot, but suddenly both of them felt awkward and didn't know how to say goodbye. This time it was Kirsty who gave him a quick kiss, just on the cheek.

When Sebastian came to school the next morning, he saw Kirsty having a lively conversation with Ivory, and immediately he felt a twinge of jealousy. Ivory was a particularly handsome boy with white-blonde, silky shimmering hair, expressive eyes and fair skin. Somehow, he reminded Sebastian of the elven 'Legolas' in 'Lord of the Rings', one of his favourite movies. No wonder that Kirsty apparently found Ivory attractive!

Should he join them? Could he kiss Kirsty here, in public? Right in front of Ivory? The next moment he stumbled as Jack tapped him on the shoulder to greet him. Jack beamed.

'Why are you grinning like a honey pie horse?' Sebastian asked him.

Jack looked at him bewildered. 'What's a honey pie horse?'

'Oops, sorry, that's my translation of a German phrase. Never mind. But why are you grinning?'

'Because Arielle is my girlfriend!'

'Super!' Sebastian was very happy for Jack. He wanted to tell him about his date with Kirsty, but something held him back. Again, he looked at her and finally she noticed him too, but nodded at him only briefly. Damn it! This was not how he'd imagined meeting Kirsty again. Had he been out of his mind thinking that she had special feelings for him?

'What's the matter?' Jack noticed the disappointed look on Sebastian's face.

'I'd thought that Kirsty and I...um ...'

'Yeah, I know all about that, mate. Arielle told me that Kirsty has a huge crush on you.'

'She did?' Sebastian asked incredulously and almost hugged Jack impulsively – in public!

# 9 RAINY DAYS

It was raining cats and dogs. Big parts of Julie's garden were already under water, and big puddles formed on the garage floor. Barbara and her siblings helped their mother to fill sandbags to be prepared for an emergency and to protect the house from flooding. The sky was dark and cloudy, and a waterfall had formed on the south-eastern side of Mount Coolum. No one went rock-climbing at the cliffs this week, but two hikers defied the bad weather and walked up the hill, not willing to deviate from their daily routine.

The rain pelted so loudly on the roof that Sebastian used his earplugs to listen to his music, looking at new messages and photos on Facebook. Lizzie visited a neighbour and Andy was at work. He had started his own business as an electrician with an Australian a few years ago, and recently he got more jobs than he wanted. Susi and Lilly were sleeping, cuddled together on a dog bed. Sometimes their legs twitched, sometimes their noses. Were they dreaming of ball games and delicious food?

Anna was sitting at her desk, busy with a watercolour painting. She intended to create a gift for her brother. Since

Sebastian was very fond of animals, she'd chosen a bright green frog catching a fly as a motif. She used a beautiful image in a calendar to copy from. After a while, Anna stopped and groaned. The frog's long tongue in her own painting looked quite repulsive and crooked. Maybe she should rather paint something else? She frowned and looked for a new idea in her collection of images. She found a photo of a border collie jumping up in the air to catch a Frisbee. Sebastian would certainly like that!

Painting with new enthusiasm, she thought of Jason, a classmate. Recently she had played tennis with him, Barbara and David, and it had been so much fun! Anna was a bloody beginner, even missing the ball completely from time to time. Nevertheless, Jason had been lovely, laughing good-naturedly and giving her helpful tips. And then, after an unexpected win against Barbara and David, he had spontaneously hugged her, and she had been embarrassed and delighted at the same time.

Now Anna dunked her brush into the water glass. Oh dear, the dog looked terrible, too. Sighing, she decided to give up her project for today. What was her brother doing? She knocked on his door. No answer! Of course, as she'd guessed, he was sitting at his computer listening to music. She tapped him on the shoulder to get his attention.

Taking off his headphones, he said excitedly: 'Anna, have a look! I thought of Thomas Cooper again and entered his name on Facebook. Although he is no longer alive, you can still see all sorts of things he liked, YouTubes, pictures and so on.'

Anna sat down and looked at the screen. A handsome, young man was depicted surfing with a Labrador in front of him. 'Wow, a surfing dog! I wonder if Susi could learn that, too?'

'I am not sure.' Sebastian moved the mouse to show her more images. Thomas had posted photos of interesting looking insects, birds, kangaroos, koalas and other marsupials, and also many pictures and texts of an environmental protection organisation. He also wrote about biodiversity loss and land clearing.

'Did you know that they call Australia a hotspot for global deforestation? So many habitats have already been destroyed, and so many mammals are endangered or even extinct. It's shocking!' Sebastian scrolled on quickly. 'And that was Maryann, his former girlfriend. Arielle couldn't stand her.'

'She does look a little stuck-up,' Anna said.

This photo was followed by several crystal-clear shots of artfully arranged cake pieces on a plate. Sebastian's mouth started to water, and his stomach rumbled. 'He liked sweets, although he was a health-conscious vegan. But I wanted to show you something else.' Sebastian scrolled back up. 'There are two men, fighting each other on the beach. And Thomas added:

'RIDING A HIGH WAVE CAN LEAD TO WAVES OF VIOLENCE'.

And you know what? One of those boxers is the same man I told you about the other day. His name is Steven. He's the guy who kicked the dog in the park. And he was lying drunk on the rocks during the wedding ceremony of Annika and Kevin.'

'It seems they are surfers. Maybe they accidentally bumped into each other in the sea, and that's what sparked the argument,' Anna said. 'Perhaps they are both very hot-headed.'

A similar photo followed with the text:

'HOT ANGER IN THE COOL WET'.

Anna saw a few other surfers and a man on a 'Stand Up Paddle' behind the fighting men, and there were two boats further in the background, far out in the sea. 'And Thomas took pictures of the guys punching each other? I'd never dare to do that!'

'Photography was one of his hobbies,' Sebastian mused. 'But yes, it's weird. And perhaps one of these fighters, or both, noticed him and attacked him later?'

'Maybe Freddie knows them as he often goes surfing. We could ask Barbara to forward these photos to him.'

'Yes, why not? After all, Freddie is now her half-brother, since her dad married Annika.' He grinned. 'Brothers are good to have, hey?'

Anna gave him a friendly smack. Lilly barked deafeningly, and both dogs raced to the front door. Lizzie was back!

'Shush, quiet, Lilly! Hi, Susi! Hello! Anna? Sebastian? I've brought you something.'

Curious, the siblings stuck their heads out of the room. Their mother held a plate with baked goodies in one hand.

'Jessica made all this food for us. Vegetable muffins, cocoa-cherry-balls, and pear-almond cakes.'

'Mm, they look delicious!' Sebastian beamed.


However, their good mood and appetite totally disappeared when they watched the local news that evening. Another man had been killed! This time, it was a twenty-three-year-old man who had died from a single blow to his head in Maroochydore. After work, he'd been in a pub, just for one beer, and then he was hit from behind on the way to his car. The reporter called it 'King Hit', a cowardly act in which somebody strikes the victim hard on the head without warning. The man named Steven Owen could not be saved, although someone had immediately called the emergency number 000 and an ambulance had arrived relatively quickly. The police had questioned three people who had been watching everything from a distance. The statements of these witnesses were rather vague, though. The perpetrator had worn a hood, partly disguising him. They said that he had a roundish face and a bulbous nose. A sketched phantom picture indicated a strongly built, medium-sized man with yellow sneakers, black jeans, and a dark gray fleece jacket.

Then an earlier photo of the victim was shown on TV, where he was smiling, holding up a huge fish on a fishing line.

'That's the same guy! I can't believe it!' Anna croaked.

'We were just talking about this Steven, and now he is dead,' Sebastian said, stunned.

'What? You know this man?' Lizzie asked incredulously.

Sebastian, usually never at a loss of words, couldn't utter a sound. So, Anna explained to her mother what she'd learned about Steven from her brother. Finally, she said: 'We'd just found a suspect, and now he's been killed himself.'

Lizzie got downright angry. 'How often do I have to tell you, children, that you must not judge other people so hastily? What a nonsense to accuse Steven! That is absurd. Please stop playing detective! This is a matter for the police, not for you!'

'Sebastian and I only try to help solve the murder!' Anna snarled at her mother.

'What's going on?' Andy came in, surprised at his daughter's grim tone of voice and the tense atmosphere.

'Mum always treats us like silly babies,' Anna cried and ran out of the living room.

'It's my fault,' Sebastian said sheepishly. 'I gave Anna the stupid idea that Steven and another man might have attacked Thomas, just because Thomas took some photos of them while they were punching and kicking each other.'

Andy didn't understand anything at all and sat down with a frown. His wife and son took turns telling him the news while he was eating the last vegetable muffins. Anna stayed in her room sulking and sent a long text message to Barbara.

# 10 DRONES & GLOVES

After school, Sebastian met Arielle, Kirsty and Jack in a park. They ate soft ice cream in a cone while Arielle told them more about her cousin. Thomas had been a talented hobby photographer who had shot many beautiful pictures, mainly of animals and landscapes. During a vacation in Thailand, he had also taken photos of strangers in their everyday life: eager salespeople in the markets, Buddhist monks in front of a temple, TukTuk drivers in heavy traffic, tourists on elephants, and a snake charmer.

'When was your cousin in Thailand?' Kirsty asked.

'About a year ago, with his parents. And after that, Thomas also took many photos of people in Australia who caught his interest. My favourite was that of an old lady with countless wrinkles on her face who grins really sweetly. But Thomas never took pictures of little children, or at least he never published them. Because that is forbidden here.' Arielle wiped some ice cream from her chin. 'At Christmas his father bought him a drone with a camera, and on New Year's Eve they took pictures of the fireworks in Coolum.'

'That's great!' Kirsty was thrilled.

'Don't you need a permit for that?' Jack asked. 'Surely it could be dangerous if a drone got in the way of a plane or a helicopter.'

'There are certain rules about security and privacy, and you can't let a drone fly everywhere.' Arielle devoured her cone. 'And I believe you are limited to a certain altitude.'

'Anyway, it sounds like a fantastic Christmas present! Did Thomas get along well with his father?' Sebastian asked.

'Yes, he did. I remember how much fun they had building a nesting box for a possum. The hardest part was to get it fixed high up on the tree! Both of his parents actually spent a lot of time with Thomas. And they were very generous! After all, Thomas is – uh, he was – a single child, just like me.' Arielle looked very sad again, and Jack stroked her hair tenderly.

'You've ice cream on your nose.' Arielle smiled through tears and gently rubbed the bridge of Jack's nose with her index finger. Jack was embarrassed, once again aware of his broad nose. Kirsty put her small hand into Sebastian's, which was a bit sticky from the ice cream that had melted too quickly.

'Not many people in Queensland wear gloves, hey?' Sebastian blurted out. 'It's not as cold here. But Thomas had a glove on one hand when we found him on that fake horse!' Remembering his childhood in Germany, he felt a pang of regret that he wouldn't be able to do any sledding in the near future. He missed the snow!

'But gloves are used for sports like baseball and so on, or for horseback riding and abseiling,' Jack contradicted.

Kirsty added: 'Many people wear gloves professionally, either to protect their hands or for hygiene reasons.'

'A grandmother of Thomas and me always wore lined leather gloves in winter,' Arielle said. 'And she went to bed with socks.'

Sebastian couldn't help smiling when he secretly imagined their granny as the murderer.

'Was Thomas wearing a lined glove?' Kirsty asked Arielle.

'No, it was a simple, thin leather glove. A woman's glove.'

Jack had a new idea. 'If you're going to commit a burglary, you wear gloves, right?'

'Yes!' Kirsty was all excited. 'Maybe Thomas had been caught stealing? And then somebody strangled him in a fit of fury!'

'My cousin wasn't a thief!' Arielle's blue eyes flashed in indignation.

'I'm sorry.' Kirsty looked onto the floor.

But Sebastian said: 'Some time ago, there were some break-ins in Coolum and also in Yaroomba.'

Before Arielle could respond, Jack said, 'So, maybe the glove did belong to a thief.'

'Can you come up with any other motives for murder?' Sebastian asked. 'Strangulation could indicate a spontaneous act of rage.'

'Many murders are supposedly committed by a family member,' Kirsty blabbered and immediately wanted to bite her tongue. Would Arielle react angrily again?

But her friend nodded her head. 'You're right! Out of jealousy or in blind rage. Or taking revenge, if you were treated badly.'

'Some people kill relatives to get an inheritance.' Sebastian put on his new sunglasses, tired of having to blink at the bright sun that had broken through the clouds a few minutes ago.

'Cool!' Kirsty smiled mischievously at him. 'Now you are looking like a gangster, Mr. Cool Man!'

She kissed him lightly on the lips and Sebastian's heart was warmed. Even though they talked about scary topics, he was incredibly happy that he and Jack now had girlfriends. How funny that they'd fallen in love at the same time!

# 11 DOG TRAINING

Some dogs get into a panic as soon as their owners leave the house. They attempt to escape, bite into doors, dig holes in the garden, bark incessantly, or howl in the highest tones, upsetting all neighbours. Lizzie bought a book about dog training and read it with interest. One suggestion was to ignore your dogs (that had been left at home) after each return for about five minutes and not to greet them effusively. This way the dogs would learn to deal better with their excitement and fear when left behind. Another trick was to leave a frightened dog alone for a very short time in the beginning and then to gradually extend the time of absence.

Lizzie and Andy took their dogs along wherever it was possible, and Susi and Lilly loved to ride in the car. Nevertheless, they sometimes had to stay at home, no matter how sad and pleading they looked. One afternoon, they were left alone and ripped a foam mattress into a thousand little pieces. Since then, Sebastian, Anna and their parents tried to follow the advice in the book. They neither looked at their dogs nor talked to them when they came home. Each morning, they went on with other activities for a few minutes before they paid attention to them. It wasn't easy to treat their beloved pets like that, but it did help in some regards! In former times, Lilly had often annoyed them with her deafening, shrill squealing upon their arrival. Now she became much more relaxed. She rarely barked, and she no longer greeted them with crazy jumps. Susi, however, still jumped up on them frequently.

In the meantime, several people had inquired about Lilly. As she was a cute and friendly dog, Lizzie and Andy had considered keeping her but decided against it. They wanted to help as many dogs as possible to find a new home, and officially, they were only allowed to have a maximum of two dogs on their property. In addition, they had cared for three young dogs in the past and didn't want to repeat that experience. It had been just for one week, but a very chaotic and stressful one. It was a mystery to Lizzie how some people could deal with a whole horde of dogs without any problems. On the walks with her three foster pets, they had pulled into different directions, their leashes getting hopelessly entangled. One of the dogs, gentle and sweet at home, had turned into a wild, snarling monster on the street, attempting to attack other dogs. The garden had also suffered immensely, plants had been bent and dug up, tomatoes had been used as balls, and a newly formed racing track on the lawn had turned into mud after rain. The three dogs, however, had enjoyed themselves splendidly in that time. And Lizzie had decided to learn more about dog training.

This morning, she was reading the newspaper in her living room while the dogs were having a snooze. A storm bird emitted its monotonous sounds without a break. Could that mean more rain to come? Lizzie was getting sick and tired of the wet weather, and today it was drizzling again. At least there had been fewer floods than the year before, and Barbara's mother's house had also been spared.

Lizzie made herself a fresh tea and continued reading. One short article aroused her attention:

The man who'd killed Steven with the King Hit had been arrested. His name was Jim, and he might have got away if he hadn't been involved in a brawl outside a nightclub later on where a police officer made the connection to his former deed. Allegedly, Jim came from a family with a criminal past. His mother was an alcoholic and known for stealing from a store, and there were several criminal lawsuits against his father for domestic violence. The police also suspected the use of drugs.

Lizzie sighed. What a terrible life some families had to endure! But why had Jim attacked Steven? The article didn't reveal any clues, and the investigation was still ongoing. She suspected the young offender had acted impulsively, being very angry for whatever reason. How cruel that Steven had to die from a single blow!

Lilly woke up, stretched and walked to a bowl of water from which she noisily slurped. Then she trotted to Susi and snuggled up to her, putting her head on her bum. Susi briefly blinked and then slept on. Lizzie had to smile about the funny and so peaceful sight of the dog friends. Dear pets could enrich the life of humans so much!

\* \* \*

'He's got a handsome butt,' Barbara whispered to Anna.

She'd already noticed Anna's admiration for their classmate Jason, and now her dreamy expression as he walked across the school grounds. Anna blushed.

'Come on, admit it, you're in love with Jason, aren't you?' Barbara grinned.

Anna hadn't intended to show her feelings so openly. 'Yeah, I think he's nice,' she admitted reluctantly. 'And I like his voice, too. It's so warm, kind of hypnotic and lulling.'

'Lulling?' Barbara was amused.

'Yes, he's such a great speaker! His presentation in the English class this morning was really good. Usually, these student's speeches are terribly boring.'

'Oh, now I see what you mean. In that regard, Jason reminds me a bit of Freddie. I always love to listen to his stories.' Barbara smiled. 'It's great to have a big brother. But watch out, he likes to flirt!'

'Did you ever send him those photos of the guys who got into a fight?'

'Yes, I did. But Freddie had never seen them before. Well, there are plenty of surfers out there.'

'You're right! It was a strange coincidence that Sebastian wanted to rescue Steven, the man who was later killed, when he was lying helplessly on the rocks. By the way, Sebastian met him again recently and Kirsty saw him kicking a dog! But now he is dead.' Anna rubbed her arms as she suddenly got goose bumps. 'How brutal some people are! I keep thinking of Thomas' body in that park and that somebody put a flipper on his foot. Hard to imagine, isn't it? It's so creepy!'

'I wonder if Thomas was just in the wrong place at the wrong time, maybe like Steven, too.'

They were both silent for a while. Then Anna had a new idea. 'Sebastian told me that Thomas had a drone. Maybe he found out something and blackmailed someone.'

'You mean, Thomas discovered something like a secret marijuana plantation?'

'Who knows? However, that wouldn't be very likely. Because planes and helicopters often fly over the area. Just the other day, for example, a man had to be rescued from Mount Coolum by helicopter when he slipped and broke his leg.'

'I wouldn't like to have a drone flying right over me,' Barbara said. 'And my neighbors wouldn't like it either, if they were lying stark naked by their swimming pool.'

'Do they swim in the nude?' Anna grinned.

'Probably not. But it's definitely wrong to take pictures of people without their knowledge.'

'But that's exactly what Thomas did! He supposedly took many photos! Maybe he did make enemies?'

It started raining, and Anna and Barbara sprinted back to the school building. On the way, they were overtaken by Jason and his friends, but to their surprise, Jason paused to take Anna by the hand and then ran on with her.

# 12 GRAFFITI

Andy was outraged. On his way home from work, he discovered graffiti on a recently painted, rendered retaining wall. Senseless stupid scrawls, he thought. He pitied the owners of the house, a nice older couple, who would now have to scrub the wall clean or to repaint it. He was glad that he'd planted a hedge in front of his own fence. As soon as he opened the door to his home, intense scents of spices and coriander wafted towards him.

'We are having Thai food today,' Sebastian told him.

A large wok was already standing on the dining table.

'Let's hope the rice will be ready soon! I was silly and forgot to turn on the rice cooker,' Lizzie said contritely.

Andy kissed her tenderly, and Sebastian grinned broadly. His father grinned back, asking, 'And where is Anna?'

'I bet she's writing hundreds of text messages again.' Lizzie put on a pout. 'These days, kids sit in front of their computers, stare at their mobile phones or watch TV for hours on end.'

'Nonsense!' Sebastian protested. 'Anna and I do a lot of sports and walk the dogs all the time. Besides, I just helped you with the cooking.'

'Did you?' Andy was impressed.

Now Lizzie giggled. 'Sebastian's girlfriend is a vegetarian. So, today we tried out an Asian recipe without any meat.'

'It certainly smells enticing.' Andy was already hungry.

'Anna, dinner is ready!' Lizzie called and spooned the rice into a pretty bowl. 'Anna?'

'I'll be right there,' Anna shouted back from her room.

Sebastian stole a fried mushroom from the wok. 'Mm – delicious!'

Anna sat down at the table, too, and smiled.

'You are looking so radiant,' her father remarked. 'Is something special going on?'

Sebastian, who was just putting a huge portion of vegetables on his plate, looked curiously at his sister. Lizzie also watched her daughter attentively. Lately, she had been worried about Anna's somewhat grumpy and rebellious demeanor. In addition, she'd sometimes seemed very tired and pale. But now Anna looked happy and her cheeks had a rosy glow.

Anna didn't answer her father's question, just saying, 'It smells great!'

'Kirsty told me that some people are allergic to coriander,' Sebastian pointed out.

'True! I'm glad we can eat anything,' Andy replied. 'I met a person once who got very ill from eating carrots.'

'Are Kirsty's parents vegetarians too?' Lizzie asked.

'Her mother is. Her father already died of cancer many years ago,' Sebastian said. 'Kirsty's little sister can't even remember him because she was only three years old at the time.'

'Terrible! So, her mother had to raise two children on her own.'

'How old is Kirsty's sister?' Anna asked.

'Ellen is ten, and she's a cheeky rascal.' Sebastian grinned. 'But Kirsty can be cheeky too.'

'Just like you!' Anna teased him. Lilly sneezed loudly, making Anna laugh. 'And you are the biggest rascal, Lilly!'

The little dog ran to her and looked at her with begging eyes.

'Daddy, it's your turn to walk the dogs today,' Anna reminded her father.

'Oh dear! Again? All right. Who wants to come along?'

'Hold on!' Lizzie said. 'Sebastian made a special dessert.'

It wasn't until they finished every little bit that Andy got up to get the leads. 'Phew, on a full stomach I don't want to go far now.'

'I'll come along,' Sebastian offered.

Susi and Lilly pricked up their ears and raced to the door. Anna decided to go along, too, and together they set off. It was already dark, and the street lamps cast just a sparse light on their path. After a while they reached the retaining wall that Andy had noticed earlier that day, and both dogs stopped to sniff extensively. Andy switched on his flashlight and illuminated the colourful, scrawly writing.

'Look at this! Isn't it mean to blemish a white wall like that? I hope they catch the guys who did this.'

'It's so ugly,' Sebastian agreed.

'Many people call themselves graffiti artists and are proud of their work, but I don't regard this as art at all,' Andy said scornfully.

Anna scoffed. 'If only they'd painted a real picture instead of those silly letters.'

'It's called 'tagging',' Sebastian explained.

'No one shall ever paint my walls without permission,' Andy said fiercely.

A man with a Spitz came towards them, quickly crossing the street before getting too close. His little dog pulled like crazy and yelped shrilly. Andy turned off the flashlight, and they continued their walk.

Anna thought about Jason. After the short run to seek shelter from the rain, she'd been breathless with happiness that he'd held her hand. Later he'd asked her for her mobile phone number and, just before dinner, he'd sent her a text message and a smiley. But why was she so excited about him? After all, he was not her type at all. She was actually more into lanky, tall, blonde boys with blue eyes – like Scott. Jason, on the other hand, was only a few centimetres taller than her, muscularly built, with dark brown hair and brown eyes. He was very attractive, though. Anyway, he ...

'By the way, have you heard anything from Scott again?' her father interrupted her thoughts.

Anna somehow felt caught out, as if it were wrong to fall in love with someone else so quickly. 'Yes, he sent me an e-mail today. He and Susan would like to meet us again and want to know when we're going to visit Aunt Paula and Uncle Sam.'

'We could go there over Easter, that's pretty soon,' Andy suggested.

Sebastian stopped unexpectedly right in front of him, and Andy almost collided with him. 'What the ...'

'There's one of those graffiti guys,' Sebastian whispered.

They were on a hilly, winding road in a suburb where most of the houses were hidden behind high fences, dense shrubs and old trees. At a distance of about fifty meters, they could see a suspicious figure right under a street lamp. A young man was busy spraying on a wooden fence, using a spray can.

'We'll teach him some manners!' Andy said grimly.

'How dare you ruin the property of others!' he shouted loudly.

The man paused, obviously startled, and then he picked up a bag from the floor and ran away, cursing. Susi growled threateningly. Lilly wanted to chase after him, and Sebastian clutched the leash tighter. For such a tiny dog Lilly was surprisingly strong. The man quickly disappeared from their sight behind the top of the hill.

'Wow, he is a fast runner!' Anna was amazed.

'Let's see if anyone is home,' Andy suggested. 'It might be easier to wash the paint off while it's still fresh.'

However, nobody replied to his knocking and calling. They stared at the fence. The only word that was emblazoned there in bright red was 'IDIOT'. Under the last letter was a thick drop. At that moment a car stopped next to them and a stocky middle-aged policeman got out. He was bald, had googly eyes and a beer belly over which his uniform was tightly stretched.

'What are you doing here?' he asked brusquely.

'Someone just sprayed this fence, but he ran away very quickly,' Andy replied and pointed to the hill.

'Damn it! My fence is brand-new.' His face twisted into an angry grimace and he clenched his fists. 'Can you describe the culprit?'

Andy shrugged. 'Well, that's difficult. He was quite far away, and he had a hood on his head. He was of medium height.'

'He was wearing a dark jacket,' Sebastian added.

'And yellow sneakers,' Anna said, suddenly realising that their description exactly matched the one of the brutal man who had killed Steven. Could it be the same man? Nah – her mother had told them at dinner that this guy had already been arrested.

'We've already seen more Graffiti today, on a retaining wall nearby,' Andy said to the policeman. 'I guess it was the scribbling of two people who called themselves SEXY BEAST and SUPERBRAIN.'

'Surely no one would call himself an IDIOT!' Sebastian chuckled.

The policeman looked at him sternly. 'There's no need for jokes, young friend.'

'Excuse me!' Sebastian muttered.

'Well, we'd better get going!' Andy didn't like this man with the ice-cold eyes, and he noticed that Susi's neck hair stood up.

Returning home, Sebastian yelled, 'Hello, Mum, we've discovered more Graffiti!'

'Idiot!' Anna called out.

'Anna, don't you call your brother that!' Lizzie scolded her.

Anna laughed. 'No, 'IDIOT' was the word someone sprayed on a wooden fence. And that fence belonged to a policeman, of all people!'

They told their mother about their discovery, while Andy poured a glass of red wine for Lizzie and himself. Susi dashed into the dining room and was disappointed to find her feeding bowl empty. Lilly, on the other hand, rolled around on the floor and kicked her feet merrily into the air.

# 13 A FINE

Andy was outraged again. Driving home after work and looking forward to a relaxed evening, he had been given a fine by the same unfriendly policeman. So much money! Three hundred and fifty-three dollars! Just because he hadn't stopped long enough at a stop sign. What a bummer! Lizzie would be mad, too.

'Hi, Daddy!' Anna beamed at him, and his heart felt lighter. It was nice to see her so happy. The next moment Susi almost knocked him off his feet, when she bounced around him joyfully.

'Papa, I'd like to play tennis again. Could you give me some money? There will be four of us, and therefore I'll only need five bucks.'

'What? Have you already spent all your pocket money?' Andy asked her sternly, inwardly smiling about her German word 'Papa' for 'Dad'.

'I bought a watercolour sketch pad the other day, and Barbara and I had some ice cream, and …'

'Never mind,' Andy agreed in a good-natured manner and rummaged in his pocket for change. 'But you'll have to do the dishes today.'

'It's my turn anyway,' Anna grinned.

'Okay, five dollars for you and five for your brother. Let's be fair, right?'

'Thanks, Daddy!' Anna smiled broadly and ran to her brother to give him his share.

'That cop treated me like a criminal, the bastard!' Andy scowled a bit later, telling his wife about the fine.

Lizzie was not at all pleased, but she had to laugh. 'Maybe it's no wonder someone wrote 'IDIOT' on his fence.'

'This policeman did look mean,' Anna said. 'And he's pretty ugly, with his bloated face. I didn't like his thin moustache and his weird beard that was split in the middle.'

'And he had cold fish eyes,' Sebastian said.

'Now you are mean! You shouldn't judge other people by their appearance! And you, Andy, better obey the traffic rules in the future!' Lizzie said firmly. But then she smiled mischievously. 'By the way, I was a kind of inspector today, checking out Jessica's garden. She'd like to adopt a dog, and a woman from the Moist Nose Rescue Organisation asked me to find out if a little Shih Tzu would be well looked after by her.'

'What did you have to check?' Sebastian asked curiously.

'First of all, the fencing. Since dogs often attempt to escape as soon as they come into a strange environment, I had to check if the garden is fenced off safely. I advised Jessica to fix one fence panel and to put some bricks or boulders in another spot where a dog could easily dig a hole and escape. But everything else was just fine, and Jessica already bought a dog bed and toys and showed me where her pet could lie in the shade and drink water when left alone.'

'Jessica? Is that the woman who made the yummy vegan balls for us the other day?' Anna asked.

'Yes, that's her! Today I got a delicious blueberry muffin.'

'Well, well, so you took a bribe? Just don't get too fat!' Andy teased her.

'Mum is slim like a willow!' Anna defended her mother. 'But you've got a little belly, Daddy!'

Andy made a face, pretending to be shocked, while Lizzie smiled in amusement. In reality, she too was not as slim as she used to be. Andy thought of the fat cop again.

'Maybe the policeman was so rude because Lilly made a mess right in front of his mailbox last night. I cleaned it up, of course, but he looked really pissed off.'

'Strange that the guy with the spray can was wearing yellow sneakers!' Anna mused.

'Not strange at all! Nowadays many people wear colourful running shoes, even the professional rugby players,' Sebastian said.

Anna scratched her head. 'I am glad that, despite the same clothes, he wasn't that brutal man from Maroochydore.'

'Who knows! Maybe they arrested the wrong guy,' Lizzie interjected.

It was a sunny afternoon with a bright blue sky when Anna played tennis with Barbara, David and Jason. They'd booked a court for one hour, and Jason supplied the tennis balls and rackets. Anna was quite nervous and hit too many balls into the net, soon getting frustrated. However, Jason patiently advised her how she could improve her game. From the way he treated her, Barbara and David assumed that he liked her a lot, and they were happy for their friend. Suddenly Anna cried out when a tennis ball hit her right on the head. But she just rubbed the spot and kept staring at the tennis court next to them as if hypnotised.

'Are you okay?' Jason asked, taking her by the hand and pulling her aside. 'A tennis ball can really hurt, but at least it was just a slow ball from Barbara. Let's have a drink of water!' he shouted to the others.

Anna smiled tentatively. In the middle of the game, she had got distracted as she'd noticed a man with yellow sneakers on the adjoining tennis court – the same guy they had seen spraying the fence. This time he was dressed in shorts and T-shirt and wore a cap on his shoulder-length brown hair. So far, he didn't seem to have recognised her. They took a short break, and just then a ball came flying, almost hitting Barbara's head.

'Sorry! Could you return that ball?' the other guy on the next court shouted. Now his friend also looked over and caught sight of Anna. Stepping closer, he said, 'Hi! You gave me a huge fright that night!'

He looked a bit embarrassed and younger than Anna had expected. She estimated he was eighteen or nineteen years old.

Anna had to smile. 'Are you afraid of dogs?'

'No, I love dogs! But that man sounded so angry. Was that your father?'

'Yes. He hates seeing anybody defacing property of others.'

'I'd never done any graffiti before in my life. And it was stupid of me! But that cop is such an idiot!'

'Why? What has he done?'

'A few days ago, he stopped some friends of mine in their car. He asked for the driver's license, checked out the car from all sides and even made them open the trunk. And then ...'

'Bruce, we're here to play and not to chat,' his friend shouted impatiently.

'Anyway, this man is mean and brutal,' Bruce said and went back to his tennis court.

Anna and her friends also continued their game. Barbara and David won the next match and Anna was annoyed with herself. She just couldn't relax in Jason's presence today, feeling awkward, sweaty and ugly. He would definitely never ask her to play tennis with him again, she thought sullenly and hit a ball into the net once again.

# 14 FATHER AND SON

Jack and Sebastian were training their skills in soccer on the sports field, and Jack admired his friend for his agility. Spotting Fiona and Arielle in the distance, both gesticulating wildly and obviously arguing about something, Jack stopped his ball.

'You know what Arielle told me yesterday?'

'What's that?' Sebastian looked at him curiously.

'Thomas' father has moved out. Since the murder of their only child, he and his wife had arguments all the time, getting worse and worse.'

'How sad! They should rather comfort each other.'

'That's exactly what I said. But the most interesting thing is that Thomas was not his biological son. And Wayne, Arielle's uncle, only found out about it now.'

'Wow! And who's the real father?'

'No idea! But Arielle told me that her Aunt Heidi had a little love affair during a holiday in New Zealand.'

'And Thomas didn't know about his dad, either?'

'Nah, apparently not.' Jack combed his unruly hair with his fingers. 'Arielle's whole family is pretty shocked. Her parents were horrified that Heidi had been cheating on her husband. However, Wayne wasn't always the best guy, either. Once he hit his wife after he'd staggered home from a pub, drunk as a pig and upset about something. But afterwards he sincerely regretted it and was never violent again, and Arielle said he really loved Thomas with all his heart.'

'I can't imagine what I would think if my mother had a secret lover and my dad wasn't my biological father.' Sebastian mused.

Jack laughed. 'You look just like your father, so don't worry!'

'Anyway, I'm glad my parents are pretty nice and almost never quarrel.'

'My parents also get along well. By the way, my mother is in charge.' Jack grinned. 'Please promise me to keep this story about Thomas' parents a secret, okay? Otherwise, Arielle will tear my head off.'

Sebastian laughed. 'I promise! It seems you are already under Arielle's thumb!'

Jack nodded, good-naturedly. 'You got it, mate!'

Sebastian's previously amused face darkened. Kirsty strolled around the school grounds with Ivory, and he could hear them laughing from afar. Why did Kirsty always hang out with him? He felt a painful sting of jealousy – and got angry with himself. He'd never liked it when partners stuck together constantly, and even though Kirsty was his girlfriend, she was a free person. Nevertheless, Ivory got on his nerves!

'What's the matter with you?' Jack asked.

Sebastian was astonished. Had his friend guessed his dark thoughts? But no, Jack was looking at Arielle who was coming towards them, her eyes red from crying.

'That stupid cow!' Sobbing, she threw herself into Jack's arms.

'Hey, sweetie, what happened?' Jack gave her a kiss on the cheek.

'Fiona is so mean!' Arielle sniffed and blew her nose.

'I never liked her,' Sebastian said. 'But I always thought you were good friends.'

Arielle scoffed. 'Yes, we were – when I didn't know her so well yet. Now I've found out how nasty she can be. All she ever wants to do is drag others through the mud.'

Jack took her hand and looked pitifully at his girlfriend. Arielle had to smile involuntarily. His brown eyes shone as warm and faithful as Max's, she thought amusedly.

'You look like my dog,' she burst out laughing.

'Don't get cheeky!' Jack pretended to growl threateningly and to bite her nose.

Sebastian grinned. 'Do you know that people often get bitten when they bend down to a strange dog? Ever since I read that, I don't pat dogs I don't know yet. In any case, I keep my face away from them and let them first sniff at me.'

'I was lucky the other day that your Susi gave me a wet, nicely meant kiss, although she hardly knew me,' Kirsty said, who'd come to them and overheard Sebastian's last words.

'Hi, Kirsty! Yes, Susi was very fond of you from the start. Amazing, as she usually is terribly suspicious.'

Sebastian nodded at Ivory. 'Hi!'

'What's wrong, have you been crying?' Kirsty asked Arielle.

'Don't worry, I was just annoyed,' Arielle replied, ashamed that she'd reacted so emotionally and even cried in front of her classmates.

Sebastian would have liked to hug Kirsty, but in Ivory's presence he felt inhibited. He wondered about what they'd talked and laughed so happily before. Ivory seemed calm and composed as always. His skin was flawless, while a nasty, thick pimple was sprouting in Sebastian's face. Again, he saw a big similarity between Ivory and the beautiful elf 'Legolas', and regarded himself as an ugly gnome.

Now Kirsty pulled Arielle away from the others, babbling away.

'There is Toby! I have to ask him something,' 'Jack shouted and left.

So, out of a sudden, Sebastian found himself alone with Ivory. He didn't know what to say. Embarrassed, he scratched his chin and noticed in horror that another pimple had already formed there.

Ivory smiled at him. 'Did you know that Kirsty was my very first girlfriend?'

'Um – no, I didn't know that,' Sebastian stuttered.

'Yes, since kindergarten. We were inseparable! And just now we were talking about how we once ran away from school when we were only eight years old. We'd had a fight with Fiona and were supposed to apologise to her, which we didn't want to do. Instead, we took off in protest and hid in the forest for hours.'

'I'm sure the teachers were really anxious!'

'Yes, two teachers looked for us for quite a long time. Unfortunately, they also called my father, because he is a policeman, and they got the idea that he might be able to use a search dog. Oh boy, was my dad angry!'

'Did he find you?'

'No! We went back to school when it started to rain. But we had bad luck. We'd been sitting in a tree for a while, and when I tried to climb down, I was too clumsy and sprained my left foot. I also stupidly stepped on a long branch that leaped up and caused a big bump on my forehead. And we got soaking wet in the rain. After that, Kirsty had a terrible cold. And so, both her mother and my parents thought that we'd already received sufficient punishment.'

Again, Ivory smiled, and Sebastian envied him for his even white teeth. The guy looks great and has perfect teeth, he thought. But meanwhile he found him much more likeable than he'd ever expected.

'So, even back then, in Kindergarten, you already had some trouble with Fiona?' Sebastian asked.

'Exactly! Kirsty once caught her trying to tear a wing off a grasshopper and we managed to save the poor animal. But Fiona ran to a teacher, whining, and said that we'd twisted her arm.'

Ivory looked at Kirsty who was still talking to Arielle in the distance.

'In reality, Kirsty had just grabbed her wrist, but Fiona was always brilliant at putting others down and making herself popular with the teachers. Better watch out, Sebastian! She can really make life difficult, and now that you're Kirsty's boyfriend, Fiona certainly hates you too.'

'It seems she already had a go at Arielle today. Anyway, Arielle was terribly upset about something Fiona said to her.'

Sebastian found it odd to talk about girls with Ivory, of all people, whom he had considered a rival until recently. Moreover, he regarded gossiping as something unmanly. But Ivory's warning had sounded serious.

# 15 DANCING IN THE STREET

Anna gazed at herself in the mirror and was dissatisfied. Her face looked blotchy, her eyes tired, and her hair seemed like a mop. She was still upset about the failed tennis game the day before. Why did she have to be so awkward and clumsy? Would Jason still wish to see her? Or did he find her far too boring and non-athletic? She bit her lips.

'Anna! Telephone!' her mother called. 'It's Scott!'

Anna hadn't expected him to call. She rushed to her mother who handed her the cordless phone. 'Hello, Scott. What's up?'

'I just wanted to see how you were doing.'

'Fine,' Anna lied, not wanting to admit that she had been close to tears a moment ago. She retreated to her room so she could talk undisturbed.

'When will I see you and Sebastian?' Scott asked. 'You are going to visit your relatives over Easter, hey? Just in case, Susan and I have already planned a little party together with Kylie and Mike.'

Anna remained silent.

'Don't worry, Anthony won't be there. But Kylie and Mike would be so happy to meet you. It's been a long time!'

Anna had to smile. 'It's great that they're still together.'

When Scott didn't respond, Anna quickly continued, 'Sebastian has got a girlfriend now, did you know that?'

'Yes, Susan showed me a picture of Kirsty. She looks cute!'

Scott didn't dare to ask if Anna had got a new boyfriend. They talked for a while until Anna said, 'We'll probably go to Aunt Paula's and Uncle Sam's on Good Friday. Maybe Sebastian and I could meet up with you on Saturday morning. I let you know later, okay?'

Anna had a sinking feeling in her stomach. On the one hand, she was looking forward to the reunion, but on the other hand, she still wasn't over the fact that Scott had a relationship with Anthony. Would she possibly fall in love with Scott again? She'd always felt so comfortable and accepted in his company, and now his pleasant voice had brought back many happy memories. Would she ever be able to behave so naturally with another boyfriend?

No sooner had she hung up the phone when she received a text message on her own mobile phone. It was from Jason! Curiously, she read his message: 'Anna, I miss you!' And a new message came in: 'Sleep well!'

Anna was immediately filled with joy. She quickly wrote back: 'Looking forward to seeing you again! Good night!'

Radiantly, she bent over to Susi. 'Hey, Susi, he seems to like me after all!'

Susi wagged her tail, first slowly and then faster and faster, hitting the floor so that it sounded like a drum roll.

Lilly was unhappy. Earlier today, she had discovered a bone in the garden. It had been buried, but Lilly had smelled it thanks to her fine nose and had dug it out. Since some painfully biting ants crawled around on it, she had to push the bone back and forth to get rid of the annoying beasts, and just when she started to chew on it with pleasure, Susi snatched it away from her. All that work for nothing! Disappointed, she now lay on her dog mattress.

'Lilly, why do you look so sad?' Sebastian knelt down and stroked her. Her dark eyes under her bushy eyebrows took on a loving expression. She really liked Sebastian, and he often hid little treats like dried liver pieces in his left trouser pocket. Hopefully, she sniffed at him.

Sebastian laughed. 'You are hungry again, aren't you? Come on, we better go for a walk, or you'll get too fat!'

In reality, Lilly was quite skinny, but his parents had advised him not to spoil their pets too much. Sebastian got up to fetch the dog leashes, calling out to his sister, 'Anna, I'm going for a walk. Do you want to come, too?'

'Okay! Just a sec!'

Walking at a brisk pace, Anna told her brother about Scott's call. Sebastian could hardly wait to meet their friends again, especially Susan.

Now Anna and Sebastian passed a house from which loud music was blasting. Four cars were parked in the front garden and a high number of cars on the street which had little traffic on most other days. 'Someone is having a big party,' Anna said.

'Good music!' Sebastian danced around Anna until Lilly started to bark and Susi jumped up on him.

Anna laughed. 'You are driving the dogs crazy. Shush, quiet, Lilly!'

'Come dance with me!' Sebastian took her hands.

Anna protested. 'We can't dance in the middle of the street!'

But then she let herself be carried away by her brother and the fast melody, and they hopped around wildly, without letting go of the dog leads. During a new song, Sebastian briefly held Susi's front paws and led her around in a circle, and Anna took

Lilly in her arms. Another car approached slowly and parked a few houses away. Anna stopped dancing and put Lilly back on the ground. She heard car doors slamming, a laugh and a voice that sounded somehow familiar. Who was that?

'Oh, hello! We seem to keep running into each other!' Bruce said, grinning broadly. This time, he wasn't wearing yellow sneakers. He was dressed all in black and carried a six-pack of beer. He was accompanied by a friend with a chubby figure, wearing tight, glittery pants and a brightly coloured shirt. His mane of raven-black hair was held in check by a red ribbon.

'And I don't even know your names yet,' Bruce continued.

'Hi! I'm Anna. And this is Sebastian, my brother.'

For some inexplicable reason, Anna blushed. Good thing it was already pretty dark!

'Hi, Anna!' Bruce put the beer bottles down on the floor, turned to Sebastian and shook his hand. 'Hi! I'm Bruce and this is Oliver.' Lilly smelled curiously at his shoes, and he bent down to pat her. Susi hid anxiously behind Sebastian's legs.

Oliver, who looked a bit like a rock star to Anna, asked the siblings, 'Are you also going to Henry's party?'

'No!' Sebastian chuckled, somewhat embarrassed. 'The music was so great and we just listened for a while.'

'Yes, we saw you dancing!' Oliver smiled at them. 'Good idea! We should dance outdoors in the fresh air much more often.'

'Yeah, well, have fun! Come on, Sebastian, it's time to go home.' Anna pulled her brother by the sleeve.

At that moment a window of the house next door opened and a curtain was pushed aside. But they couldn't see anybody.

Oliver said, 'I bet the old grump has already called the police again. At every birthday party of Henry's, this neighbour complains about the noise.'

Bruce raised his eyebrows. 'Really? It's still early in the evening!' Susi noticed that her friend Lilly enjoyed being stroked by him and now she also nudged him with her nose.

'You are beautiful dogs,' Bruce said in such a funny, unnaturally high tone that Anna had to laugh. Both dogs pressed themselves against him, keen to get his attention, and he patted them. Anna and Sebastian were amazed. They had rarely seen Susi behaving so trustingly with a stranger!

'Here they come!' Oliver frowned.

A police car had stopped nearby and two policemen came towards them. 'Oh no, it's that idiot!' Bruce's voice sounded normal again and much deeper, but since he mumbled the words into Susi's ear, only the dog understood him. Susi stiffened and watched the men suspiciously.

'Are you also part of the celebration, or what are you doing here?' the fat policeman asked, staring at them with his bulging eyes.

'One of the neighbours complained about unbearable noise,' the other policeman explained, who, despite his size, seemed less threatening to Sebastian than his colleague whom they had met before.

Oliver winked at Bruce. 'See?' he whispered.

The fat policeman looked sternly at the siblings. 'I know you! You're always hanging out where there's trouble.'

Anna got angry. Although she was usually rather shy, she said snottily, 'We are taking our dogs for a walk, just like the last time we saw you. And then we didn't make any trouble at all, but just wanted to tell you about the graffiti on your fence.'

Sebastian was surprised at his sister's harsh tone of voice. What had gotten into her?

Bruce said, 'It's just a birthday party.'

'But the music is much too loud,' the tall policeman said. With long steps, he went to the entry and knocked on the door. 'Police!' he shouted. No one opened. 'Hello!'

Apparently, nobody could hear him inside. Anna saw the curtain from the neighbouring house moving again.

'Wait!' Oliver quickly fetched his mobile phone and dialled a number. 'Hi, Henry, you have visitors!'

Lilly sniffed at the trousers of the policeman standing next to Anna, and she quickly pulled her away. 'Stop it!' Once again, she said to her brother: 'Come on, let's go home!'

But Sebastian didn't move from the spot. He was keen to find out what the police would do. A young man now appeared at the entrance with a beer bottle in his hand. He froze when he saw the policeman standing next to Oliver.

'Are you Henry?' the man in uniform asked politely. 'Happy Birthday! However, there has been a complaint. Can you please turn down the music?' Then he joked, 'I'd love to join the party, but I'm on duty.'

Henry grinned: 'No problem!'

Bruce and Oliver said goodbye to Anna and Sebastian, and finally Sebastian turned to go back with his sister. But the unfriendly policeman unexpectedly put his hand on Anna's arm and hissed, 'I warn you! You better stay away from these guys!'

His breath blew hot and foul-smelling into her face and she instinctively took a step back. What a creep! To their relief, the other policeman patted his colleague on the shoulder. 'All right, Tim, it's just a harmless party.' He winked at the siblings.

Sebastian was still perplexed that Anna had answered Tim so defiantly. And later he remembered that he had been warned twice today. Once about Fiona and then about Bruce and Oliver.

# 16 THE SNAKE

The Easter weekend went by in a flash. The Kuhlmanns immensely enjoyed their time with Uncle Sam and Aunt Paula. Susi loved swimming in a pond full of duck weed, and both she and Lilly got along very well with the bigger dogs Lola and Missy. Initially, Anna had been worried about the meeting with Scott, his sister and Scott's best friends. Luckily, it turned out much easier and nicer than she'd expected. At first, she hugged Scott a bit awkwardly, but after a while their friendship overcame all bad feelings. Kylie and Mike were still in love with each other, and they joked and laughed a lot. None of them talked about Anthony. Susan, high-spirited and bubbly as usual, bombarded Sebastian with questions about his new girlfriend.

After several days in the hinterland, the Kuhlmanns and their dogs were back in Coolum. On Wednesday morning, Lilly was overjoyed when she found an old bone. To her surprise, Susi graciously left it to her. Andy went to work, and Sebastian tried out a new computer game. He already missed Kirsty who'd gone to Hervey Bay for a week. Lizzie was busy in the garden, while Susi was keeping her company. Hoping that Lizzie would throw sticks for her, Susi kept bringing her various tiny twigs. Finally, she dropped a big branch at her feet. Lizzie sighed. 'You never give up, Susi! But we can't play all the time. Can't you help me weeding?'

Susi's eyes lit up with anticipation.

'Oh, dear. You've heard the word 'play', haven't you?'

Lizzie got up, stretched her aching back and went to the shed to look for a rubber ball. Once again, the pleading gaze of those beautiful dog eyes made her combine gardening with ball throwing. She laughed when Susi let the ball plop directly into the container full of weeds.

'Okay, Susi, new rules: From now on you must catch the ball and drop it into a bucket.' She brought an empty, smaller bucket, and in the end, she caught many balls herself with that bucket, running around almost as much as Susi.

Anna got up late. She chuckled when she discovered her mother romping around with Susi.

'Hi Mum, I am going over to Barbara's!' she called to her after breakfast.

On the way to her friend, she was feeling a bit sad, wondering about her relationship to Jason. Sometimes, he was attentive and very nice to her. But much too often, he seemed disinterested, hardly listening to her. Did he regard her just as a quick flirt? So far, they had only cuddled up in the cinema once. And he had a strange sense of humor. In any case, she had found the movie that he'd loved far too silly and ...

A loud squeak tore her from her brooding.

'Watch out!' someone shouted. Anna turned around in shock. She'd almost got run over by a car!

'Oh, it's you! Wow, that was really close,' Bruce said through the open window of a light gray car. 'Shall I give you a ride?'

Anna hesitated.

'Come on, get in!' Bruce urged her as a car behind him had to slow down. No sooner had Anna got in than he drove off. He put his hand on her leg for a moment. 'I'm so glad you're okay!'

His fleeting touch triggered an intense, pleasant tingling in Anna. Normally she hated being touched by someone she hardly knew, but she was magically drawn to Bruce. Very confused and without saying a peep, she put on her seatbelt. Her mouth was terribly dry.

'Where are you going?' Bruce asked.

'To my friend Barbara.' Anna found her voice again and gave him the address. 'I was completely lost in thought,' she admitted. 'So silly to cross a street without looking.'

'Good that my brakes work well. I can still rely on my dear old car.' Bruce smiled at her.

Wonderful how his whole face lights up when he smiles, Anna thought. She said aloud, 'Strange that we run into each other all the time. Do you actually live near that unfriendly policeman? Or how did you know his address so that you could spray 'IDIOT' onto his fence?' At the same moment, she was a bit shocked about herself. Usually, it was her brother who asked inconsiderate questions and could be too nosy.

Bruce stopped at a red light. 'Yeah, I live just around the corner from him. But not for very long yet. Just recently I moved there from my parent's house in Mooloolaba. Because of my new job in Coolum, I am living in a shared house now, so that I don't have to drive that far to work.' He grinned briefly. 'It was time to move away from my parents anyway.'

'And what kind of job do you do?'

'I am a salesman in a plumber's store. It's only part-time, but better than nothing.'

'Sounds great!' Anna watched him from the side. He looked really good! And then an idea sprang up in her mind. 'Have you planned anything special for this morning? Would you like to come with me to Barbara's? I could ask her if that would be fine with her.' She blushed again and was annoyed that she did.

The light turned green and Bruce stepped on the gas. Anna admired his slender, muscular hands at the wheel. She felt her heart race as he almost touched her right knee while shifting gears. He replied, 'I was going to do some shopping, but yes, why not?'

Anna wrote an SMS to Barbara with nimble fingers, and her answer came immediately: 'OK.'

'And where are your brother and your dogs today?' Bruce asked.

'Probably busy with computers, ball games and old bones.'

Bruce laughed. 'I love dogs.' A shadow flew across his face. 'And they are more loyal than humans.'

'That's so true,' Anna sighed.

They looked at each other and smiled sheepishly. Anna had the crazy impulse to caress Bruce's cheek when his distinctive features took on a distressed expression. What was wrong with her? A moment ago she had been thinking about Jason, and now she was so fascinated by another guy? What would Barbara think of her bringing him along? Her heart was beating so loudly that she thought Bruce could hear it too.

Anna was surprised when Barbara's little brother opened the garden gate and Lisa and Freddie were right behind him. So, all the siblings of her friend were at home. Lisa looked at Bruce with undisguised curiosity. 'Who are you?'

Bruce smiled and introduced himself. Freddie shook his hand and gave Anna a kiss on the cheek.

'Come in!' Tom said and marched ahead of them into the garden. When Barbara greeted them, she smelled of shampoo and her hair was damp. 'I've already mowed the lawn and needed a quick shower after that,' she said. 'Hello, I'm Barbara!' she turned to Bruce.

'Hi, we'd met before on the tennis court.'

'Would you like something to drink? Lemon tea, juice or lemonade?'

'I'll get it,' Freddie volunteered. 'Lisa and Tom, you could give me a hand. Come on!'

Anna sneezed violently. Bruce flinched, and Barbara grinned. She had gotten used to Anna trumpeting as loud as an elephant.

'Do you suffer from hay fever?' Bruce asked.

'No, thankfully not.' Anna blew her nose. 'I even love the smell of fresh grass cuttings.'

They sat down at a table under a big tree. Freddie, Tom and Lisa soon returned with glasses decorated with fresh orange pieces. Anna was thirsty and drank half of it. 'Freddie, you should become a waiter! You have got a real talent for mixing cocktails – even anti-alcoholic ones.'

'What is it?' Bruce asked suspiciously and held his glass against the sun. The liquid inside shimmered greenish. Lisa giggled. 'Top secret!' Freddie smiled. 'Just try it!'

Tentatively, Bruce took a few sips, and his face brightened. 'Delicious!' He wondered not only about the unusual taste but also about Anna. When he'd seen her playing tennis with an extremely good-looking boy, he had considered him to be her boyfriend. But earlier in the car today, he had sensed her admiration for himself. And then she'd unexpectedly invited him. But who was this Freddie? He frowned.

'Just admit it if you don't like the juice,' Barbara said, misinterpreting his frown. 'My new brother always tries out new drinks of all kinds. Most of the time it's very tasty, but now and then it's disgusting. And right now, he's on a health trip and likes to mix kale leaves and stuff like that to make freshly squeezed fruit or vegetable juices.'

Freddie cut her a long nose.

Bruce was still confused. 'What is a 'new brother'?'

Freddie laughed and told him about his mother's marriage to the father of Barbara, Lisa and Tom. Because he was an accomplished speaker, in the end Bruce felt that he knew everything about the family relationships. Then they got to talk about Steven Owen, the fisherman, whom Sebastian wanted to help during the wedding ceremony at the sea. The same man who was later killed by a King Hit in Maroochydore. Anna suddenly remembered guiltily that she had suspected Bruce for a short time! Just because the perpetrator had been described with similar clothes and yellow sneakers! In the meantime, she could no longer imagine that Bruce was such a brutal guy. On the contrary, she found him nicer from minute to minute!

Her mobile phone rang. Oh no, why did Jason call her right now? 'Hello?' Her voice sounded a little strained.

Everybody was looking at her. Anna was glad that Lisa and Tom started a loud argument, thus distracting the unwanted attention from her. She got up and went to another part of the garden where nobody but Jason could listen to her.

When she returned, Barbara was still trying to placate her little siblings. Freddie looked at Anna curiously, and she feared a stupid comment like, 'Was that your sweet-heart?'

She took a seat at the table and quickly asked Bruce,

'How was the party at Henry's house?'

'Super! But the police had to come back later that evening because some guys were making trouble. They hadn't even been invited! And one chick was so drunk that she staggered to the neighbour's front garden and threw up there.' Bruce laughed. 'In the garden of the man who'd probably called the police before!'

'And then?' Anna asked.

'The same two policemen returned, and Tim, the big one with the fish eyes, almost got into a fight with somebody. But the friends of that guy pulled him away in time. He was lucky, because Tim can be brutal.' His face darkened. 'He once hurt a friend of mine, just because he didn't get out of the car fast enough for him, during a traffic control. And he groped his girlfriend! But they couldn't prove it.'

'Was that the reason why you were so angry and did ...', Anna paused, because she didn't want to tell Barbara's siblings too much about the spraying attack on the fence of the 'IDIOT'.

'Yeah. This cop should be locked up and ...'

A blood-curdling scream interrupted him. Barbara jumped up as if stung by a tarantula. 'Mum?'

Julie, her mother, appeared at the corner of the house. She held a pair of by-pass loppers in her hand and called out:

'Come on, everybody, I have to show you something!'

She led her children and the guests to the back of the house and pointed to the timber fence, which was mostly hidden behind a lushly growing bougainvillea.

'I was cutting back this climbing plant as it was already spreading out over the roof, and that's when I suddenly discovered the snake, right in the middle of that thorny bougainvillea. Incredible, hey? I almost cut it in half with my by-pass loppers! I only spotted it at the last moment!'

A huge python was stretched out on the top of the fence.

'It's looking quite grim and not very friendly!' Bruce said.

'You have destroyed its hiding place, Mum,' Barbara said accusingly.

'Look how thick it is in the middle!' Lisa cried.

'Our neighbours have been missing their little cat since yesterday!' Tom croaked. 'Do you think the snake has eaten it?'

Barbara and Lisa looked at their brother in horror, but their mother replied, 'Don't worry, I've heard the kitten has already returned. Maybe the snake has eaten a lizard or a fat rat.'

Freddie carefully stroked the back of the python that remained completely still. 'It's so full after its meal that it's too lazy to move.'

'Better leave it alone, Freddie!' Julie warned. 'Anyway, I'll finish my gardening for today.'

Freddie winked at the others. 'You must try my new juice creation, Julie – fruit juice with snake blood.'

Barbara said indignantly: 'Don't talk such nonsense! We don't kill any snakes or other wildlife.'

Bruce laughed good-naturedly. 'Maybe you should tell us the ingredients of your last cocktail, Freddie!'

'No chance! That's a secret. But it's purely vegan.'

'That's right!' Lisa confirmed.

Bruce was easily persuaded to have another drink and then he said goodbye after writing down Anna's mobile phone number. Barbara's siblings and her mother moved into the house so that Anna and her friend could finally talk in private.

'Bruce is very nice!' Barbara said. 'And you look like you're in love! But what about Jason?'

Anna didn't know what to say. She hardly knew herself what was going on with her. And Jason? During their chat on the phone, he hadn't even asked her once about her reunion with her old friends over the Easter weekend.

'I'm not sure if Jason is really interested in me. It seems he prefers to talk about himself. Besides, he always makes silly jokes and laughs about them like crazy.'

'Yes, I'd also noticed that. But Bruce seems to be a good listener. Do you know how old he is?'

'No idea! Definitely older than us, eighteen or something. Anyway, he already has a car.'

'He looks cool!' Barbara smiled. 'And you're smitten with him, hey?'

'Was that so obvious?'

'For me it was.'

Anna had to agree with her. After all, she'd constantly watched Bruce, admiring his chestnut-coloured hair and his figure. The blue T-shirt he was wearing today suited him well. He seemed quite athletic, and she'd already experienced that he could run fast. But most of all, she was fascinated by his face that brightened so wonderfully with every smile and was made even more beautiful by his radiant eyes. And somehow, he smelled so good!

'By the way, David, Freddie and I will go to the movies this evening,' Barbara said. 'Would you like to come with us? It's a science fiction called 'LEATHERSKIN'. I heard it's really good.'

'No, I can't. I'm supposed to watch over Sebastian tonight. My parents are going to a party.'

'What? Sebastian is old enough to stay alone, isn't he?'

'Of course he is! But sometimes our mother treats us like little children. Really annoying!' Anna glanced at her watch. 'Oh boy, it's almost noon, I'd better go home quickly.'

She also said goodbye to Freddie who gave her a short hug and a light kiss on the cheek. She liked him very much, and she thought it was wonderful that Barbara now had a 'new brother'. Anna became aware that Jason hadn't reacted jealous at all before Easter when she'd told him about the planned meeting with her ex-boyfriend. Perhaps it was nice of him, but she rather regarded it as proof that she was not that important to him.

# 17 THE CLIFFS

Sebastian lost his patience. The new computer game was too difficult and he hated losing all the time. His stomach growled and he realised with astonishment that he had been sitting in his room for hours. He rubbed his stiff neck and looked out the window. Bright blue sky! He wondered what Jack would do this afternoon. Maybe they could get a few friends together and play rugby. At the same moment, a message arrived on his mobile phone. Great! Jack had planned a soccer match on the sports field. Arielle and a few other girls would join in, too. He looked around his messy room. Where were his favourite shorts? Oh man, he'd have to tidy up again. Well, later. First he had to eat something. In the kitchen, Lizzie was stirring in a large pot.

'What are you cooking, Mum?' Sebastian stuck his head over the pot, and his stomach growled even louder.

Lizzie smiled. 'A lentil soup for you and Anna. It's for the evening, though, as Andy and I will be away. But you could set the table for our lunch. I'm sure Anna will be home soon.'

Sebastian took mayonnaise, cheese, salami, mustard, jalapeños, a green lettuce and cucumbers from the fridge and cut off thick slices of the home-baked bread. Immediately, the dogs came running and sat down expectantly right next to him.

'No chance! You won't get any food until this afternoon.'

Sebastian noticed a nasty smell and turned up his nose in disgust. 'Lilly, you stink! Did you roll in something?'

His mother laughed. 'Lilly devoted several hours to an old smelly bone.'

'Bah, it's disgusting!'

Lilly wagged her tail. Susi alternately watched her dog friend suspiciously and her human friends attentively, hoping to get some yummy tidbits.

'That reminds me: your room also stinks. Did you forget a pair of dirty socks in your gym bag? Or a sweaty T-shirt?' Lizzie asked her son.

Sebastian had just shoved a piece of cheese in his mouth and mumbled something no one could understand.

'Hello!' Anna stormed into the kitchen. 'I am so hungry!'

Susi greeted her effusively, while Lilly had her eyes fixed on Sebastian. Anna stroked Susi, who was leaning heavily against her legs, and then complained to the other dog, 'Well, you disloyal doggie, it seems that food is more important to you than I am!'

'Perhaps Lilly decided to ignore us for five minutes whenever we come home,' Lizzie said.

'Oops, sorry, I patted Susi at once and forgot about our new rule,' Anna replied with a rueful smile. She washed her hands and bit heartily into one of the sandwiches that Sebastian handed her. Tears shot into her eyes. 'How many jalapeños are in there? That's hot as hell,' she croaked and picked out most of the spicy pieces. Then she turned to her broadly grinning brother. 'What are your plans for today? Freddie, Barbara and David want to go to the cinema this evening. But I'll have to baby-sit you.'

Sebastian sulked. 'I'll get along just fine without you!'

Lizzie feared an upcoming fight but then discovered the sparkle in Anna's eyes. 'As long as you're not having a wild party, Sebastian!' she joked.

His mobile phone rang. 'Hi, Kirsty! How are you enjoying Hervey Bay?' He quickly moved into his room.

Lizzie checked her watch. 'I hope Andy can tear himself away from work in time. We'll already go to our friends in the afternoon, although the official celebrations won't start until 7 p.m. Will you be okay? You will have to feed the dogs and let them out later to pee in the garden. And don't forget to switch off the stove after warming up the soup!'

Anna pouted. 'Mum, we're no babies anymore!'

Lizzie hugged her. 'I'm sorry, Anna. It's just kind of strange when the children grow older and suddenly have love affairs. I'll have to get used to that.'

'Who's having a love affair?' Andy asked.

'Hi, there you are! We were just talking about you.' Lizzie gave her husband a kiss.

'Well, I hope you don't have a new lover!' he joked.

'Not yet, but maybe I will find one tonight.' Lizzie pointed to the plate of sandwiches. 'Well, you might as well fortify yourself, just in case. Sebastian has prepared our lunch and made far too many sandwiches. And slices of bread so thick you can hardly get them into your mouth.'

A little later Lizzie cursed. Having intended to wear a wine-red dress, she now realised that her belly had become too fat and she had to look for something else. After a while, she emerged from the bedroom in an elegant, dark blue dress. A gold chain with a pretty opal adorned her neck and two narrow gold rings embellished her wrist. Like Anna, she had blonde, curly hair that fell softly around her face.

'You're snazzy!' Anna marvelled. 'You'll charm all men!'

Andy wagged his index finger at them. 'What are you women up to?' Then he added with a funny expression, 'I guess I must dress up too. Oh boy, that's not really my thing!'

To Anna's delight, her father put on a fashion show in front of them, dancing around in a silly way. At the end of the show everyone agreed on a chic suit for him, combined with a light blue tie with dark blue kangaroos on it. Meanwhile, Sebastian was searching around in all wardrobes and bags, as he was missing a sneaker. He gradually became angry until he finally found it under his bed. Now it was time to cycle to the sports field. Shouting: 'Bye, have fun!' at his parents, he left.

'He was in a big hurry,' Andy said.

'For the first time in his life, he will play soccer in a mixed team,' Anna explained. 'It's a pity that Kirsty is still on holiday. Sebastian only found out from Jack today that Arielle and Kirsty belong to a soccer team.'

'Kirsty is a nice girl and seems to be a good match for Sebastian,' Andy said. 'And what about you, Anna? Are you going to meet your new boyfriend?'

Anna was perplexed. How did he know about Bruce? No, surely he meant Jason. Sebastian had probably told his parents about him. Weird, even though she hardly knew Bruce, she'd immediately thought of him instead of Jason. Her father still looked at her expectantly.

'Nah, I don't have a real boyfriend,' she said, embarrassed. 'I'll probably just keep the dogs company, take them for a walk, and maybe do some painting.'

Andy felt she was hiding something but let it go.

'Just don't forget the key when you leave,' he admonished.

Anna moaned. 'Dad, don't you start treating me like a little kid, too.'

Andy chuckled. 'Well, I'd left my bunch of keys in the ignition before and locked my old car at the push of a button. After that,

I could neither get into the car nor into the house. Fortunately, a good friend of mine had a spare key for my front door, and at home I had a second car key. But as I didn't have a mobile phone at that time, I had to walk many kilometres.'

'See, I always told you mobile phones are handy to have!'

\* \* \*

Anna was alone at home, painting a sunrise by the sea. Susi and Lilly slept peacefully on a dog mattress, close together. It was unusually quiet, and Anna flinched when the phone rang shrilly. It was Aunt Paula. She talked like a waterfall and hardly let her speak. Anna yawned, getting a bit bored. But the next moment she opened her eyes in horror.

'What? That's terrible!' Now she was listening intently.

'Well, it happened many years ago. Back then, everybody called it death by suicide. The man had apparently thrown himself off a high cliff in the evening. In any case, several men found him the next morning after having abseiled from above. Looking for a good place to climb, they walked along the bottom of the cliffs and discovered the body. What a shock for these four men! They'd come from Brisbane expecting to have a good time, and then that!'

'Scott and Susan are members of the 'UP & DOWN' climbing club. But they never mentioned a suicide at Mount Tinbeerwah.'

'As I said, it was several years ago. At that time, your friends were far too young to be in a climbing club.'

'And why did this story come to light again?'

'Colin has hinted that the Crime Squad made a connection with the dead man on the horse sculpture. And now they are investigating whether this older case could have been a murder and not a suicide.'

'What sort of connection? DNA traces or something?'

Aunt Paula laughed at Anna's eager tone of voice. 'I can hear that you want to play detective again.'

In the background, Anna heard Uncle Sam's voice.

'Sorry, I have to go, Anna! Sam has just reminded me of something. Give our love to everyone, will you? Bye!'

'Bye!' Anna remained sitting on the couch in the living room, lost in thought. Another murder on the Sunshine Coast? Somehow it seemed much worse to get bad news when they'd happened nearby. Lilly rolled around and fell off the mattress. Confused and a bit drowsy, she looked around. And now Susi woke up too, stretched herself extensively and then sneaked up to Anna for a pat. Anna gave her a kiss on her beautifully formed head. 'Oh, my Susi, you are such a loyal friend!'

Anna was also very fond of Lilly, but she loved Susi dearly. Besides, little Lilly would have to move to a new home at some point. Unfortunately, the world was not as safe as people sometimes thought, and life always had surprises in store.

She finished her painting, observed it critically and decided to give it to her mum for Mother's Day. Later in the afternoon, Sebastian came home hungry and with a scraped knee.

'Hi, Anna, you should have watched our game! Arielle was a perfect goalkeeper and our team won. And I scored a goal, too.'

Anna had to smile at her brother who looked very young with his dirty sports clothes, shaggy hair and red cheeks. But she was startled when she saw his leg.

'You're all bloody! And you have dirt in your wound! Should we treat it with iodine right away?'

'Nah, I'll take a shower first.'

Whistling happily, he went into the bathroom, and soon he was singing loudly. Susi and Lilly pricked up their ears, listening to the unusual sounds muffled by the sound of water. Afterwards, Anna and Sebastian ate a bowl of soup, and Anna told him about Aunt Paula's call.

'Colin is the nice policeman we once met at Aunt Paula's and Uncle Sam's, isn't he?' he asked.

'Yes, that's right. They are good friends, but he told them very little. He probably has to keep certain things secret.'

'The father of a boy in my class also works for the police.' Sebastian held up his spoon broodingly in the air.

'Really? In which area, crime or traffic?'

'I don't know! I will ask Ivory.'

'By the way, the two policemen had to come to the party a second time recently,' Anna said.

Sebastian looked at her without understanding.

'Remember Henry's party, where we danced in the street?'

'I see. For a moment you completely confused me! How do you know?'

'I happened to see Bruce again.'

Anna told her brother how she'd met Bruce and then spontaneously taken him to Barbara's. Sebastian was surprised. But he was much more interested in the news about Thomas. What had the police found out? Hopefully the murder would be solved soon. Or rather: the two murders, if that man at the cliffs had been killed, too.

# 18 PLAY WITH WATER

After Bruce had finished his apprenticeship as a plumber, he applied for a part-time job in a shop in Coolum Beach. To his surprise, his application was successful, although he had no work experience as a salesman. His new boss was very nice, and Bruce enjoyed serving the customers and learning more about the products in the shop. He really liked his job! This afternoon, however, he could hardly concentrate. He was constantly thinking about Anna. His previous girlfriend had offended him badly, so he didn't really want to get involved with anyone else yet. But the pretty girl with the sky-blue eyes, who had already run into him several times – and once almost got run over by his car – was always on his mind. Should he call her tonight? She had similar hair to his ex-girlfriend Maryann, but she seemed completely different, so wonderfully natural and honest.

He flinched when a colleague impatiently called his name. Darn! He was still on probation and should rather pull himself together than dream away. Quickly he collected all the items on his list and took them to the checkout – and saw Gordon, his previous boss. 'Hi! What a surprise!'

'Hello! You work here now?' Gordon laughed. 'Well, it surely beats fixing clogged toilets.' He turned jokingly to one of Bruce's colleagues, 'Watch out, Bruce loves to play with water!'

'What's that supposed to mean?' Bruce protested.

Gordon laughed even louder, and his broad face turned turkey red. 'I'll never forget how you accidentally broke a water pipe in your first week of training and got a woman and yourself soaking wet!'

'Better don't remind me of that!' Bruce grinned coyly. The woman had screamed like a banshee when a huge torrent of water had completely soaked her!

Two new customers came into the shop and the whole afternoon passed in a flash as Bruce was very busy and had to run back and forth. It wasn't until he got home that he thought of Anna again. Hesitantly, he picked up his mobile phone and dialled her number. Suddenly feeling shy, he almost hung up again when she answered, sounding a bit breathless, 'Hello!'

'Hi! It's Bruce. I just wanted to call you and ...' He heard a car in the background. 'Are you out on a road?'

'Yep! I'm walking the dogs.'

'Where are you? Maybe I can join you.'

'I'm almost at that nasty cop's house. You know who I mean.'

Bruce laughed. 'Okay, I'll find you. See you!' Shortly afterwards, Bruce stepped out of a somewhat shabby wooden house and waved to her. 'Hi, girls!' Again, Bruce spoke in that funny voice to the two dogs who immediately snuggled up to him.

'Lilly and Susi are crazy about you,' Anna said, amazed. 'You must be a kind of dog whisperer.'

'Dogs like it when you talk to them in a high voice,' Bruce explained, squatted down and stroked them. Susi looked downright ecstatic. He cuddled them for a while and then straightened up. 'Excuse me! It happens to me again and again that I talk first with the dogs and then with the people.'

Anna smiled. 'No problem, I'm glad you like dogs. Could you take Lilly's leash?'

'Sure.'

Together they walked down the street and Anna felt elated. Bruce seemed so attractive and masculine to her, and she found herself wanting to snuggle up to him just like the dogs. She had to giggle and was angry with herself because she didn't want to appear a silly brat. Now they were just passing Tim's house and she pointed out that a part of his fence was freshly painted.

Bruce told Anna that he had found a spray bottle nearby by chance and spontaneously written the word 'IDIOT'. 'It was absolutely childish, and I was an idiot myself,' he admitted.

'That cop really is unpleasant. Anyway, he gave me the creeps the other day.' Suspiciously Anna looked to the house, anxious that Tim might show up right now.

Bruce asked, 'Do you often go for walks here? Where do you live?'

'Our house is only a block from here. And yes, we come here quite often, but mostly we go to the beach. And you live in a shared house?'

'Yes, with two other guys and a young woman. You should come for a visit!'

'I'd love to, just not today, as I have to look after my brother. But why don't you come and visit us? The dogs would be happy.' Anna gazed at Bruce. Would he accept? To cover up her embarrassment, she joked, 'But I must warn you: Sebastian can drive people nuts with all his questions.'

'Oh, I am used to that! I have two little sisters who are very curious.'

'How old are they?'

'Short of eleven. They're twins.'

'Really? Do they look exactly alike?'

Bruce laughed. 'Yeah, it's hard to tell them apart. They've teased my parents and me many times.'

Anna tried to imagine what it would be like to have two almost identical brothers, when Susi suddenly pulled on the leash like crazy. 'What's the matter?' Anna hadn't paid any attention to her surroundings as she was so excited to go for a walk with Bruce. Now she saw that they had arrived at a park. Gradually it was getting dark and it was time to turn back.

'No hunting!' she reprimanded Susi as a large black bird with a red head, an Australian Brush-Turkey, ran away from them. To her surprise, Bruce pushed Lilly's leash into her hand and ran into the park.

'What are you doing there?' he asked in a loud voice.

A boy and a girl Sebastian's age were hitting something in the lawn with golf clubs.

'Leave it alone!' Bruce angrily grabbed the putter of the boy who was about to swing it.

'Those disgusting, poisonous toads should be killed,' the girl replied snottily.

'But not in such a brutal way! You might just injure them and then they'll die a slow and painful death! And are you even sure they are cane toads and not native frogs or toads?'

'Come on, Fiona, we'd better get out of here,' the boy said and pulled her by the arm.

With a grumpy look, the girl followed him. A fat toad hopped away in the other direction, and this time it was Lilly who got into a hunting fever. Bruce took the leash off Anna again, saying grimly, 'I hate it when people kill animals and regard it as a sport.'

'I think that toad got away,' said Anna.

Bruce bent over briefly to look at another one. 'Here is a dead one. Off! Lilly, leave it!'

'I always fear that one of our dogs might eat a poisonous toad and die from it.'

'I've seen a dog that got totally high from licking the glands of a cane toad. His mouth was already full of foam, and we quickly rinsed it with water, but he still raced around the garden like a crazy puppy and was totally psyched. Thank God he didn't get sick! It's so sad that dogs and many other animals often die from the poison.'

'Terrible!' Anna agreed. 'We also had a few frightening experiences. Once, we had a young foster dog that collapsed out of the blue! We took him to the vet immediately and he gave him something to make him vomit. And back at home, he was as fit as a fiddle again. We suspect that he had been chewing on a wooden slat that had been treated with a poisonous stain. A few weeks later, the same dog pooped a bright pink pile, and we were worried about an internal injury. It wasn't until the second poop that we realised he'd eaten an old pink sponge.'

Bruce laughed and Anna told him more dog stories. Soon they arrived at Anna's parents' house. Anna led Bruce into the living room and offered him a glass of water.

'Hi, Sebastian! We're back,' she shouted. Susi ran to greet Sebastian while Lilly ran to her feeding bowl.

'Your place looks nice,' Bruce said appreciatively. 'The house we are renting is quite run-down and needs new paint desperately. And I fixed a leaky faucet the very first day I moved in.'

'It's great that you can do that! You've really learned a practical trade.'

Before Bruce could respond, Sebastian walked into the room.

'Hi, Anna! Oh, you have a visitor.' A sassy grin came over his face. 'The man with the yellow sneakers!'

As Bruce looked confused, Anna explained, 'The man who killed somebody with a King Hit had yellow running shoes, and we thought it was silly of him and not the best camouflage if you want to commit a crime. Well, the guy probably didn't plan it.'

She now told Bruce that she'd momentarily feared that he had performed the cruel King Hit, as the perpetrator had been dressed similarly according to the statements of some witnesses.

'Oh no!' Bruce made a grimace. 'What a coincidence! Good thing they didn't arrest me!' He took a sip of water and patted Susi and Lilly who had settled at his feet.

'How is your knee?' Anna asked her brother, seeing that he had stuck a large plaster over his wound.

'It's throbbing and quite hot. But a cat has nine lives!'

'What have you done?' Bruce asked.

Sebastian told him about his fall at the soccer game, adding joyfully that his team had won.

'Sebastian can run as fast as the wind! And he also scored a goal, even though he usually only plays rugby.' Anna was obviously proud of her little brother.

Bruce smiled. Then, with a serious expression on his face, he asked Sebastian, 'When did you get your last tetanus shot?'

Sebastian pondered and looked at Anna questioningly.

'I think a couple of years ago.'

'Well, wait till tomorrow. If the wound looks worse, you'd better go to the doctor to get a professional cleaning.'

They chatted for hours on end, and it didn't bother Anna at all that Sebastian stayed with them, eagerly yapping away, because that way she could secretly watch Bruce and didn't feel forced to talk all the time herself. She loved his voice, his laughter and his beautiful, expressive eyes.

Later, they finished the soup, and it was only when Sebastian started yawning that Bruce noticed the time and left. Sebastian went to bed and fell asleep straight away, but Anna was still very giddy with excitement.

# 19 NICOLAS

The next morning, Sebastian was the first to wake up. His knee still hurt, but at least it didn't seem to have got worse. He replaced the plaster with a bandage that he laboriously wrapped around his knee. As he didn't feel like going for a walk with the dogs, he went into the back garden to play ball with them.

Anna woke up from a squeal. Was it a bird? Oh no, it was Lilly's new toy. Smiling, she opened the curtains. The sun was shining and a few white clouds were sailing in the blue sky. A beautiful Saturday! Eating her muesli, Bruce came to her mind again. He was really nice, and very handsome to boot! She knew she had to end her relationship with Jason! But how? Should she call him, or just send him a text message? What should she write? IT'S OFF? No, that would be mean and cowardly. On the other hand, she'd never even felt like his girlfriend yet. She sighed deeply, when her parents came into the kitchen.

Andy's hair was disheveled from sleep. Lizzie looked tired and had the mark of a crease from the pillow on her left cheek.

'Morning! How was your party?' Anna asked.

'Super! We made some new acquaintances and danced a lot,' Andy said. 'Lizzie got a bit drunk.'

'Good morning!' Sebastian, followed by the dogs, came back from the garden. 'Did we wake you up?'

'Yes, that awful loud squeaking thing might not have been the best idea,' Anna said, but grinned good-naturedly.

'What did you do, Sebastian?' Andy asked as his eyes fell on his son's knee that was wrapped in a bandage.

'It's just a scratch. I fell down during the soccer game yesterday.'

'Oh, dear, we'll have to look at it later,' Lizzie said, preparing herself a cup of tea.

Andy made himself a coffee and sat down with the kids.

'Aunt Paula phoned yesterday. She hadn't known about the party and was surprised that Sebastian and I didn't go with you,' Anna reported.

'Well, you haven't missed anything. It was a bunch of older people, just as we'd expected.' Andy winked at Anna. 'And poor Lizzie didn't find anyone to flirt with and had to dance with me most of the time.'

'But you flirted with another woman!' Lizzie said, jokingly wagging a finger at him.

'No way!' Andy protested. 'I was just feeling sorry for Jessica.'

'Why?' Anna asked.

'Jessica had drunk too much wine and became quite maudlin,' Lizzie explained. 'She lost her husband in tragic circumstances some years ago. And seeing the happy Golden Couple in front of her now, she became very sad.'

'And so, I comforted her a bit, talked to her and also asked her to dance,' Andy said.

'To a slow blues, of all things.'

Andy smiled. 'I didn't know what song they'd play next. But I think the dancing helped Jessica to talk and relax. Anyway, her tears finally dried up on our third dance.'

'What did her husband die of?' Sebastian asked.

'He jumped off a high cliff at Mount Tinbeerwah and died instantly.' Glancing at his wife, Andy was not sure how much of this spooky story he should tell the children. But to his big surprise, Anna and Sebastian got very excited, both shouting almost in unison: 'Really? That was Jessica's husband?'

And Anna added, 'Was it suicide or murder?'

'What are you talking about? Murder?' Andy asked, confused.

Anna passed on what she had learned from Aunt Paula, finally saying, 'And now there's going to be a new investigation.'

Lizzie put her piece of toast back onto her plate.

'Sometimes the world does seem like a village. You know almost as much as we do. But Jessica is quite certain it was suicide, because Nicolas, her husband, had suffered from severe depressions. He had been prescribed medication for this, but later on he stopped taking it. And one day, he took his own life.'

'How sad! And she'd never told you this before?' Sebastian inquired.

'I'd known that he'd died, but nothing else. She had mentioned his death as one of her reasons for adopting a dog, as she often felt lonely.'

Lizzie took another bite, and now Andy continued, 'Recently she heard from the police that her husband had a son. And guess who that was: Thomas, the murdered boy! Yet Nicolas had never mentioned anything about a son. This was a new shock for Jessica.'

'That's crazy!' Sebastian called out. 'I thought Thomas' biological father was in New Zealand!'

Now everybody was stunned. 'What?' they asked.

'Please don't tell anyone! Jack told me in confidence that Arielle's aunt and uncle, the parents of Thomas, split up as they had too many arguments. And in one of their ongoing fights, Aunt Heidi blurted out that Wayne, her husband, wasn't the biological father. Allegedly, she had a love affair in New Zealand. And bingo, she got pregnant by the other man.'

'Who knew about this?' Anna asked.

'Nobody – except Thomas' mother.'

'Unbelievable! So, Jessica's husband had no idea he had a son!' Lizzie pondered.

'And now father and son are dead!' Andy was utterly shocked.

'How did they actually discover that Nicolas was the father of Thomas?' Anna asked. 'Does the police keep DNA from all dead bodies for many years and then compare them with the DNA from other victims?'

'Good question! I suspect that the DNA profiles are stored in a database whenever a person's death is unnatural,' Andy said.

'I wonder if Thomas's father was also vegan.' Sebastian just remembered Jessica's delicious muffins. He would like to eat one of those now, even though he'd already had breakfast.

'Do you know if Jessica has ever met Thomas?' Anna asked. 'Maybe there's a vegan club or something like that.'

'You two always ask weird questions!' Lizzie sighed. 'The main thing is the murderer is caught! But now back to your sore knee, Sebastian. Would you like to show it to me?'

'Oh, no, I've just put the bandage on. Besides, I have been vaccinated against tetanus. That's what Bruce asked about directly.' Bummer, now he'd blabbed again; he always had trouble keeping things secret! Well, his sister hadn't asked him not to mention Bruce, but he didn't know whether she had intended to hide his visit from their parents.

'Who is Bruce?' Andy asked curiously.

'A new acquaintance,' Anna quickly said. 'I met him by chance on my walk with the dogs yesterday and spontaneously invited him.'

'He is really nice! And he was absolutely delighted with your vegetarian lentil soup, Mum!' Sebastian smiled at his mother.

Lizzie returned the smile. 'I already wondered why there were no leftovers.'

Anna now told her family about the two children and the cane toads in the park, and strangely enough, she didn't blush at all speaking about Bruce. But she still couldn't figure out how to deal with Jason. She spent most of the weekend brooding, getting angry with herself and with Jason when she repeatedly tried to call him without any success. She had to admit that she was a bit envious of her brother who seemed to have such a beautiful and uncomplicated relationship with Kirsty.

# 20 STOLEN DOGS

Monday morning was a bit hectic, as Lizzie had forgotten to set the alarm clock. They all overslept and had just a banana for breakfast. While Sebastian couldn't wait to meet Kirsty again, Anna felt uneasy about Jason. Seeing him in the classroom, she thought again how good-looking he was, almost too perfect. The lesson had already begun and everyone was looking at her curiously. She muttered an apology and sat down hastily in her seat beside Barbara.

During the break, Jason was just on his way to Anna when he was approached by Wendy, another classmate, who spoke to him eagerly. Jason smiled briefly at Anna but turned to Wendy and kissed her on the cheek. Anna did not know whether to be outraged or relieved. Well, her friend Audrey had already warned her that he was a womanizer. It wasn't until the next break that Anna had the opportunity to talk to Jason. He beamed at her as if nothing had happened, causing her anger to flare up again.

'You totally disappeared during the holidays,' she said pointedly. 'I tried to call you a few times, but I could never reach you.'

Jason kissed her on the cheek and said ingratiatingly, 'When you're mad, you're even prettier.'

Anna was speechless for a moment. She pulled herself together and stated, 'You know what, Jason, I'm in love with someone else.' There – now it was out! She was glad, although she knew she was once again turning bright red like a tomato. Her legs seemed strangely wobbly.

Jason was taken aback but replied calmly, 'No problem, Anna. I've already noticed that we are not really a good match. And I've fallen in love with Wendy. Um, I didn't intend anything like that, but I met her by chance during the holidays. We went swimming and ...'

Anna saw Wendy standing in a small group of friends, giving her suspicious looks. 'Well, you'd better go back to your Wendy quickly,' Anna snapped at Jason. She turned around and marched away from him.

*　*　*

Kirsty told her friends about the giant pelicans she'd seen on a long pier in Hervey Bay. The birds, not shy at all, had been sitting right next to some fishermen, apparently hoping to catch a fish. Sebastian was as happy as Larry to see his girlfriend again and his face was beaming with joy. Only after a while did he notice that Arielle was very silent. 'What's wrong?' he asked her.

'Somebody has stolen the pets from a family in my street. From Kate, actually! Their two dogs were taken from their own backyard in broad daylight when Kate and her parents were shopping in Maroochydore. And now I worry about my Max.'

'That's mean! And none of the neighbours noticed anything?' Kirsty asked incredulously.

'No, unfortunately not. Kate lives just a few houses away from me, and that's why we became friends.' Arielle replied. 'One of her dogs is a black Labrador. He is only three months old and his name is Patrick. The other dog is a female Jack Russell called

Abby, about half a year old. She's a funny little animal with a black patch around her eye – like a pirate with an eye patch.'

'Then it should be easy to spot Abby,' Jack speculated.

'Not if the thief will hide them well,' Kirsty argued.

'So, both are purebred dogs. I bet the thief wants to sell them for a lot of money,' Sebastian said. 'Labradors and Jack Russells are very popular breeds, after all.'

'That's right!' Arielle almost felt relieved. 'Then maybe I won't have to worry about someone trying to steal my Max, cos he's a half-breed.' After that she quickly went on, so not to seem too selfish: 'But I feel so sorry for Kate! And for the poor puppies too! I wonder how they are treated.'

Kirsty looked grim. 'I hope they get enough to eat and drink!'

Sebastian suddenly got a horrible image in his head. 'I told you I was looking at Thomas Cooper's Facebook pages, didn't I? Anyway, there was a photo of many young dogs locked up in a kennel. They looked so miserable and distraught and I wanted to rescue them all! And the text below this photo called for action against illegal dog breeders.'

Horrified, Kirsty and Jack wondered about the fate of the missing dogs while Arielle thought of the dead Thomas.

'Do you think anyone around here could have an illegal puppy farm?' Jack asked. 'Perhaps Thomas had found one, threatened the owners, and was therefore killed by them!'

Kirsty and Arielle were doubtful, but Sebastian thought it was possible. 'Yes, who knows? People who abuse animals are often brutal and have no compassion for others.'

'Jack and I offered Kate to help her with handing out leaflets about the missing dogs in Coolum and surrounding areas, not sure yet where exactly.' Arielle shrugged her shoulders.

'I can join in, too,' Sebastian kindly suggested.

'That would be awesome!' Arielle smiled gratefully at him. 'Kate's mother gets them printed this morning. We just have to figure out where we could distribute them. In any case, we'll put up some posters in the car parks of the beaches where dogs are allowed.'

'You could also stick some on the public information boards. I will help, too,' Kirsty offered.

'Thank you!' Arielle said and added thoughtfully, 'I actually used to like Kate. And for a while we also had a good time with Fiona. But at some point, I realised that Fiona tried to play us off against each other. And I found out that she said some very nasty things about me behind my back. She wanted us both to be her friends, but she intended to destroy the friendship between Kate and me. Crazy, isn't it?'

# 21 MEAT DISHES

Anna was feeling like a child short before the Christmas presents, looking forward to meeting Bruce again. Her heartbeat accelerated rapidly when she got closer to the house where he lived, and she hardly noticed the light drizzle. After her initially too tentative and then stronger knocking on the front door, a young woman appeared in a dark green patterned dress. She had a round face and a red-blonde, slightly tousled mop of hair and smiled at her in a friendly manner.

'Hi, you must be Anna! Come in, Bruce has already told me about you.'

'And the dogs? They are wet and dirty.'

'No problem, come in! Here, take this!' She handed Anna a towel that had already been lying next to the door and shouted,

'Bruce, your visitors are here!'

Anna dried the dogs' paws as best she could and then looked around the living room curiously, surprised how cosy it was. From the outside the house looked rather scruffy. Inside, the brownish carpet was a bit shabby and worn, but soft and clean. Several huge pictures decorated the beige walls and she also liked the rustic wooden furniture. One painting depicted an old, somehow wise looking turtle that was ridden by a cute tiny monkey.

The woman grinned. 'Do you like it? I painted it myself!'

'Super!' Anna was impressed.

Now Bruce appeared, looking even better than she'd remembered him. 'Hello, Anna!' He beamed at her with that special smile that made his eyes shine. 'Hi dogs!' he approached Susi and Lilly who were just as delighted as Anna to see him again. He stroked them briefly and then said, 'Okay, let's go! See you later, Lucy!'

Bruce took Lilly's leash as soon as they stepped out of the house. It was still drizzling and they put the hoods of their rain jackets on. The sky was grey, but the air was pleasantly fresh. They walked briskly, stopping occasionally to let Susi and Lilly sniff the scents of other dogs. Anna gladly allowed them this pleasure as long as they didn't stop at every tree and post. When she told Bruce the story of the stolen dogs, he too was outraged.

'How horrible! Hopefully the leaflets will help to get some information! Too bad it's raining now, because they'll get soggy and illegible in a sec.'

'I think Kate's parents have made quite sturdy posters which won't dissolve so quickly. And they've also asked for help via the Internet to find Abby and Patrick.

'But if their dogs end up far away, they'll probably never see them again.'

'I'd be heartbroken if someone tried to steal our dogs!'

'Me too! Who knows what that thief will do to these pups? Well, he'll probably sell them. Good that nobody here in Australia eats dogs! My parents met a woman in the Philippines once whose beloved dog had disappeared without a trace. She was desperately looking for it everywhere. Many months later, she found out that a neighbour had stolen and eaten it! Isn't that shocking? And on a different island, my dad chatted with a cook in a small restaurant who suddenly told him a secret: at certain festivals, they'd be making meat dishes from dogs, even though this had already been officially banned.'

'Oh no!' Anna felt nausea and a great protective instinct for Susi and Lilly kicking in.

The dogs stopped at a bush to pee. Bruce pushed the hood deeper into his face as the rain now came down harder.

'Some time ago we fostered a little terrier who hated to walk in the rain.' Anna smiled at the memory. 'Once we got caught in a heavy shower, and it was crawling under a shrub, refusing to go any further. In the end I had to carry it home.'

They talked casually about dogs and then moved on to other topics, both feeling at ease in each other's company. Bruce often made Anna laugh, and she liked his humour and way of talking. And unlike Jason, he was a good listener. She was falling more and more in love with him!

Bruce was a bit confused. All of his previous girlfriends had been about the same age as himself, while Anna certainly had to be two or three years younger. Therefore, it would be impossible to take her along to a pub or disco with his other friends. But he felt so comfortable in Anna's presence, and he'd already missed her so much since they had met last. He loved her beautiful blue eyes, her gentle smile, and her natural behaviour. And she had a good figure and pretty curls – even if he couldn't see much of them right now.

'Oops!'

Not watching her steps, Anna stumbled over her dog, when Susi picked up an ancient, tattered tennis ball. Anna would have fallen on her face if Bruce hadn't caught her. Without thinking, he instinctively pulled her into his arms, held her close and kissed her on the mouth. Then he laughed sheepishly and released her again.

'Oops!' he repeated.

Anna grinned, and butterflies seemed to perform a wild dance of joy in her belly. 'Well, I understand why a dog should actually 'heel'! It's not the first time I've almost fallen down because of Susi. But it would be far too boring for her if she always had to trot beside me.' Secretly, she was very grateful to Susi this time. Just because she'd stopped out of the blue, Bruce had hugged and kissed her! Susi looked at her expectantly, but Anna shook her head. 'No, we don't play ball here. It's too dangerous on the street.'

As if Susi had understood each and every word, she dropped the ball. Bruce felt a bit self-conscious, but still put an arm around Anna's waist. Anna was only too happy to wrap an arm around him, too. And a little later, when both dogs were once again sniffing at some scent marks, they kissed again.

\*   \*   \*

Sebastian was tired. For almost two hours, Kirsty and he had walked around in the rain, fixing many posters with drawing pins or tape in different locations. Each poster showed a photo of the two missing dogs and a short text explaining what it was about and who to contact.

'I've had enough,' he said. Although his injured knee hardly hurt anymore, he now had blisters on his heels. Because of the rainy weather he had put on brand new, freshly waxed leather shoes instead of his comfortable sneakers. Wrong choice! He would have preferred wet feet to sore heels!

'I've only got one poster left anyway,' Kirsty replied. 'Come on, we can quickly tack that somewhere.'

She stepped towards an electric pole that seemed appropriate and Sebastian handed her the hammer.

'What are you doing?' someone snapped at them. 'It is forbidden to put up signs without permission.'

'It's only a poster about missing dogs,' Kirsty defended herself and hit the last pin into the wood, unmoved by the strict voice. Sebastian looked behind him and saw the broad grinning Ivory together with a smiling police officer who looked familiar to him. Yes, he had met him outside at Henry's party that one evening.

Kirsty turned around. 'Oh, it's only you! To frighten me like that!'

'Sebastian, this is my father,' Ivory introduced him politely.

'Hi, we'd already met before.' Mr. Little shook Sebastian's hand and then approached Kirsty. 'You didn't sound frightened at all but rather rebellious! Well, you always were a bit of a rebel.' He winked at Sebastian and read the text on the poster. He frowned. 'Um, we'll keep our eyes open. But presumably someone will buy the dogs who won't care about a microchip or any papers. I don't think there's much hope for the rightful owners to get Patrick and Abby back.'

Ivory contradicted his father. 'But the thief must advertise the dogs in order to sell them. There must be a way of catching the bastard!'

'Maybe he will check out ads from people who want to purchase a dog, for example at 'Gumtree' or 'Marketplace' or elsewhere on the Internet,' Sebastian said.

'Then we should place such an ad ourselves,' Kirsty suggested excitedly. 'That way, we could bait the thief!'

Mr. Little, the tall policeman, nodded appreciatively. 'Not a bad idea, Kirsty! However, it would be better if someone else did it in another region. Not too close but not too far away, either.'

'I've got relatives and friends in the hinterland – they'll certainly help us,' Sebastian called out.

'But if you find out anything, call the police straight away, okay?' Mr. Little urged them. 'Don't do anything stupid, especially no wild rescue operations or anything like that!'

Noticing their soaked clothes, he asked, 'Shall I drive you home, Kirsty and Sebastian?'

* * *

Anna was almost back at home, when she saw Sebastian getting out of a police car. Oh no, what had he done? She was relieved when she heard him laughing.

'Bye, see you tomorrow!' A girl's voice came from the car.

The dogs pulled on the leash like crazy to greet Sebastian, and Anna struggled to keep her balance and upper hand. She growled at them and gave them a stern warning to heel the rest of the way. At the entry gate, both dogs sat down obediently and let her enter first, just as she had taught them. In the meantime, Sebastian had already rushed into the house, eager to take off his tight shoes and wet clothes.

At dinner he told his family about their plan to set a trap for the dog thief.

'And why did the police take you home?' Anna finally asked.

Lizzie and Andy looked stunned.

'That was Ivory's father. He and Ivory met Kirsty and me by chance and gave us a lift home,' Sebastian explained.

Later he was on the phone for a while. And then he shouted enthusiastically, 'Yippee! Our friends will help us! Susan and Scott will pretend to look for a Jack Russell; and Kylie and Mike will place an ad for wanting a young Labrador.'

Sebastian left it to his mother to call Aunt Paula. As expected, Lizzie had to endure a huge verbiage from her cousin before she even got a word in. But in the end Paula also offered her assistance to track down the dog thief. It was worth a try anyway, she said. Paula also informed Lizzie about some other news she and Sam had received from their friend Colin:

Wayne, Arielle's uncle, was suspected of having killed Thomas and possibly Nicolas, Thomas' biological father, too! Colin had expressly warned Paula and Sam not to shout this from the rooftops, and Lizzie also promised to keep it secret.

The next night, Lizzie was wide awake while Andy was snoring softly next to her. Although she didn't know either of these two dead people personally, the whole story aggrieved her very much. After all, she had been right there when Thomas was found on the fake horse, and she knew Jessica who had been married to Nicolas. What had really happened to her husband? Had it been a suicide or another homicide? Could the same person have killed both father and son? But why?

Suddenly freezing cold, she pulled the doona over her head and snuggled up to her peacefully slumbering husband.

# 22 ARRESTED

Arielle was utterly shocked when her parents told her the news. Uncle Wayne was suspected of murder! And Aunt Heidi had reluctantly confessed her love affair with a man called Nicolas. She had met him, a handsome guy from Noosa, during a first aid course in Tewantin. Both of them had fallen in love with each other, head over heels, and had secretly met a few times. But as she'd already been married to Wayne, she quickly broke off all contact with Nicolas. However, purely by chance, they'd met again in New Zealand where he had been travelling around in a rented motorhome. She'd ended up in his bed after a romantic dinner and had promptly become pregnant. After days of desperate brooding, many tears and sleepless nights, she'd decided never to see Nicolas again and to pretend that Wayne was her kid's father.

Nicolas had called her just once afterwards – many months later – to tell her that he was going to marry another woman called Jessica. Heidi had no idea why he'd even told her. And she hadn't known about his severe depressions, either.

She was completely perplexed when the police now hinted that her husband might have been responsible for the death of her former lover and her son Thomas. After the embarrassing interrogation by the homicide detectives, she confided in her sister, Arielle's mother, and she fiercely defended Wayne. 'He loved Thomas so much', she stammered again and again, sobbing so hard that Arielle's mother could hardly understand her.

Arielle couldn't help telling her friends the whole story the next day.

'But why is your uncle a suspect now? You said he didn't know anything about the love affair!' Jack was confused.

'And he'd always assumed Thomas was his real son,' Kirsty said, also puzzled.

'Well, it was known to the police that Uncle Wayne was once involved in a nasty brawl in a pub, something like you'd see in the Wild West movies. Although that was ages ago, it was held against him,' Arielle reported. 'In any case, when the detectives found out that Thomas was Nicolas' son, they became suspicious. Two mysterious deaths in one family? That couldn't be just coincidence, could it?'

Jack gazed at his girlfriend. 'So what? Why would your uncle have killed them?'

'No idea! But he must have known Nicolas, as they fought in unison against two other men in that pub. And one of their opponents was a police officer.'

Jack whistled through his teeth. 'Wow! But that doesn't prove a thing!'

Arielle shrugged her shoulders. 'Well, my aunt wants to visit us this weekend, maybe then we'll find out a bit more.'

'Could you imagine your uncle being a murderer?' Sebastian asked.

Arielle's blue eyes flashed angrily for a moment, but then she grinned a little crookedly. 'To be honest, I've been wondering about that myself. But I don't think so. He had a bit of a temper sometimes, but I can't believe he could ever commit murder, or even a double murder.'

Kirsty said, full of genuine empathy, 'I'm so sorry for your uncle. It must have been a terrible shock for him that Thomas was murdered. And then to be accused himself by the police ... and all the stress with his wife ...'

'Hello!' Kate walked towards them, beaming with joy. 'Our little Abby is back! My mum has just sent me a text message.'

'Really? Fantastic! How did that happen?' they all shouted.

'It looks like Abby could escape from her thief and found her way home. I am so happy! And you were so nice to help us with the distribution of those posters! I just wish Abby could tell us where Patrick is.'

'What are we going to do with the posters now?' Arielle asked. 'Should we write a note on each one, saying Abby's been found in the meantime?'

Sebastian sighed. Oh boy, that would mean heaps of work again! Jack, on the other hand, looked at his girlfriend with admiration. 'Good idea! Sure, let's do it.'

*   *   *

When Anna came home from school, Jessica was sitting in the living room, talking animatedly to Lizzie. Anna greeted her and informed her mother that Sebastian wouldn't be home until later as he and his friends were going to update all the posters about the missing dogs. Lizzie and Jessica were delighted that at least one of Kate's family's stolen dogs had turned up.

'By the way, I've seen you with your boyfriend and your dogs a few times,' Jessica told Anna.

Anna blushed and her mother looked at her curiously.

'Oh, I didn't know you've got a new boyfriend. I was wondering why you've been volunteering to walk the dogs so often lately.' Lizzie was tempted to ask her daughter to introduce her boyfriend soon, but she was afraid of a snide remark.

'You haven't met my dog yet, have you?' Jessica realised she had unintentionally revealed a secret. She bent down and looked under the table. 'Where is he? Marcus, come!'

Her Shih Tzu, a fuzzy, silver-grey ball of wool, came out from behind the sofa where he had been blissfully sleeping. Anna tried to pat him, but he retreated and barked with a thin voice.

'He's very shy,' Jessica said. 'He must have had some bad experiences in his young life.'

'But he looks cuddly!' Anna loved the little creature with the dark, round eyes at first sight. She stretched out her hand and he timidly came a step closer but then leaped backwards, barking again. Smiling, Anna spoke in a gentle voice to the tiny dog. Marcus sat down in front of Jessica's feet, carefully watching Anna who now pretended not to notice him at all. Promptly, he moved a little closer to her. 'Doesn't he get along with other dogs?' Anna asked, as Susi and Lilly were left outdoors.

'Luckily, he has no problems with dogs!' Jessica chuckled. 'You should have seen how wildly the three dogs played together today! But after that, Marcus was utterly exhausted.'

Both Susi and Lilly pressed their noses against the glass door, obviously keen to come in. Jessica checked the time and shouted, 'Oh my goodness, I was here much longer than intended. It's time for dinner! Your dogs must be hungry, too.'

'Has Marcus also become a vegan?' Anna asked curiously.

Lizzie thought amusedly that her daughter resembled the nosy Sebastian much more than many suspected.

Jessica laughed out loud. 'No! He loves his meat! And I wouldn't even know what to give him otherwise. Many things that are healthy for us humans can be poisonous to dogs, such as nuts and avocados. Come on, Marcus, let's go!'

No sooner did she open the door than Lilly and Susi barged in and tried to play with Marcus. Jessica promised them to come back another time. 'Goodbye, sweet dogs!'

'Jessica is really nice,' Anna said as soon as the visitors had left.

'She is!' Lizzie agreed with her. 'And she seems much happier since she adopted Marcus. She was very lonely after Nicolas' death.'

'Did she never try to find a new husband?'

'Yes, she tried it with a partner search on the Internet and also with advertisements in a newspaper. Unfortunately, she hasn't found the right one so far.'

'What a pity! Why do you think it never worked out? She looks quite good and isn't that old and wrinkled yet.'

Lizzie felt a little offended because Jessica was several years younger than herself. Well, at Anna's age, adults over twenty-five probably seemed ancient.

'Some people get lucky, but she only met strange men. It's funny that you should ask about this right now, because only a little while ago Jessica told me about a weird fellow. At first, she felt attracted to him, but he constantly feared he was being watched. He was almost as afraid of the parachutists as our Susi! He assumed they were secretly filming him. And one day he actually discovered a drone above his garden, and he totally flipped out and kept babbling about a spy.'

Anna cried out in disbelief. 'Really? Was Jessica there, too?'

'No, but he quickly fled into the house and called her. He whispered and turned on a tap so that nobody else could overhear their conversation.'

Anna grinned. 'Maybe he'd read or watched too many spy stories!'

'Anyway, Jessica found him too tiring. He just couldn't relax at all and made her nervous too. She rather longs for an uncomplicated, cheerful person.' Lizzie sighed. 'She really had enough trouble with Nicolas who was so often depressed. And even if it's complete nonsense, she still blames herself for not being able to help him. She was devastated when she was told that he had thrown himself off a cliff.'

'So cruel! It must have been terrible for the people who found him there. Even worse than what Barbara and I experienced.'

Lizzie looked at her with pity. Some time ago, Anna and Barbara had come across a corpse in a forest, that is, they had discovered a foot on a muddy bank and had raced away, screaming for help. It had turned out to be a murder which fortunately had been solved. Lizzie shuddered. Why did they always get involved in shocking crimes? Why had it been Sebastian who'd discovered the hand of the dead Thomas in the 'Garden of the Seven Senses'? To take her mind off things, Lizzie now said, 'Did you notice that Jessica talks to the dogs as if they were humans? She has a good connection to animals.'

'Just like Bruce!' Anna replied. 'Um, he's my new boyfriend. He always talks to Susi and Lilly in a funny tone, kind of high and squeaky, and they are besotted with him.'

'That's great!' Lizzie marvelled. ''Even our shy Susi?'

'Yes, especially her! She adores him.'

'How did you two meet?'

Anna told her mother the truth, starting with Bruce's graffiti spraying, pointing out that he had only followed a spontaneous idea at the time. 'By the way, he was really scared of dad when we caught him red-handed.' Anna grinned broadly. 'Of course, he didn't know that daddy wouldn't hurt a fly.'

Lizzie also smiled and then looked at her watch.

'I've been yapping so much; I haven't even started our dinner yet. Would you like to give me a hand?'

# 23 THE PLAN

Sebastian received a phone call from Kylie. After chatting animatedly for a while, he put the call on speakerphone. Now Anna and her parents could hear Kylie saying:

'And then the man said he'd be happy to show us his dogs, without any obligation. He actually has two Labradors for sale, a black and a golden one, both only a few months old.'

'Did you arrange a meeting?' asked Sebastian.

'Yes, on Saturday morning we'll meet him and his girlfriend in Marcoola. No way Mike and I'd reveal our own addresses and we thought that a dog park would be an appropriate place. We told him that we'd like to test the puppies' behaviour towards other dogs. And Mike's brother Peter will drive us there.'

'Super!' Sebastian cheered.

'But how will we know if one of the dogs is Patrick?'

'Kate or her parents must come, too!' Anna butted in.

Sebastian remembered something. 'Kylie, I gave a policeman, the father of a classmate, the promise to inform him if we'd find out anything at all.'

'Oh no ...' Kylie didn't sound too thrilled.

'He's very nice, don't worry!' Sebastian appeased her. 'He would be a reliable witness and could help to catch the thief!'

'Careful, son! Maybe that man is just an honest person trying to sell two dogs. Perhaps he is a professional breeder,' Andy said. 'Have you asked about health checks, Kylie?' he now spoke towards the phone. 'And if the parents of those two puppies are free of hip and elbow dysplasia?'

'What's that?' Sebastian asked.

'They're diseases of the joints that are hereditary, sometimes so bad that surgery is necessary. Certain breeds are particularly susceptible, especially large dogs, such as Labradors, Golden Retrievers, German Shepherds and Rottweilers. It's so sad when the dogs have to limp and are in constant pain. And that's why smart people should demand a veterinary examination of a puppy's parents to rule out these joint problems, before spending a lot of money. However, a good breeder should only sell healthy dogs anyway.'

'How much do you usually have to pay for a purebred dog?' Sebastian asked.

'About a thousand dollars or so,' said Andy, just guessing.

'Much more,' Lizzie interjected. 'The other day a lady told me her husband had almost bought an eight-week-old mastiff for two thousand five hundred dollars. But then they adopted a five-year-old Greyhound instead. Its owner wanted to get rid of it because it could no longer win any races. And a friend of them spent three thousand dollars on a poodle puppy! Some dogs even fetch 5000 dollars nowadays. Crazy prices, hey?'

Kylie cleared her throat.

Andy continued, 'Sorry, Kylie! Did you ask that man if he had any dog breeding papers?' The next moment he frowned. 'Actually, many breeders never give away the pedigree documents anyway, because they don't want other people to compete with their own business.'

Lizzie sighed. 'I don't care if a puppy is purebred or not. The main thing is the dog is healthy, happy and friendly!'

It was only now that Kylie had her say. 'Um, we didn't ask him about any health checks or papers like that, but we did ask if he could show us a vaccination certificate from the vet. His response to that was pretty weird, and now he came across a bit suspicious!'

'How much money did he ask for?' Anna wanted to know.

'Seven hundred dollars – for each dog,' Kylie replied.

Andy said, 'Kylie, we're gonna have a brief discussion and call you back, okay?'

'All right. Talk to you later.'

'Thanks for your help!' said Sebastian, ending the phone call. 'I'm going to call Ivory. Let's see if his father is at home,' he then suggested, feeling a bit anxious to talk to a police officer.

'Barry Little speaking,' a deep voice answered after four rings.

'Um, good evening!' Sebastian stammered. 'I'm Sebastian, a schoolmate of Ivory, and...'

'Hello! Yes, I remember you! Just a sec, I'll call Ivory.'

'No, stop! I must talk to you!'

Anna had to wipe that grin off her face. Her brother wasn't normally shy at all, but now he was visibly embarrassed when he told Ivory's father about the two Labrador dogs. Barry listened patiently before replying: 'I'll go to the dog park as well. I'll have Saturday off, and Ivory and I intend to visit some relatives near Marcoola anyway.'

'Perfect!' Sebastian said. 'Thanks so much! We will let Kylie and Mike know and also call Kate and her parents.'

Patrick's owners were over the moon when they heard the news about the two Labrador retrievers. Could the black puppy be their beloved Patrick?

# 24 MARYANN

Anna knew that Maryann had been the girlfriend of Bruce before she started a love affair with Thomas Cooper. Anna would have liked to find out more, but Bruce became quite taciturn and grumpy every time he talked about his ex. On Saturday, Anna's curiosity was partially satisfied when Bruce revealed a bit more of his past. After a short walk, they were sitting on a bench in a park. It was a sunny morning, and they could hear the humming of several lawnmowers. Another young couple walked by, holding hands, and smiled at them.

Anna whispered, 'They must be fresh in love! It can't be coincidence that they have similar clothes, glasses and hairstyles!'

Bruce replied: 'Maybe! They seem to be very happy!'

His amused facial expression changed into a distorted smile. 'The question is, how long will that last?' He sighed. 'I was not very lucky with Maryann! I met her at a friend's party, and I was totally smitten with her straight away. She's very pretty, and I was fooled by her looks and her charm. But then I found out that she was quite vain and arrogant. Her name is Maryann King and she acts as if she really were a queen, the whole world at her feet. She is a real schemer, sly and deceitful!' He smiled apologetically.

'Sorry, Anna, I'd better not talk about Maryann at all. I was distraught when she secretly started an affair with Thomas. It's pretty silly as she's not even my type. For example, she doesn't like animals and doesn't care for the environment. And that bothered me right from the start. She's also terribly unreliable. I never knew whether she would actually show up or not. Sometimes she made me wait for hours.'

A lawn mower made a popping sound and died. The blades had probably hit a rock or another hard object. Bruce laughed unexpectedly. 'Maryann suffered from hay fever. Some days she would sneeze all the time and get red, watery eyes.'

'No wonder she prefers to sit indoors instead of going out into the nature,' Anna replied.

'Well, she is not a couch potato. She loves going to parties, dancing and flirting. And she's quite a boozer.' Bruce frowned. 'It was Maryann who puked at Henry's neighbour's garden the other night. Nobody had invited her, but somehow, she heard about the party and showed up with some friends. With a lot of beer and a bottle of some self-mixed, high-proof alcohol. Maryann always liked to mix cocktails. And you know what? She and Simon, her new boyfriend, wrote 'SEXY BEAST' and 'SUPERBRAIN' on the wall back then. I happened to see them from a distance. Later I discovered a spray bottle underneath a shrub, and I used the red paint to spray the word 'IDIOT' on Tim's fence. And that's where you caught me!'

He grinned, and Anna was once again fascinated by the various expressions on his beautiful face. His brown eyes had such a warm glow when he smiled. He gave her a short kiss and said,

'Totally idiotic of me, but at least I got to know you that way!'

A kookaburra, also called 'Laughing Jackass', started a loud laughter in a tree above them, and other birds joined in.

Anna chuckled. 'The kookaburras often wake me up while it's still dark, but they always sound so happy that I can never be angry, no matter how early they start singing.' She kissed Bruce again. Her heart was fluttering and her knees trembling, but at the same time she felt indescribably comfortable in his presence.

'Yuck!' Bruce shouted, interrupting the kiss and her romantic feelings. Confused, she looked at him and then laughed as he wiped fresh bird shit off his leg. The kookaburras began a new deafening concert that rose and fell. And another wet blob hurtled through the air and landed on Anna's hand. Anna and Bruce jumped up and left the bench quickly.

'Did Maryann actually break up with Thomas or was it him breaking up with her?' Anna asked a little later, instantly regretting that she'd brought up the subject again.

'Oliver told me that Thomas was fed up with her once he got to know her better. After all, good looks aren't everything.'

'Was Oliver a friend of Thomas?'

'Not really, but they met from time to time. Oliver is the main singer and guitarist in a rock band, and Thomas took photos of them for a promotion at some point. He had a knack for taking pictures.'

'What's the name of the group?'

Bruce laughed. 'Hot Ears. Funny name, hey? They are not famous yet, but I love them! Their songs are great for dancing!'

A thought struck Anna. 'I heard that Thomas had been in a disco before he was murdered. But how had he got in? He was only seventeen.'

'Stuart, the older brother of his friend Daniel, was working as a bouncer there, so I guess it was no problem for Thomas to sneak in.'

'Do you think that drunk man who punched Thomas in that disco could have killed him later?'

'Nah, I never heard that he was suspected of murder.'

'Well, I keep wondering who could have strangled Thomas. And why did he go away in the middle of the night without telling his friends? At least he could have left them a note. Did he have trouble sleeping and went for a little walk? Or did he want to meet someone? Can you think of a reason?'

'If someone asked me for help, I would run out of the house right away. Especially if it were a good friend or a family member. So, if you ever get into trouble, Anna, call me quickly and I will come to your rescue at once – just like 'Superman'!' He smiled, but Anna was sure he wasn't just joking, and it made her feel warm all over. On the way back to Bruce's home, he invited her to come in for a while.

'I better wash off the bird shit from my hand,' she said as they entered the house.

'I'll show you the bathroom.'

While Anna washed her hands, Bruce hugged her from behind, sniffing at her hair. Then he cleaned a spot above his knee with soapy water and grinned mischievously. 'It's supposed to bring good luck when you get hit by bird poop!'

'At least it didn't land on our heads!' Anna giggled.

'Then we'd have a shower together and wash each other's hair now,' Bruce replied with a broad grin.

Anna blushed, but Bruce laughed and led her into his room. Her temporary self-consciousness quickly gave way to a very pleasant feeling. It was simply wonderful to cuddle up and to chat with him. She would have loved to spend the whole day with him, but Bruce was going to visit his family in the afternoon. Before Anna went home, he played a few songs from the Hot Ears and they danced around until they finally fell into each other's arms, breathless and happy. They kissed each other tenderly to say goodbye.

# 25 PATRICK

Sebastian's knee had healed reasonably well and he'd played rugby today. As hungry as a wolf and very dirty, he appeared in the kitchen, where Andy was cooking something. Wonderful scents filled the air.

'Off to the shower,' Andy commanded after a single glance at his son. 'No food until then!'

Sebastian went into the bathroom and surprised his sister who was looking at herself critically in the mirror.

'Who is the fairest of them all?' he teased her. 'Are you counting your freckles again?'

Anna stuck her tongue out at him.

Andy had prepared a delicious meal, and Anna and Sebastian enjoyed it without saying a word.

Lizzie grinned, amused. 'Are you having an eating contest?' Her smile faded when the doorbell rang. 'Oh, no, who is that?' she moaned, not willing to interrupt her lunch.

Sebastian ran to the entry door, still chewing. And there was Kate, looking radiant, and hugged him tightly.

'It was our Patrick, we got him back!' she called out.

'Awesome! Come on in!'

'Nah, my parents and the dogs are waiting in the car, I just wanted to let you know and say thanks.'

'Thanks for what? I haven't done anything.'

'You have organised your great helpers. But I'll tell you about it later. Bye!'

'Patrick is home again!' Sebastian shouted happily to his family.

The Kuhlmanns had just finished their lunch when they got a phone call from Kylie and Mike. Thrilled about the events in the dog park, they took turns in talking, both in high spirits.

'We were getting a bit nervous because the damn old car of my brother wouldn't start,' said Mike. 'But we arrived at the dog park just a few minutes too late and saw the couple with one golden and one black Labrador right away, heading towards a bench.'

'So, Mike and I walked to them while Peter stayed in the car,' Kylie butted in. 'Suddenly a Jack Russell jumped all over the black Labrador puppy. And both of them were so happy that it was obvious they'd already known each other.'

'Was that Abby?' Sebastian asked.

'Yes, Kate and her parents had stayed at the other end of the park. But they'd been there much too early, and they let Abby off the leash to play with the other dogs. As soon as she spotted her friend Patrick, she ran straight to him, followed by her owners.'

Anna smiled, calling out, 'And then?'

'Well, when we all appeared in front of this couple at the same time, they knew something was wrong and tried to get away.'

'But Peter had observed everything from the car and already blocked the exit of the fenced dog park. You'd met him before, he's a strong guy, over two meters tall and scary looking if you don't know him,' said Kylie. 'And so, they quickly took off towards the other exit, dragging the two Labradors behind them.

Abby chased them and barked shrilly, and Kate's parents screamed in rage. The other people in the park were stunned!'

Mike said, with triumph in his voice, 'But at the other exit, another man and a boy were stopping the thieves.'

'Ivory and his father?' Andy asked.

'Yes, that's right. Sebastian, it was good that you asked Ivory to send us a photo of his dad and himself because that's how we recognised them,' Kylie said. 'Mr. Little was not in uniform but very authoritarian. He identified himself as a police officer and forced the thieves to answer his questions.'

Mike laughed. 'You should have seen their faces!'

'Kate and her parents cried with joy and hugged their Patrick all the time,' Kylie reported. 'Abby raced around them in big circles. And after the first round, two other dogs joined in. They all had a great time!'

'And the other stolen Labrador?' Anna asked.

'The poor puppy was quite timid and confused, but Ivory comforted him very nicely,' Kylie replied.

Mike continued, 'After a while, the thieves confessed and even admitted that they'd stolen other dogs besides Abby and Patrick. Tiny Abby had escaped by digging under their fence, but they'd already sold two other dogs before. So, the police will have to look into those cases too. If the dogs had a microchip, it should be easy to prove who the rightful owners are. And the golden Lab is from Brisbane. Ivory and his father have temporarily taken him into their care.' Mike scoffed. 'It's a terrible thing to steal pets! They are family members!'

Sebastian asked, 'Has that couple been arrested? And how will they be punished?'

'Mr. Little was not on duty, but he informed a colleague who will deal with the guys.'

'It was wonderful that you helped us!' Sebastian said, feeling chipper.

'No problem! Everything worked out great, even if it looked dicey at first because of Peter's car.'

'Say Hi to Peter and thanks from all of us!' Anna said. 'And you should visit us soon!'

\* \* \*

Kate and her parents decided to celebrate the reunion with their beloved dogs straight away, and they invited Sebastian, Kirsty, Arielle and Jack to join in. Ivory couldn't take part as he was still out with his dad visiting relatives. Kate was beaming when she opened the door to her guests, and everybody was overjoyed to see Abby and Patrick romping around in their own home and garden, safe and sound. Sebastian stared at the table, loaded with various cakes, nuts and biscuits.

Kirsty whispered to him, 'Heaps to eat!'

Arielle watched the young dogs playing. 'It's hard to believe our plan worked out!' she said with a smile. 'You'll have to tell us exactly what happened, Kate.'

Although Sebastian already knew most of the story, he didn't mind listening. Kate's parents let Kate speak and only added a few comments now and then. Kirsty's green eyes sparkled with excitement, and Jack forgot to eat for a while.

Finally, Kate said gratefully, 'It was a brilliant idea, Kirsty, to trick the thieves and pretend to look for a particular breed of dog. And you all helped us so much!' She swallowed, visibly moved to tears.

Her mother smiled at her daughter. 'You've got great mates!'

Sebastian felt bad because he hadn't really liked Kate at first, and Arielle and Kirsty also seemed to be embarrassed.

'Oh boy, now we'll have to take down all the posters again,' Jack said dryly. He made a droll grimace and everyone laughed.

'By the way, where is Fiona?' Kirsty asked. 'She'd also put up posters, hadn't she?'

'No! At first, she was all sympathetic and said she'd help, but then she had flimsy excuses. Therefore, I didn't invite her to this party.' Kate's heart-shaped face took on an angry expression. 'Also, Fiona made a completely stupid remark. She doesn't seem to understand at all how much the dogs mean to us, because she asked me, «Why don't you just get new dogs?» Can you believe that? As if our pets were objects that could easily be replaced!'

Arielle was outraged. 'What a bitch! I was worried that someone might also steal Max. I love my dog, and he's my best friend! Besides you, Jack.'

Jack joked, 'You already compared us the other day, saying we had similar eyes. I hope you won't put me on a leash!'

Kirsty's expression remained stern. 'I've known Fiona since kindergarten. Even as a small child, she liked to torture animals, like ripping the wings off all sorts of insects.' Fiona had also done something horrible to a cat one day, but Kirsty preferred not to talk about that. Looking at Kate, she said, 'To be honest, Fiona became my worst enemy. I was glad to have Ivory as a friend because he always stood by me and saved me whenever Fiona tried to beat me up with her brother.'

'It was awesome that Ivory and his father helped you in the dog park,' Sebastian said to Kate and her parents.

'How did the thieves manage to steal your dogs in the middle of the day?' Kirsty asked.

Kate's mother grimaced. 'We don't know! These guys, Simon and his girlfriend Maryann, did a clever job, because nobody in the neighbourhood noticed anything at all. Even though the woman's surname is 'King', she certainly wasn't acting in a royal way.'

'Let's hope nothing like that will ever happen again!' Kate's father said in a grim tone. 'And we should train our dogs not to accept treats from strangers.'

'Speaking of treats, we'd like to give some presents to Kylie, Mike and Peter,' Kate's mother said kindly. 'And to Ivory, too.'

'We should also hand a gift to Mr. Little,' her husband reminded her. 'Without him, the thieves might have escaped.'

'By the way, where was Mrs. Little? Did she also come into the dog park?' Jack asked. 'You didn't tell us about her.'

'Ivory no longer has a mother,' said Kirsty. 'Unfortunately, she died a few years ago. She had some incurable kidney disease that she'd inherited from her father.'

'Oh no! I didn't know that.'

'My father also passed away.' Kirsty smiled sadly. 'A year ago, my mum and Ivory's dad fell in love with each other. Ivory and I were already looking forward to becoming brother and sister, as we've always got along great. But somehow nothing came of it. Well, they are still good friends anyway.'

Sebastian thought how often he'd been jealous of Ivory. In the meantime, he accepted him as Kirsty's old buddy, and he even liked him! A pity that he wasn't here now to celebrate with them! He shared another piece of cake with Jack, and then the teenagers went into Kate's room.

'Your parents are really nice!' Jack smiled at Kate.

'Yeah, they are! And we are so glad to have our puppies back!' Kate replied. 'We were totally distressed when we thought we might never see them again. And because of that fear, my parents became nervous wracks and had some bad arguments.'

'Relationships can be quite complicated,' Arielle remarked. 'Imagine this: my Uncle Wayne is now reunited with his wife!'

'How come?' Jack asked.

'Ever since he was suspected of being a murderer, my aunt fervently defended him, and so they have reconciled!'

'That's fantastic!' Jack took Arielle's hand in his and squeezed it tenderly. 'Definitely good to know that you don't have a gangster in the family,' he teased his girlfriend.

Arielle had to smile. 'You may have criminals among your ancestors yourself. After all, many of the first settlers in Australia were prisoners, as we recently learned from Mrs. Wilder.'

Kirsty eyed Jack critically. 'According to your appearance, you could be the descendant of an Aborigine.'

'You're right, Kirsty!' Jack said. 'My great-grandmother was an Aborigine and lived in Mackay.'

Sebastian accompanied Kirsty to her home, and they were silent for a while. The talk about Arielle's relatives and the murder story were still buzzing around in their heads.

'Ivory's father pointed out that the police would sometimes be too quick to label someone as the perpetrator. Just to make themselves look better in public, they pretend to have solved a case,' Kirsty finally said. 'But in reality, nobody has a clue.'

'Maybe the detectives are on the right track after all. Jack told me that Arielle's uncle had beaten his wife once. So, Wayne could have a tendency to violence.' Sebastian frowned. 'Oh bummer, I was supposed to keep this a secret. Please don't tell anyone! It was just a single slap, ages ago, and Wayne was very upset about himself after that.'

'That's disgusting!' Kirsty gazed at him in horror. 'I don't mean you, because you blabbed, but that he would beat his wife. I can't understand why women don't leave men like that!' Kirsty kept brooding for a while, and then she shouted: 'That would explain it! We wondered why Thomas left Daniel's house in the middle of the night. Perhaps his mother called him in despair because her husband threatened to hurt her. And when Thomas tried to help her, his father strangled him in his rage! Afterwards, he had to get rid of the body as fast as possible. What could he do? And then he had an idea: he took Thomas to the park and put him on the fake horse with the help of a rope. And to make it look like the act of a lunatic, he put a snorkelling fin and a leather glove onto his body.'

Sebastian was by no means convinced. 'Then Arielle's aunt would have known about it, too! Why should she protect her husband if he was so cruel?'

'Because she's afraid of him!'

'Nah, I think this Uncle Wayne is wrongly suspected. Arielle and her Aunt Heidi seem to agree on this after all. And apparently, he really loved Thomas.'

'Well, we're still in the dark, and we're no better than the police.' Kirsty suddenly smiled. 'And I was already regarding myself as the heroine of the day, having found a motive for the murder.'

'In any case, you are my heroine,' Sebastian said gallantly and hugged her.

\* \* \*

Returning home, he heard loud music coming from Anna's room. 'Hi, Sebastian!' his mother shouted. She was busy cleaning up the living room, sorting out old newspapers. 'How was your afternoon?' Sebastian flopped down on the couch and moaned exaggeratedly. 'Pooh, I've eaten far too much!'

Lizzie laughed at his feigned tortured expression.

'Does Anna have visitors?' Sebastian asked curiously.

'Her friends Audrey and Brenda are here.'

'It sounds like a wild party! And where's Dad?'

'He's out with Susi and Lilly. Just when we were about to leave together, Aunt Paula called, and Andy didn't want to wait for me. You know him, patience isn't exactly his strength. Paula was talking up a storm, and then I also chatted with Sam.' She looked at her watch. 'Andy should be back any minute, because I've been on the phone for at least an hour.'

'With all that noise?'

Lizzie smiled. 'I took the phone outside.' Inwardly, she was glad Anna and her friends played pleasant music, even if it was too loud for her taste. But it could be much worse! Some ghastly songs on the radio or in movies triggered either aggressive feelings or thoughts of escape in her. The music stopped now, and Anna accompanied her friends to the front door, where Audrey giggled. She made a remark that Sebastian and his mother couldn't understand. 'I really love those hot ears, they are cool!' Brenda said aloud. 'Bye!'

Lizzie looked puzzled. 'I still have hot ears from talking on the phone. But Brenda certainly meant something else, didn't she?'

Anna sat down and chuckled. 'It's music from a CD that Bruce lent me this morning. The musicians are his friends and call themselves Hot Ears.' Addressing her brother, she said, 'Oliver is the lead singer, and he's also fantastic on the guitar.'

'Awesome!' said Sebastian.

'Does Bruce also play any instruments?' Lizzie asked.

'He used to play the guitar in the past, but not anymore.'

A thought occurred to Sebastian. 'Anna, you mentioned a woman called Maryann recently, the one who was the girlfriend of Bruce and later of Thomas. Do you know her last name by any chance?'

'Yes, why? Her last name is King.'

'Wow!' Sebastian yelled. 'That's the same woman who stole Kate's dogs!' He told his sister and mother what he'd learned from Kate this afternoon.

'Incredible!' Lizzie exclaimed.

'It's a small world!' Anna said.

# 26 MOTHER'S DAY

Gradually, the nights became cooler and the days shorter. Lizzie had never got used to the fact that the sun in Queensland already set between 5 and 7 p.m., depending on the season, and she still missed the long summer days in Germany. On the other hand, she enjoyed the beautiful sunrises on the Sunshine Coast. Before she'd had a dog, she would never have thought of going for a walk at the first light of dawn. But in the meantime, it had become a lovely ritual for her to take the dogs to the beach prior to breakfast. One Sunday in May, she woke up, stretched and was about to fall asleep again when she heard voices in the house. She sighed and stood up.

'What's the matter with you people?' she asked. The whole family crew already gathered in the kitchen, obviously wide awake and full of energy. 'It's still pitch black!'

'Happy Mother's Day!' everyone chanted. Andy hugged his wife and lifted her high into the air, and Anna giggled.

'We want to walk to Peregian Beach and have a picnic on the beach,' Sebastian explained.

'We've already packed everything into three backpacks. And you won't have to carry anything, Mum,' Anna said.

'That sounds wonderful! Okay, I'll be ready in ten minutes,' Lizzie replied, stifling a yawn.

The mouth of Stumers Creek offered different views all the time. On some days the creek dammed up to form a lake that was separated from the sea by a sandbank; on other days there was a shallow stream. It was a wonderful place for kids, dogs and adults alike! In summer, the water could be as warm as in a bathtub. Often, parts of the black coffee rocks near the dunes were exposed, and children played in the mud and smeared it on their bodies. The course of the stream also constantly changed, and now and then you could see small waterfalls and rock pools. At other times, there was a torrential river that no one could cross. In the last rainy season, the sea had even surged wildly up to the road above, and the thundering, brown foaming waves of the so-called KING TIDE had amazed many curious spectators.

When the Kuhlmann family arrived at this beach, still very early on Mother's Day, the sea water was flowing into Stumers Creek. Only a small strip of sand separated the dunes near the car park from the creek. Susi and Lilly had to swim to get to the other side, and Sebastian's shorts got wet while wading through. At a brisk pace they walked north towards Peregian Beach. The rising sun created a golden light on the waves and a happy smile on their faces. Andy searched for beautiful shells in the light-colored sand and Lizzie hoped to discover a treasure. Sebastian and Anna played ball with the dogs. Apart from them, there were already a few other people out and about, some alone, some with their dogs. Anna thought Susi was especially pretty when she was running around on the beach as she was doing now, carefree and full of life. Her velvety brown eyes were shining expectantly and her bushy tail was proudly pointing upwards.

Anna once again took a swing with her ball thrower, and the rubber ball flew about twenty meters through the air, hit the ground, bounced to the side and then ...

'Oh no!' cried Anna, startled. The ball landed right on top of a woman's head who turned around indignantly.

'Excuse me!' Anna shouted to her.

How embarrassing! The woman said nothing, but her sour expression spoke volumes. Anna hoped that the soft ball hadn't hurt her too much!

Susi was joyfully chased by a German Shepherd for a while, and Lilly made it her business to support her friend, chasing the huge dog. The sun rose rapidly higher, hiding behind the clouds every now and then. Meanwhile, the Kuhlmanns almost reached the end of the beach where dogs were allowed to roam freely; and they chose a suitable spot for their picnic. Lizzie was impressed with the amount of food her family had provided. There was tea, coffee, juice, rolls with peanut butter and honey and bananas. The dogs got fresh water and a few treats.

They all ate and drank with gusto, until Sebastian complained, 'I have sand in my teeth.'

'And I've eaten too much!' Lizzie sighed, yawned, lay down in the sand and closed her eyes. But the very next moment, she jumped up, fast as a rocket. Bouncing around, Susi had accidentally hit Anna, causing her to dump a full cup of water over Lizzie's stomach.


The way back seemed longer to them than the opposite route earlier on, and when they finally reached the mouth of Stumers Creek, they were surprised how high the water had risen in the meantime. They had forgotten about the tide coming in.

'Let's keep going to the right,' Andy suggested.

Followed by his children and the dogs, he stepped into the gurgling stream, immediately up to his waist in the water.

Sebastian and Anna took off their backpacks and held them high above their heads, marching through the water. Susi and Lilly were drifted off a bit but made it to the other side. They shook themselves extensively and waited for their human friends. Lizzie chose another spot to cross the river, believing it would be easier there. However, the bottom under her feet suddenly dropped. She submerged up to her stomach and then even deeper into the water. She felt the strong suction and became frightened when a thick branch passed her, grazing her slightly. Her leg hit a rock with a painful impact. In the end, only her head stuck out of the creek. Some strangers shouted encouraging words and a young man with an extravagant haircut stretched his arms out to her. Gratefully, she grasped his hands, and he pulled her to the safe shore.

'Thank you very much!' Lizzie stood there like a doused poodle. 'Phew, the water is much deeper than I thought.'

'You've picked the wrong place,' cried Andy mockingly and without the slightest hint of pity.

She glared at him, furious. Why hadn't she married a more caring man?

They arrived home dripping wet, and after a warm shower Lizzie felt better, although she had a huge bruise on her leg and a scratch on her arm. Her anger at Andy quickly passed. And now she received her Mother's Day gifts: a cook book from Sebastian, a framed painting from Anna, and an amber necklace from her husband. She was thrilled and hung Anna's beautiful picture of a sunrise on a wall in the living room. Afterwards, she studied the cook book, admiring the colourful illustrations.

'The dishes look delicious! Sebastian, which recipe shall we try first?' Then she grinned at her husband. 'And I finally got my treasure! Long time ago, we used to look for amber in our holidays at the Baltic Sea.'

In the late afternoon, Bruce came to visit and gave Lizzie a small plant in a pot, nicely wrapped.

'This is a spinach plant for you from my mother,' he explained somewhat embarrassed. 'She's an avid gardener and has written its botanical name on the pot. She said you can steam or boil the leaves briefly, or make a tea out of them.'

'Lovely, thank you very much!' said Lizzie. And it's so nice to meet you!' she beamed at him.

'Maybe this spinach will help us take long walks without getting sore muscles. Or cross rapid streams!' Andy winked at his wife and then smiled at Bruce.

Anna told her boyfriend about their adventurous crossing of Stumers Creek, and Bruce replied, 'Yeah, it can be tricky to wade through there at times. Some people who don't like dogs, or are afraid of them, suggested in the past to change the off-leash area. They wanted to reduce it to designated sections to the north of the creek only. But that would be silly! It would be much too dangerous or even impossible to get to the other side when it's more like a torrential river. And some puppies could also get in trouble and drawn out into the sea.'

Sebastian was flipping through the cook book.

'Here's a great sounding recipe! We could make spinach and feta puff pastry for dinner.'

'Better give this tiny plant some time to grow before you eat it straight away!' Bruce joked.

Anna was curious to see how her parents would react to her boyfriend. Would they accept him? Parents often seemed to have weird expectations. She inwardly moaned when her father asked him about his job. That was typical! Parents always wanted to know whether someone earned enough money and was successful. As if a good job were the most important thing in life!

# 27 THE DIARY

The morning sky was grey with a few pink clouds. Kate had a suspicion and didn't know how to deal with it. Heading towards the main entry of the school building, she met Ivory. Smiling at him, she asked, 'How's the young Labrador? Have you tracked down his owners?'

Ivory nodded, looking a bit sad. 'Yes, and they picked him up straight away. I would have loved to keep him, he's so cute! But they were thrilled! It was a family with two small children and they'd almost given up hope of ever seeing him again.' He smiled now. 'The kids and the puppy were crazy with joy!'

Kate decided to confide in Ivory. 'I must tell you something! Yesterday evening a woman called us, as she'd noticed a girl who pulled two dogs roughly behind her, even though the leash had wrapped around one of the smaller dog's legs. When she pointed it out, the girl freed the Jack Russell's leg but gave her a pathetic reply. Later, this lady spotted a poster in a car park, wondering if she'd seen our missing dogs. And when my mother asked her what this girl looked like, she described someone who looked exactly like Fiona!'

'Really?' Ivory's eyes widened.

'Well, it could have been someone else. But the girl allegedly had shoulder-length, dark brown hair, a narrow nose, a large birthmark on one cheek, and slightly too far apart brown eyes. And she was about thirteen years old.'

'That does sound just like Fiona! The woman was very observant!' Ivory was impressed. 'If I were to describe someone I'd only seen for a very brief moment, I would find it very hard. And where did the woman see her?'

'Not far from our house. Therefore, it popped into my mind that Fiona could have helped the bloody thieves, probably getting paid for it.'

'But why would Maryann and Simon put her up to that?'

'Perhaps because a young girl would arouse less suspicion. Or maybe because Fiona knew me and had been to my house before. If someone had caught her coming out of our garden with the dogs ...'

'Then she'd have simply claimed to be doing you a favour, walking the dogs,' Ivory interrupted her excitedly. 'That makes sense! And I wouldn't put it past Fiona to do something so mean.' Spontaneously, he squeezed Kate's hand as he saw how distraught she was. 'It's too bad you have to sit next to her in class,' he said pitifully.

'Well, it's just a hunch. Don't tell anyone about it, okay?'

'It's a deal!' Ivory promised.

When Fiona saw Ivory talking to Kate, her face darkened. She'd never liked him! And Kate had been acting strangely towards her lately. She would have loved to know what was going on inside her. She decided to be especially kind to Kate, trying to win her back. After all, she didn't have many friends.

Sebastian had massive hiccups and Kirsty laughed at him. For fun, she tried to hold his nose and he fought her off in a good-natured way, hiccupping on and on.

'Will you... hiccup... will you come to Jack's place for a game of... hiccup... table tennis this afternoon?' he asked her.

The next moment he unintentionally fell into Kirsty's arms and looked around in indignation as soon as he had regained his balance.

'Oops, sorry!' Jack grinned. 'I forgot what a flyweight you are.'

Shocked by the friendly slap on the back, at least Sebastian's hiccups had passed.

'Yes, sure!' Kirsty said. 'But I must take my little sister along.' She made a grimace. 'My mother is going to get a haircut today. I think she's met a guy she wants to impress.'

'Sounds great!' Sebastian said.

'That depends! Before she flirted with Ivory's father, she'd had a really stupid boyfriend. Ellen and I couldn't stand him.'

'You never told me that.'

'I'd rather not even think about him! He gave me the creeps, but my mother found him fascinating.' Kirsty sighed. 'I hope her new boyfriend is nicer.'

Jack smiled even wider.

'What's so funny now?' Kirsty asked.

'Look at Arielle! She's wearing different socks again!'

'Hi!' His girlfriend arrived at the group, kissed Jack briefly and brushed the hair out of her slightly sweaty forehead. Her cheeks were red and she was breathing fast.

'Whew, I had to cycle very fast so that I wouldn't be late. This morning, Max hid my socks somewhere, and he also nibbled on my school uniform and tore off a button. I had to sew it on in no time. And when I scolded him, Max grabbed one of my shoes and ran off with it.'

Kirsty laughed. 'I thought he'd only attack visitors' shoes!'

'Well, I thought so too! He's such a rascal!' Arielle smiled and turned to Jack. 'This afternoon I'll better leave Max at home because otherwise he would probably keep mugging the ping-pong ball. He might accidentally swallow it.'

Since Jack's parents had given their son a ping-pong table for Easter, he'd already invited his friends to play several times. They all enjoyed the games. This time, however, there was a bit of a row when Kirsty and Sebastian lost a match against Ellen and Jack. Kirsty became very agitated and accused Arielle of counting wrong. Sebastian was quite startled about his girlfriend's behaviour. But then Kirsty apologised, admitting her own mistake. After a few games, they sat in Jack's room and ate a chocolate cake his mother had baked. Ellen quickly took the biggest piece, Sebastian noted amusedly.

'Do your mothers keep a diary?' Arielle asked her friends.

'I don't have a clue! Why do you ask?' Jack wondered.

'Aunt Heidi and I discovered something interesting. She donated most of Thomas' things, his clothes and stuff to various charities. She also gave me many things, and we both had to cry again. Thomas had quite a few books, and by chance we found some photocopies ...' Arielle cleared her throat.

'So what?' Jack asked curiously.

'Aunt Heidi was completely shocked! In one of those books, she discovered three folded sheets that were copies from her own diary. Apparently, Thomas had found it one day. And he had copied the pages where she'd written about Nicolas, her former lover, and their baby. So, Thomas knew that my Uncle Wayne was not his biological father!'

'And he kept this a secret?' Kirsty was amazed.

Ellen looked uncomprehendingly from one to the other, not knowing what they were talking about.

'Thomas was the dead man on the horse sculpture,' Kirsty whispered into her ear. 'And a cousin of Arielle.'

Ellen promptly forgot her cake and listened intently.

Arielle poked around on her plate with a fork.

'My aunt assumes that Thomas found her diary shortly after their holidays in Thailand, as suddenly he behaved brusquely and dismissively towards her, but was particularly nice to her husband.'

'Why?' Sebastian asked.

'I don't know! Did Thomas feel sorry for his dad, I mean Uncle Wayne, because my aunt had a secret love affair in the past? I suppose that Thomas was angry with his mother. Firstly, because she'd cheated on Uncle Wayne, and secondly, because she'd kept everything quiet. It must have been terrible for Thomas to hear about Nicolas, his real father, in this way!'

Jack raised his eyebrows. 'Why did he copy those pages? He wouldn't blackmail his own mother, would he?'

'Blackmail?'

'Yes, he could have demanded money, threatening to tell your uncle if she didn't.'

'Oh no!' cried Arielle. 'I'd never have thought of such a thing!'

'You mentioned once that Thomas was rather curious. Perhaps he was trying to find his real father.' Sebastian rubbed his chin.

'Well, who knows? But Nicolas has been dead for some time now. And we can't ask Thomas anymore.' Tears came to Arielle's eyes, and she quickly brushed her nose.

Jack comfortingly put his arm around her shoulder, causing Arielle to cry even harder. Kirsty handed her a new tissue and looked at her pitifully.

'What else did Thomas discover in this diary? More secrets?' Ellen asked. But nobody paid any attention to her.

# 28 LEATHER SKIN

Anna was sitting with Barbara and David in Tickle Park. All of them were dressed in warm clothes, as the temperature had cooled down in the last few days and today there was an icy wind blowing. Anna was amused about the bright green beanie on David's head. Barbara watched a group of skateboarders in the skatepark nearby. She was very impressed with the acrobatic jumps and turns of an older boy, until she heard him curse in a rather vulgar and unsympathetic voice.

'Did you like the movie 'LEATHER SKIN' the other day?' Anna asked.

'Yes, but it was scary!' Barbara replied. 'Some scenes are still haunting me.'

'At one point Barbara even screamed loudly in the cinema.' David grinned broadly.

'I was terrified when this monster unexpectedly grabbed the child with its claws! And then its huge, bloodshot eye ...'

'Hey, stop, don't tell me the whole story, after all I want to see the movie myself!' Anna interrupted her quickly.

'The creatures from the newly discovered planet were very frightening,' said Barbara. 'These aliens were highly intelligent, but extremely cruel. And they seemed so real!' She shuddered, and Teddy, who was sitting on her lap, looked at her reproachfully. 'Sorry, Teddy!' Barbara stroked the little dog under its chin and it licked her hand briefly.

Susi nudged Anna with her nose and Anna automatically scratched her behind the ears. Feeling that Anna was elsewhere in her mind, Susi put a paw on her leg. Anna laughed. 'No, Susi, you are much too heavy to sit on my lap. Why don't you sit nicely next to Lilly?'

'Maybe those two are getting cold bums.' Barbara smiled.

'The leathery skin of those dangerous creatures in the movie was a good protection for them,' David said thoughtfully. 'A kind of natural armour, supple yet so strong that they were almost invincible. And it was great how they could adapt their colour to their environment, like chameleons ...'

'Now you're telling too much!' Barbara admonished David.

'At least now I know where the movie got its title from,' Anna said.

'No!' David objected. 'The title refers to the unusual sclera of the eyes from the aliens. They had special abilities, using their eyes not only to see, but also to ...'

Barbara gave him a warning look.

'Okay, I'm not gonna tell you anymore, Anna!'

'Teddy is getting impatient anyway,' said Barbara, putting the fidgeting dog on the floor. 'Let's go to the sea.'

\* \* \*

The next day, the wind was howling, and Anna was in bed. She had caught a bad cold and high fever, and her limbs were aching. So annoying! She was very disappointed because she had planned to go to the cinema with Bruce that evening. She'd already imagined how she would cuddle up to him, enjoying his closeness and his scent. Of course, she'd also been looking forward to the movie, a thriller that you had to watch with three-dimensional glasses. Crap! Now she wouldn't meet her boyfriend at all this weekend as she didn't want to infect him. Disgruntled, she turned around in bed and stared at the pictures on her wall.

'Anna, it's for you!' Her mother entered her room and handed her the phone.

'Hi, Anna. It's me, Scott!'

'Oh, I didn't expect you!' Anna coughed.

'You sound terrible,' Scott said pitifully.

'I have a cold,' Anna croaked.

'Should I rather call another time?' asked her ex.

'No, but I'll let you do the talking. What's new?'

Scott laughed softly. 'Kylie and Mike are getting a baby!'

'What?' Anna sat bolt upright. 'I can't believe it!'

'Well, they surely hadn't taken birth control too seriously. At first, they were completely shocked and at a loss, but Kylie's parents are great! They offered them their full support. I think Mike's parents are still very perplexed.'

Anna was stunned. 'Wow, to be a mum at sixteen – or how old is Kylie now?'

'Um, yeah, she'll turn seventeen in July and Mike eighteen in October. Still, very young indeed! However, they're a great couple and I hope that they'll manage. Mike will start an apprenticeship as a mechanic. Your Uncle Sam, who is a friend of the boss, has kindly put in a good word for Mike.'

For a moment, Anna was overcome with sadness. She had once overheard Susan, Scott's sister, whispering to Kylie that Anna and Scott were a beautiful dream couple! Well, that dream was over ...

'I am sure Kylie will phone you soon and tell you all about it herself!' Scott said gleefully. 'Maybe the baby will be born on the same day like you. Kylie said she's pretty sick in the morning, but other than that, she's okay. And after the initial shock, Mike is already acting like a proud father!'

Anna smiled. 'I can well imagine! And I'm looking forward to seeing you all again. Maybe sometime in June?'

Scott chatted away, without mentioning Anthony, and then said goodbye. Anna had hardly hung up when her mobile phone rang. This time it was Bruce, and her heart leapt.

'Hello, you sick mouse!'

'Hello, Bruce!' Oh dear, her voice had become even hoarser!

'I just wanted to wish you a quick recovery. And tomorrow morning I'll come over. Wrap yourself up nice and warm, okay?'

Anna was touched that he was so compassionate. Tears came to her eyes, but she quickly wiped them away when she heard the quick steps of a two-legged person and two four-legged friends.

'Hi, Sis!' Sebastian handed her a glass of orange juice. 'Here, some vitamins for you!'

Susi and Lilly looked at Anna expectantly.

'I'm sorry, but I can't walk with you today.' Anna coughed and sneezed, and Susi pricked up her ears. Lilly tilted her head to the side.

Sebastian grinned. 'They are definitely wondering about your different voice. Dad and I will take them to the beach now. See you later!' He bent down to stroke Susi and Lilly. 'Better don't kiss Anna today, or you'll catch a cold, too.'

Anna had to laugh, which immediately triggered another coughing attack.

Later, she lay in bed thinking about Scott and Bruce. She hardly wasted anymore thoughts on Jason. He had already ended his short affair with Wendy and seemed to have new girlfriends – or flirts – all the time. Anna was glad that she still got along well with Scott, and happy to be with Bruce. She was totally in love with him! It wasn't just the strong physical attraction he exerted on her, but his whole demeanor.

It suddenly occurred to her what he had once said to her:

'... if you ever get into trouble, Anna, call me quickly, and I will come to your rescue immediately – just like 'Superman'!'

She trusted that she could rely on him one hundred percent. However, she was a bit concerned about his feelings. Maryann, his former girlfriend, was so completely different in character from herself. That had worried her right from the beginning of their relationship.

And it was strange that Thomas had also been Maryann's boyfriend. Both Bruce and Thomas felt compassion for animals. Why had they been attracted to Maryann who turned out to be a nasty dog thief? In general, she didn't seem to be a nice person, according to what Anna had heard so far. But she'd probably beguiled them with her good looks and her charm. None of the relationships had lasted very long, though. And now Thomas was dead.

The previous night, Anna had a horrible dream in which Thomas was attacked by an alien monster. Even though she hadn't seen the movie 'LEATHER SKIN' yet! But David's description of the aliens had reminded her of a sculpture in the 'Garden of the Seven Senses' – and of the leather glove on Thomas' hand! And once again, she mused about his last night. Had Thomas run out of the house in a great hurry? Had he heard something suspicious and tried to be 'Superman' to help someone? However, none of the neighbours had noticed anything unusual. Only one elderly lady had reported hearing loud barking, a pathetic whining, and a suppressed cursing in the middle of the night.

Anna sat up in bed so quickly that she became dizzy for a moment and her feverish head began to throb. Her thoughts twirled around. A whimper? A dog in need? A rescue attempt? Thomas had been very fond of animals – so that could have been the reason! Excited, she picked up her mobile phone and sent an SMS to Bruce:

*MAYBE THOMAS WAS MURDERED WHILE TRYING TO PREVENT A DOG THEFT!*

Her mother came into the room to bring her a cup of chicken soup.

'Thank you!' Anna wanted to say, but now her voice was completely gone. Lizzie heard only a very soft whisper.

Looking at her daughter with concern, she said, 'Poor child! If you don't feel better tomorrow, I'll take you to the doctor.'

Anna had no appetite at all, but managed to eat the soup. Then she sent the same text message to her friend Barbara and added:

*CAN'T SPEAK TODAY. WILL YOU CALL ME TOMORROW?*

Afterwards she felt so tired that she only wanted to sleep. And soon she fell into a deep slumber.

# 29 COLD

Anna felt much better on the next day and her fever had also dropped. She noticed that Bruce had texted her two replies, one ending with: 'See you soon, my sweetheart!' Barbara called early in the morning, keen to know what she'd meant by her text message. Still a bit croaky, Anna relayed her idea that Thomas might have attempted to prevent a dog theft in the night of his murder.

Barbara was impressed. 'You are clever! We should find out if there are any dogs in the street where Daniel lives.'

'I could take Susi and Lilly for a walk in that area,' Anna suggested. 'It's always easy to start a conversation with a dog owner if you have a dog yourself. But today I'm still too weak. This daft cold is really getting on my nerves.'

'Yeah, you sound pretty awful,' said Barbara sympathetically.

Anna laughed hoarsely. 'Last night I couldn't speak at all.'

'You know what? I'll check it out with David and Teddy. I'll call him straight away. Bye!'

Anna didn't want to stay in bed any longer and got up, although her head still hurt slightly. In the dining room she met her brother who was having his second breakfast. He'd already played rugby, and he'd got new scratches and bruises on his arms and legs. Only now did Anna get the chance to tell him about her suspicions. Sebastian thought her idea was a bit far-fetched and told her so honestly. However, after another bite into his bun, he said, 'Well, it actually sounds quite plausible that Thomas might have heard something that made him rush out onto the street. But I can't believe that a dog thief could have killed him.'

Anna's eyes widened as a new thought crossed her mind.

'Perhaps Maryann and Simon did it! Maybe they tried to steal another dog that night and Thomas caught them doing it.'

Sebastian almost choked. 'No way! Maryann used to be his girlfriend! Do you really think she could be that mean?'

'Who's mean?' Bruce asked, standing next to them with Lizzie.

'Oh, you're already here! I hadn't expected you so early,' Anna stammered. She was embarrassed, as she had neither washed herself nor brushed her teeth yet.

'How are you, Anna?' Bruce tried to give his girlfriend a tender hug, but she pushed him away. 'You better keep your distance from me!' And as if to warn him, she sneezed violently.

Bruce smiled affectionately at her and Lizzie winked at Sebastian. Her amusement disappeared when the conversation led back to the murdered Thomas. She had intended to leave the young people alone, but now she sat down and listened to Anna's account. Bruce remembered with consternation that he had discovered a bandage on Maryann's hand at a concert of the Hot Ears. And that had been shortly after Thomas' murder! Had she really tried to steal a dog that night and got bitten by it? Had Thomas caught her and Simon in the act? But Bruce could hardly imagine that the two of them were capable of murder. Or were they? Had Maryann hated Thomas with all her heart because he'd broken up with her? And Simon? He knew him only by sight and had the impression that he was quite under Maryann's thumb. He shivered at the thought that one of them might have strangled Thomas.

'Are you cold, Bruce?' Lizzie asked. 'I'll make some tea! And let's go into the garden. Perhaps the sun will chase away your germs, Anna.'

No sooner were they sitting outside than Jack came to visit unexpectedly, as agitated as Sebastian had never experienced before. Jack gushed out, 'I've fallen out with Arielle! She kicked me out of the house and doesn't want to see me anymore!'

Sebastian was stunned. 'Why is that?'

Jack ran his hand through his hair. 'Because I said something stupid! I accused her Uncle Wayne of being a murderer!'

'Well, the police suspected him, too,' Sebastian interjected. 'But nothing was proven.'

'I know, and Arielle and her aunt always believed in his innocence. However, after Arielle's story about that diary, I suddenly thought of a motive. So, Thomas discovered who his biological father was. Perhaps Wayne, Arielle's uncle, had also learned at some point about his wife's secret love affair with Nicolas. Wayne became so jealous and angry that he ambushed Nicolas one day, pushing him off the cliff. And somehow Thomas found out, blackmailed his father, namely Wayne, and was therefore also murdered by him. Uncle Wayne – as I call him – was aware that Thomas was at his friend's that night, and so he lured him out of Daniel's house somehow. Then he strangled him in the darkness and took him to the park so that no one would associate him with his son.'

His listeners remained silent for a while. It was hard to digest Jack's wild fantasies! Anna wanted to know what the diary was about and Jack told her about the three copies that had been hidden in one of Thomas' books.

'No wonder Arielle is mad at you now!' Sebastian said.

'She never wants to talk to me again!' Jack swallowed hard. 'Her face was white as chalk when she told me that. And she didn't yell at me, but was calm and cold as ice. I thought that was even worse! What am I going to do?'

'Oh boy! Really stupid that you blurted out your unfounded suspicions like that,' Sebastian said.

'You could've done that, too,' Anna said to her brother. 'You talk without thinking all the time!'

Sebastian made a grimace. Bruce smiled and then turned to Jack. 'Have you and Arielle often quarreled?'

'No, never! Or just a bit. But now it's over.'

'You will work it out,' Sebastian tried to comfort Jack. 'You could give her a nice present and tell her how sorry you are.'

Jack didn't look very convinced. 'I tried to apologise, but she didn't even let me in. Standing at her doorstep like a bloody salesman, I kept knocking and shouting, but she wouldn't give in. And she doesn't answer her mobile phone, either.'

'Oh boy!' Sebastian repeated. 'I wonder if Kirsty could calm her down somehow. Shall I ask her?'

'I don't know,' Jack said despondently. 'I wish I'd kept my mouth shut!'

To distract him, Bruce now told him about Anna's ideas about a connection between a dog theft and the killing of Thomas.

'But as long as we can't prove anything, they're just fantasies,' Anna pointed out. She was grateful that Bruce didn't hold it against her that she'd suspected his former girlfriend of such a horrible deed.

Later that afternoon, Barbara called Anna. 'David and I walked around that area where Daniel lives, and quite a lot of dogs barked at Teddy. So, it wouldn't be unusual to hear some whining there at night. But we talked to a lady with a very unusual dog ... um, I can't remember the name of this breed. Something rare. I have to ask David again. But Brownie...'

'Brownie?' Anna interrupted her friend. 'That's a strange animal name! I've only ever met dogs or horses called Blacky.'

'Yes, me too. Anyway, her dog was really pretty, and she had to pay heaps of money for him. When we asked her if she'd ever been afraid that someone might steal Brownie, she told us that a couple had actually tried to steal him once, but that he'd bitten one of them! She was quite startled, because Brownie is normally sweet and trusting. And he was friendly with us and Teddy too.'

'Was she at home when this happened?'

'Yes, she and her husband heard their garden gate open in the middle of the night because it was squeaking. They became concerned and quickly switched on an outside lamp. The next moment, their dog growled terribly and then someone cursed and they saw two people running away. And the next morning they discovered some drops of blood on the path by the gate.'

'That could have been Maryann and Simon! I bet they'd tried to steal other dogs before they were caught in the dog park!' Anna said, excited. 'And could Brownie's owner remember the date of that attempted robbery by any chance?'

'Yes, she did! She even remembered the night very well, as she and her husband had stayed up until midnight to celebrate her birthday. But this happened after Thomas had been killed! Well, we found out more than we'd expected, and yet we still don't know much at all. The murder still is a mystery!'

'At least Maryann and Simon won't be stealing dogs anymore! At least I hope so! In any case, I'm glad they've been caught red-handed.'

'And I am completely exhausted. It's been a long walk and even Teddy is worn out.'

'Thank you, Barbara, for doing all this research!'

'No problem. I hope you'll get better soon! Bye!'

# 30 A LID FOR EVERY POT

Arielle sulked for a whole week. Neither Jack's beautiful bouquet of flowers nor the coaxing by Kirsty and Sebastian mollified her. Although Arielle felt unhappy and lonely, she wouldn't give in. Jack's accusations had deeply upset her, and she wished so much that her cousin Thomas were still alive! She was only comforted by her beloved pets who often made her laugh despite her deep grief.

Jack was sad. How could he win back Arielle's friendship? He started many letters to her, but then he tore them up into thousand little pieces because he just couldn't find the right words. He felt miserable, and he also had a terrible cold. He didn't know whether Anna had infected him or whether he had become ill out of sheer frustration. Except for his sore, red nose, he looked pale and cheesy, and Sebastian took pity on him and tried to cheer him up.

Ivory noticed that Fiona seemed to be pleased that Arielle and Jack were not on best terms. How could she be so mean? Some people were horrible! Like Tim, his father's colleague! Recently his dad had complained about Tim, pouring his heart out to Ivory. Barry had never told anybody before that he detested working with Tim, a corrupt and brutal man who'd often used unnecessary force. Just as an example: in an attempt to break up a brawl between three young people, Tim had broken several ribs of one guy. Afterwards, Barry argued with him, getting so mad that he almost had a fight with him, too!

When he confessed this to his son, he was quite embarrassed. Why had he lost his temper? And he hated the feeling of helplessness. Although he had intended to tell his superior the truth, he kept his mouth shut. After all, he couldn't prove Tim's guilt as one of the youths had pulled out a knife and everything had happened incredibly fast; in a dark street with no other witnesses. Nevertheless, Tim had not acted in self-defense in Barry's opinion, because he had already successfully fended off the clumsy attack of the drunken young man. After kicking the knife out of his hand, he'd beaten him up, while Barry had dealt with the other two men without injuring anybody.

Barry was boiling with rage again, thinking of how Tim had been bragging about the arrest of the three youths to other colleagues back then. Well, at least nobody had been killed. In his entire career as a police officer, Barry had only been personally involved in manslaughter once, and just remembering it made him sick. He hated violence! Sometimes he wondered why he hadn't chosen another profession. Baker, for example – then he still would have to work night shifts, but he would be able to work with fragrant rolls instead of dealing with stinking drunks or brutal colleagues.

Ivory usually got along very well with his father, and in many ways, he admired him and regarded him as his role model. Barry Little was an honest, reliable person who could be quite strict, but was also very soft-hearted. He was fit, sporty and handsome. Similar to Ivory, he had white-blonde hair, grey-blue eyes and smooth skin with a pale complexion.

Ivory was happy that his father confided in him. Ivory had occasionally met Tim, and from the first moment he hadn't liked him at all. Tim could be funny and jovial when he was in a good mood, but even when laughing and joking, his eyes remained cold and scary.

Ivory's thoughts drifted to Kate and her dark brown, warmly shimmering eyes. Although he had initially looked down on her as Fiona's friend, his feelings for her changed. Lately, he got the impression that Kate was not as close a friend of Fiona as he'd always believed, but that she was simply very good-natured, feeling sorry for the rather unpopular schoolmate.

When they'd actually managed to find Patrick, the missing Labrador, in the dog park, he could have kissed Kate – if he'd dared. She had played so lovingly with her two dogs! At the sight of her tears of joy, and seeing her initially timid, incredulous smile turn into a radiant one, he promptly fell in love with her. However, he had no idea what Kate thought of him. In his daydreams he imagined them cuddling and laughing together, but in reality, he had only squeezed her hand once when she told him about her suspicion that Fiona might have stolen her dogs.

\* \* \*

Anna had meanwhile recovered from her cold, fortunately without passing it on to her family or Bruce. She hadn't gone to school for several days, and now it was Friday evening. Tonight, she and Bruce would watch the thriller with the 3D glasses in the cinema in Maroochydore. Oliver and Angus, another member of the Hot Ears, would come along, too. The Kuhlmann family had just finished their dinner when the doorbell rang. Andy opened the door and was shocked to see two wild looking guys. One was quite chubby, had raven black, long hair and looked like a rocker, the other was very thin, had a half-shaven skull and short, light blonde hair on the other side of his head. He wore a yellow T-shirt depicting a hissing black Tasmanian devil with bright red ears. The skinny boy smiled at him friendly and Andy discovered a piercing on his lower lip. Before Andy could say anything, Oliver greeted him cheerfully, 'Hello, Mr. COOL MAN! We've come to pick up Anna.'

Well, he wasn't the first one to make jokes about their last name KUHLMANN that almost sounded like COOL MAN.

'I'm coming!' cried Anna. 'Bye, Daddy!'

And she whizzed past him. Lizzie noticed her husband's perturbed expression, watching the youngsters from the window getting into a car. She grinned. 'I'm sure the boys are all right. Bruce's friends might look a bit scary, but they seem to be nice. Anyway, Anna has told me a lot about the rock group.'

'You think so?' 'Andy asked sceptically, raising his eyebrows.

'Yeah, Angus and Oliver are cool!' Sebastian confirmed. 'And their music is brilliant!'

Andy was concerned, though. What kind of people had Anna got herself involved with? And she was still so young! Since he'd found out that Kylie was pregnant, he worried even more about his daughter. He didn't like the fact that she was now leaving with three young men, all of them a few years older than her. What a pity that she was no longer in love with Scott, such a nice boy who was of the same age! he thought.

Anna, Bruce, Angus and Oliver sat next to each other in the cinema and didn't say a peep. They were completely under the spell of the exciting thriller and its fascinating scenery. The action took place in the tropical rainforest in the north of Queensland and partly at the Great Barrier Reef. The 3D glasses made everything look so realistic that they thought they were right in the middle of the action.

'Wow – this underwater world was so beautiful,' Anna enthused later on the way back. 'But at some point in the movie, I got somewhat dizzy. It felt as if I were sitting on the shark myself, speeding through the water so fast!'

'I loved the lush rainforest and the way the couple abseiled down the thundering waterfall to escape their pursuers,' Angus said.

'I nearly twisted my neck when the crocodile snapped,' Oliver said. 'I believed the huge beast was right in front of me.'

Bruce laughed. 'Me, too! My body also moved involuntarily. If the seat hadn't had a backrest, I would have flown backwards in shock. But I was even more scared of the mean people in this film.'

He looked briefly at Anna. It was a pity that he now had to take her straight home. He would have loved to spend more time with her – preferably all night! But she was only sixteen! Oliver had once joked that Bruce was a 'cradle-snatcher' – which was of course exaggerated, as she was only a few years younger than him. But unfortunately, at her age, this really turned out to be a problem. Some of his friends had already complained that they hardly ever met him in pubs or discos anymore. But somehow it seemed wrong to him to enjoy the nightlife without Anna. And he also wanted to avoid meeting Maryann as much as possible. He had been shocked when she'd come to Henry's party uninvited, getting silly and terribly drunk. He sighed.

'What's wrong?' Anna asked. She put one hand on his leg.

'Nothing!' Bruce lied.

His good mood had suddenly evaporated. Anna sensed that something was bothering him and pulled her hand away, but Bruce took it, squeezed it tenderly and put it back on his leg. Angus and Oliver continued their lively conversation while Anna and Bruce remained silent for a while. A light drizzle had set in and the wind-screen wipers made a soft, squeaking sound. The narrow moon hung pale in the sky and did little to illuminate the single-lane highway. Anna turned around to the friends on the back seat, amused, when Angus made a witty comment and Oliver laughed out loud. In the next instant, she cried out in shock as Bruce abruptly braked, cursing loudly. Another car had boldly overtaken him, despite an oncoming truck and the continuous centre line, then slowed down again. By a mere hair's breadth Bruce avoided to slam into the back of the car!

'What an idiot!' Oliver scolded. 'Why did he overtake and then brake at the next moment?'

'Look out!' Anna shouted. 'There's something on the road!'

The car in front of them now stopped on the side and Bruce carefully parked his car behind it. Only a very narrow hard shoulder separated the highway from a steep grassy embankment that descended to a wetland. Anna stared anxiously at the bundle in the middle of the road, which was hard to define in the dark and from the distance. What could it be? Had somebody hit an animal? Was it a dead kangaroo? Unconsciously, she held her breath as she and her friends got out of the car. She could hardly believe her eyes when she recognised one of the people coming out of the black Audi: it was Tim, the policeman! This time, he was not dressed in uniform but in jeans and sweat-shirt. The other person was a middle-aged woman, also wearing blue jeans and a jumper. She was fairly pudgy and seemed to be swaying slightly on her high heels. Bruce immediately noticed her strong alcohol breath.

'Hi, folks,' she whispered. 'We have to ch … ch … check what's over there, don't we, Timmy?'

'Wait here!' Tim commanded in a harsh voice. 'I'll check it out!' Armed with a torch, he stepped forward. The woman started to follow him, but stumbled after only one step and quickly held on to the side of the car. She must be pretty drunk! thought Bruce. A car came towards them, slowed down briefly, but then drove away as Tim waved the driver on.

Oliver looked back onto the highway, worried. 'Be careful not to get run over!' he warned his friends.

Angus shivered in the cold night air.

Tim now bent down to the thing in the road.

'It's just a rucksack,' he shouted.

Everyone was relieved. Not only Anna had feared to find an injured or dead animal, and Oliver had even thought of a human corpse, for his mind was still churning with movie scenes and images, with all the exciting chases, shootings and other acts of violence. Tim couldn't believe how heavy the backpack was, which he could only carry with difficulty. He opened it in the headlights of his car.

'What is it, Timmy?' the woman asked him. She brushed a dark curl from her roundish, heavily made-up face and lit a cigarette with a shaky hand.

'Climbing gear,' Tim said. 'Ropes, carabiners and stuff like that.' He rummaged around and pulled out various devices, a hammer and a helmet and then stuffed everything back into the rucksack. 'Apparently someone has lost his luggage! Pretty dumb not to secure it sufficiently.'

He turned his gaze towards the young people, but was blinded by the headlights and blinked. 'And you better get going again! It's dangerous to stand here on the motorway. Come on, Astrid, let's go!'

He took his girlfriend – or was it his wife? – by the arm and pushed her ahead gently. She giggled and then burped loudly. 'Goodbye!' she shouted to them. Tim heaved the rucksack into his boot and grunted briefly: 'Bye!'

Anna and her friends also got back into Bruce's car. In that very instant, another car drove past them, so quickly and so close that the car seemed to shake. Tim dashed off in pursuit.

'Now that idiot would wish to have his police car and siren, guaranteed!' Bruce said.

'Do you know this guy?' Angus asked in surprise.

'Yes, that Timmy is a policeman. A nasty guy who lives near me. Anna and Oliver have already met him as well.'

'It's weird that the owner of the rucksack didn't realise he'd lost it,' Angus said.

'He'll probably find out soon,' Bruce said and started the engine.

'What is Tim going to do with it?' Anna asked.

'There is a kind of lost and found property office at the police station.' Oliver explained. 'I once picked up my house key there. Nice when people hand in stuff!'

'That lady was pretty drunk,' Angus said. 'Is she his wife?'

'I don't think so. Perhaps his new girlfriend,' Bruce replied.

Anna shuddered. 'Bah, I find Tim disgusting! How any woman could get involved with such a man is a mystery to me!'

Oliver laughed. 'Anyway, she called him Timmy affectionately! Maybe he has some good qualities.'

'There's a matching lid for every pot,' Angus said and grinned broadly.

# 31 A BROKEN LEG

'Arielle has broken her leg!' Kirsty called out to Sebastian and Jack from afar when they arrived at school on Monday morning. 'She's in hospital!'

Jack exclaimed, 'Oh no! Did she fall over Max again?'

Some time ago, Arielle had slightly injured her wrist when her boisterous puppy had accidentally knocked her over.

'No, Arielle was skateboarding at Tickle Park, practicing a special jump. Karen, Arielle's mother, called me yesterday. She didn't tell me much, but she offered to take us to the hospital this afternoon.'

Jack pulled a face. 'I don't think Arielle wants to see me!'

'Nonsense! You're coming, too!' Kirsty said firmly.

On the way to Nambour, Jack was unusually silent, and he was grateful that Kirsty was talking to Karen with ease, as if they were old friends. It was tricky to find a free parking space, and then they had to walk quite a long way to the hospital. When Karen finally registered them all as visitors at the reception, Jack felt really queasy. For the whole last week, Arielle had been avoiding him. What should he do if she refused to see him now?

He would have preferred to run away to avoid such shame. Lost in thought, he followed the others through the hospital corridors and almost collided with a nurse. He took a deep breath as they entered Arielle's room. How would she react?

Arielle was lying in bed with her right leg up. It was stuck in a dark blue plaster bandage that reached from the foot to just below the knee. She looked tired, but was radiant when she saw her unexpected guests.

'Hi, dear, how are you feeling today?' her mother asked, patting her arm gently. 'You are looking much better already! Yesterday you were still pretty dazed!'

'Hello, Mum! I didn't know you were here yesterday.'

'Dad and I have both been with you ever since the accident. But after the operation and all the painkillers, you were naturally groggy.' She smiled. 'You were high on drugs and said all kinds of nonsense.'

'Really?' Arielle's gaze wandered from her mother to her friends and stayed with Jack.

'Hello! How nice of you all to come! Oh, Jack, I missed you so much!'

Jack leaned over to her, kissed her briefly on the cheek and dropped onto a chair next to her bed. 'I missed you, too,' he murmured. The next moment he jumped up and offered Arielle's mother his seat, but she refused his offer and smiled.

'Just stay there next to your girlfriend!'

She sat down on the bed and put her hand back on her daughter's right arm. Jack took Arielle's left hand and smiled tenderly at her.

Kirsty and Sebastian grinned. They fetched two chairs from another corner of the rather large room. Two other patients were lying in beds. An elderly woman, carrying one arm in a sling, was reading a book. A younger woman seemed to be fast asleep. She had one bandage on her head and one on her wrist, and her face was disfigured by a blueish swelling. Just as Sebastian looked at her pitifully, wondering what had happened to her, she opened her eyes. He quickly averted his gaze, turning to Arielle.

'How long do you have to stay here?'

'Just a few days! I was lucky to be operated on immediately.'

'What exactly have you been doing?' Kirsty asked.

'I was skateboarding on Saturday morning, heading for the shops to buy a new ball thrower for Max. And then I spontaneously decided to do some training in the Tickle Park. But after just a few jumps and turns with the skateboard, I fell down so stupidly that I broke my ankle. It hurt like hell, and I couldn't even get up.'

'Did anybody help you?' Jack asked.

'Yeah, sure! At least five children and three teenagers ran straight to me, and an older boy took his mobile phone and called an ambulance in no time at all, before I could say a single beep! And he also called my parents after I gave him the number.'

'Awesome!' said Sebastian.

'Well, I was quite embarrassed to be the centre of attention. And then some adults came along and started talking to me.' Arielle smiled a little crookedly. 'But I don't really remember what happened after that. I think the nurses gave me some strong painkillers that made me pretty woozy.'

'Are you still in pain now?' Arielle's mother wanted to know.

'No, luckily not. Yesterday I was puking. And I'm still groggy and feel kind of wrapped up in cotton wool. But otherwise, I feel fine!'

'Thank God! Dad had actually planned to come and visit you after work today, but by then visiting hours will be over. But he'll try to finish work earlier tomorrow and see you then! And now we'll let you sleep. You look very tired!'

Sebastian glanced furtively at the patient with the head bandage, who had fallen asleep again. Her blanket had shifted a little and he could see another thick bandage on her leg.

Arielle whispered: 'The poor woman was hit by a car on Friday night, and the driver did not stop but took off. What a nasty thing to do!'

Before Sebastian could reply, several women came into the room. One was carrying a tray with all kinds of pillboxes and medicine bottles, another had a large notepad in her hand. They gathered around the elderly lady in the bed next to Arielle and addressed her in a friendly manner. When one of them started to read information about the patient to the others, Karen said,

'We better get going, Arielle! It seems another team is in charge now. Get well soon, hey?'

'Thanks, Mum!' Arielle squeezed her hand and then looked at Jack. 'I'm so sorry!' she said softly. 'I've been an idiot! I know you didn't mean any harm.'

Jack grinned broadly, jumped up and hugged her passionately. Not only Kirsty and Sebastian were smiling now, but even the lady with the puffy face and all the staff members. However, Jack didn't give a hoot about that. He was incredibly happy! And on the way home, he chatted with Arielle's mother in a cheerful and relaxed mood while Kirsty and Sebastian cuddled up in the back seat, holding hands.

# 32 HIT AND RUN

Barbara was appalled. 'Hard to believe that someone could be so heartless! I do understand that you may be in a state of shock after hitting someone by accident, but to commit a hit and run? And a second car sped by that evening without helping the victim.'

'The way some people drive really is irresponsible! When we came back from the cinema the other day, we almost crashed into another car that cut us off,' Anna said. 'The crazy driver was a traffic cop, of all people, imagine that! He drove much too fast and, what's more, he shouldn't have overtaken us at that point anyway. And later he chased another car that didn't respect the speed limit, either. Such idiots!'

She described the incident in detail, while they were walking to David. Susi and Lilly trotted along. Anna had wrapped the loop of Susi's leash around her wrist so that she could put both hands in her jacket pockets. Nevertheless, they were icy. During the day, it had been sunny and warm, but as darkness fell, the temperatures dropped rapidly. The night before, they had only had 5 degrees Celsius. Barbara stopped suddenly, and Lilly, who was about to sniff at a bush, looked at her with irritation. She pulled with all her strength on the leash, but she couldn't reach the interestingly smelling shrub.

'Wait a sec, Lilly!' said Barbara. 'Anna, when exactly did you go home? I heard the accident happened on David Low Way in Coolum, near the surf club, on Friday night. Could it be that the car chase that you watched was done by the same guys?'

'You're absolutely right! That could well be! Were there any witnesses? Or could the woman herself describe who hit her?'

'Yes, some people watched the accident happen. A car came from Beach Road, turning much too quickly, and knocked down a woman who was about to cross the street. It seems the driver tried to brake and also swerved to the side, but still hit her – but then he just drove away! And a second car followed him at the same hellish speed, almost running over that poor lady! Fortunately, a man came to her aid and also called the police.'

'What did the cars look like?'

'Nobody could read the number plates so quickly, but one witness stated that the first car was a white Ford Falcon and the second a black Audi.'

Anna called out, 'It can't be a coincidence! Tim, that policeman, was also driving a black Audi that evening, one of those fast R8 sports cars. And the other car that flashed past us on the motorway was white.'

'So, that must have been them indeed!' Barbara was all excited. 'We should inform the police!'

'You think so?' Anna didn't sound very thrilled. The next moment, she almost fell, because Susi made a huge jump to catch a colourful parrot. 'Off!' Anna yelled.

Barbara laughed. 'Susi's dinner almost flew right into her mouth. Come on, let's go! David's probably waiting already.'

Susi watched the bird flying to a huge tree. Countless parrots had already gathered there, making a deafening spectacle. Why did they all meet in a single tree?

'You know what, I'll ask Sebastian to call his mate's father,' Anna said. 'Mr. Little seems to be a very helpful policeman. Maybe he can find out more.'

'Good idea!'

Barbara walked faster, and Anna had to hurry to keep up with her speed. Her hands finally got warm again.

After they'd arrived at David's house, the dogs played happily with Teddy. Anna called her brother, telling him briefly about the cars. Although Sebastian liked Mr. Little, he resented being told by his sister to phone him. But then the image of the swollen, bruised face of the woman in the hospital came into his mind, and it filled him with compassion and unrestrained anger. How could someone leave an injured woman lying in the middle of the street? So, Sebastian called Mr. Little and was relieved when Ivory picked up the phone. He told him Anna's news and asked him to pass them on to his father as soon as possible.

When Anna went home with her dogs, it had become dark. She was annoyed that she'd forgotten to bring a torch because some areas were not lit very well. Nevertheless, Anna walked relatively fast. After all the frolicking with Teddy, both Susi and Lilly seemed to be a bit tired and trotted along beside her, well behaved. Once something rustled in a bush close by, startling them. Several dogs barked excitedly behind various fences, walls and hedges as they approached. Anna stumbled over a tree root on the verge and flinched when a particularly loud dog kept throwing itself fully against a timber fence, sounding as if it wished to eat them all alive. She hoped that the fence was solidly built! Oh no! For a fraction of a second, she spotted a huge dog's head above the top of the fence, which stood out as a dark silhouette against a brightly lit window. The wild beast wouldn't be able to jump over the fence, would it? Susi growled softly as she felt Anna's fear, and Lilly leapt to one side in shock and started to bark as well. Someone shouted a harsh order, and the dynamic jumper behind the fence yelped half-heartedly once more and then fell silent. The dog was certainly harmless, but Anna still wanted to leave this place as quickly as possible. But now she had to wait because Lilly was making a poop. And once again, that dog bumped angrily barking against the fence while Anna collected Lilly's mess in a special bag. A car stopped next to her.

'What are you doing here?' Bruce asked and got out to greet her.

As an explanation Anna lifted the 'poop bag' with a grin. Lilly and Susi did a dance of joy, and Anna hugged her boyfriend. The invisible dog was howling in a high-pitched tone now, triggering other dogs nearby to join the chorus.

Anna said hastily, 'We better get out of here! The beast in this garden is scary! Do you have time to drive us home?'

'Yeah, sure, get in!'

'No, Susi, I want the front seat!' Anna had to shoo her dog onto the back seat.

Bruce had visited his friend Angus and was now on his way home. He chuckled, amused about her fear. 'I know this dog! And funnily enough, his name is Angus, too! If you meet him, he's totally sweet and rather submissive. He always throws himself on his back to be stroked and licks your hands like crazy.'

Anna was not convinced. 'Well, you are a real dog whisperer! All dogs seem to like you, and even a vicious mutt would lovingly kiss your feet. Anyway, I was glad that this fence is so high, although I usually find it sad that so many properties are completely hidden behind tall fences.'

'Well, most people do love their privacy.'

That's when they turned into the street where Tim lived. His house was also surrounded by a high timber fence. Only a faint glow of light indicated that someone was probably at home. Anna told Bruce about her conversation with Barbara and he replied, 'Yeah, I just heard about this accident. It's so lucky that the woman survived!'

'That Audi is quite a flashy car. Does it belong to Tim's girlfriend, Astrid?'

'No idea! In any case, it would be good if the guy who hit that woman was caught. So far, the news only covered the hit-and-run and nothing about an arrest,' Bruce said. 'Shall we give the police a tip about that wild car chase that we witnessed? But Tim is a police officer himself.'

'Strange that he apparently didn't report anything. But on the other hand, he might be anxious to get in trouble for his own dangerous driving!'

'Yes, they could blame him for the accident. And who knows, maybe he had too many drinks before and shouldn't have been driving that night? His girlfriend was tipsy for sure.'

'You couldn't tell if Tim was drunk or not. His eyes always seem to be glassy,' Anna said. 'What a chain reaction! If the backpack hadn't fallen out of a car, Tim and we wouldn't have stopped, and the white car would never have overtaken us on the motorway. And then the accident in Coolum wouldn't have happened, either.'

'That's true!' Bruce turned around to the dogs. 'Almost home, sweeties!'

Andy heard the slamming of a car door and looked curiously out of the window. At this moment his daughter said goodbye to her boyfriend and let the dogs out of the car.

'Hi, Daddy!' Anna shouted to him in a good mood, stepping into the house.

'I thought you'd gone to Barbara's?' Andy hissed. 'I don't like you seeing Bruce in secret.'

'Are you crazy?' Anna was upset. 'I was with Barbara.'

'Don't lie to me! I've just seen Bruce!' her father snapped at her.

Now Anna was fuming. 'It was a pure coincidence that he drove past me on my way home. And it was very kind of him to give the dogs and me a ride, as it would've been quite a long walk.' Her tone was icy, although an inner turmoil was raging inside her.

'Hello, Anna!' Sebastian said. 'I've called Ivory, and his daddy will ...'

With an angry look at her father, Anna interrupted her brother: 'I'll be right in your room, but I have to go to the bathroom first.'

Sebastian had already crouched down with the dogs that were rolling around on the floor, excited to play with him, and therefore he missed the grim expressions of both his father and his sister. Anna was mulling over her dad's attitude towards Bruce. Why didn't he like him? She was thinking: 'Bruce has a decent job, is polite, incredibly nice, smart, and an animal-lover. He's a wonderful person! And Dad is really mean and unfair!'

She brushed her disheveled hair so hard that she almost burst into tears. Trying to suppress her anger, she splashed cold water on her face and took several deep breaths. She didn't find any time to talk to Sebastian alone, as the food was already on the table when she left the bathroom. Lizzie sensed immediately that something must have happened. Anna looked grumpy and Andy also seemed to be in a bad mood. Earlier today, he'd already grumbled that they would have Brussels sprouts for dinner; he would hate them. Lizzie was glad that at least Sebastian was in an excellent mood and had a good appetite as always.

'How was it with Barbara?' she asked her daughter.

'Please tell Dad that you dropped me off yourself at Barbara's house this afternoon!' Anna said, in a new rage. 'He doesn't believe me that I was there and that Bruce met me just by chance later on. By the way, Barbara and I also visited her boyfriend, if you want to check every step I took!'

Sebastian looked at his sister in bewilderment. Why was she so snotty?

'Excuse me, Anna!' Andy skewered a Brussels sprout on his fork and looked at it suspiciously. 'I do trust you and of course you're an honest person. I was just surprised to see Bruce outside the house earlier.'

'What have you got against him?'

Her father sighed. 'Nothing at all! It's just … um … he's much older than you. And I don't know if his friends are good company for you. For example, that guy with the blonde half-shaved hair and the piercing …' He paused, not sure how to express his concerns.

'We're worried because Bruce is an adult and might hang out with people who drink a lot of alcohol, have sex, go to pubs and discos and so on,' Lizzie explained openly. 'And we are far from ready to become grandparents. But I hope you'll be more careful than Kylie!'

Sebastian swallowed audibly, Andy looked startled, and Anna blushed. She had never had 'real sex' with anybody yet, but she would never tell her parents. Even with her best friend Barbara she had never talked about such topics.

Lizzie smiled unexpectedly. 'You know what? I've been wondering all along why Angus looked so familiar to me. He stretched out his hands to me on Mother's Day when I waded through Stumers Creek, already up to my chin in the water. Even though half of his hair is shaved off and he looks a bit wild, he seems to be very kind and helpful.'

Andy timidly bit off a piece of a Brussels sprout and was pleased that it tasted much better than he'd thought. As a child he had always found them terribly bitter. Anna sabered furiously at a piece of meat. When Lilly could no longer resist the delicious smell and came to her to beg for a bite, Anna growled at her threateningly and Lilly immediately disappeared with her tail between her legs.

Sebastian laughed. 'Anna, you have completely frightened our poor Lilly! I didn't know you could growl like a vicious dog!'

Lizzie smiled. 'They say the best way to train dogs is to speak to them in their own language!'

'Bruce is particularly good at it,' Andy said to Anna's amazement. 'Whenever he praises Susi and Lilly and his voice is so high and sweet, they are ecstatic. But he only has to make a throaty, disapproving sound once, and they stop making nonsense straight away.'

Sebastian grinned cheekily. 'Does Bruce speak to you in such a tone when he is alone with you, Anna?' In an exaggerated high voice, he said, 'Oh, my love, how beautiful you are!'

Anna tried to kick her brother but only caught the leg of a chair. But she now had to giggle, and Lilly, who had watched her suspiciously from a distance, wagged her tail in relief. Everyone was grateful that the general mood had improved again.

No sooner had they finished dinner than Barry Little called. While her parents and brother listened curiously, Anna told Ivory's father about the events on Friday, at first haltingly and then more and more fluently. She said it was very likely that the policeman named Tim was involved in the accident that night. Barry promised to investigate. He was keen to find out what had happened to the driver of the car his colleague had been chasing.

# 33 A LUSH GREEN PYTHON

Bruce came over after dinner on the following day and seemed somewhat agitated. As soon as he sat down in Anna's room, he said contemptuously, 'It seems Tim is a bloody thief! I just talked to Angus who got some information about that lost rucksack. He told me that an acquaintance of him in Brisbane shares a flat with a German guy called Walter. So, Walter visited a friend in Bli Bli and then someone in Mount Coolum, and only there he noticed that his luggage had flown off the roof rack. He drove back and forth and got really pissed off when he found nothing. But later he went to the police station in Coolum and got his rucksack back. At first, he was elated and totally grateful, and he ...'

Anna interrupted him, feeling confused. 'I don't get it! Then why are you saying that Tim is a thief?'

'Because some items were missing, like some carabiners and devices that are used for a 'Flying Fox'. Tim must have stolen them! Walter is very upset as he'll have to buy new gear for his next abseiling tour.' Bruce looked grim, but then he grinned.

'Angus had been on such a tour before, and today he raved about it like a happy child. He and some others hiked through a gorge, and from time to time they had to abseil from cliffs with waterfalls. And finally, they attached themselves to a rope and glided over a river – and landed with their butts in the water. Afterwards, they walked back through a rainforest and had to fight off some painfully biting giant ants.'

'Wow, that sounds adventurous, almost like that movie the other night!'

'Yes, their tour must have been great – except for the biting ants. A pity that I am afraid of heights! But Angus loved it! By the way, we were wondering if Tim would have kept the whole rucksack if we hadn't been there when he found it.'

'Did Walter check it out straight away at the police station, and did he complain about the missing items?' Anna asked.

'Yes, he did. But I bet Tim will just deny that he stole anything from it.'

'Hey, Anna!' Sebastian shouted excitedly and burst into Anna's room without knocking. 'I've seen a lush-green python!' Only now did he realise she was not alone. 'Oh, hello, Bruce!'

'Hi, Sebastian!' Bruce replied. Spotting the dogs behind Sebastian, he said in a different tone of voice, 'Hi, cuties!'

Anna approached her brother, 'Are you pulling my leg? Do green pythons even exist?'

'Don't you believe me? Here, I have proof!' Sebastian fumbled around in his pocket and pulled out his mobile phone. Then he showed Anna and Bruce the pictures he'd taken of the giant snake.

Anna was amazed. 'Beautiful!'

'How pretty!' Bruce said admiringly.

The photos depicted a bright green snake, lying partly on a wooden fence and partly on a branch that was reaching far over the fence. The tree was densely covered with leaves, making it hard to detect the animal.

'Is this a native snake?' Anna asked. 'Where did you see it?'

Sebastian grinned. 'On Tim's fence!'

'What?' Anna and Bruce asked in unison.

'Yes, Susi suddenly stopped, stiff as a board, and simply refused to go any further. And when I pulled on the leash, she barked as if she wanted to warn me! And then I discovered the reason for her excitement and took some photos in a flash, before the python disappeared in the tree.'

'How do you know it's a python?' Anna asked.

'Because I am smart!' Sebastian chuckled. 'Well, yesterday I checked out snake descriptions on the internet. Susan had texted me that she and Scott had seen a black and white coloured snake in their garden. And so, I was keen to find out what it might have been. Looking at all sorts of snakes, I also noticed a nice picture of a green python snake. It lives in tropical rainforests in Papua New Guinea and on the Cape York Peninsula in Australia.'

'Then how did it get to Coolum Beach?' Anna asked.

'Tim must have smuggled it!' she exclaimed in the next moment.

'He must be angry as hell that the python escaped,' Sebastian said.

'Better take it easy with your accusations! Who knows where this snake comes from.' Bruce cautioned them. 'Perhaps it has already been in my garden too. It might be hungry, looking for food.'

'Good thing it didn't strangle our Lilly!' Sebastian shouted. 'I'll go and tell Mum. Maybe she could call the organisation that looks after wild animals. She had saved a sick possum with their help once before, when it had been attacked by crows.' And he took off, calling out, 'Mum, I've found a green python!'

'Your brother has quite a temper,' Bruce smiled. 'He reminds me of my sisters. Always running around at breakneck speed, talking away and not caring if you're busy with something else.'

'Hopefully I'll get to know your little sisters soon.'

'Yes, definitely! I already told them so much about you.'

'I hope only good things?' Anna asked, snuggling up to him.

Lizzie was surprised to learn of such an unusual snake in their surroundings. She looked up the phone number of a woman who volunteered to help wild animals in need and called her for advice.

Shortly afterwards, Sebastian got a phone call from Kirsty.

'Hi! We all want to meet at Arielle's tomorrow afternoon. Do you want to come along? She'll leave the hospital tomorrow morning. But because she still has to walk on crutches, and her parents' house has far too many stairs, she will live with her relatives, Aunt Heidi and Uncle Wayne, for a while.'

'Oh! Does she like the idea?'

'Well, it will be strange to move into Thomas' room. But her relatives' house is accessible for wheelchairs, so that she can easily roll around.'

Sebastian laughed. 'Better not too fast! Otherwise, she might fall down again.'

A shrill scream echoed from the laundry room, and Lilly barked.

'Sebastian!' Lizzie called.

'Bye, Kirsty, I've got to go, my mum's calling. I'll see you tomorrow.' He rushed to the laundry room. 'What's wrong?'

Lizzie stood by the washing trough next to the washing machine, desperately trying to repair a faulty tap, from which the water was gushing out as if from a cannon.

'This stupid thing keeps falling off,' Lizzie scolded. 'And I can't screw it back on.'

'Let me have a go!' Sebastian offered.

But he couldn't close the valve, either. 'I'll get Bruce! He's a plumber after all!'

He burst into Anna's room again and stunned the young lovers who were just cuddling tenderly. Anna sent him an angry glare, but before she could say anything, Sebastian turned to Bruce:

'Come quickly! We need your expert help!'

'Oh, sure!' Bruce jumped up immediately.

'Anna, can you turn off the main water tap outside?' Sebastian shouted as he ran back to the laundry, closely followed by Bruce.

In no time at all, Anna's boyfriend fixed the problem, replacing the faulty valve with a new one. And Lizzie was very happy when he also repaired another dripping tap in the garden.

# 34 ARIELLE

Arielle felt uneasy sitting alone in her cousin's room. Her parents had bought her a second-hand wheelchair which was a bit too small for her. But it served its purpose. Her new crutches were leaning behind the door. She was to stay here for a week and had to practice moving around on her own. Aunt Heidi and Uncle Wayne had given her Thomas' computer so she wouldn't get bored. She looked around the large, light-flooded room and into the back garden. An oval swimming pool had been designed to look like a natural pond, surrounded by rocks, tropical-looking plants, palms and a tiny sand beach. The lawn had recently been mowed and a faint scent of hay wafted towards Arielle. The bright blue sky was almost cloudless, and a light breeze made the leaves of the trees and the curtains at the window rustle softly.

Arielle's bulging travel bag was still standing unopened on the floor. Although Aunt Heidi had already cleared out the wardrobe, giving away most of her son's belongings, the room still maintained a certain aura of Thomas. On the shelf were quite a few books, a small jade elephant and the wooden figure of a kangaroo, and on the walls were some posters, printed pictures and several framed photos. On one of them, Arielle saw her cousin and herself as little children, happily screaming and shooting at each other with water pistols.

'Oh Thomas, I wish you were still here!' Arielle whispered. She felt like an intruder, hardly daring to touch anything.

'Who could have hated you so much, Thomas?'

Reluctantly, she took a book from the shelf which she could reach from her sitting position. It was an old, slightly tattered book by Jules Verne: 'Around the world in eighty days'. She put it back and studied the covers of the other books. Thomas had obviously liked science fiction and thrillers. He had always loved to travel and had been fascinated by everything to do with science and faraway lands.

'You wanted to see the world and experience so much more, and now you're lying in your grave – dead as a doornail!' Arielle said angrily, taking out another book from the bottom row of the shelf.

She flinched when someone knocked at the door and the thick book crashed noisily onto the floor.

'Is everything all right?' Aunt Heidi asked anxiously.

'Um … yes!' Arielle stammered sheepishly, wondering if her aunt had heard her. Had she actually spoken aloud?

Aunt Heidi sat down on an armchair and smiled sadly at Arielle. 'I also still talk to Thomas sometimes. Many people would probably declare us crazy, but for me it's quite normal. I feel so close to him! And I will always love him …'

She swallowed, and tears came to both their eyes. They avoided looking at each other, otherwise they would have cried for sure.

Aunt Heidi noisily blew her nose. 'I just wanted to ask you if we should put a TV in your room. Wayne kept an ancient one that still works. Otherwise, you can watch telly in the living room, of course. Make yourself at home.'

'Thank you, Aunt Heidi. You guys are so sweet. No, I don't need my own TV. And I've got plenty to read here.' She bent down to pick up the book.

'Are you comfortable in the wheelchair?'

'Yes, that's fine. But I still have to get used to the crutches.'

'By all means, let me know if you need help!'

'Of course, don't you worry, Aunt Heidi!'

Arielle missed her pets Max and Sniff. But she was glad that she had reconciled with Jack again. Thinking of him, a warm feeling of happiness spread through her, chasing away all spooky thoughts. In the afternoon she would see Jack and her friends again! She began to read, but couldn't concentrate properly, even though the book was written in a captivating way. Putting it away, she rolled to her desk and turned on the computer. Uncle Wayne, after several failed attempts, had found out Thomas' secret code to log in. How he had managed that remained a mystery to Arielle.

Again, she was overcome with an uneasy feeling when she entered the password 'SWaRM xXx', thus gaining access to Thomas' private life. But soon her curiosity took over. She was impressed that her cousin had saved everything neatly in folders. For example, there were 'Emails from Arielle'. She was touched when she read some of her own old letters to him. A few tears dripped on her hands, while a white cloud briefly moved in front of the sun. A black bird croaked hoarsely and then grabbed a poor little worm in a flash.

Arielle wondered how Daniel and John must have felt when they learned of the death of their best friend. She had only known them superficially. In all probability, they had been the last people – besides the murderers – to see Thomas alive. Tentatively, she clicked on 'Emails from Daniel', and later she also read 'Emails from John'. Her guilty conscience stirred unpleasantly in her, but she quickly put it aside. At least she had a good reason for her espionage, namely to find out what might have led to the murder of Thomas. After skipping over a few mails by other friends, she stopped. Thomas had not saved any e-mails from Maryann. Would she still find any photos of her? Had Thomas actually known Simon too? With renewed zeal, she searched the data in the computer.

* * *

Sebastian looked critically at himself in the mirror, relieved to find only a tiny residue of an old pimple on his nose. In the morning, he'd seen Kirsty chatting amiably with Ivory again, but this time, he hadn't been jealous. Perhaps Kirsty's remark that Ivory had a crush on Kate had helped? He grinned happily and combed his unruly hair.

'Sebastian, hurry up!' Anna banged on the door. 'What are you doing in the bathroom so long? I want to take a shower!'

'I've finished!' Sebastian opened the door, calling out: 'What's wrong with you? You're bright red!'

'I went for a bicycle ride with Audrey and Brenda. Pooh, I am completely exhausted! And I got too much sun.'

'A sunburn in winter? And I bet you've got at least three new freckles!'

'You're mean!' Anna boxed him slightly on the arm, but smiled.

A bit later, Sebastian swung himself onto his bike. On the way to Arielle's, he noticed that he had forgotten his helmet, but he didn't want to return because he was already late anyway. When he arrived at Arielle's relatives' house, everyone except Kirsty was already there.

'Hi, Arielle! How are you doing with that cast on your leg?'

'Phew, it's tiring! And tricky to carry something when you have to move around with crutches and your hands are full.'

'I have a solution for that!' Sebastian put on his little backpack, grabbed Arielle's crutches, and hopped around the room on one leg to demonstrate his idea.

Jack was impressed. 'You're clever! But a shoulder bag would be even better.'

Arielle grinned amusedly.

'Do your parents visit you here every day?' Kate asked.

'No, my mum had to go to the Gold Coast this week to take care of her sick mother. Because my grandma also fell down recently and broke her shoulder. What a bad timing! And that was actually the main reason why I moved in with Aunt Heidi and Uncle Wayne. As my dad has to go to work, otherwise only Max and Sniff would keep me company during the day.' Arielle chuckled. 'Max was pretty naughty yesterday. He tore a roll of toilet paper from its holder and played with it. My father was very upset when he discovered the mess!'

Kate laughed. 'Our dogs also did that once, leaving little bits of paper everywhere.'

'It's too bad you couldn't bring your four-legged friends here,' Ivory said to Arielle.

'Well, Aunt Heidi wouldn't like that, and she's allergic to animal hair, especially from cats.'

At that moment, Jack sneezed loudly and everyone laughed.

'Excuse me!' he said.

Sebastian thought it was strange that you should apologise for sneezing in Australia, while in Germany the others were wishing you 'good health'.

'It's weird that Kirsty isn't here yet,' he said, looking at his wristwatch.

'Maybe she's lost,' said Ivory. 'I've turned into the wrong street myself.'

'You fool!' Kate teased him.

Ivory blushed, and Sebastian was surprised to see him so embarrassed. Was he really in love with Kate? Now that he knew Kate a bit better, Sebastian quite liked her, and also found her much prettier than before. She had a somewhat voluptuous but shapely figure, a sweet heart-shaped face, and expressive dark eyes that created an interesting contrast to her blonde hair. However, he found Kirsty and her unusual green eyes a thousand times more beautiful! Once again, he glanced at his watch. Where was his girlfriend? She was already half an hour late now. A dreadful fear rose in him when the image of the patient came back to his mind who had been hit by a car. He hoped nothing had happened to Kirsty!

As if Ivory had read his mind, he said: 'By the way, my dad told me they found the car that caused the accident the other day. It was sitting in a ditch, just slightly damaged.'

'And what about the driver?' Sebastian inquired.

'He escaped. However, the owner of the car is on holiday in Bali.'

'Really? So, someone stole the car?' Arielle asked. 'No wonder he didn't want to stop when someone chased him.'

'It was a couple,' Ivory said. 'Thanks to the testimony of Anna and her friends, my father could inform his boss about Tim's wild driving on Friday evening. And then Tim admitted that he chased the car until the driver lost control, ending up in a ditch. But the couple took off. They disappeared into the bushland, and Tim didn't even attempt to follow them on foot.'

'Where was that?' Kate asked.

'Somewhere along the way towards Noosa, just after the exit into Murdering Creek Road. And now Tim is in trouble for that dangerous chase on the motorway and through the town with such a hellish speed. It was a blessing that the woman who'd been hit by the first car survived.'

'And good that nobody else was hurt,' Kate continued. 'Or did the couple get injured when they crashed the car?'

'I don't know! At least they could still run away.'

'That's a scary name, 'Murdering Creek Road'!' Sebastian pondered.

Jack snorted in outrage. 'This street name recalls a massacre in which a group of Aborigines were ambushed and murdered by white men long ago. Incredibly, not a single one of the brutal assassins was brought to justice.'

Sebastian was horrified. And then he remembered that Thomas had allegedly argued with someone about Australia Day, the public holiday, just before his murder. He decided to learn more about the atrocities committed since that invasion. The white immigrants had brutalised and even slaughtered so many Aboriginal people and snatched countless children from their parents, it was hard to believe! Sebastian hated violence and injustice! Maybe he should become a judge and work hard to ensure that criminals received their due punishment!

Arielle asked, 'Has Tim been suspended from duty?'

'Not yet. But there will be a thorough investigation,' said Ivory, hoping that his father wouldn't have arguments with other policemen because he had accused a colleague.

# 35 KIRSTY

Kirsty had got into a fight with her sister and was still furious as she set off on her walk to Arielle's. Actually, she was even more annoyed about her mother than about her sister. Why had her mum taken Ellen's side instead of supporting her? It was so unfair! After all, Ellen had borrowed one of her favourite books, without her permission, and then she'd stupidly dropped it in the bathtub. Kirsty could understand that it was fun to read in hot soapy water on a cold winter's day, but her book was now completely soaked. Ruined! When she had angrily demanded compensation, Ellen had just become snotty.

Kirsty now marched ahead, with a face so grim that an approaching older man frowned. His tiny dog, which he kept on a leash, even turned away in fear. Only in the next moment did Kirsty understand that the little fellow was not afraid of her but of a huge Weimaraner whose nose was almost at the back of her knee. Startled, she stopped, while the old man and his dog hastily walked on.

'Don't worry, he doesn't bite,' said a cheerful voice. The owner of the grey hunting dog smiled at Kirsty. 'Many dog owners want to save their pets when they see my Buddy, even though he is the dearest dog in the world. As a puppy, he had two Maltese dogs as best friends, and since then he loves little dogs and gets pretty excited when he spots one that looks similar to his mates. Unfortunately, most people mistake his demeanor for hunting fever, fearing that he wants to eat their pets.'

Kirsty smiled back and stroked Buddy, whose short coat felt silky and smooth. The Weimaraner stepped on her foot accidentally, and she grunted. 'Whew, you're heavy!'

'Buddy!' The woman pulled him back and apologised to Kirsty. Then they kept moving, chatting away, and Kirsty's mood improved rapidly, although her left little toe hurt. She now wished she had accepted her mother's offer to drive her to Arielle's.

'By the way, my name is Kristie!' the woman said.

'And I'm Kirsty!'

Kristie grinned. 'Then we've probably got the same name – Christine!' She briefly fingered her hair, which was silver-grey and short.

Just like her dog's, Kirsty thought amusedly. But despite the grey hair, the woman looked very youthful, and her clothes were both sporty and elegant. 'That's right! My sister called me Chrissy for a while, but I didn't like that.' Kirsty now told her about Ellen's misfortune, and Kristie laughed out loud.

'Good that it wasn't an e-book reader that fell into the water!'

Buddy took a sudden leap to a garden fence. He sniffed excitedly and lay down flat on the ground. What was he up to? Now he pulled something from the bushes behind the fence.

'Stop that!' Kristie demanded.

Too late! Buddy already carried something in his mouth, very gently, and dropped it at her feet, looking at her expectantly.

'What is it?' Kirsty asked. None of them had ever seen such an animal before! It appeared to be dead. They bent down to take a closer look. It was a large, white bird with a salmon-pink shimmer, obviously a kind of cockatoo.

'It's still alive!' Kirsty shouted as she noticed a faint movement, gazing with pity at the seemingly very sick animal.

Buddy whimpered softly but didn't move. 'Good boy!' Kristie patted him affectionately. 'We have to take this poor bird to a vet! Could you help me and wait here? I live very close by. I'll just take my dog home and then return by car. I'll be back in a sec, okay?'

'All right, no problem.' Despite these words, Kirsty felt a little queasy as she sat beside the bird, tenderly stroking its plumage. She hoped it wouldn't die! To her relief, Kristie quickly reappeared with a large cardboard box and a pillow in it. Carefully they bedded the bird on it, and lifted the box into the car. 'Would you like to come along?' Kristie asked.

Kirsty nodded. After a short drive they arrived at the vet's surgery and didn't have to wait for long. They were told that they had found a Moluccan cockatoo. Fortunately, it only seemed to have minor injuries to one wing, one foot and the beak. Most certainly it would recover, the kind veterinarian informed them. He suspected that the exotic bird had been kept in captivity and had been grossly neglected. In any case, it was severely dehydrated and emaciated. They would have to nurse it in the surgery for a while.

'I'm glad that Buddy discovered it!' Kristie said when they left. 'I like cockatoos. But it's terrible when they get locked up in a cage! I much prefer watching them in the wild, although they often nibble at the passion fruits in my garden.' She looked at Kirsty. 'And thanks for your help! Shall I drive you somewhere?'

'That would be great! I'm already late anyway!' She checked the time and gave a horrified scream. 'Oh no, my friends must be worried. I should have been there an hour ago!'

'Well, let's go!'

Her friends were relieved when Kirsty finally showed up. However, the afternoon ended with a bad surprise for Sebastian! Not far away from his house, police officer Tim stopped him and fined him for riding his bicycle without a helmet. Damn! One hundred and twenty-one dollars! Sebastian was boiling with rage. Would his parents deduct it from his pocket money?

# 36 PEPPER

Back at home, Sebastian informed his parents about his fine, expecting a lengthy sermon. Luckily, his father reacted in a friendly manner. Andy reminded him that he had already received an even higher fine from the same policeman. Only because he hadn't stopped at a stop sign long enough.

Lizzie frowned. 'Good that you didn't fall off your bike, Sebastian! You should always wear your helmet! And both of you should be smarter from now on and obey the traffic rules!'

Sebastian wiped a grin off his face.

'Hopefully Tim will get punished for his own sins too!'

He told his family what he'd learned about the car chase and the Ford Falcon in the ditch.

'That must have been a nasty surprise for the car owner,' Anna said. 'But at least he has a good alibi for the time of the hit-and-run if he is in Bali.'

'I hate people who drive much too fast! They endanger the lives of others and their own,' Lizzie said grimly. 'I wonder if the couple will be caught one day.'

'I doubt it!' Andy said.

'And you know what's weird? Kirsty found an exotic bird today! A Moluccan cockatoo that was half-dead!' Sebastian kept chatting away, talking about Kirsty's experience.

'Where are the Moluccas, anyway?' he finally asked.

'It's a group of islands somewhere in Indonesia, I think,' Andy said.

'That's right! They're also called Spice Islands.' Lizzie had to smile at her husband's impressed look. 'I read only yesterday that nutmeg and cloves are found there. And the area is said to be a paradise for divers.'

'But why would anyone smuggle such a cockatoo into Australia?' Anna asked. 'We have so many fascinating birds here anyway! For example, the colourful rainbow lorikeet or the Australian King Parakeet, and we have native cockatoos here, too. I think they are all very pretty!'

'Unfortunately, some people have a silly desire for something special,' Lizzie sighed.

'Like a pink cockatoo and a green python?' Sebastian asked.

'Yes! Often, there is big money involved. And therefore, people try to smuggle all kinds of plants and animals. And then they sell them at a high price, regardless of whether the species are endangered in their home country or not.'

Andy took the pepper shaker and generously seasoned his potato salad. Anna was astounded by the amount of pepper he used.

'How could anybody sneak in a big bird or a snake from abroad? Or other living animals? Without the notice of the Australian customs officers?' she asked.

Andy now reached for the salt.

'Well, perhaps these crooks just transport the eggs of reptiles and birds to let them hatch later.'

'Or they cram the poor animals such as small lizards, turtles and insects in tiny containers and hide them somehow, either on their own bodies or in their luggage. Many animals die in agony in the process. It's disgusting what people do!' Lizzie said with contempt in her voice.

'It can't be coincidence that I spotted the unusual snake the other day and Kirsty discovered an exotic bird this afternoon,' Sebastian exclaimed. 'There must be a smuggler in our town!'

'We must find out where these animals came from,' Anna said, just as excited as her brother. 'But how?'

'Customs officers often use Labradors or Beagles as sniffer dogs. Not only to detect hidden drugs, but also prohibited food, plants or animals. Maybe Susi and Lilly could help us,' Sebastian said. 'After all, Buddy, the Weimaraner, has discovered the Moluccan cockatoo with his excellent nose.'

Anna shouted enthusiastically, 'Yes, great idea! And our Susi is a Labrador-mix!'

Both dogs listened curiously, and Susi now sat down next to Anna with shining eyes. What was going on?

'Hello, customs dog Susi!' Anna kissed the dog's beautiful head briefly and then cuddled her lovingly.

Lizzie roared with laughter. Normally it bugged her seeing her children playing detective, but now she couldn't stop laughing. Andy got some pepper up his nose and had a violent sneezing fit, Sebastian choked and had to cough, and Lilly barked and ran around in circles.

'We are a pretty crazy family, Susi, hey?' Anna whispered into the dog's ear, and Susi wagged her tail in confirmation.

Lilly now tried to hop onto Sebastian's lap, Susi jumped up at Anna, and only after a while did everyone calm down again.

A few days later, the Kuhlmanns heard that someone in their neighbourhood had spotted the green python in his garden. He had called a professional snake catcher, and now the snake was in a terrarium in Noosa, in the care of somebody with a license to keep certain wild animals. The neighbour didn't know what would happen to this exotic snake later on. Maybe it would end up in a zoo. Or would it be transported back to its home country?

In any case, Lizzie was relieved that the python hadn't been hiding in her water pipe, in the garage, or even in her bed!

A week and a half later, Sebastian caught his parents dancing around to loud rock music in the living room when he came home from rugby training.

'What's the matter with you?' he asked in amazement. 'That's pretty wild music!'

Lizzie laughed. 'Dad has bought a second-hand radio cassette recorder for five dollars at a garage sale this morning. All he really wanted was a radio for his shed when he's tinkering around there. But we are happy as the seller also gave him a stack of old cassettes from his parents, which surprisingly still work. Isn't that nice?' She pointed to the table. 'You can read the names on the sleeves.'

'MELISSA ETHERIDGE, WORKING WEEK, FURY IN THE SLAUGHTERHOUSE, THE CURE, THE MISSION, THE PRETENDERS, SISTERS OF MERCY, CAMEL …' Sebastian paused. 'Camel? Some of these names are funny!'

'Just like HOT EARS!' Anna shouted.

'Hello, Anna! I didn't hear you come in!'

'No wonder with this loud music! The whole house is shaking! Someone might call the police for disturbing the peace any moment!'

'Now, now, don't exaggerate!' Andy jokingly threatened her with his finger when the doorbell pinged. Andy opened the door, still smiling – and turned pale seeing a cop in uniform before him! Andy was so startled, he couldn't speak.

'Good morning, Mr. Little!' Sebastian said. Then he noticed Ivory behind his father's tall figure. 'Oh, hi, you're here too! What a surprise!'

Andy regained his composure. 'Good morning! Please come in!'

'You may call me Barry!' Mr. Little said amiably.

Lizzie felt flustered and bright red, hot and sweaty after dancing. She disappeared into the kitchen to splash some water on her face before returning with some cold drinks. They all sat down in the living room.

Ivory was the first to speak. 'We were looking at a garage sale nearby and I suggested we drop in for a quick visit.'

'Did you buy anything?' asked Sebastian. 'My dad got a radio cassette recorder.'

'No, I guess we were too late! Nothing worth buying! But it never hurts to look at old junk.' Barry smiled and turned to Anna. 'Hello, Anna! We'd spoken on the phone before. Thanks again for telling me about your observations. By now, we have found out why Tim didn't want to give up the pursuit at that time. Originally, that white car caught his attention just because of its high speed. But then he discovered that it had been stolen.'

'How did he do that?' Anna asked.

'Tim recognised the car. He's acquainted with the owner and knew that he was in Indonesia at the time.'

'He could have lent the car to someone else,' Andy interjected.

'Tim didn't think so. Unfortunately, the car chase led to the accidents, and the fact that Tim tried to hide his involvement makes things even worse for him. And there are other incriminating aspects against my colleague.'

'Was he drunk that Friday night?' Anna asked, remembering Tim's tipsy girlfriend.

'No idea! But the interesting thing is: the remains of a broken reptile egg were discovered in the stolen Ford!'

'Really?' Sebastian called out.

'Wow!' Anna marvelled. 'Did Sebastian tell you about the green python? There must be a connection!'

'Yes, I bet! And Ivory also told me about the Moluccan cockatoo.' Barry took a sip of his orange juice. 'And that's why I was alerted straight away when the police found the eggshells from an exotic lizard.'

'Did someone steal the car to transport illegal animals in it?' Lizzie asked. 'That doesn't make much sense!'

'I rather think that the couple took the car just for a joyride. There were three other cars reported stolen some time ago, and they turned up the very next morning in various locations, in one case even back on the owner's driveway. Perhaps these thugs are the same thieves. However, I don't believe they are responsible for the smuggling of wildlife.'

Barry cleared his throat and drank again from his glass.

'But who is it then? Could that guy in Bali be a smuggler?' Sebastian asked. 'What kind of lizard egg was that? Does it come from the Moluccas by any chance? Or from the home of the Green Python?'

Barry smiled. 'You are just like Kirsty, always asking thousands of questions! Kirsty and Ivory were inseparable in kindergarten and primary school, doing all kinds of mischief together. When they were eight years old, they ...'

'Dad!' Ivory cut in. 'Don't change the subject!'

'Um, sorry! What they discovered in the car was the remains of a Borneo earless monitor egg that didn't survive the transport. Maybe it was better that way, otherwise the poor creature might have died soon after hatching anyway! In my opinion it is completely brainless to take lizards like this from their natural home and to keep them as pets. After all, they are both light-shy and nocturnal. They like to dig themselves into the mud during the day. So, what's the point of having them? Moreover, they often refuse food in captivity and die miserably. People should leave them alone!' Barry glanced at his watch. 'I must go, I have work to do! I've already yapped too much at the garage sale. Shall I give you a lift home, Ivory, or would you like to stay here for a bit?'

Before Ivory could answer, Sebastian quickly said, 'I could show you my new computer game, Ivory!'

Ivory smiled. 'I'd bet I'll win!'

They dashed off into Sebastian's room. Mr. Little said goodbye to everyone else with a firm handshake. Even Lilly gave him a paw, while Susi hid suspiciously behind Anna. Then he drove away in his police car, which he had parked directly in their driveway. What would the neighbours think? Lizzie wondered.

Anna smiled amusedly at her father. 'At first you really looked like an embarrassed little schoolboy, dad!'

Andy laughed. 'Yes, I thought someone had indeed complained about our loud music! It gave me quite a shock when the tall policeman appeared at our door. But at the same time, I was relieved that it wasn't that unsympathetic Tim.'

Lizzie said: 'Isn't it weird how quickly you feel uncomfortable whenever you spot the police? It makes me feel queasy seeing a police car in my rear-view mirror, even though I always drive according to the traffic rules.'

Later Andy prepared lunch, humming along to some soft background music. Anna and her mother made themselves comfortable in the living room, both reading a book. Lizzie had lit a few logs in the fireplace, and the dogs lay on a colourful rug at her feet. Lilly snored softly, and Susi looked dreamily into the fire, listening to the crackling of the flames. Every now and then computer noises, voices and laughter emanated from Sebastian's room. A sudden loud bang, followed by Ivory's howl of victory and Sebastian's protest, startled Susi.

'It's all right, my sweetie!' Lizzie reassured Susi. 'The boys are just playing some stupid war game.'

Ivory cheered and clapped his hands, winning a second time. Sebastian grinned benignly but was beaming when he won the next game. And then he blurted out that he'd been jealous of him for a long time. Ivory was completely stunned.

'No reason for that! Kirsty and I were never in love with each other. We were always very close, but more like siblings. We probably bonded so well as we'd both lost a parent at a very early age.' A shadow flew over his face, but then he smiled.

'I'm glad you are going out with her and not some bloody fool!'

Sebastian chuckled. 'Yes, me too!'

He would have liked to ask Ivory if he had a crush on Kate, but at that moment his parents called them for lunch.

* * *

After hours of reading near the fire place, Anna visited Bruce, and his room now seemed quite cold to her. To get warm, they snuggled up under a blanket on the sofa and drank hot tea. Then Bruce asked, 'Shall we take a trip? It's much warmer outside in the sun than in our house.' He grinned mischievously. 'Would you like to drive?'

'Me? I can't do that!' Anna protested.

'Well, I'll teach you. We could go to the industrial park. Nobody will be there at the weekend.'

Reluctantly, she agreed. But when they arrived there and Anna got behind the wheel, she got nervous.

'What if I cause an accident?'

'Nonsense, there's not another car in sight for miles, and everything is flat and easy here. The main thing is that you don't forget where the brakes are,' Bruce said. 'Wait, I'll adjust the seat a bit. Is the rear-view mirror fine with you? Here we go!'

Taking a deep breath, Anna timidly turned the key in the ignition. And stalled the engine as soon as she tried to start it!

Bruce remained calm. 'Try again! Let the clutch out very slowly ... yes, super!'

Anna drove off at a snail's pace and hesitantly accelerated a little more.

'You're a natural!' Bruce praised when Anna unexpectedly took off, almost hitting a kerb.

'Wow, better slow down!' He laughed.

Anna drove around, not very smoothly and rather meandering, glad about the wide and empty streets. There were vast stretches of lawns on lots that were still for lease or for sale. They were very close to the lake where one of their foster dogs, little Sally, had once disappeared and remained missing for a whole night before she was reunited with the Kuhlmanns. Anna was just about to tell Bruce about Sally when a rabbit suddenly ran across the street in front of them. In her shock, Anna braked so hard that her head almost hit the windscreen. Then the car dashed off with a jerk as she stepped on the gas again. 'Sorry!' she shouted. 'Are you okay?' She didn't dare to look at Bruce but kept looking straight ahead, her whole body tense. She held the steering wheel so tightly that her hands hurt a little and her knuckles turned white.

'All good, just take it easy!' Bruce replied.

He put one hand on her knee to calm her down, but Anna immediately yelled, 'Oh no, don't distract me!'

Even through the fabric of her long trousers, she could feel the crackling electricity emitted by her boyfriend, which she would have enjoyed under different circumstances. Bruce grinned and quickly took his hand away. He glanced in the side mirror and spotted a car in the distance.

'Oh boy, someone is coming! Better turn left and stop!'

Anna didn't brake as abruptly this time and parked a full meter from the kerb. In no time at all they changed seats and Anna had to giggle, even though her heart was pounding in her chest. A small dark blue truck now drove past them, slowed down and parked near some bushland at the lake. Two men, whom Anna estimated to be in their mid-twenties to early thirties, got out. They unloaded a mattress and threw it on the lawn.

Without thinking, Bruce dashed off, stopped his car right behind the truck and yelled at them, 'Hey, you can't just dump your rubbish here!'

The men laughed sneering. One of them called back:

'And what are you going to do about it, mate?'

But the word 'mate' didn't sound friendly at all, and Anna got goose bumps. The men were relatively slim but seemed strong. One of them had eyes that were a bit too close together, giving him a bit of a sinister appearance. And his crooked nose looked as if it had been broken at least once. His shirt sleeves were rolled up, showing heavily tattooed arms, and a gold chain sparkled on his black-haired chest. He had a thick beard, but sparse, short-shaven hair on his head. The other man was dressed in shorts and T-shirt despite the cool winter day. He had many tattoos all over his body, but they were partly hidden by his clothes and by his long blonde hair. Dark sunglasses and a brown floppy hat overshadowed his face. He said something to his friend that Anna could not understand.

Then he grinned suggestively. 'We could have some fun on the mattress with your pretty girl,' he shouted.

'Pigs!' Bruce said angrily. 'We'd better leave!'

He hadn't turned off the engine, so they could drive away quickly.

'Sleazy bastards!' Anna said in disgust, feeling a bit shaken. Scary guys! But the next moment she smiled again and drew her friend's attention to an ibis flying elegantly across the lake, offering a picturesque sight against the bright blue sky.

\* \* \*

Sebastian and Ivory spent the whole afternoon together and got along brilliantly. After dinner Andy offered to drive Ivory home and to take the dogs for a walk.

'Let's go to the lake! We haven't been there for a long time,' Sebastian suggested.

'Yes, why not? We better won't lose a dog there again, though!' Andy replied, thinking of their former foster dog Sally.

After dropping Ivory off, he drove to the lake and parked near the edge of the forest. No sooner had they walked a few steps than Andy spotted several old car tyres in the bushland and a queen-size mattress on a lawn near the water.

'More and more people dump their rubbish in the natural environment and litter the streets,' he said grimly. 'Recently I even found an open container of used motor oil in the forest. What a mess!'

'Look, Daddy!' Sebastian shouted in a joyful voice. In the middle of the mattress, there was a tiny frog, apparently enjoying a sunbath. Its light colour exactly matched the colour of the mattress, making it hard to spot.

'How cute!' Andy bent down to the animal.

'I wonder if this froggie was smuggled into Australia, too,' Sebastian mused. 'I have never seen a white frog in my life.'

'Well, it's not snow white, it's more light beige. I'll take a photo, then we can find out later if it's exotic or native.'

The dogs couldn't understand all the fuss about this small, motionless animal and were quite bored until they got going again.

Back at home, Andy and Sebastain learned that the frog was a native Red Desert Tree Frog, which was not as unusual as they had assumed. The colour palette of this frog species ranged from light grey to reddish brown.

'Strange that it was sitting right in the sun and not in a cool, damp place,' Sebastian said.

'I am glad you spotted it! It was cute, hey?' Andy replied.

When Anna learned that her father and brother had also been at the lake that afternoon, she almost choked and feigned a coughing fit. If her father had caught her driving, he would've been furious! Not just at her, but at Bruce too! What a luck that they hadn't met in the industrial park!

One of the nasty guys who had brazenly dumped the old mattress had looked familiar to her. Anna pondered about it for a long time, getting no results. But when she woke up in the middle of the night, it suddenly occurred to her: Sebastian had shown her a picture of the bearded man on Thomas' Facebook page some time ago. She now remembered the photo of him (and the crooked nose). It was showing him and another surfer in a fight. And that other man was Steven, who was later brutally killed by a King Hit. But why had Thomas taken those photos back then? And who was his murderer?

An icy shiver ran down her spine. Good thing Bruce didn't mess with the guys at the lake! Would she have helped him if necessary? In any case, she always got annoyed when the hero in a movie was attacked and his girlfriend just stood around idly. Anna hoped that she would never be so cowardly. And she wondered whether Susi, her faithful dog, would stand by her in a case of imminent danger. She loved Susi so much! She was her best friend, her beautiful, cute pet, and an irreplaceable family member. With Susi, she was free to fool around and play merrily, and she could always tell her everything, whether it was sad or funny, sensible or silly. Both had complete trust in each other!

Anna couldn't comprehend why some people did not like dogs. She smiled involuntarily, thinking of her boyfriend. It was wonderful that Bruce was very fond of animals and even seemed to have a very special relationship with dogs. And she enjoyed being with him tremendously!

# 37 DEEP GRIEF

Arielle woke up in the middle of the night. The full moon shone right into her face and some palm fronds moved gently in the wind. Something in the house creaked softly. What was that? Did she hear footsteps coming closer and closer? For a moment she was gripped by sheer horror, and she hurriedly grabbed her crutches, until she remembered that she was still in Thomas' room. She had already wondered about strange but harmless noises before. Mostly they came from some creaking beams or from nocturnal animals in the garden or on the roof. Silly wimp! she scolded herself, wishing to be as brave as Kirsty.

Her friend, a whole head smaller than her, almost never showed fear. Well, in the animal world, height didn't mean everything. Tiny dogs could intimidate bigger ones with their behaviour. Once she'd seen a huge Great Dane with its tail between its legs running away from a Dachshund. Max, her own big puppy, was pretty boisterous and yet very gentle and good-natured, allowing Sniff to be the boss. The little cat was definitely the 'alpha animal' in her family.

Arielle was looking forward to playing with her pets again. The very next evening her mother would return and pick her up. Arielle couldn't wait! Aunt Heidi and Uncle Wayne had been extremely kind and caring to her. But having her own space was something special!

During the last week she had spent countless hours on the computer, gathering information about her cousin. Although she'd been plagued by gnawing remorse and crying attacks, her inner urge to continue the research had repeatedly gained the upper hand. She had feared that her relatives might catch her in her dishonorable acts, but to her relief they never burst into the room and always knocked politely first. They were really incredibly nice! In the meantime, Arielle had the impression that she knew them and Thomas much better.

By pure chance she had opened a computer file called 'LIVING ON THE BEACH' the day before, which was a kind of diary of her cousin. Here, Arielle learned more about his dreams and hopes than she could ever have imagined. To her amazement, she found out that Thomas had fallen in love with Claudia, Daniel's girlfriend, while he was still in a relationship with Maryann. And that had really thrown him off track. Daniel had been one of his best friends, and therefore he had tried to suppress his feelings for Claudia ...

Arielle's train of thought was disrupted by another strange sound. This time, it was definitely coming from within the house. She sat up straight and moaned as a sharp pain shot through her foot. She hopped to the door on one leg and listened. It was a sob! That must be Aunt Heidi! What could she do? Should she rather leave her alone? Filled with pity, she decided to comfort her aunt.

But when she came into the living room, she saw her uncle sitting on the couch in the golden light of a floor lamp, crying bitterly. 'Uncle Wayne,' she said softly. 'What's the matter?'

She was startled when she saw his face, marked by the deepest sorrow. His hand trembled as he rubbed his reddish eyes and brushed his nose. On the low table stood a half-filled glass and a half-empty whisky bottle.

'We'll miss you, Arielle! It did Heidi and me so much good to spoil you a little, but now ...,' he sniffed and dabbed his eyes again. 'But now Thomas' room will be empty again, and the silence... that awful silence ...'

He sobbed loudly, and Arielle's eyes filled with tears as well. She sat down with him on the couch, and they both remained silent for a while, overwhelmed by their emotions.

'Oh, Uncle Wayne, it's so sad! But I'll visit you very often,' she said. 'And thank God Aunt Heidi has reconciled with you again!'

'Yes, that really is a great comfort! She's a wonderful person!' He took a sip from his glass. 'We loved Thomas very much. And although it won't do him any good anymore, I still hope that the police will find the murderer soon. Because as long as he's still on the loose, I just can't find peace.'

'That's what Aunt Heidi said, too. And I am feeling the same.'

'Heidi thinks she's done something wrong; she's still wondering why Thomas was so hostile to her for a while. But she will never find out now.'

Arielle's stomach cramped up at these words and she struggled with herself as to whether she should reveal her discoveries to him and Aunt Heidi. All this time she had feared being caught spying, but now she believed Thomas' parents were entitled to know everything.

'I have to confess something!' she said timidly.

Uncle Wayne looked at his niece in surprise. Before he could say anything, Aunt Heidi asked, 'What do you have to confess?' With dishevelled hair and a light blue bathrobe over her pyjamas, Arielle's aunt stood before them.

'I'm sorry, I didn't mean to wake you up,' Arielle said quickly. 'You'd better go back to bed! I can talk to you in the morning.'

'Bullshit! Now I'm already awake anyway and much too curious! But I'll quickly make some tea. Do you want one too?'

Both nodded and Uncle Wayne carefully pushed an armchair over to Arielle so she could put her legs up and he handed her a woollen blanket. 'The whisky has warmed me up inside, but I'm afraid I can't offer you that, little one.'

Arielle had to smile. Although she was now the same size as her uncle, he still often called her 'my little one' with affection. And although he was a bit doped up on alcohol, he didn't seem aggressive at all, just melancholic. His dark blonde fluffy hair stood on end, and with his brown jumper and slightly worn beige corduroy trousers, he reminded her of a teddy bear. Thomas really didn't look one bit like him, she thought, perplexed that she had never noticed that before.

Aunt Heidi soon returned with three steaming tea cups, which she carefully balanced on a tray, and sat down on another chair.

'Well, shoot! What's on your mind?' she asked her niece.

Arielle turned red. 'It's pretty embarrassing.'

She tried to sip her tea, but it was still much too hot. She made a grimace and said, 'I've been snooping through Thomas' files.'

She expected horrified looks or shouts of protest, but instead she only saw two sad but tense pairs of eyes in front of her. And so she began to tell them everything.

'It was really nice of you to give me the computer. And if Thomas were alive … I would never have interfered in his private life.'

This apology sounded a bit lame in her own ears, but Aunt Heidi nodded to her encouragingly. Uncle Wayne finished his whisky glass in one go and then took the teacup in his hand.

Arielle continued, 'At first, I wondered why Thomas had saved many e-mails from all sorts of people, but none from his former girlfriend Maryann. But then I read his personal messages on

Facebook and found out a lot. The tone of voice between him and Maryann has changed dramatically over time, namely from declarations of love to nasty comments and sarcastic remarks. They must have really hated each other in the end! But even before he broke up with her, he fell in love with Claudia who'd been with Daniel for a long time. And that must have been horrible for Thomas, because there was no way he was going to take Daniel's girlfriend away from him.'

Uncle Wayne took a spoonful of sugar and stirred it around in the teacup longer than necessary.

'Was Claudia in love with Thomas too?' Aunt Heidi asked.

'Well, he wasn't sure, but he had the feeling that after a certain party at John's, she felt more than friendship for him, too, but she didn't seem to want to admit it.'

'Um. I wonder if Daniel suspected it,' Uncle Wayne said.

A terrible suspicion came up in Aunt Heidi.

'Do you think Daniel killed our Thomas out of jealousy?'

Arielle blushed again. 'For a moment, I did suspect Daniel! And I tried to imagine what could have happened back then. Perhaps something like this: Daniel didn't drink any alcohol in the disco as he still had to drive. But at home he drank several bottles of beer much too quickly and became very cheerful until his mood suddenly changed. After John went to bed, it came up for some reason that Thomas and Claudia had feelings for each other – and Daniel got mad. Sometimes, drunk people can be brutal!'

Arielle paused, angry with herself. Oh boy, why had she uttered these words about drunks? She glanced at her uncle, anxious how he would react. After all, he had been in a fight after drinking too much booze and certainly didn't like to be reminded of those former times. But Uncle Wayne continued to stare into his tea, as if he wanted to find the truth in it.

'So, you mean Daniel strangled Thomas?' Aunt Heidi asked. Her normally pleasant voice sounded shrill.

Arielle shook her head.

'No, that was just a stupid idea. Sorry, I should have kept that to myself! It doesn't make any sense. Because Daniel is a really nice person. He wouldn't hurt a fly, for sure. And he, John and Thomas were best friends!'

'But who killed him? And why?' Uncle Wayne asked in a flat voice and pained expression.

'I believe Thomas was on the trail of a smuggling ring,' Arielle said. 'And that Claudia was indirectly involved.'

'What?' her uncle cried.

'A smuggling ring?' her aunt asked. 'You mean drug dealers?'

There was a loud crash and Arielle screamed in horror. The silhouette of a black cat appeared for a tiny moment at the window, with sparkling eyes and all four legs stretched out wide, and then disappeared again.

'Damn neighbour's cat!' Aunt Heidi shouted, annoyed. 'She keeps trying to catch our geckos. She has already scratched my fly screens several times.'

'And she scared me almost to death!' Uncle Wayne said. 'Although she is actually a cute pet,' he added with a smile.

'Phew, I need some chocolates to calm my nerves.'

Aunt Heidi went to the kitchen and came back with three small plates full of chocolate pieces.

'Thank you! Mm, I love chocolates!' Arielle said with a smile. 'But I've probably put on a few pounds while I was staying with you. You spoiled me so much!'

'Nonsense, you look great!' Uncle Wayne said, pinching her cheek gently. 'But now go on!'

'Thomas liked photography and had the habit of observing his surroundings closely, always looking for an interesting shot. And when you flew back from Thailand to Australia, he noticed a man at the Brisbane airport who seemed quite nervous. A rather strong guy kept pulling up his trousers and was fiddling with his jacket pockets.'

'He probably had to take off his belt for the customs check and was now afraid of losing his pants,' Uncle Wayne said amusedly.

'In any case, Thomas casually mentioned this in an e-mail to Daniel and John.' Arielle looked at her aunt. 'And in the same e-mail he mentioned you as well. During your holidays, he got upset with your snide comments about him being a vegan.'

'Really? What did I say? I don't remember anything like that at all!' Aunt Heidi was stunned.

'Well, Thomas enthusiastically described the beautiful landscapes and friendly people in Thailand. But he didn't always like the food in the restaurants. And then he complained bitterly that you once told him that Thai food is delicious and he shouldn't make such a fuss.'

'Oh dear! I guess I was in a bad mood! Well, it generally is quite difficult to get vegan food in restaurants – not only in Thailand. But is that the only reason why he was so unkind to me for a while? And I've been wondering for ages what the reason might have been.'

'Thomas was a very sensitive boy, and he could feel offended far too easily,' Uncle Wayne said.

He clasped his teacup as if to warm his hands, and Arielle slipped him one half of the blanket. Outside, a gecko snapped at a moth on the window and just missed it, while another gecko inside was loudly chirping from the ceiling.

'And what else did you find out?' Aunt Heidi asked in a fragile voice. She furtively wiped a tear from her eye and toyed with the idea of pouring a good shot of whisky into her tea. Instead, she took another piece of chocolate.

'What was going on with that guy at the airport? Was he involved with drugs?'

'Thomas didn't think about that incident anymore until months later when he happened to see the same man again in Coolum. He was the new boyfriend of Claudia's mother. Claudia had celebrated her birthday with some girlfriends and also with Daniel, John and Thomas. And suddenly this guy came along and gave Claudia a turtle in a terrarium. She was very happy, but Thomas was concerned as it was an Indian star turtle.'

'So what?' her uncle asked impatiently.

'Thomas wrote that he had never seen such a turtle in a pet shop and that it had most certainly been smuggled.'

'But why didn't Thomas tell anyone?'

'For various reasons. He didn't want to upset Claudia; he couldn't prove anything anyway; and besides, the mother's new boyfriend was a policeman.'

Aunt Heidi gave a little whistle, and another gecko chirped cheerfully.

Arielle took a piece of chocolate. 'Thomas has always been a keen conservationist. And after Claudia's birthday party he secretly watched this Tim. He even let his drone fly over his garden once in a while.'

Uncle Wayne looked at his niece in disbelief and suddenly started sobbing again. 'I gave Thomas that drone as a special gift, and he loved it!'

Arielle swallowed, close to tears. Aunt Heidi sat down with her husband, leaned against him and tenderly took his hand in hers. Arielle drank her tea. Finally, she reported about the experiences of her friends Kirsty and Sebastian and their discoveries of other exotic animals.

'Why didn't you tell us all this right away?' Uncle Wayne asked, and Arielle was startled by his reproachful, harsh tone. Would he now flare up and possibly become violent after all? She looked suspiciously at the whiskey bottle. How much had he already drunk tonight? Aunt Heidi now also seemed to look at her with a stern, probing look. Or did her reading glasses gave her a wrong impression? She usually wore contact lenses.

Arielle pulled herself together. She was as sensitive as Thomas! She said somewhat timidly: 'I was about to confess everything last night. And today too. I kept thinking back and forth how I could start. But I just didn't dare and I was afraid you would hate me!'

'Oh, child, that's nonsense! We love you almost as much as we love our own child!' Uncle Wayne said.

And again, everyone had to sob. It took a while before Aunt Heidi declared:

'Tomorrow we'll report this to the police. Even though the smuggling stories probably have nothing to do with Thomas at all, it is worth a try to shed more light on these incidents.'

At that instant, the gecko caught the moth at the window and greedily devoured it. Arielle would never have thought that her cousin's life could also come to an abrupt and cruel end.

# 38 A SILKY CLOTH

Sebastian was not particularly interested in his parents' conversation and kept looking at his mobile phone. He didn't even notice his mother's reproachful expression. Lizzie hated the smartphone addiction of her children and other teenagers, constantly exchanging text messages and getting totally absorbed in their own world. Moreover, she had just asked her son a question that he brazenly ignored. When she repeated the same question a little louder and he still didn't respond, she was boiling with rage.

'A strange way of communicating, to deal more intensively with people in the distance than with those around you,' she said angrily. 'Hello!' She waved her hand in front of his nose, trying to get his attention.

'I was only reading what Kirsty had written to me,' Sebastian sulked.

Andy grinned and pretended to grasp his son's smartphone. 'And what does your girlfriend write? Let's have a lookie!'

'No! That's a secret!' Sebastian protested.

'What's a secret?' Anna just came home at that moment.

Lizzie hissed, 'Nothing! Sebastian doesn't pay any attention to me and just reads his stupid texts all the time.'

Anna was surprised how bitter her mother sounded, but Sebastian was getting furious too, shouting: 'They're not stupid at all!'

'Now, now, don't argue!' Andy tried to calm them down. 'I'd suggest we all turn off our mobile phones during lunch or dinner. And also, when we watch telly. Because I don't like any pings, buzzes or beeps in the middle of the most exciting movie or documentation! Deal?'

'But what if something really important happens at that exact moment?' asked Sebastian. 'Like an emergency?'

Just as Andy was about to answer, his mobile phone rang.

'Andy Kuhlmann speaking!' His amused, sparkling eyes soon changed to a worried expression as he listened. Turning to his family, he then said: 'I have to leave! Someone tried to fix an electrical fault and received a shock. Thank God his girlfriend was clever enough to turn off the electricity at once and call an ambulance. Fortunately, it is not far away!'

Andy sighed. Well, it wasn't the first time that he had to rush to work unexpectedly. Sometimes he'd even been called out in the middle of the night to repair some cables or install new switches.

Sebastian grinned triumphantly. 'You see, this is exactly what I meant, and that's why ...'

'That's why Dad should always have his mobile switched on, but not you,' Lizzie interrupted him. 'I hardly think your messages could be that important!' She still sounded pissed off.

Anna bent down to Susi and Lilly to caress them. What was going on with her mother? She was in a terrible mood! She cast a warning glance at her brother. Unfortunately, Sebastian had no sense of when to shut up. She could see that he was about to say something impudent. Luckily, at that instant, the house phone rang. Just at the right time before a real fight broke out! Lizzie took the call and started beaming: it was an old friend from Germany, what a nice surprise!

Anna had to smile as her mother chattered away eagerly, now and then giggling like a child. 'The coast is clear again,' Anna whispered in Susi's ear, and her dog galloped through the living room while Lilly happily chased after her.

When Andy parked his car between an Audi R8 and a Mazda MX-5 he realised that he had been called to the address of Tim, the policeman. An elegantly dressed woman opened the door for him and introduced herself as Astrid. Under normal circumstances he would have found her quite pretty, but currently her eyes were swollen, and tears had dissolved her makeup, leaving colourful marks on her face.

'My poor Timmy!' Astrid said tearfully. 'It was such a shock!'

Her thick hair looked like a shaggy bird's nest and gave Andy the impression that she had been electrocuted herself. With difficulty, he suppressed a grin.

'What exactly happened?' he asked as he followed her into the house.

'Timmy was in the garage tinkering with something. He's very handy! He was welding when suddenly the TV in the living room went off. And nothing worked in the garage, either. And that's when Timmy tried to find out where the fault might be.'

'And he didn't switch off the electricity?' Andy asked.

'Oh, well, he did at first. He tried all kinds of things and kept running to the meter box to turn the power on and off. But apparently, he got it wrong once, because suddenly I heard a short scream and then a thud. And my Timmy was lying on the floor and wasn't moving!'

'Is his life in danger?'

'I hope not! An ambulance came very quickly and they gave him an EKG. They are still investigating whether the electric shock could have caused any cardiac arrhythmia. And therefore, Timmy has to spend the whole night in hospital. I just got back from there.'

'Good thing he wasn't alone in the house,' Andy said.

Astrid now showed him the meter box and Andy went to work. It didn't take long before he found two sources for the trouble: a damaged cable and a faulty kettle. However, he was horrified at how inexpertly many of the power lines had been laid. As if Astrid had guessed his thoughts, she said:

'Timmy has often wondered who installed the electrical wiring in this house, because some things seem a bit chaotic and not very professional. For example, if you want to turn on the fan in the bedroom, the light often goes on instead.'

'Shall I have a look?'

'Yeah, why not?'

After an hour, Andy had repaired everything that needed fixing, and he wrote out an invoice for Tim. Astrid offered him a glass of beer, which he declined with thanks. She seemed to be a nice woman. Why was she involved with Tim of all people? he mused. Tim was such an ugly and unpleasant man in his opinion. It was only when he said goodbye that he noticed a large square object, covered by a dark blue fabric with printed images of silvery fish.

'What a beautiful pattern! Is this a cloth from Indonesia?' he asked.

'No, it's from Thailand. Timmy's been on holiday there lots of times.' Astrid smiled at him. 'Recently he gave me a similar wall decoration with a lovely turtle motif.'

Andy would have loved to know what was hidden under the silky cloth. Perhaps a bird enclosure? Once he had done a repair in a house where two cockatoos had screamed so loudly that he'd hardly been able to understand his own words. The tenant had quickly covered their cage to stop that noise. Perhaps Astrid also wanted to prevent any birds from screeching too noisily? Or did Tim have a talking parrot that liked to tell secrets? Andy grinned. But he didn't want to appear too curious and refrained himself from asking further questions.

Astrid thanked him warmly. 'I wish there were more tradies you could rely on. Sometime in February, for example, I called a plumber who promised to come straight away but never showed up.'

'It's really annoying when people make you wait forever and don't even bother to cancel an appointment. Well then, goodbye! And let's hope Tim will get better soon!'

'Bye, and thanks again!'

Sleek Mazda! Andy thought in admiration as he got into his car, wondering if the red car in front of him belonged to Astrid. On the way home, he sang along to a song on the radio, loud and a bit crooked. He took a bend too fast, causing the tyres to squeal. And suddenly his children's report came into his mind. What had they said about the chase and the hit-and-run in Coolum? So, the black Audi had to be Tim's! And now the scales fell from his eyes. If Astrid had indeed hidden an animal – or more than one – in a cage covered with a cloth, then she could be Tim's accomplice in the illegal wildlife trade!

# 39 A NEW CAST

Arielle and her mother were very happy to return home again. At first, Max kept his distance, obviously feeling insulted that they'd left him alone for days on end. But then he sniffed curiously at Arielle's crutches and her plaster leg, and later he and Sniff slept peacefully in the wheelchair. Arielle thought that the pets were as cute as ever, just a bit bigger around their tummies. Her father had probably spoiled them with too many treats in the last week. Well, she had also gained weight during her stay with Aunt Heidi and Uncle Wayne. She sighed. Normally, she would quickly lose excess weight when jogging or playing soccer, but now she couldn't do any sports. Well, at least she had got used to the crutches quite well by now. And she was finally allowed to use her right foot since she 'd got a new cast and a special boot. She could hardly wait to see her boyfriend again! He seemed to feel the same way, because as soon as they met the next morning at school, Jack hugged her tightly.

Arielle squealed with delight, and Sebastian and Kirsty, who'd followed Jack a bit slower, grinned. Kirsty studied the supporting boot critically. 'You look cool, like someone in a science fiction movie! It would be great if we could all take a trip to the moon together!'

'What did I miss?' Arielle asked, opening her eyes wide. Her exclamation, however, was in no way referring to any new research or tourist trips into space, but to Kate and Ivory walking hand in hand. However, Kirsty, Jack and Sebastian were equally astounded.

Arielle had no difficulty following lessons after her long break, but the subject of mathematics gave her some headaches. Sebastian offered his help, and in the afternoon. he cycled to Arielle, this time with his helmet on. Arielle was very grateful, and she was truly impressed how fast he could calculate in his head. She constantly used a calculator and feared that Sebastian might find her terribly stupid. But he had the patience of a saint and obviously enjoyed helping her.

'I wish you were our math teacher and not Mr. Riddles,' Arielle said at the end. 'You explained everything so well!'

Sebastian beamed. 'Thanks! By the way, Jack would like to join in next time, as he also has some trouble with mathematics. And I wouldn't mind if we'd all practice together once in a while.'

'That would be great!'

'And perhaps you could help me improve my English! Kirsty often laughs about me when I use a wrong word. She can be really mean!'

'Sure! But your English is fine!'

Arielle gently pushed Max aside, who was trying to put his big paw on the calculator. 'The other day, Sniff ran across my computer keyboard and was shocked when a new picture appeared on the screen and she was facing a huge tiger.'

She added sadly, 'Actually, it was Thomas' computer that Aunt Heidi and Uncle Wayne gave to me.'

After a short hesitation, she revealed that she'd done research about her cousin, feeling that she could trust Jack's best friend. Sebastian listened carefully. Hearing the news about Tim, he was amazed.

'Are you sure it's the same Tim, that cop who is the boyfriend of Claudia's mother? And is her name Astrid by any chance?'

'Yes, exactly. Why do you ask?'

'What a small world! My dad met her yesterday. And Anna and Bruce had already met her, too!'

Sebastian alternately petted Max and Sniff, and after a while Sniff jumped on his lap and cuddled up to him. She was so cute! He had actually never been very fond of cats, but he'd fallen in love with Sniff at once. She purred softly, and Max put his huge head on Sebastian's right knee, close to the little cat's head.

'My father has considered whether Astrid and Tim could be smugglers,' Sebastian said. 'But he's asked Anna and me not to tell anyone.'

Arielle grinned at him cheekily. 'Am I nobody?'

Sebastian drew a pout. 'Oh boy, I'm obviously not very good at keeping secrets.'

Sniff purred loudly and made Arielle laugh. 'Nevertheless, Sniff likes you!' Then she said, this time in a serious tone:

'I don't understand why people would buy exotic animals. Do they want to show off? They should rather adopt a dog or a cat! There are more than enough of them in shelters and they can become such wonderful, loyal friends!'

# 40 A SPOTTED POND TURTLE

Ivory was full of joy and felt like dancing on the table! He was still baffled that Kate had asked him to go with her – just like that, with a somewhat mischievous expression. When his father came home from shopping, he immediately sensed that something nice must have happened. And so, Ivory told him, a bit shy and embarrassed, but with shining eyes, about his new girlfriend.

'That's wonderful! I've got news, too!' Barry replied. 'However, I don't really know whether they are good or bad.'

'Why? What's up?' Ivory asked excitedly.

'We have wronged Tim! It seems he has nothing to do with the smuggling of animals.'

Barry stowed away the groceries he had bought and then took out a bottle of beer from the fridge. After a big sip he continued, 'After the police had received several calls from people suspecting Tim of being a smuggler, his whole property was thoroughly searched. Tim was boiling with rage! And just imagine: There was indeed something unusual in his house, namely a Spotted Pond turtle, swimming around happily in an aquarium!'

'Really? But then ...'

Barry interrupted his son.

'Of course, everyone thought that this would clearly prove his guilt! This kind of turtle comes from India, Nepal, Bangladesh or

Pakistan, and its international trade is prohibited. Nevertheless, many Spotted Pond turtles are still being secretly taken to other countries, such as Thailand. And from there they are sold on, as some people like to eat them.'

'What? Oh no, I'd thought that buyers were only interested in exotic turtles to keep them as pets! But to eat them? That's horrible!' Ivory was appalled.

'Yes, it's sad! So many species become extinct anyway because their natural habitats are disappearing. If you take endangered animals out of their habitats, squeeze them into tight containers and handle them completely wrongly – or even eat them – biodiversity will continue to decline. At some point, we'll probably only be able to look at certain animals in a zoo or an animal park. We can only hope that all those species are treated well and according to their specific needs. And that they are given sufficient space. After all, who would be happy in a small enclosure or in a cage? Besides, only those animals that can cope with their new living conditions in the long term survive in captivity anyway. And...'

'But what about Tim?' Ivory butted in.

'I would never have believed it, but Tim seems to like many animals and especially turtles!' Barry smiled somewhat distorted. 'Stupidly, he tried to expose a smuggling ring on his own initiative. He had accidentally stumbled upon some shifty-looking guys while on holiday in Thailand. And he saved this Spotted Pond turtle from certain death in a soup pot.'

Ivory was bewildered. The often brutal, aggressive Tim should be an animal lover with a soft heart for turtles?

His father saw his raised eyebrows and grinned.

'Yes, it's pretty crazy, hey? But Tim had been tailing a man on the Sunshine Coast for quite some time. And one day, he discovered this turtle and also an Indian star turtle. But instead of going through the legal process and making official charges, he stole the two turtles and continued to spy on this man. He suspected that someone else here in Australia might be in cahoots with him.'

'But who would eat these turtles?' Ivory asked.

'Well, some people like to try new things and would probably eat almost anything. But the Indian star turtle is usually sold for its pretty appearance and not as potential food on the illegal market.'

Barry frowned. 'Without further ado, Tim gave one of the turtles – in a large terrarium – as a gift to the daughter of his girlfriend Astrid. And he kept the other turtle for himself.'

'I guess that would be regarded as a criminal offence as well, wouldn't it? But who belongs to this smuggling ring? What else did Tim admit? And how are the two turtles doing?'

Barry laughed. 'Take it easy, son! I can't answer so many questions so quickly. Besides, my stomach is growling. There again – did you hear it, too? Let's cook and eat first.'

'But please no turtle soup!' Ivory said, and his father gave him a friendly slap on the back of the head.

While Barry busied himself with the preparation of a pasta dish, Ivory read aloud what he found out on the internet:

'The Indian star turtle is an endangered species. It is difficult to keep these turtles as pets because they need high humidity, a certain temperature, and overall special conditions to survive. Wrong food is a common cause for diarrhea. In captivity they often die from respiratory and other diseases.'

Ivory handed his smartphone to his father, saying: 'That was, in a nutshell, the most important thing about this species. Look, here is a picture of such a turtle!'

Barry pulled a face as he'd just burned the tip of his tongue tasting the hot sauce. Then, looking at the picture, he exclaimed, 'What a pretty pattern! That's beautiful!'

He put a noodle in his mouth and said, 'Okay, all done! Time to eat!'

At dinner, Ivory asked, 'And what about Tim's friend, the owner of the car in which they'd found the eggshells of a Borneo earless monitor?'

'According to Tim, that guy wasn't his real friend but just an acquaintance. His name is Martin. For some time, Tim has suspected him to be involved in illegal animal trades. Despite his indignation, Tim didn't want to reveal anything about it yet. He rather tried to conduct further secret investigations about that smuggler ring.' Barry snorted contemptuously. 'I bet Tim would've liked to get all the credit for catching the thugs by himself.'

'Um, what a story!'

'By the way, Martin is a wealthy man who owns an elegant yacht, often cruising around. Apparently, there is no solid evidence yet to arrest him. In any case, I'll keep you informed. But now tell me more about your Kate!'

Long after their dinner, they still pondered about Tim. Was he really innocent? Even though he was acquainted with a smuggler? And Sebastian had seen the green python very close to Tim's house. Was that a coincidence?

# 41 NEW NEIGHBOURS

Very early, even before dawn, the cackling laughter and loud hoots of a kookaburra woke Lizzie. She stretched and moaned as this caused a cramp in her leg. 'Darn!' she cursed softly and limped into the kitchen. Susi got up and bounced around her excitedly. Lizzie went on, her face distorted in pain, without paying attention to her dog. She hadn't had such a horrible cramp for a long time. She drank half a glass of water, rubbed her calf and was about to go back to bed when she heard a strange sound, something like a sob. Was Anna lovesick? But no, the sound seemed to come from the garden. So, she switched on the outside lights and in no time both Susi and Lilly were next to her, pressing their noses against the glass door. Lizzie shivered, whether from feeling cold or discomfort, she did not know.

A few weeks ago, new tenants had moved into the house on the adjoining property. So far, Lizzie had only seen the couple from a distance. But she intended to visit or invite them soon. Although she found the woman's voice very loud and somehow unpleasant, almost vulgar, she'd like to establish a harmonious relationship with all neighbours.

'Well, maybe it was just my imagination,' Lizzie mumbled and limped back into the bedroom. She massaged her leg for a moment and then cuddled up to her slumbering husband.

Andy woke up and wondered how his wife could keep on sleeping despite the annoying ringing of their alarm clock. Sebastian had already got up and let the dogs out. Right now, they were pulling wildly on a small rope, growling happily. When Andy turned on the kettle, Anna came into the kitchen.

'Did you also hear any strange sounds last night, almost like a crying child?' she asked her father and yawned loudly.

'No, but I bet it was just a movie. The new neighbours seem to like watching TV at night, and it's often much too loud. Lately, I had the feeling of being in the middle of a war as I could hear the rattling and thundering of machine guns and explosions. Terrible! I preferred the snoring Staffi of the former neighbours!'

Anna put two slices of bread in the toaster when Sebastian joined them. 'Morning! Whose turn is it to walk the dogs?'

'Yours!' Anna said.

'Oh no! Again?' He looked into the garden. 'Actually, Susi and Lilly can occupy themselves quite well without me.'

'No excuses!' Andy admonished. 'After all, we agreed to participate equally in the care of our pets. Sometimes I don't feel like walking them, either, but I do it anyway.'

'Okay!' Sebastian grumbled. 'But only after breakfast!'

He snatched away a piece of toast from Anna, who grinned benignly and put more slices in the toaster. Shortly afterwards, Sebastian got ready and put on his old, comfortable sneakers. As soon as he grabbed the leads, the dogs danced around him with joyful excitement, making him smile. 'Yes, I know how much you like your hikes. Where shall we go today?'

Anna noticed amusedly that Sebastian's voice sounded higher than usual. Was he trying to imitate Bruce?

'See you!' Sebastian said in his normal voice to Andy and Anna. At the same moment his mobile phone vibrated. 'Hello!' he said in a happy tone.

'Hi, Sebastian!' Kirsty sounded abnormally soft-spoken and doleful.

'What's wrong? Has Ellen been driving you crazy again?'

'No. My mother's terribly ill!'

'What's the matter with her?' Sebastian asked, concerned.

'It seems she has an upset stomach. She can't even get away from the toilet and she keeps spitting and puking.'

'Oh no! Should my mother take her to the doctor?'

'I don't know! Well, I'll stay here and see how she is doing. Could you tell our teachers that I won't come to school today?'

'Sure, I'll do that. And if you need anything, give us a call, hey?

At noon, Kirsty rang Sebastian's mother and told her that her mum was in hospital now. After a visit to the doctor, they'd found out that Kirsty's mother would need an appendectomy as soon as possible.

'If she needs surgery, she'll probably have to stay in hospital for at least four days,' Lizzie said thoughtfully. 'You and Ellen can't stay alone.' She had no idea whether the siblings had other relatives nearby, but she spontaneously suggested, 'You know what: Ellen and you can stay with us during that time!'

'Really?' Kirsty asked, incredulous.

'Yes, no problem! You can move into our tiny guest room!'

'Thanks so much!' Kirsty felt relieved. Their neighbour who had taken her mother to the doctor had already offered her help, too, but she was a strict lady with a grumpy husband. It would be more fun to move in with the Kuhlmanns!

Sebastian and Lizzie picked the girls up in the early afternoon. Kirsty still looked pale and visibly shaken. Susi felt her sadness, nudging her with her wet nose and putting her head on her feet. But Kirsty's mood didn't improve until Lilly tried to scratch her ear, lost her balance and fell over. Kirsty had to laugh. Ellen was thrilled with the dogs and asked if they would sleep in her bed.

'No way!' Sebastian replied. 'The guest room is a taboo zone for the dogs anyway, and they're not allowed in bed at all.'

Ellen was disappointed. But Kirsty grinned.

'That reminds me of a funny story. Before my mother met my father, she'd had a boyfriend with a dachshund. That dog was very jealous and kept trying to kick her out of bed. Not very helpful when you want to cuddle!'

Lizzie was on the phone for a while and got some good news: Kirsty's mother was due to be operated on the same day and would probably only have to stay in hospital for two days.

That night, it was Sebastian who woke up from an unusual sound. Had Susi growled to warn the family? But why should she do that? Half asleep, he rubbed his eyes and went into the living room. Susi jumped up on him, while Lilly walked to the door into the garden, sending him a pleading look. 'Do you have to pee?' He opened the door and both dogs ran outside. Sebastian went into the kitchen to search for little snack. A bit of cheese? Or something sweet? He decided on a chocolate bar. Delicious! In the middle of chewing, he paused and listened. Apparently, the new neighbours were arguing. Now he could clearly hear the young woman's nagging, 'If you hadn't drunk so much, this wouldn't have happened! The woman could have been dead, just like that poor girl back then!'

'Shut up!' the man yelled back.

'You're lucky I haven't turned you in yet, you stupid man,' the woman cried angrily. 'But if you go on ...'

A door was slammed shut and a window closed, muting the voices so that Sebastian could no longer understand them. Not very nice neighbours, it seemed! Suddenly he thought of Kirsty. She could be very hot-headed, and he'd already experienced several of her tantrums which fortunately had never lasted long. Still, he was a bit worried. Would they also scream at each other in rage one day? Usually, he tried to keep his mouth shut when Kirsty was freaking out, but he wasn't sure if he could always bear her moods so calmly. He finished his biscuit and then let the dogs back in, still pondering what the neighbour might have meant. To which woman had she referred, and who was 'that poor girl'?

The next morning, Anna came across Ellen in the corridor, who was trying to plait two braids in front of the large mirror on the wall. 'Shall I help you?' Anna offered.

'Yes, please!' Ellen looked at her trustingly. 'Normally my mum does this.'

Anna was no more adept than Ellen, and they both giggled foolishly. In the end, Anna said amusedly, 'You look almost like Pippi Longstocking now.' Totally cute, she thought secretly. She liked Kirsty's younger sister with her reddish hair and blue-green eyes. Ellen didn't seem at all as cheeky and naughty as Sebastian had described her, but calmer and gentler than Kirsty. Anna had often wished for a little sister, and she was sometimes sad that all her cousins lived in Germany. Well, at least she had her brother whom she adored and loved (most of the times). She really didn't want to miss him. It would be terrible if something happened to him! How sad that Arielle had lost her cousin ...

'What's wrong?' Ellen noticed Anna's changed expression. 'You suddenly look as if you've seen a ghost!'

Anna said distractingly: 'Oh, I'll have an English exam today, which I'm dreading. But now tell me what you want for breakfast! Maybe toast with honey? Or yoghurt with fruit?'

She didn't want to tell Ellen that the murdered Thomas had crossed her mind. Kirsty and Sebastian were already sitting in the dining room, chatting animatedly.

'The new neighbours had a fight last night,' Sebastian said.

'Did they? I slept like a log,' Kirsty said.

'So did I!' Ellen spread a thick layer of Vegemite onto a slice of toast and took a big bite.

'How can you eat Vegemite?' Sebastian wondered. 'That stuff is disgusting!'

Ellen grinned. 'I like it!'

'Me too!' said Kirsty. 'I'm glad you thought of it, Ellen!'

Besides stuffing a bunch of other things into her backpack the previous day, Ellen had also taken a jar of her beloved yeast extract with her that Kirsty now enthusiastically smeared on her second slice of bread. Sebastian shook his head. Many Australians loved this spread that he'd only tasted once in his life – and surely never again.

'I wonder if Susi and Lilly would like some Vegemite,' Ellen asked, looking around for the dogs.

'Don't you dare feed them!' Anna warned her. 'And certainly not here at the table! My parents would get mad at you!'

'Hello, kids!' Andy had already gone for a walk with the dogs and returned, a bit out of breath from the quick pace.

'I'll drive you to school later, but only if you've left me something for breakfast!'

'How about Vegemite?' Anna asked, motioning to the jar.

''Yuck, no way!' Andy turned up his nose.


Only much later, in the middle of his English lesson, Sebastian thought of something. The nightly conversation he had overheard might have had something to do with the hit-and-run. Because the neighbour had said: 'that woman could have been dead!'

Restlessly, he moved back and forth in his chair, until Jack asked him curiously, 'What's wrong?'

'I'll tell you later!' Sebastian whispered.

# 42 OLIVER AND OLIVIA

When the doorbell rang, Anna opened the door quickly. She had already been waiting for Bruce, constantly looking at the clock. For the last five minutes she'd nervously walked back and forth in the house. Of course, her obvious anxiety had been transferred to Susi and Lilly. Both of them followed her wherever she went. What was going on? And why was there a travel bag in the hallway? The dogs sniffed at it suspiciously. But now they greeted Anna's friend with joy.

'Hi!' Anna beamed at Bruce, saying with admiration, 'That jacket looks great on you.'

Bruce smiled. 'Even my little sisters told me that the other day. So, there must be some truth in it!' After stroking the dogs, he gave Anna a kiss. 'Well, are you ready?'

'Yep, let's go!'

'Wait!' Sebastian shouted. 'Do you have that music for me, Bruce?'

'Sure!' Bruce grinned and handed him a CD. 'This is the very first recording from the Hot Ears. Back then, they also had a didgeridoo player and a female singer.'

'Cool! Thanks!' Sebastian took the CD. Reading the title, he frowned. 'Oliver & Olivia? Is that the same group?'

'Yes, Olivia was the singer. She had an incredible voice, kind of smoky and sexy. And she was Oliver's girlfriend. But one day she fell in love with the manager of another rock group, and so she left Oliver and his band.' Bruce sneered. 'That other guy promised her a paradisical career in the music business.'

'And did she become famous?' Anna asked.

Bruce cleared his throat. 'Um, no! Olivia is no longer alive. About six months ago, she had an accident on her moped, and she died of her injuries shortly afterwards. The car driver who'd hit her just took off, and nobody found out who it was.'

'Oh no!' Sebastian stared at him in horror.

'Yes, it was such a shock! Oliver took it badly, and for a while I was afraid he'd turn into an alcoholic.' Bruce sighed. 'Luckily, he pulled himself together again. But better don't talk about Olivia in his presence, okay?'

'And why did the didgeridoo player leave the Hot Ears?' Anna asked.

'He decided to travel around Australia for a year. But now we have to go, Anna, or my parents will get angry if we're late for dinner.'

Sebastian smiled. 'Have fun!'

'Thanks! Bye, my darlings!' Anna patted the dogs. 'Sorry, you can't come along this time.' Susie and Lilly were disappointed. They'd already guessed that the travelling bag would mean no good! But to their relief Sebastian took them for a walk now, accompanied by Kirsty and Ellen.

Anna and Bruce got into his car and fastened their seat belts, and as they drove off, they waved goodbye to the group.

Bruce said, 'You are looking particularly pretty today! My parents and siblings will be smitten with you.'

'You think so?' Anna was feeling a bit awkward. Would she get along with them? She tugged at her sleeves and listened only half-heartedly to Bruce who kept talking about Oliver and the

Hot Ears. Silly that she was so jittery about meeting her boyfriend's parents! Annoyed with herself, she sighed softly.

'It's getting too hot, isn't it?' Bruce turned down the heater that was running at full blast. 'Well, we are almost there. I bet you can't tell my sisters apart.'

Anna laughed. 'All right, bet accepted! If you lose, you'll have to shout me a sundae or something like that!'

'Okay! And if I win, you'll have to buy me one!'

In spite of the increasing darkness Bruce spontaneously took a small detour to get a glimpse of the sea at Alexandra Headland. In the last light of day, they could see the gentle waves and the silhouettes of a few pedestrians. Bruce was driving slowly along the promenade, which was lined with solitary Bunya pines, Casuarinas and Pandanus trees. The windows and balconies of the hotels and skyscrapers on the opposite side of the street truly offered a magnificent view to the ocean. A car driver behind Bruce honked impatiently, and Bruce accelerated his pace again. A few minutes later he turned into the narrow driveway of his parents' house. It was located near a shopping centre and didn't look very attractive from the outside.

Anna's concerns disappeared as soon as she met the Williams family. Charlotte, Bruce's mother, embraced her as if they had known each other for a long time. She was fat and cheerful and a real chatterbox. Her chestnut brown, curly hair was already streaked with a few grey strands at the temples, but she made a youthful impression and was smartly dressed. Her blue eyes behind the modern reading glasses shone affectionately.

Cliff, Bruce's father, was a tall, well-built man with a shock of silver-grey, slightly wavy hair. Despite his imposing figure, his eagle nose and his broad chin, he almost seemed shyer than Anna. He had a mischievous smile, and Anna liked him at once. Then she met the twins who Anna couldn't tell apart for the life of her. As Bruce had already warned her, they talked incessantly, bombarding her with all sorts of questions. They guided her to the guest room where she was to spend the night and showed her the whole house. The interior turned out to be an architectural marvel with different living areas on two levels, a modern kitchen and a huge living and dining room. Impressive large abstract paintings were hanging on the walls. Outdoors, Anna admired an oval plunge pool that was surrounded by tropical plants. It was looking very romantic in the dim light of some solar lamps. A white rendered retaining wall separated the small garden from the street.

Meanwhile, Bruce set the table in the dining room.

'Mm, something smells delicious!' Anna smiled when the girls finally took her back into the house.

'We are having roast beef and fried potatoes,' the twins shouted in chorus.

'And broccoli!' Mia added.

Or was it Emily?

During dinner, the girls and their mother chattered away cheerfully, and everyone burst into loud laughter as Charlotte told a joke with droll facial expressions. Her round cheeks were rosy from excitement. After eating and cleaning up, Bruce explained to his sisters that he and Anna would go out for a while, and that they'd go alone.

They left the house through a gate in the garden, and after a short time they reached the Mooloolaba Esplanade.

'I haven't been here very often,' Anna said. 'How convenient that your parents live so close to the town centre! And your house is fabulous!'

'Yes, it's not bad! By the way, every New Year's Eve there is a stunning firework on the beach. It's always a crazy bustle, but still wonderful! Maybe you could come along next time!'

# 43 THE YACHT

They strolled along the street, enjoying the pleasant ambiance. Quite a lot of people were out and about. The restaurants were well attended, and some tourists were even sitting outside, despite the cold air on this winter evening. Two young men with beanies on their heads were dining with obvious appetite, sitting at a tiny table next to a gas heater. Anna stopped in front of a cosy looking café and grinned mischievously at Bruce.

'Instead of the promised ice-cream sundae, you could actually buy me a drink. Because you owe me one!'

'Why?' Bruce asked, and then it dawned on him. 'Because of my sisters?'

'Exactly! I discovered a tiny scar on Mia's chin. So, you've lost your bet!'

Bruce laughed good-naturedly and studied the drinks menu.

'All right! How about an anti-alcoholic cocktail? Hum, I wonder if they serve as good ones as Freddie made for us. Remember his yummy drinks at Barbara's?'

'That was ages ago! Let's check it out!'

They found a seat in the back corner and were still thinking about what to drink when someone slapped Bruce on the shoulder and smiled at Anna. 'Hello! What are you doing here?'

'Oh, hi, Angus!' Bruce hadn't expected to see his friend. 'I didn't know you're a waiter here.'

'I'm just filling in for my older sister.' Angus glanced at his watch and moaned. 'And I won't be off work for another hour. What can I get you?'

Anna ordered an orange-papaya juice and Bruce asked for a strawberry-vanilla lassi.

'Shall we go to the harbour afterwards, and look at the boats?' Anna suggested. She was a bit irritated when Bruce didn't answer. He was apparently interested in a woman near the entrance. 'Bruce?'

'What? Um, yeah, sure. What a small world it is! First, we meet Angus, and now there is Stuart, Daniel's brother.' He whispered, 'Over there, next to the blonde woman in the bright red jumper. I'd told you about him before.'

For a few seconds Anna was puzzled, but then it came back to her: Stuart was the doorman at the disco who had let Thomas in, even though he was still a minor. Curious, she observed Stuart. He actually looked rather small and inconspicuous and not at all like someone who could break up a nasty brawl. With his tousled, light blonde hair and a wide blue-grey jumper, he appeared very young and harmless.

Anna grinned somewhat mockingly. 'Well, would you have noticed him without the pretty blonde?'

'Are you jealous?' Bruce smiled disarmingly.

At the same moment Stuart and his girlfriend left the restaurant without noticing Bruce. Not much later Anna and Bruce said goodbye to Angus who was busy at the bar counter, pouring drinks into glasses and decorating them with slices of fruit.

'Nice of him to help his sister!' Anna said as they made their way to the harbour.

'Family ties are really worth something,' Bruce said.

'Is Stuart still living with his parents? No one said anything about him after Thomas was murdered.'

'No idea! But I guess Stuart has his own place.'

'Does he still have a key to his parents' house?'

'And if so? I kept my old house key. It's only natural.'

'Um, I was just thinking if Stuart could have come home and had a fight with Thomas that night ...'

'And killed him, without Daniel and John hearing anything?' Bruce cut in. 'Nah, he probably had to work at the disco until 3 a.m. or so. And I can't think of any reason why he should kill his little brother's friend anyway.'

'You're right!' Anna said sheepishly. 'Sometimes absurd thoughts pop into my head. I just find it so mean that the murderer still walks around freely, maybe even in our own neighbourhood.'

Bruce hugged her. In the meantime, they had arrived at the port. Boats of different shapes and sizes lay moored side by side. The night was cloudless and the water shimmered in the moonlight. Now and then they heard a soft splash as they walked across the wooden landing stage.

'Wow, what a huge catamaran!' Anna said admiringly.

'Beautiful! And look, there's a sleek yacht back there! It must belong to a rich bigwig,' Bruce said, impressed.

'Oh, who is sitting there all alone?' Anna asked.

Close to the Underwater World Museum, a dark, motionless figure sat on a bench. It turned out to be a man-sized seal sculpture. It had a blue ball in its fins and grinned friendly.

Anna giggled.

'Sit next to it, Bruce, and I'll take a picture of you!'

Bruce leaned against the seal, putting on a big smile for the photo. In a good mood, they snapped a few selfies of both of them, with the artificial seal in the middle, and then went back again.

'It is so quiet here!' Anna said after a while. 'Where have all the tourists gone?'

'They are all sitting in the restaurants and pubs, I guess. Or watching a movie.'

Everything was silent and peaceful, yet suddenly a strange and sinister feeling came over Anna. Was it due to her reoccurring thoughts about the murder of Thomas? The air which she had found fresh and pleasant before now smelled somewhat musty of fish and seaweed, and the water of the Mooloolah River seemed to be unfathomably deep, like pitch-black oil. A muffled bang from one of the boats made her flinch. Bruce stood at the railing, staring at the long, elegant motor yacht.

'Someone seems to be in there!' he said. 'I've just seen a light.'

In the distance, someone sneezed and a woman belched loudly. And then something splashed into the water. However hard Anna and Bruce tried, they couldn't make out what it might be. Again, something banged, but this time it sounded like an explosion. And then a real inferno erupted: the beautiful yacht was on fire!

Anna and Bruce cried out in horror and Bruce clasped Anna's hand without realising it. Another deafening blast resounded, followed by the wild crackling of the fire. Thick smoke drifted to their nostrils, and the water glowed with twitching colours like a show of lights.

'Bruce, someone is swimming over there!' Anna cried.

'Where? I can't see a thing.'

Anna strained to identify the object in the water. Or had she been mistaken? Was it not a man but a big fish? Could it be a shark? Then they heard loud cursing and wheezing.

'There are two people fighting,' Bruce remarked in surprise.

'Help!' someone yelled hoarsely, and then there were more calls, now shrill and panicky, until the last word died in a gargle.

Anna released her hand from that of her friend and said in a trembling voice, 'We must help him!'

'But how?' Bruce asked. 'Oh, I better call the fire brigade!'

He rummaged through his pockets. 'Where is my phone? Damn it, I must have left it at home! Just when I need it most! Give me your phone! Anna? Anna, no!'

Without thinking for long, his girlfriend took off of her shoes, jacket and pullover and jumped into the dark water, feet first.

'What are you doing? Are you crazy?' Bruce shouted.

Helplessly, he ran a hand over his hair, not knowing what to do. He had never felt so miserable and useless in his life! What would happen to Anna? He remained frozen, but then he pulled himself together and looked for Anna's mobile phone. As loudly as he could, he also screamed for help until he found the phone and called 000. Meanwhile, Anna was swimming briskly towards the men.

'Anna, come back!' Bruce called out.

Just as he was about to plunge into the river to help her, another explosion roared, sending burning boat parts and wild sparks into the air, and Bruce felt the ground swaying beneath him. A dense cloud of smoke rose, briefly obscuring the view. As he felt a hand on his shoulder, he turned around instantly and almost struck out in shock.

'Bruce, what's going on? Are you okay?' Stuart asked, concerned. He and his girlfriend had heard his screams and rushed to him, stunned by the flames and smoke.

'Anna is … ,' Bruce was so excited he could hardly speak, and he swallowed hard. ' … My girlfriend is over there!'

'Let go of me!' one of the men in the water cried, and Bruce recognised Tim's voice. What was he doing here? And where was Anna? Then her blonde mop of hair appeared right next to the policeman's head.

'Anna, watch out!' An icy fear ran through Bruce and tightened his throat even more.

He had already experienced that Tim was a brutal person and he couldn't stand him! What would he do to his beloved girlfriend? But to his surprise, Anna clasped the arm of the unknown man, and she seemed to help Tim. With a cry of rage, Tim now hit his enemy's jaw, making him collapse. To stop him from drowning, Tim turned him on his back, went behind him and grabbed underneath his arms, holding his face above water with both hands and kicking only with his legs to move back to the wharf. Once there, Stuart and the woman in the red sweater helped him pull the unconscious man ashore, where he fell to the ground like a wet sack. Tim stayed in the water and turned around to Anna. She arrived just seconds after him, pulling a wooden box along.

'Give us a hand! Be careful!' Tim grunted.

Together with Anna, he lifted the crate up so Stuart and his girlfriend could take it. Bruce then grasped Anna's hands and pulled her towards him, while Tim, with some effort, climbed onto the pier by himself.

Bruce almost cried with relief and hugged Anna.

'You're crazy jumping into the water like that! What were you thinking? And what's in that box?'

Anna's teeth chattered, and she snuggled up to him.

'You'd better bring her into the warm quickly,' Tim said harshly.

But without his uniform, in soaking wet clothes and shivering with cold, he looked less frightening than usual. He took off his wet T-shirt, and they were startled to see blood dripping from his left arm. Furthermore, he had a gaping wound on his stomach! Bruce handed Anna her clothes which she hastily slipped on.

'Hey!' Stuart shouted and quickly grabbed the stranger, who'd regained consciousness and tried to pounce on Tim. Stuart held his arms behind his back and Anna noticed that the bouncer was stronger than he looked.

'What is going on?' Stuart's girlfriend looked at Tim's wounds in dismay and was glad to hear the sirens of police and fire brigade.

'This man is a smuggler and a murderer,' Tim said full of contempt. 'And when he saw no other way out, he set the yacht on fire.'

'His own yacht? And what's in that crate?' Stuart asked.

'Don't open it!' Tim warned. 'I think it's full of snakes.'

'Snakes? Are you serious? And who else was on board?' Bruce worriedly watched the wild flames that lit up the harbor.

By now the fire had spread to two other boats. With a half-choked scream, the man freed himself from Stuart's grip and kicked at Tim, who, despite his enormous body weight, swerved gracefully to the side. Stuart lost his balance and would have fallen into the water if Bruce hadn't caught him. Once again, the man fought against Tim but was overwhelmed by him. Both Tim and Stuart then held him firmly between them.

'It's over, Malcolm!' Tim hissed. 'And your drugs are gone, too!'

Addressing the others, he said, 'Malcolm was working for Martin, the owner of this yacht.' He frowned and glanced at the flames. 'I met Martin a long time ago, just by chance, in Thailand. And soon enough, I found out that he was involved in a drug trade. Only later I discovered that he also sold wildlife. Mainly turtles and certain lizards, but now and then also birds and snakes.' Tim paused, trying to stop the blood from his belly with his T-shirt.

'You need a doctor!' Anna said.

Although she still found Tim repulsive, she felt sorry for him. Swimming to the men, she had seen Malcolm repeatedly stabbing Tim with a knife, and when she got close and he'd tried it again, she'd grabbed his arm. She couldn't explain why she had done this. Usually, she didn't regard herself as very brave, and now she felt sick. He could have killed her! She put her hand over her mouth to suppress vomiting. Her legs seemed to be like pudding, and she hastily sat down. Bruce squatted down next to her and embraced her lovingly. Then he took off his jacket and put it over her legs in the soaked jeans to protect her a little from the cold winter air. They could hear the sounds of a helicopter and a boat in the distance.

'Tim is a miserable liar!' Malcolm burst out angrily. 'It was him who set the yacht on fire! Tim is a drug dealer, and he was Martin's partner! But when Martin established his wildlife business they started to argue. And now Tim killed him! And he tried to kill me too! He almost managed to drown me, but luckily, I carried my pocket knife in my shorts and could fend him off. But poor Martin is stone dead! Tim shot him!'

Anna stared at him in disbelief until she remembered the blood-curdling cries for help. They had made her instinctively jump into the river to assist the victim. Could Malcolm's story be true? Had she helped the wrong man?

Tim laughed derisively. 'Such a nonsense!'

'I'm so glad you came along!' Malcolm said to the others. 'Because with you as witnesses, he couldn't make me disappear so easily, and ...'

Before he could continue talking, he was interrupted by excited shouts and loud commands. A crew of firefighters got down to work, and several policemen and paramedics joined the group on the wharf. A young woman crouched down to Anna who was sitting on the floor shivering, an older nurse looked at Tim's wounds, and someone else put a blanket around Malcolm. Soaking wet, he also trembled heavily, and every now and then he was coughing and spitting.

'I'll take Anna home right away and take care of her,' Bruce said. 'She needs to get out of her wet clothes. But before that, I have to discuss something with a policeman.'

He glanced at Tim, and in the light of a torch that someone had switched on, he saw how an angry expression briefly turned Tim's face into a demonic grimace.

'I am a policeman myself,' Tim exclaimed furiously. 'Don't believe a word this guy says!' His googly eyes stared at Bruce grimly.

'We'll listen to each one of you!' an elderly policeman said in a firm voice.

His gray hair was cut short in a military style. Everybody now gathered around him, and the atmosphere was tense. Bruce, Malcolm and Tim started talking at the same time, but the police officer raised his hand and said authoritatively:

'Stop! Not all at once!'

Stuart's friend Belinda was the first to report her observations. As soon as the policeman heard about an alleged murder, he gave the command for an immediate search for an injured person or dead body. Looking at the burning yacht, he had little hope of finding a shot person still alive, even though the fire brigade did their best.

Bruce added a few details to Belinda's report and explained why Anna had jumped into the sea. Finally, he told the police officer everything he'd previously learned from Anna and Sebastian about various smuggled animals – such as a green python, two turtles and a Moluccan cockatoo.

Then he pointed to the crate. 'According to Tim, there might be snakes in it.'

A younger policeman who had toyed with the idea of sitting down on the wooden box, jumped to the side with a cry of horror. Tim laughed scornfully and the gray-haired policeman frowned.

'All right. We'll get Tim and Malcolm treated by a doctor and take them to the police station. And we'll also examine what's in the box. I need everybody else's addresses and phone numbers, and then you can go home.'

Calmly, he gave his colleagues a few orders. Then, with a stern face, he said to Anna, 'You're a daredevil, young lady, and I hope you don't get sick. So, get warm quickly!'

Malcolm was shaken by a wild coughing fit and had to spit, and Anna wondered how much water he had swallowed. Had Tim really tried to drown him? And had Tim killed Martin before? Once again, she almost felt like puking. When she got up, she swayed a bit and Bruce looked at her worriedly.

Luckily, they didn't have to go far, and Anna and Bruce arrived at his parents' house in no time at all. As expected, his little sisters were already sound asleep, but his parents were still sitting in the living room watching a movie. They were consternated to see Anna in her soaked state and Bruce more distraught than they'd ever seen him before. While Anna took a very long hot shower, warming up her numb limbs, Bruce told his parents everything. He bitterly reproached himself for being such a coward and for not supporting Anna. Although his parents assured him that he had acted wisely in calling the fire brigade, he was close to tears and felt miserable.

# 44 SUSPICIOUS

Sebastian, Kirsty and Ellen took the dogs for a walk. As they were about to cross a street, they stopped to let a woman on a moped pass by. Involuntarily, Sebastian mumbled, 'Poor Olivia!'

'Who?' Kirsty cast him an irritated look.

'Olivia was a singer in a band called 'Hot Ears', and she was riding her moped when some car hit her, and she died! And the son of a bitch just took off. And now I was thinking ... um, ... it could have been our neighbour who'd killed Olivia! And perhaps he also hit that other woman who luckily survived! The one on David Low Way.'

'What?' asked Ellen.

Sebastian now told them about the quarrel he had overheard at night.

'The woman from next door nagged, «If you hadn't drunk so much, this wouldn't have happened! The woman could have been dead, just like that poor girl back then!» Well, she could have talked about the recent hit-and-run accident in Coolum. And 'that poor girl from back then' could be Olivia.'

Kirsty was confused. 'That's a wild accusation, Sebastian!'

'It's only a guess,' Sebastian defended himself. 'That woman who's our neighbour also threatened her husband to testify against him. That means, he must have committed some crime, I'd say!'

'She certainly won't accuse her own hubby,' Kirsty butted in. 'Who would do such a thing?'

'A woman who wants to get rid of her partner,' little Ellen said wittily.

Sebastian had to laugh. 'You make a face as if you were trying to start a scheme of your own!'

Kirsty smiled. 'Better be careful! My sister might try to destroy our relationship!'

'I would never do that!' Ellen protested indignantly. 'After all, I like Sebastian! He is all right! Not like the stupid guy Mum used to have as a boyfriend.'

'Thanks for the compliment!' Sebastian said amusedly.

'Well, I didn't get along with that man, either. But Ellen made life difficult for him. One day, for example, she put two teaspoons of salt instead of sugar in his cup. He immediately spat the coffee out in a high arch, on a brand-new white tablecloth of all things, and Mum was really mad!' said Kirsty.

'That was mean of you, Ellen!' Sebastian said, but couldn't help smiling.

On the way home Ellen was chatting away happily. When they turned into the street where Sebastian lived, she pointed to a person with long, thick hair who was talking to a man next to a dark blue truck. Both were gesticulating wildly.

'The woman has beautiful blonde hair,' Ellen said admiringly. Getting closer, she realised that it was a man, and she giggled.

'This is our new neighbour,' Sebastian whispered.

'The one with the long hair?' Kirsty asked.

'Nah, the other one with the short haircut and the black beard.'

'His arms are tattooed in all sorts of colours,' Ellen said. 'And his neck too! Ugly!'

'Hush!' Sebastian reprimanded her. 'Your loud voice can be heard for miles!'

Kirsty grinned. 'Can you now understand why my little sister drives me nuts sometimes?'

Ellen boxed her on the arm and drew a pout. The men, however, were so engrossed in a heated debate that they paid no attention to the children.

'You still owe me two thousand five hundred dollars,' the blonde guy said angrily. 'I don't care how you get the money, Gabriel, but if you don't pay it soon, you'll be in trouble! Can't Melissa lend you anything? Your lady must have some money!'

'Leave my wife out of this!' Gabriel shouted back in indignation.

'Then sell your shiny necklace or your car or whatever! Think of something!'

The long-haired man jerked Gabriel towards him by his gold necklace, so that they stood nose to nose, eyeballing each other angrily.

To Sebastian's horror, little Ellen giggled again, arousing the attention of both men. The blonde man let go of the necklace, pushed Gabriel away and said in a completely changed, exaggerated friendly tone of voice: 'Well, see you on Saturday, and many greetings to your dear wife!'

He got into the blue truck and drove away. Gabriel straightened his shirt and cleared his throat.

'Hello, I'd seen you a few times before, but we haven't introduced ourselves yet. I am Gabriel, your neighbour.'

'Hi! My name is Sebastian, and these are my friends Kirsty and Ellen.'

'And these are Susi and Lilly,' Ellen pointed to the dogs.

'Well, you've got many girlfriends, Sebastian,' the man smiled, revealing a gap in his teeth.

When he tried to stroke Susi and Lilly, Susi jumped back half a metre.

'She is very shy towards strangers,' Sebastian explained.

'She liked me right away,' Ellen objected.

Kirsty nodded, but said nothing. Gabriel smiled and then said goodbye. With a slight limp, he went to his front gate, pulled a face and muttered to himself: 'I'd wish Martin had paid me my thousand dollars this morning as he'd promised! You can never rely on him!'

At home, Sebastian said, 'This blonde guy was scary! Don't you think?'

'Yes, he was creepy!' Kirsty agreed.

'They both stank of oil and grease,' Ellen said. 'And they had dirty fingernails.'

'Maybe they're mechanics or something like that,' Kirsty thought.

'No idea if Gabriel even has a job. He must be having money problems,' Sebastian mused.

# 45 GARAGE SALE

When Anna got up at 7:00 a.m., Bruce, his sisters and parents had already prepared everything for their garage sale. They were sitting in the driveway of the house, amidst a lot of junk, spread out on blankets on the floor and on a few tables. One visitor was rummaging around in a box of old tools, another was testing an office chair, and two women were looking interestedly at some books for sale. Seeing his girlfriend, Bruce jumped up and gave her a big hug.

'How are you doing, Anna? Did you sleep well?'

'Yes, like a bear!'

'Let's go to the kitchen, I haven't had breakfast yet, either,' Bruce said. 'Should I bring you anything?' he asked his family.

'No thanks!' Everyone shook his head.

Anna was a bit embarrassed. Back in the house, she said to Bruce: 'Oh dear, and I had offered to help with the garage sale!'

'No problem! We can give my parents a break later in the morning. Mia and Emily want to stay outside all the time anyway as they are keen to use all their charm and sell as much as possible!'

Anna laughed. 'I'm sure they are very good at that!'

Her thoughts, however, were not on the garage sale, but on the events at the harbor from the day before.

'Have you heard any news today?' she asked Bruce who'd just turned on the kettle and now started to prepare scrambled eggs on toast.

'Yes, I did. On TV they showed the fire brigade trying to extinguish the fire. However, the yacht and another boat almost burned to crisps. Some other sailing boats and a catamaran were also damaged. Pretty bad! And the police did find a body on the yacht!'

'Oh no! Terrible! Was it Martin?'

'Probably! The reporters didn't give many details yet. However, they indicated that it could be a case of drug dealing, murder and arson.'

Bruce put two plates and cups on the table and took Anna's hands in his.

'Anna, I'm so sorry I let you down yesterday! I keep thinking about the moment when you dived so bravely into the water. I really wanted to come to your aid, but I was simply petrified! I am a useless coward!'

'Bullshit! I was crazy, not you! And without you, the police and fire brigade would never have come so quickly, and everything would have turned out much worse. In any case, you were much smarter to phone for help instead of following me into the deep water.' She smiled. 'It wasn't that icy, by the way. It was only afterwards that I almost froze my butt off.'

'But how did you get the idea to help Tim?'

'Well, I suddenly saw the knife in Malcolm's hand, and since Tim is a policeman, I assumed that he was the victim. But who knows, perhaps Tim is the killer?' She shivered. 'What's the news about the body they found? It must have been completely charred in that wild fire! And did you see how Tim looked at us both in the end? As if he wanted to kill us too!'

'Hopefully he will end up in jail as soon as possible. Then he can't hurt us anymore.' Bruce squeezed Anna's hands briefly and turned his attention back to the scrambled eggs.

During breakfast he said, 'They didn't say much about the body at all. But it was implied that the man was already dead before the flames reached him. It probably won't take long until the police will determine his identity. And of course, they will be looking for clues to the perpetrator.'

'Somehow it seems to me as if it was just a bad dream.'

'I feel the same way!' Bruce sighed. 'What else went through my mind: If Tim is the bad guy, then why didn't he shoot Malcolm too? That would have been easier than to fight with him.'

'Maybe Tim didn't know that Malcolm was also on the yacht and he'd already thrown the murder weapon into the sea after he'd killed Martin.' Anna carefully sipped her hot peppermint tea. 'Malcolm may have jumped overboard to save himself but couldn't swim away fast enough.'

'I wonder who owned the gun or rifle or whatever it was. I heard a muffled bang before the explosion.'

'Hum. If it was a registered gun, it should be possible from the bullet in the corpse to find out who the owner was. But it probably was an illegal or stolen weapon. And I guess the culprit intended to destroy all other traces by spilling gasoline and starting the fire.'

'And what about the snakes?' Bruce asked.

'I was quite perplexed when Tim asked me to pull the box by the loop. He shouted to me that there was an animal in it that we absolutely had to bring ashore. Well, we might never get to know the whole story. My mother often complains that you constantly read exciting headlines, but later you'll hardly hear any new information.'

'So true! By the way, my parents and I watched the news on TV very early in the morning. We haven't told Mia and Emily anything about these incidents and our involvement. We didn't want to scare them or spoil their fun at the garage sale. So, please don't say anything when we join them, okay?'

'Yes, it's a deal!' Anna promised.

The rest of the morning passed by in a flash. Anna and Bruce helped Mia and Emily sell all kinds of stuff while the sun rose higher, temporarily making them forget the dark events of the previous evening. At 2 p.m. the family ended their garage sale and brought all the leftover junk back into the house, storing many items in boxes. Only after Mia and Emily had counted their earnings, proud about their success, did their brother tell them what he and Anna had experienced. They listened spellbound to his story.

To Anna's surprise, Emily suddenly threw her thin arms around her neck. 'I am so glad that nothing happened to you, Anna!'

# 46 PLAYING DETECTIVE

Later in the afternoon, the Williams family thanked Anna for her diligent help, and the twins hugged her, giggling. Then Bruce drove his girlfriend to her home in Coolum. Just as she was about to get out of the car, Anna saw her new neighbour for the first time, pruning a sprawling shrub in his front yard, and her body got tense.

'Hey, Bruce, that's one of the men who chucked the old mattress on the lawn the other day! And the same man who'd fought against the guy who later died from a King Hit.'

'Are you sure?'

'Yes, I noticed his crooked nose when Sebastian showed me the photos of the fighting surfers on Thomas' Facebook page.'

'And now this man of all people is living next door?' Bruce asked, feeling uneasy.

'Well, come in, my mother texted me earlier to invite you for dinner.'

Heading towards the house they waved to the neighbour, who in turn moved his head to the side, greeting them in a typical Australian way. His smile was friendly.

'Hello, Anna and Bruce!' Lizzie shouted happily. 'You're just in time, dinner will be ready in a sec! Sit down!'

'Hi, Bruce! How was your garage sale? I hope Anna didn't sell anything too cheap?' Andy asked, pushing the bowl with the sweet potatoes closer to him.

Bruce laughed. 'No, on the contrary, I'd never thought that Anna would be such a great salesperson! She was really smart!'

Anna grinned. 'Otherwise, I would have got in trouble with Mia and Emily for sure. Those two are shrewd saleswomen!'

'How much did you earn?' Sebastian asked.

'Almost four hundred dollars,' Bruce replied.

'Super!' Kirsty and Ellen said in unison.

'Maybe Gabriel should have a garage sale, too,' Sebastian said.

'Who is Gabriel?' Andy asked.

And now Sebastian told them about the conversation that he, Kirsty and Ellen had overheard when they had returned from their walk, and about Gabriel's trouble to pay off a debt.

'I didn't even know his name until now,' Lizzie said. 'I must invite him and his wife sometime.'

'Oh, no, don't do that!' Anna burst out, and everyone looked at her, perplexed. She blushed. In no way did she want to reveal anything about her first driving attempts and her unpleasant encounter with Gabriel! 'I don't know, but this man seems to be a hothead. His nose was probably broken in a fight. Do you remember the pictures of the fighting men that you once showed me on Facebook, Sebastian? Well, one of them is Gabriel!'

'Oh, wow! Um, when I heard our neighbours arguing in the middle of the night, both of them sounded quite nasty. And they gave me the idea that Gabriel might have had something to do with the hit-and-run.' Ignoring the grim look on Lizzie's face, Sebastian expressed his suspicion. Finally, he said, 'But just a moment ago, he didn't seem so bad. In any case, he was nicer than the blonde guy who demanded the money from him. He made a really dangerous impression to me.'

Ellen nodded her head vehemently. 'To me, too! Although the man was very handsome and had such beautiful long hair!'

Anna and Bruce glanced at each other, thinking of the nasty guy they had met in the industrial park before.

'By the way, didn't you watch the local news today?' Anna asked her family, wondering why nobody mentioned the events in Mooloolaba.

'Nah, we were busy all day long,' Lizzie said guilelessly. 'Dad was at work, and the rest of us visited Kirsty's and Ellen's mother in the hospital this morning, and in the afternoon Jessica and Marcus were here.'

'Why?' Andy looked at his daughter in dismay. 'Has something bad happened?'

Bruce blurted out, 'Anna tried to save someone yesterday. She is a true heroine!'

Anna was quite embarrassed when he recounted their experiences of the previous evening and her daring act. Listening intently, Lizzie turned completely pale. She jumped up so suddenly that her chair tipped over and Susi and Lilly, who had been lying under the dining room table, fled into the living room. 'Oh child!' Lizzie cried, hugging her daughter tightly. 'How could you be so reckless?'

'One policeman called me a daredevil!' Anna murmured. sheepishly.

'Bruce, did you just say 'Martin'?' Kirsty wanted to know. 'Gabriel also muttered something about a Martin who supposedly owes him a thousand dollars!'

'Yes, exactly!' Ellen exclaimed. 'Gabriel might never get that money if Martin is dead.'

'You have good ears; I didn't hear anything like that!' Sebastian said.

Andy scoffed gruffly, 'What a nonsense! Who says it's the same Martin? Kids, why must you always interfere in matters that don't concern you?'

Lizzie supported her husband. 'I am sick and tired of you playing detective! How often do I have to tell you? Leave it to the police! I don't like it at all when you snoop around and ... '

'Anna endangered her own life to save another one!' Bruce interrupted her angrily. 'She was selfless and adorable! This has absolutely nothing to do with childish detective games.'

Lizzie looked at him in surprise, and Andy's angry expression suddenly changed to a soft, vulnerable one.

'Lizzie and I just worry about you, Anna!' He lovingly squeezed his daughter's hand. 'I'm really proud of you! But I don't want to imagine how bad it could have turned out! One of those men could have hurt or even killed you! And then there was the explosion, the fire, the poisonous smoke, and the icy water ...' His voice broke, and he wiped his eyes.

Lizzie blew her nose and tried hard not to cry.

'Bad weeds grow tall!' Sebastian shouted cheekily and winked at Anna. Kirsty and Ellen grinned, although they too were shocked and their smiles were rather tense and timid.

Bruce remained serious. He felt like a miserable loser, and besides, Tim's threatening looks had scared him more than he wanted to admit. Was he a murderer indeed, and would he end up in prison? Or was Malcolm the real culprit? And what was going on in Anna's neighbourhood? Would Gabriel pose a danger to the Kuhlmann family? Could he really have a connection to Tim and Martin?

# 47 IN THE BOX

On Monday morning, Sebastian told his friends at school about the adventures of Bruce and Anna. Arielle could hardly believe that Anna had so recklessly plunged into the cold water at the harbor.

'Madness! Your sister is a knockout!' she said to Sebastian.

'Your sister is a complete idiot,' said a scornful voice behind them. Apparently, Fiona had sneaked up on them, eavesdropping. 'What was she thinking? She was crazy to swim to the dangerous men, in winter and in the dark!'

'Shut up!' Kirsty snarled at her furiously. 'You'd never save anyone! You only think of yourself! I bet you even enjoy the suffering of others!'

'You silly cow!' Fiona shouted, full of hate. 'You always pretend to be so nice and friendly, but in reality, you are a bitch, circulating stupid and false stories about me behind my back! And what's more, you have snitched my girlfriends!'

'That's not true,' Kate interfered now.

Her voice was calm and controlled, but her flashing eyes and reddened cheeks betrayed her inner turmoil.

'You're the one, Fiona, who likes to slander others and to spread rumors, and you constantly post all sorts of lies on Facebook. I used to stand by you, but I'm getting sick and tired of you! And finally admit it: you worked for Maryann and Simon and stole Patrick and Abby! My beloved dogs! How could you do that? You are so mean!'

Fiona stared at her in shock and burst into tears. And then she ran away.

Arielle looked sad. 'She makes her own life difficult! But she probably wouldn't have expected you of all people to say anything against her!'

Kate replied: 'I did feel sorry for her, but I am fed up with her! Besides, I can't stand the way she treats animals. And I will never ever forgive her for stealing my dogs!'

Ivory put a hand on her shoulder to comfort her. 'I'm so happy that your pets are home again!'

'Fiona stole your dogs?' Sebastian asked in surprise.

'I believe so!' Kate said. 'Meanwhile, my mother was approached by three people who'd noticed a girl dragging a Labrador and a Jack Russell roughly along. And according to their descriptions, it most definitely was Fiona!'

'Why did she do that?' Arielle shouted indignantly.

'I bet she got some money from Maryann and Simon,' Jack said.

Sebastian said, 'Your dogs must have been totally frightened!'

'Yes, my poor darlings! I hope they didn't suffer a mental crack!' Kate said, shivering, and Ivory put his arm around her.

Arielle nodded. 'It's disgusting that anybody would steal pets! And I also hate people selling endangered wildlife!'

'Were there really snakes in the box your sister was transporting that night?' Jack asked Sebastian.

Sebastian opened his mouth to reply, but Ivory beat him to it. 'My dad told me they found five snakes in that crate, all squeezed together tightly.'

'Poisonous snakes?' Kirsty asked. 'And where are they now?'

'They landed in the zoo. But two of them were already half-dead. The poor creatures!' Ivory said. 'However, my father's colleague didn't know yet what kind of snakes they were.'

'I wonder if snakes bite each other when they are crammed together in a small space. Um, a python might rather try to strangle the others,' Sebastian mused.

'What a horrible thought! And the animals probably didn't have enough air in the crate anyway,' Kirsty said, appalled.

'Did Tim really kill Martin?' Jack wanted to know. 'And why did he blabber so much on the wharf instead of keeping his mouth shut?'

Before Sebastian could utter a peep, Ivory responded to Jack's questions.

'My father told me a bit about Tim and Martin. The police received calls from concerned residents who believed that Tim might be involved in illicit wildlife trafficking, and so they searched his house thoroughly. Nothing was found, though, except for a single turtle that actually looked well and happy. But the police also checked out the car that had been stolen from his acquaintance Martin, and they figured that Martin had tried to sell Borneo earless monitors, or their eggs. When Tim was now interrogated, he stated that he had rescued this turtle. And that he had been watching Martin for some time, convinced that he was a smuggler of wildlife. Allegedly, Tim was still waiting for more information, hoping to expose more smugglers, and drug dealers too.'

Ivory frowned. 'But I'd suspect that Tim was in cahoots with Martin. However, the whole affair became too risky for him.'

'That makes sense!' Kirsty shouted. 'Tim didn't trust Martin, his partner, anymore and decided to get rid of him.'

'Maybe! That would also explain why Tim was so eager to talk at the harbor. He tried to accuse Malcolm of murder! But it's strange that the police couldn't find any evidence against

Martin at all! After all, they already suspected him since his stolen car was found in a ditch. What could have served as an excuse for the lizard eggs in that car?' Sebastian asked. 'And how did Martin manage to hide the drugs on his yacht? Or did Tim lie about them?'

Ivory shook his head.

'No, that part of Tim's statement has been verified. Despite the arson, the firefighters found several bags and burnt remnants of various substances on the yacht and in the water. And another interesting fact: A medical examination detected strangulation marks on Malcolm's neck and some other wounds on his body. So, Tim must have really tried to kill him. Unless he was just acting in self-defense, as he claims!'

Sebastian shivered in horror. 'Thank God Anna got away safely! Even if Malcolm only tried to defend himself against Tim, he could have easily hurt her with his pocket knife!'

'I wonder who else besides Martin, Tim and Malcolm was involved,' Arielle pondered. 'I'd thought for a while that my cousin might have been murdered because he'd learned about a secret animal smuggling operation in our area.'

Kirsty let out a surprised cry and Kate asked, confused, 'What had Thomas got to do with these men?'

Arielle faltered for a moment and then continued: 'Thomas met Tim at a birthday party of Claudia. She's the girlfriend of Daniel, one of Thomas' closest friends. Tim had been with Claudia's mother Astrid for some time. And now he gave Claudia an unusual turtle, namely an Indian star turtle. Thomas became suspicious at once. Especially because he had already noticed Tim earlier at the airport in Brisbane, where he'd acted strangely. After he unexpectedly met Tim again at this party and found out his name, he stupidly tried to spy on him. He even used a drone with a camera once! Crazy, right? However, I still don't know if Tim really is guilty of illicit wildlife trafficking or not. But then you, Kirsty and Sebastian, suddenly discovered an exotic snake and this pink cockatoo, and the green python was in Tim's garden.'

Kirsty was shocked. 'You think Tim, Martin or Malcolm could have killed Thomas because he was on to them?'

'Or all of them together? It must have been impossible for a single person to put Thomas on that high horse,' Jack said.

'I wonder if Astrid, Tim's girlfriend, also knows about it, or even took part in it?' asked Sebastian.

Arielle looked as if she could pass out at any moment. 'Poor Thomas!' she whispered teary-eyed.

'How do you know all this, Arielle?' Kirsty asked.

Arielle blushed. 'I read quite a bit on Thomas' computer. But unfortunately, he only wrote about his suspicions without revealing any results.'

'What about his best friends? Perhaps he'd told them more.' Kate said.

'No idea!' Arielle replied. 'I only know Daniel and John by sight.'

Kirsty flinched when a bird croaked loudly in a tree nearby.

'It would be interesting to know if your neighbour Gabriel had something to do with that Martin who'd been killed on the yacht,' she said to Sebastian. 'In any case, I'd never met anybody called 'Martin' before.'

'I met a few in Germany,' Sebastian said. 'But here in Australia it is quite a rare name, isn't it?'

'I know someone with a last name like that,' Kate said.

'Now I am lost! What's the story about your neighbour, Sebastian?' Jack asked, puzzled.

'My little sister and I overheard last Saturday that someone named Martin owed Gabriel a thousand dollars,' Kirsty replied.

'Perhaps we can find out more,' Sebastian said eagerly.

'Better be careful!' Arielle warned. 'I don't want you to end up dead on a horse, too!'

* * *

On the same day, the mother of Kirsty and Ellen was released from hospital and the siblings moved back into their own home. As a farewell, Ellen tenderly stroked the two dogs, whispering into their ears how much she would miss them. Kirsty gave her boyfriend a kiss and thanked him for the wonderful time.

'You have such a great family!' she said, 'I am still so sad that my daddy passed away so early.'

'Yes, I can imagine! You must miss him terribly!' Sebastian said compassionately. 'Um, by the way, what do you think of your mother's new boyfriend?'

'Well ...' Kirsty hesitated. 'You met him when we visited my mum in the clinic. He's not very handsome, but he seems nice. And he cheered her up so well after she'd found out that she had to stay in hospital longer than expected.'

# 48 THE EMPTY BOX

A few days later, Anna peered through the window and saw the man with the long blonde hair getting out of his truck. She watched him walk to the neighbours' house and knock. No response. Strange! Just before, Anna had heard Melissa's voice on the phone to someone.

The man shouted, 'Hi, Gabriel, Melissa! Is anyone at home?'

But nobody answered him. After another knock, he gave up, got into his car and drove away. Anna felt relieved without being able to give a good reason for it. She simply didn't like the man! A wet nose nudged her hand.

'Susi, my cutie! Are you bored again? Why don't you play with Lilly?' Susi wagged her tail. 'Where is Lilly? Is she outside? Let's have a look!'

Susi followed Anna into the garden. After a rainy night the grass was still wet, the air fragrant, and the leaves of the plants were glistening and shimmering. A lizard rushed to the fence and disappeared on the other side, and a bird screeched loudly. But where was the little dog? 'Lilly!' Anna shouted. Susi sniffed around and finally ran behind a bush, where Anna now discovered a fresh pile of soil and a small pit. Oh no, had Lilly burrowed her way underneath the fence? She had never done that before! 'Lilly!' Anna cried fearfully. 'Come back!'

Susi was eagerly digging with her front paws, deepening the existing hole and throwing lumps of soil at Anna.

'Yuck!' Anna rubbed her eye to remove a piece of dirt. 'Stop it!'

Susi lay down on her tummy and then jumped back when a filthy little creature appeared in front of her.

'Lilly, you are looking like a pig,' Anna scolded, but she bent down to Lilly and patted her tenderly. 'Since when have you turned into a runaway? And what's that in your mouth?'

Lilly dropped a small plastic container, barked shrilly and promptly tried to disappear through the hole again. At the last moment Anna caught her, holding on to her tightly as the dirty doggie was wildly struggling in her arms, trying to escape.

'What's wrong, Lilly?'

Lilly was visibly excited. But Anna didn't release her and looked around for something to block Lilly's new tunnel. Her gaze fell on an empty but rather heavy clay pot in a planting bed nearby. Quickly she moved it to the gap in front of the fence and let Lilly go.

'There, now you can't run away so easily again! And don't you dare dig a new hole!'

Susi had nimbly snatched the little container, happily racing around. Then she ran to Anna, dropped it at her feet and looked at her expectantly.

'This is not a toy, Susi!' Anna picked up the container. Although the sticker on it was somewhat faded and dirty, she could decipher that it had contained sleeping pills.

Lilly now began to dig wildly in a place next to the pot.

'Stop!' Anna yelled and grabbed her collar. In the meantime, she was getting worried, sensing something dreadful. She tried to peer through the narrow gaps in the fence into the adjoining garden, while Lilly was barking in the highest tones.

'What's all this noise?' asked Lizzie, curiously coming towards them.

Anna was standing on the big pot, peeking over the fence. Her discovery rendered her speechless and made her so frightened that she almost lost her balance.

'Anna!' Lizzie said indignantly. 'What are you doing? Are you spying again?'

'Call a doctor, quick!'

'Why? Let me have a look!' her mother demanded, and Anna let her take the place on the pot. Lizzie was also startled when she saw Melissa. Their young neighbour was hanging like a wet sack half on a garden chair, half on the floor, not moving.

'Is she dead?' Anna asked in a trembling voice. Quick-wittedly, she showed Lizzie the empty pill box.

'Oh no!' Lizzie yelled and rushed into the house to call an ambulance.

\* \* \*

Both Anna and her mother were still very distressed and a little nauseous at the thought of the lifeless figure, when Sebastian returned from his rugby training.

'Good that you weren't here to see this, Sebastian!' Anna croaked. 'Melissa tried to kill herself! She was white as a sheet, and Mum and I really thought she was dead. But luckily, the doctors revived her.'

'What? Oh no! What exactly happened?' Sebastian asked, suppressing a groan as he took off his dirty, sweaty T-shirt and accidentally touched a deep scratch on his elbow.

'Melissa took an overdose of sleeping pills, but thanks to Lilly her stomach was pumped out in time!'

'What has Lilly got to do with it?' Sebastian marvelled.

'She discovered Melissa and was smart enough to alert us,' Anna said. 'She is the heroine of the day, and Gabriel was here an hour ago to give her and Susi a toy.'

Lizzie had to grin when she noticed Sebastian's confused expression. After explaining more precisely what had happened, she finally said: 'And so, Gabriel came over to thank us for our help, because without us his wife might have died. He hadn't been at home and only found out about her attempted suicide when someone from the hospital rang him.'

'Sebastian, why are you standing around half-naked in the kitchen? It's much too cold! And what's wrong with your arm?' Andy just returned from shopping, putting two full bags on the kitchen counter.

'I am already on my way to the bathroom! And it's just a new scratch, not too bad,' Sebastian replied. 'What's for lunch today?' he then asked. 'Did you buy something yummy, Dad?'

'You always think about food,' Anna said reproachfully. 'I don't know if I can even eat anything, I'm still feeling queasy. I guess I couldn't be a doctor or a nurse.'

'Me neither,' Lizzie said. 'But at least I won't faint at the sight of the blood on your arm, Sebastian. But now go and have a shower, and then we'll all have something to eat.'

Andy was totally shocked about the news, too.

'But why did Melissa want to kill herself?' He asked a bit later at lunch. 'What a sad story! And how will she be doing from now on? Maybe we could help her somehow.'

Anna chewed and swallowed hastily. 'Gabriel mentioned that she is bipolar.'

'What is that?' Sebastian snorted.

'She's manic-depressive,' Lizzie explained. 'There's nothing to laugh about, Sebastian! I don't know much about this mental disorder, but according to Gabriel, she's had severe mood swings. Sometimes she was in high spirits and full of energy, sometimes she was stuck in such a sad phase that she only wanted to lie down and do nothing. Furthermore, she was often irritable and aggressive. Gabriel also suffered immensely from her behaviour, more and more often seeking comfort in alcohol, which of course didn't help either of them. Their arguments became even more vicious after he'd lost his job.'

'Gabriel has willingly told you all this?' Andy wondered.

'We were pretty amazed too, but it was obviously good for him to talk,' Lizzie said. 'At first, he could hardly utter a word, but then he started talking like a waterfall. Unfortunately, he smoked like crazy and lit up one cigarette after another. It's hard to believe that people remain chain smokers in spite of their money problems. He was fired some time ago when the car company where he was employed closed down.'

'Does Melissa have a job?' Andy asked.

'She used to be a hairdresser, but she got allergic to the chemicals in the hair care products and dyes. Then she did some cleaning jobs for a while, but although she wore gloves, her skin condition only got worse, probably because of the constant moisture in the rubber gloves. But without gloves it was not possible at all.'

'Oh dear, that really doesn't sound very rosy,' Andy said. 'Well, the rents in Australia, and almost all costs in general, are getting higher and higher, so it's no wonder that many people find themselves in financial difficulties or even become homeless. Just the other day I met a man in the parking lot at the beach who lives in his car.'

'Really?' Anna's eyes widened. 'I could imagine to live in a big van to some extent, but in a car? How can he cook and sleep in it? And where does he put all his stuff?' She thought of her own crammed wardrobes, her many pictures and posters on the walls, and the shelves overflowing with books and knickknacks.

'I'm sure he only has got very few belongings, the poor guy! At least the winter here in Queensland is not as icy as in Germany, but still – it must be terrible not to have a real home.' Lizzie sighed.

'Well, Melissa and Gabriel will certainly get some unemployment benefits,' Andy said. 'Otherwise, they might have moved to a cheaper area.'

Anna said, 'Who knows? By the way, that blonde man was at their house again! I wonder if he was trying to collect his money? But at that time Melissa was probably already lying half dead in the backyard. And Gabriel was not at home.'

Sebastian looked at Anna thoughtfully. 'You told us earlier that you'd heard Melissa on the phone in the morning, just before she tried to commit suicide. Could you understand her words? Did she sound very depressed?'

'Hard to say, and I couldn't understand a thing.' Anna brushed an unruly lock of hair behind her ear. 'Although, I did hear a short scream. Perhaps she got some terrible news.'

Her father frowned. 'So, this phone call might have made her think about killing herself!?'

'I hope she'll get better soon,' Lizzie said pitifully.

'And from my conversations with Jessica I know how hard it must be to be the partner of a bipolar person. Jessica will probably never get over the fact that Nicolas, her husband, could not overcome his depressions and jumped off a cliff back then.'

She looked sad, but then a tiny smile played around her mouth. 'At least Marcus, Jessica's cute dog, has brightened up her life now.'

# 49 FISHY

Susi and Lilly were playing with the new rubber crocodile that Gabriel had given them. Growling and grunting, they dragged it across the lawn, ignoring their old piggy toy. During their wild game, they trampled over a few small plants, stopped for a while, panting loudly, and then started again with new energy. Lizzie would go ballistic when she'd discover her damaged flowers! Anna called the dogs just in time to stop them from flattening a vegetable patch. 'Come on, let's go!' She took the dog leashes, ready to go for a walk. The dogs bounced gleefully around her, but Anna didn't take them outside the entry gate until they had calmed down. After all, she had to prove that she was the boss!

After breakfast, Sebastian went into his room to read a book. However, he found it quite boring, although it was a bestseller. A soft noise echoed from his laptop on his desk. A new e-mail! Curious, he checked who'd written to him, but to his disappointment it was just a stupid 'SPAM'! Allegedly, he had inherited a huge amount of money from a deceased relative in England. What a nonsense! Nevertheless, he imagined what he would do with such a pile of money. And then his thoughts turned to his neighbours and their worries. Was it true that Melissa's parents were wealthy? They must have been completely shaken by her suicide attempt. Would they be able to help her deal with her depression? And would they lend Gabriel money to pay off his debts?

He suddenly thought of Kirsty and Ellen. Their mother had also been in financial difficulties for a while. In that time, they had eaten a vast array of carrots because they'd been cheap. Kirsty had told him that her skin had already turned yellowish-orange. Had that been a joke? Well, at least carrots were healthy, and he was sure his girlfriend would look pretty even with a 'carrot complexion'! If he were rich, he would spoil Kirsty with particularly tasty delicacies, and she'd never have to starve, he promised in his mind. And then he had to grin. Anna was right, he really did think about food all the time! Spontaneously, he called Kirsty and invited her over.

Lizzie and Andy were going to meet six friends for a game of Bocce. To his sorrow, Andy found out that his favourite shorts pinched him uncomfortably in the stomach. He must have gained a few kilos! A bit disgruntled, he put on a different pair of shorts. 'Hey Lizzie, shall we take the bicycles?' he asked.

Lizzie squealed. 'That far? We will be tired by the time we get there!'

'Come on, the fresh air will do us good!'

And so, they took their slightly dusty bicycles out of the garage, removed some cobwebs and inflated the tires. On the way, they passed their daughter and the dogs and happily waved to Anna. 'See you later!'

Anna was amused. 'My mother put on her helmet the wrong way round. Doesn't she look droll?' she asked the dogs as if to expect an answer. Susi scratched her stomach extensively while Lilly pulled wildly on the leash, trying to run after Anna's parents. 'Hey, slow down, Lilly, we have to go in a different direction! We are going to see Bruce!'

Although it was still winter, the sun was already burning very hot. Lizzie groaned while riding up a steep hill. Oh dear, she was really not very fit! Should she rather walk and push her bicycle? Nah, she didn't want to make Andy laugh about her with malicious joy! With her last ounce of strength, she pedalled, inwardly happy to hear her husband panting loudly behind her. It seemed he wasn't in the best shape, either. When they finally arrived at the park, they saw their friends just choosing their partners for the Bocce game. Exhausted, Lizzie sat down on a bench, taking off her helmet and wiping her forehead. 'Phew, first I need to catch my breath!'

Andy also had a bright red head and was a little sweaty. His knees felt wobbly and his butt hurt from the hard saddle.

'Hey, you keen cyclists, we've already decided about the teams,' Bob shouted. 'Andy, you are going to play with me!'

'Okay, no problem!' Andy replied and smiled.

He liked Bob, a tiler who he'd met many months ago, during a house renovation in Marcoola, a neighbouring town. Andy had installed new electric cables there; and while moving a ladder, he'd accidentally knocked over a stack of tiles. Despite this unpleasant first encounter, they had become friends. Bob was a small, wiry man with a wrinkled skin on the back of his neck, indicating that he must have spent a lot of time in the sun. No wonder, since he was an avid surfer and had lived by the ocean all his life.

Lizzie was now to join forces with Bob's wife Rosie, a petite lady with bright blue eyes. Her raven black curls spilled out from under her light blue cap. Apart from her leathery decolletage, she still looked very young. Besides them, two other couples were present, ready to compete against the others.

Rosie laughed mischievously and said to Lizzie, 'Bet that we'll win? Come on, we'll show our husbands!'

There was much shouting and laughter, and Andy and Bob were beaming with delight when they narrowly won the first game. Lizzie hadn't played Bocce for a long time. In one of her tries, the heavy ball rolled much further than intended. It rolled down a slope and disappeared in thick bushland. The others jeered at her, making crude jokes, but Lizzie smiled benignly and searched for the silvery ball. Where could it be? She crept under a shrub and squealed as she touched a sticky spider web. Ugh! Repulsive! She rubbed her nose. And then she discovered something shimmering nearby. Was it her ball? She had to crawl on all fours to reach it, and a thorny plant hooked painfully into her left calf. Just as she was about to retrieve the ball, she was attacked by several ants, and she cursed loudly.

'Bloody beasts!' Bah, what was that smell? What was that? Oh no, that couldn't have been ... that wasn't ...

'Andy!' she screamed loudly and in complete panic.

Andy and his friends fell silent when they heard her scream, and Andy immediately ran down the hill to help her. His heart was racing. Had his wife hurt herself? Or got bitten by a snake?

Rosie and Bob also rushed to Lizzie's aid, reaching the edge of the lawn in the valley even sooner than Andy.

'What happened, Lizzie?' Bob asked, peering anxiously into the dense shrubbery from which Lizzie emerged a few seconds later, slightly scratched. In one hand she held the bowling ball, with the other she pulled a travel bag behind her. She smiled. somewhat embarrassed, and put the bag down hastily so that she could rub a very itchy spot on her leg.

'Oh, it was just ... for a moment I thought I'd found a dead baby! It stank so horribly, and then I saw a pale arm sticking out of this bag.' She plucked a twig from her hair. 'But it's only a doll!'

They all looked curiously into the bag. Inside was a huge, naked and bald doll with outstretched limbs, lying on its stomach. The back had burst open in one place, and something slimy stuck to it. Reluctantly, Andy took it out, and they studied the face with the light blue eyes and long eyelashes.

Lizzie shuddered with disgust. 'I've never liked dolls. Somehow the staring, lifeless eyes give me the creeps!'

Rosie turned up her nose. 'I do like dolls, but I prefer them with hair and clothes. And what is that horrible smell?'

Andy turned the doll around again and pointed to the hole in the back.

'Yuck!' Bob said. 'It smells like rotten eggs or dead fish!'

'It's even worse!' Lizzie burst out, holding her breath.

Rosie was checking out the bag. 'Look, there's more of that nasty mash in here!'

'Yuck!' Bob repeated. 'Is it a decomposed animal?'

'What are you doing down there?' Alice was shouting from above. 'Have you found the bowling ball? We want to play on!'

'We'll be right there!' Andy yelled back.

And then he grinned unexpectedly. 'Jacqueline is a biologist! I'm sure she can figure it out.'

Soon after, everyone gathered around Jacqueline. She looked interestedly at the doll and the contents of the bag and, to Lizzie's horror, even put her nose very close to it.

'Do you know what this could be?' her husband asked impatiently.

Jacqueline sniffed at the doll again, saying: 'Hum, this slimy stuff could be the rest of a drug that was eaten by an animal and then vomited up again. Look here!' She pointed to a seam on the back of the doll that was barely visible to the naked eye, and to various scratch and bite marks. Then she showed them the countless tiny plastic parts in the bag. 'So, here is my vague theory: someone was hiding drugs in this doll and, for whatever reason, put the bag in this dense shrubbery. Maybe it was there for a while, because it looks quite rotten and the zipper is broken and rusty. And at one point, an animal tried to eat the contents of the doll. Perhaps a cat –  they often roam around in this area.'

Andy stared at her in disbelief. 'Why would a cat eat drugs?'

'Well, I don't know what kind of substance it is. It would have to be tested in a laboratory.' Jacqueline looked around for a stick, found one and carefully touched the unsightly mud in the bag with it.  'This mush could be a mixture of some powder and water. There was a bit of a drizzle in the early morning today, and judging by the stench – well, maybe some cat tried to nibble on it last night and puked it out.'

'Do you think the poor animal survived it?' Alice asked, feeling sick from the horrible smell.

'In any case, I'm not going to crawl under the bushes again to look for a carcass!' said Lizzie.

Andy was still amazed. 'Another smuggling story? But a drug that attracts cats?'

'Maybe it was a rat!' Jacqueline's husband said.

'Well, we'd better call the police,' Andy suggested. 'Whatever was in that doll seems to be fishy. And it could be dangerous stuff!'

'Good idea! I will deliver the bag and the doll to the police later. I guess you won't want to transport the stinking thing on a bicycle, Andy!' Bob winked at Lizzie.

After hanging up the smelly bag on a tree branch far enough away from them, they played another round of Bocce. Rosie and Lizzie won big-time and cheered. And then they all had a picnic in the shade of a large tree, sharing the various treats that Alice and her husband had brought for everyone. In the end, the smelly bag would have been forgotten if Jacqueline had not reminded her friends. She was desperate to know what kind of strange substance they had unexpectedly come across.

# 50 DRUG X

Jacqueline and her friends had to be patient for quite a while before getting any hints about the weird stuff. Finally, it was announced that a new narcotic had appeared in Australia, mainly in the north but also in various other regions. It was a very dangerous drug that had been produced in a secret laboratory on an island in Queensland. The chemical substance hidden inside the doll was the same poison that had been found on Martin's yacht in Mooloolaba. Even a slight overdose could lead to severe nausea, dizziness and kidney failure, or even cause cardiac arrest and death. The greenish powder could easily get into the wrong hands – or the wrong mouth – as it was neither smoked nor injected but consumed as a drink, mixed with water or juice. According to the statements of certain users, the drug dealers had praised the wonderful effects. Just a minimal dose, i.e., half a teaspoon dissolved in a glass of water, would produce hours of ecstatic euphoria, while a whole teaspoon would put an adult into a relaxed trance. However, the real effects were not at all like that! A witness, whose identity was concealed, reported about a tranquil and dreamy feeling after consuming the drug. To his disappointment, however, that pleasant feeling had only lasted for about half an hour before rather grisly visions popped into his mind. And worst of all, he had suffered from hellish headaches, stomachaches and an itchy rash all over his body during the following days. He would never touch that stuff again! Strangely enough, the intoxicant had another unusual side effect: it contained certain fragrances that attracted both reptiles and cats.

* * *

The Kuhlmann family was discussing the news over dinner. Bruce was there, too as Lizzie and Anna had invited him.

'Then it could have been a cat eating the stuff in that park, just like Jacqueline suggested!' Lizzie said.

'Poor animal!' Andy said pitifully.

'On which island did they make the drugs?' Sebastian asked, once again with his mouth full of food.

'And who discovered the lab?' Anna wanted to know.

She took a second helping of the delicious vegetable casserole before passing the bowl on to Bruce, smiling at him. The rain was clapping so heavily on the roof that Andy had to raise his voice for the others to understand him.

'I believe the name of the island or the drug hasn't been revealed yet. And I am not sure if it's true, but I'd read on the internet that the laboratory had been detected by some bird watchers who'd got suspicious and raised alarm with an environmental agency. During an excursion, a group of bird experts had found many dead birds very close to a lonely house. And the laboratory had been located in that house! It seems as if somebody was careless and didn't store the drugs safely enough, thus causing the death of the birds. Luckily, this laboratory and all remaining drugs in it have been destroyed now.'

'Oh yes, I remember!' said Lizzie. 'I did hear about a mysterious mass dying of birds in northern Queensland! However, nobody mentioned any man-made drugs back then.'

'Birds? What have they got to do with it?' Sebastian asked, puzzled. 'I thought this specific drug would only attract reptiles and cats!'

'You silly boy, the birds must have eaten some poisoned geckos or other small lizards, and therefore they have died, too!' Anna said.

Sebastian drew a snout. 'Stop calling me silly all the time!'

Bruce said thoughtfully: 'It could be that many animals died miserably that way! You know, from passing on this terrible stuff in the food chain.'

'The cockatoo was sick, too!' Sebastian shouted. The rain was pattering and the wind whistled around the house. Sebastian's voice was loud with excitement. 'I mean the pink cockatoo that Kirsty and the other lady found on the street. The vet said it was badly weakened and dehydrated, but who knows, maybe it had also eaten a small amount of the drug.'

'That's an interesting thought!' Bruce said.

Sebastian continued eagerly and with bright red cheeks:

'And now I also understand the context – hey, I finally understand everything! This man, Martin, originally only dealt with this Drug X, as I simply call it. And he transported it on his yacht. Because of the extremely strong effects of the chemical, he could earn a lot of money with small packages, which made smuggling easier. Purely by chance, he then discovered that the powder attracts certain animals. And so, he got the idea for another source of income: he persuaded other people in Asia to use tiny amounts of the Drug X as bait for rare and endangered lizards. Of course, everyone had to be very careful that the animals wouldn't eat too much of it, as Martin wanted to sell them alive, as exotic pets.'

Sebastian looked around triumphantly, taking a deep breath. 'Or maybe he fed the animals just the right amount, so that they were slightly dazed and could be transported more easily.'

Lizzie laughed resoundingly. 'You have a wild imagination, son!'

But Anna was deeply impressed. 'Wow, you're not so dumb after all, Sebastian!'

Her brother grinned and started another speech.

'Tim, the policeman, was initially Martin's partner in the drug trade. However, since Tim is fond of animals, he didn't agree with the animal smuggling. He got into an argument with Martin and Malcolm, which then led to the arson and the fatal gunshot. And it is only because of you, Anna, that Malcolm is still alive!'

Bruce swallowed audibly and gazed at his girlfriend with an expression she didn't quite know how to interpret. Quickly she reached under the table for his hand and squeezed it gently.

Andy poured himself a glass of wine, saying:

'In any case, this Drug X seems to be very dangerous! Not only to people but also to the environment. I'm glad that the police or the drug squad found and destroyed that laboratory on the island! And I hope they will catch all the drug producers and dealers! Whether Tim was also involved and whether he killed Martin remains to be seen.'

'Is Tim actually in prison?' Anna asked. 'And Malcolm? What happened to him?'

'No idea!' Bruce replied. 'Hum, last night I saw the lights on in Tim's house when I drove by.'

'I didn't like that guy from the start, maybe because of his staring bulging eyes,' Anna said.

Lizzie suddenly thought of the huge doll whose lifeless eyes had made her shiver. She also poured herself a second glass of red wine and then said, 'International animal smuggling is certainly much more difficult than transporting drugs, even if the animals were sleeping blissfully, slightly intoxicated from that drug as you suggested, Sebastian. But what about this doll that I discovered in the park? Who would hide drugs inside a doll? That doesn't make sense! Nowadays, the customs officers are very clever. I bet they already know many of the smugglers' tricks, and the controls are becoming more and more intensive. Besides, sniffer dogs are often used at airports.'

'But Drug X is supposedly not coming from abroad, but from an island in Australia,' Bruce interjected.

'That's right. And if you don't have to go through customs, it's easier to transport illegal stuff. Martin was unlucky that his car was stolen and that the police discovered these special lizard eggs. Or the pitiful remains of them,' Anna said.

'It's kind of grotesque to imagine Tim being a drug dealer and a killer. A policeman who carries out traffic controls! Unbelievable, isn't it? Although, hum, he is a nasty guy who even harasses harmless people in their cars,' Bruce said grimly.

'He has already fined me,' sighed Andy.

'And me too!' Sebastian said. 'Even when you only ride a bicycle, you're not safe from him!'

Lizzie had to suppress a grin. Anna was grateful that Tim hadn't caught her making unauthorized driving attempts.

Bruce put down his fork. 'I wonder if Martin was the leader of this gang and if he had many associates. How did the drug dealers find their customers? How long has this Drug X been around? And how many people have suffered as a result? Do they become addicted? Perhaps it was too expensive for some?'

'Nobody has mentioned any deaths. So, this drug is certainly relatively unknown even in drug circles. And I would also like to know why this travel bag with the leftovers of the narcotics landed in the bushes. In a park of all places! Good thing that no children came into contact with it! Besides, it's horrible that animals can be lured by such a dangerous poison, get sick or even die in agony from even the smallest dose.' Andy stroked Susi who had put her head on his knee. 'We should definitely train our dogs not to eat anything they find along the way!'

Lilly suddenly became restless.

'Well, are you jealous?' Andy smiled. But then his face darkened. 'Oh God, do you hear that, too? The neighbours are arguing again!'

Everyone listened spellbound.

Melissa cried, 'You are so mean! Where did you hide my doll?'

'You'll never touch that stuff again!' Gabriel shouted. 'It doesn't help you at all but just makes you sick and ugly! And it's because of you that I'm in all this trouble! I don't want to steal cars and worry about money all the time! I'm gonna end up in jail one day, and then what?'

Melissa replied, but her words were incomprehensible.

Sebastian whispered: 'Kirsty and Ellen should be here now; they have super good ears!'

'Shh!' Anna and Lizzie hissed.

'How am I supposed to pay for your drugs? And your parents are tired of helping us! We won't get a cent from them anymore!' Gabriel's voice became quieter. 'If they only knew why you...'

'Don't you dare tell them anything! They'd take me straight to rehab.'

'That's where you belong!' Gabriel yelled furiously.

'Are you trying to get rid of me, you son of a bitch?'

Something rattled, and then something crashed to the floor. Melissa cried out in horror.

Andy jumped up. 'We've got to do something, or there'll be murder and mayhem!'

'I'm coming with you!' Bruce said spontaneously.

'We're all coming,' Sebastian said.

'No!' Lizzie objected. 'Better leave it to the men!' Quickly, she reached for her son's arm as another bloodcurdling scream rang out. Andy and Bruce ran to the house next door.

Anna asked her mother, 'What shall we do?'

Lizzie bit her lips. 'I hope Gabriel doesn't become violent! But we can't all go there together!'

'At least I'll go onto the street,' Sebastian said resolutely. 'If I have to, I'll shout for help!' And he tore loose from his mother's grip and dashed away.

Arriving at the neighbour's house, Andy hesitated for a second and then knocked energetically on the front door. As expected, nobody answered. Bruce pressed his ear to the wooden door but heard nothing. The silence was almost more eerie to him than the sounds before. What had happened? Andy took a deep breath and moved the knob. The door was not locked. He nodded conspiratorially at Bruce and stepped inside the house. A fresh smell of lime and orange mingled with the disgusting smell of cold cigarette smoke. They moved quietly through the dark hallway, and Bruce could barely suppress a hysterical laughter. It felt like a crime thriller! Would Gabriel jump at them at any moment, armed with a knife? What had he done to his wife?

'Hello!' Andy shouted now. 'Gabriel? Melissa?'

Oh no, someone moaned pathetically! Andy got sick to his stomach. Were they coming too late?

In the living room, they found the couple crouching on the floor amidst broken glass. Gabriel stared dazed as Melissa pressed a wet towel against his bleeding head wound, crying.

'I didn't want that! Gabriel, say something!' Melissa begged. With red eyes widened in shock, she looked at the unexpected visitors. 'What... what are you doing here? How dare you!' she stammered. For a brief moment her face distorted in anger, but then she turned to her husband again, frightened.

'We heard shouting and were worried,' Bruce replied calmly. 'And we knocked on the door but didn't get an answer.'

Andy crouched down next to Gabriel. 'What happened?'

Gabriel wanted to say something, but all he could get out was a rattle.

'We argued, and I threw a bowl against the wall and smashed a vase over his head,' Melissa confessed. 'He fell down like a sawed-off tree!' She was sobbing now. 'I was so angry because he'd taken something from me, and then...'

'A doll?' Bruce asked.

Melissa jumped up as if stung by a tarantula and ran to the hallway where she collided with Sebastian. Confused, she stopped on the spot.

'Sebastian, I told you to stay put!' Andy snapped at his son.

'Um, I just wanted to make sure nothing happened to you and Bruce,' Sebastian said, 'and the front door was wide open.'

Curious, he looked at Gabriel who now had a tiny, if slightly distorted, smile.

'Hi!' Gabriel croaked. 'You're without your four girlfriends today?'

Sebastian grinned, slightly embarrassed.

'Go and ask your mother to call an ambulance, and the police too. Quick!' Andy ordered. 'Tell Mum that Gabriel is bleeding heavily and may have a concussion or worse!'

'Okay!' Sebastian mumbled and rushed off.

Melissa walked back to the others, slowly and bent over like an old woman, and plopped down on a chair. 'It's all over,' she said softly. Gabriel tried to get up, but Andy held him back.

'Don't move!' Despite his harsh words, he carefully wrapped two clean tea towels around Gabriel's head, which Bruce had found in the kitchen.

'I don't want him arrested,' Melissa whined. 'It's all my fault!'

'Shut up!' Gabriel yelled at her.

But Melissa was unstoppable. 'It's my fault we're short of money, and Gabriel was just trying to help me. I was often so terribly depressed! One day, I sat on the beach for hours on end, thinking about swimming further and further out. But then a man came along, sat down beside me and asked why I was so sad.

And he told me about a wonderful new medicine that could help me.' She faltered.

Gabriel scoffed. 'Medicine? No way! This wacko sold you a damn drug and made you addicted to it. And this so-called miracle drug 'FUN' didn't help you at all, on the contrary! You just became more aggressive, and depressed, too. On top of that, you got nasty pimples all over your body, and often you had to puke. And recently you started to lose tufts of hair! Without your new wig, you can hardly dare to go out among people anymore.'

'Yes, the drugs had some nasty side effects, but sometimes I was so happy afterwards, and I could sleep like a log.'

'And I couldn't sleep at all,' Gabriel said bitterly. 'This 'FUN' was so expensive that you made me a common thief.'

He seemed to have forgotten that shortly before he had told his wife to be silent, because now he said, 'Go ahead and tell the men what I've done!'

He looked at Melissa, but she cowered on the chair crying, without saying a peep. So, he went on himself:

'Yes, first we asked Melissa's parents for money, pretending that we were only in trouble because we'd both lost our jobs. But the amount they gave us was far too small to pay for this drug. Melissa didn't need much of it to get high, but it was insanely expensive. I was desperate! Then someone gave me the idea of stealing cars. Here by the sea, it was easier than I'd thought. A lot of people go surfing or swimming and leave their stuff on the beach. And so, I often grabbed a car key, went to the car park, and – Bingo! Every time I pressed the button, the signal told me from a distance which car I could get into. I always wore sunglasses and a wig, or a big floppy hat, so that nobody would recognise me. It was more difficult to sell the cars, but that's what ...' He paused.

Bruce noticed that his eyes looked glassy. When would the ambulance arrive? On the one hand, he hoped it would be soon, feeling concerned about Gabriel. On the other hand, he wanted to know much more about Gabriel's story. Andy was curious too, while Melissa sat there motionless. She seemed petrified. Her long, dark hair and the bright red jumper made her look very pale. Without her coarse-pored, impure skin she would be quite pretty, Bruce thought.

Andy wondered at the same moment whether all the pimples on her face were caused by the Drug X or 'FUN'. And what would her real hair look like?

'I'm a well-trained mechanic and always had a knack for cars,' Gabriel now said with a proud undertone. 'After the car company where I used to work closed down, I worked in a garage in Brisbane for a while. But Melissa wanted to live here on the Sunshine Coast, and I wanted to make her happier, so we moved here. I was hoping to find a new job.'

Melissa started sobbing again.

'But nothing worked out. There seemed to be hundreds of applicants for every vacant position. Finally, I placed an advertisement for a job as a handy man and ...'

'What about the car thefts?' Bruce interrupted impatiently as he already heard a siren in the distance.

Andy frowned grimly.

Gabriel said, 'Thanks to my ad, I finally got some small jobs. Like disposing of rubbish for older people, trimming hedges, or mowing lawns. And one day, I met an oddball. For him, I washed stolen cars and sometimes painted them. Well, he also made me steal cars from time to time. He had good connections and no problems selling the cars. Unfortunately, he's dead now! And he still owes me a thousand dollars.'

'Was that Martin?' Bruce asked.

Melissa was startled. 'Did you know him?'

'No, but I heard he was dealing with drugs and got killed.'

'Drugs? No way, there must be a misunderstanding! He only stole cars and boats. And got stinking rich,' Gabriel said.

'The money is no use to him anymore,' Melissa said. 'He's dead as a doornail.'

Andy and Bruce were confused. Was it true that Martin had had nothing to do with drugs? They would have loved to ask more questions, but now two policemen and the ambulance arrived. After an initial interrogation and a quick examination, Gabriel was carefully placed on a stretcher. In addition to the cut, he'd probably got a concussion from the heavy vase. Furthermore, he had broken a cervical vertebra when he'd fallen down, hitting the edge of the table.

Melissa wanted to accompany him to the hospital, but was first questioned by the police. Bruce and the Kuhlmann family were also asked to make a statement.

# 51 PUCK THE PUG

Due to their busy schedules over the next few days, the Kuhlmanns didn't spend much time to think about their neighbours. But on Saturday morning Sebastian woke up early from a shrill barking in the street, and his mind was immediately occupied with images of Melissa and Gabriel. He had the feeling that he had learned something important but simply couldn't grasp it. What a pity that his brain didn't work like a computer! What was it? His thoughts kept going round and round. He knew that Melissa had hidden her drugs inside her doll so that no unexpected visitor would accidentally come across them. And then Gabriel chucked that doll. But why was it stark naked when Lizzie found it in the old bag? And was it true that Gabriel was so worried about his wife? In spite of their horrible quarrels?

And there was something else he couldn't get out of his mind. Bruce had told them that, according to Gabriel, Martin had got rich by stealing. And now Martin had been killed. Would his relatives inherit his possessions? Or would they be confiscated by the state, because he had acquired most of his money illegally? Sebastian suddenly remembered the e-mail about an alleged inheritance from an uncle in England. Complete nonsense! He didn't have any relatives in England, and if he did, Anna would be entitled to inherit as well – but she wasn't mentioned in the fake message. Of course, in case of a real inheritance, he would give her the half and throw a rollicking party for his friends. And he would also buy special presents for his parents and the dogs, he decided. He couldn't understand the nasty people all over the world who plotted mean intrigues or committed murders in order to gain power and money. How could anyone be happy after killing another person, perhaps even a family member?

He turned pale. Only recently he'd spoken to Kirsty and Ellen about intrigues and about Melissa, who had once threatened to denounce her husband to the police. Kirsty had asked, «who would turn in his own husband or boyfriend?» And Ellen had replied, «a woman who wants to get rid of her partner!» But who knows, maybe it was the other way round, and Gabriel wanted his wife out of the way? He'd already admitted that she made his life hell!

Sebastian ran excitedly into Anna's room and gushed out: 'Hey, Anna! Maybe Gabriel wanted to get rid of his wife and it wasn't suicide at all! Or maybe he influenced her to do it!'

Anna had just been lying comfortably on her bed, reading a book. Rather amused than angry about the interruption, she said, 'Maybe you should write a thriller, Sebastian! You certainly have a vivid imagination!' She put the book aside. 'But Melissa took the sleeping pills when she was alone.'

'Yes, she did. But only after she got a phone call.' Sebastian flopped onto a chair. 'Gabriel was sick and tired of bickering with his wife. It occurred to him that his life would be much easier without her. He would no longer be forced to steal money for her, and he might also receive the inheritance from Melissa's rich parents one day. So, even if he didn't kill her, he could've threatened her with divorce. Or perhaps he told her that he'd stop buying those expensive drugs.'

'Um, I don't know. It all sounds pretty far-fetched to me.'

Sebastian grinned. 'By the way, Melissa wears a wig, Dad told me. The drugs caused her hair to fall out.'

'Really? That's awful!'

'And this stuff also gives you a nasty rash and stomach aches. I'd never use it!' Sebastian touched his chin involuntarily, which fortunately was free of pimples right now.

'How is the mother of Kirsty and Ellen doing?' Anna asked. 'Is she well again?'

'Yes, she's fine. And she is totally grateful that we took such good care of her daughters while she was in hospital.'

'Our parents have really pampered Kirsty and Ellen. They can be so warmhearted and generous!' Anna smiled briefly, but then she made an indignant face. 'I just wish Daddy would be nicer to Bruce, instead of ...'

'Come on, Dad's okay. I get the feeling he really likes your friend and just doesn't want to admit it.'

'You think so?' Anna asked doubtfully.

'Sure! And I also think Bruce is great! You fit together really well.'

Anna beamed. 'That's what Barbara was saying the other day, too.'

At that moment, her mobile rang out. 'Oh, speak of the devil! It's a message from her.' She read, 'Teddy swallowed a ball! But he's on the road to recovery. I'll be right over.'

'The poor dog!' Anna cried pitifully.

Shortly afterwards there was a knock at the front door and Anna dashed off to let her friend in, with Susi and Lilly overtaking her on the way.

'Hi, Barbara, that was quick! How is Teddy doing?'

'David and his parents took him to the vet, and I came along, too. Poor Teddy! But he was so lucky that he didn't suffocate! Although the ball got stuck in his mouth and blocked his windpipe, he could still breathe a bit, otherwise the vet wouldn't have been able to save him.'

'Was it a tennis ball?' Sebastian had followed Anna and the dogs to the door.

'No, it was a rubber ball that Teddy had found somewhere. He was happily chewing on it, when it somehow slipped down his throat and got stuck there. Really horrible! David and his parents were out of their minds with fear!' Barbara patted Susi and Lilly. 'Hi you two, better be careful not to do such nonsense!' Then she approached the siblings, 'By the way, I learned something interesting in the waiting room.'

'Hello! Why are you all standing around in the hallway? I didn't expect such a great reception,' Andy joked, who had just returned home. The dogs immediately greeted him effusively.

'Teddy had to be rescued,' Sebastian shouted so loudly that Lizzie came out of the garden to see what was going on.

Finally, Barbara had to tell the whole story again in detail. Sebastian prepared tea for everyone and they sat down on the patio. There was a light breeze, but it was still warmer outside than inside the house. Anna watched her dogs playing with their old rubber toy, concerned. Could Susi swallow the piggy by mistake?

Barbara suspiciously sniffed at the Mexican Tarragon tea in her cup. It smelled spicy and vaguely familiar. Like anise or liquorice? Carefully she sipped it. 'Oh, yummy!' she said, pleasantly surprised.

'And what happened in the waiting room?' Sebastian asked impatiently.

Barbara took a deep breath. 'An elderly woman was sitting next to me with her black pug who'd injured its left eye. We chatted about dogs for a while, and then she told me about Thomas and Daniel. Alison –   this is the lady's name – lives in the same street as Daniel, where Thomas spent his last night.'

'Who are Thomas and Daniel?' Andy asked, confused.

'Thomas was the boy who was found murdered in the AIRY TOES park. And he'd often visited Daniel, one of his best friends. Alison is very thankful to Daniel. A long time ago, she was due for a hip replacement. Initially, she was very worried about her dog. Who would look after her beloved Puck – that's the name of her pug – during her operation? To her surprise, Daniel offered her his help, although she only knew him by sight. He cared for Puck while she was in hospital, and later he also took him for walks until she could move around better again. Alison was very happy. Um, and because of Daniel she also got to know Thomas, who was very fond of dogs, too. They had a little chat almost every time they met. And now, of course, Alison is terribly sad about his death.' Barbara swallowed. 'Well, the important thing is that she couldn't sleep in the night of the murder and she noticed something.'

'What?' Anna asked, shifting restlessly on her chair.

Lizzie clasped her steaming teacup with both hands, anxious to hear Barbara's reply.

Barbara briefly tugged at her dark green patterned flannel shirt and crossed her legs. 'That night, Alison heard a muffled bang and a soft curse. As she peered out the window, she saw two men checking out their cars. But there were no arguments at all and the drivers seemed to know each other. At first Alison thought that one of them was a woman because he had very long hair until she heard his deep voice.'

'What did he say?' Sebastian asked.

'Something about a small dent. She couldn't understand the exact words, but in the light of the street lamp she could see them standing between the cars, looking at the bumpers. She guessed that the man with the long blonde hair had braked too suddenly and the driver behind him had hit his car. To her surprise, the long-haired man handed the other guy, a rather big man, a very thick envelope. Just then Puck started barking and she quickly pulled away from the window.'

'Weird! And that was in the night of the murder?' Lizzie looked up at Barbara. 'Did Alison report this to the police when she learned of the murder?'

'No, she only told some neighbours about it,' Barbara said. 'And by chance, she saw the one man again later, at a traffic control, discovering that he was a policeman. She described him as an unpleasant guy with a protruding stomach and googly eyes. And suddenly she giggled and said that her little Puck had eyes like that and was still very sweet and nice.'

Anna grinned. 'Yes, pugs are rather ugly and yet cute!'

'I wonder if that was Tim?' Sebastian exclaimed excitedly. 'But why didn't Alison make a statement? This meeting sounds suspicious, like a bribe! And on the very street where Thomas was that night!'

'Actually, Alison wanted to report her observations to the police as soon as she heard about the corpse in the park, wondering if those men could have killed Thomas, but she changed her mind as there was no evidence.'

Andy looked at Barbara thoughtfully. 'Well, we should all be careful not to spread unfounded accusations, especially when it comes to murder! But it is an uncanny story. Did Alison say anything about the makes of the cars?'

'Yes, the policeman had a dark, sleek-looking car. The long-haired man had a small truck with a few boxes piled up on the loading area.'

'This could be the man to whom Gabriel owes money!' Anna said.

Lizzie choked on her tea and coughed. 'I'm getting scared! Murder, arson, drugs, an attempted suicide, money in an envelope ... and the gangsters might be right here, next door? Somehow, we seem to be indirectly involved in all these events!'

Andy took her hand and squeezed it lovingly. 'I'm feeling uneasy, too, but somehow I have an inkling that everything will be over soon.'

'I still don't understand why Thomas left his friend's house. Even if he, like Alison, could have heard the car crash or the voices in the street, it doesn't make much sense, unless ...,' Barbara paused.

'Unless he had an appointment with those men,' Sebastian shouted.

Anna looked at her brother in dismay. 'You believe Thomas was in cahoots with them?'

'Did Alison actually mention the time of her observations, Barbara?' Lizzie asked.

'Yes, it was long after midnight. Since she'd trouble sleeping, she got up again at 11 p.m., watched a movie, drank some herbal schnapps and didn't go back to bed until after 1 o'clock. And soon after, she noticed these two men.'

'She has told you a lot of things,' Andy marvelled.

Barbara grinned. 'Yes, we both had to wait a while at the vet's, and she was a chatter box indeed! And her Puck was so cute! I hope his eye will heal fast!'

'Would you like some more tea?' Anna asked her friend.

Barbara refused. 'I'd better get going! I will have to baby-sit my little brother and sister, as my mother wants to do some shopping in Maroochydore.'

'I can drive you home, Barbara,' Lizzie suggested, still a bit worried about her neighbourhood.

'No thanks, that's kind of you, but I'd rather jog. See you soon!'

'Bye!' the Kuhlmanns said in unison, and Anna accompanied her to the front yard, hugged her and watched her jog away, her ponytail swinging.

Later at lunch, Lizzie noticed that Sebastian was unusually quiet and didn't eat much. 'Aren't you hungry?' she asked him. 'Or don't you like it?'

Sebastian hastily swallowed down his last bite. 'Well, I'm still pondering why Thomas was killed. Apparently, he had been spying on Tim for a while, even with the help of a drone. Who knows what he discovered?' He briefly poked around on his plate with his fork, finally cutting a new slice from the pizza. The knife squeaked horribly, giving everyone a shiver.

Sebastian smiled apologetically. 'And if one of these guys that Alison described, had been Tim, maybe Thomas knew about their planned meeting, so he went out of the house to listen in on them. Or to take photos of them secretly? Unfortunately, he was caught and ...'

'And was killed in the middle of a residential neighborhood? Or was dragged into a car against his will?' his father asked in disbelief. 'Then he would have called for help.'

Lizzie shuddered. 'Horrible! The poor boy!'

'You know what else is strange? Arielle mentioned that Thomas had watched a movie on Daniel's computer, using headphones so as not to disturb his two friends who'd already gone to bed. But then he couldn't have heard any noise outside at that time. And yet he left the house. Why? Could it be that he wasn't watching a film at all, but was spying on Tim – if it really was Tim – and the other man? Maybe Daniel's parents had installed video surveillance? So, Thomas discovered the two men out there and found their behaviour suspicious. And therefore, he snuck out of the house to ...'

Suppressing a grin, Andy interrupted his son again.

'I think your imagination is running away with you again, Sebastian! You've obviously watched too many James Bond movies! I'm sure that the police interrogated Thomas' friends as well as Daniel's brother and parents, and they must have checked out all mobile phones, computers, cameras, videos and so on that could possibly provide clues to the murder. However, it is a pity that Alison has not made a statement. Could she be persuaded to go to the police now?'

'We don't even know her!' Lizzie interjected.

'Well, I could speak to the vet. He won't give me her phone number, but maybe he could ask her to call me.'

'Good idea!' Lizzie said. 'Such a statement could be very important and help to find the murderers.'

'This Tim is definitely behaving suspiciously,' Sebastian said. 'And if the other man whom Alison was describing is really the acquaintance of our neighbours, we may even have two murderers close by!' And again, everyone was shivering.

# 52 HEDGE

Sebastian decided to have another chat with Arielle. He was keen to know if Thomas' camera and mobile phone had been stolen. Had his killers destroyed them, or had they just deleted any photos that might show a connection to them?

Anna decided to keep an eye on her neighbours Melissa and Gabriel. Who was this blonde man to whom they apparently owed money? What did he have to do with Tim? And what had become of Malcolm after his desperate fight against Tim? Just thinking of the night at the harbour in Mooloolaba and of the murdered Martin made her feel queasy.

Andy decided to get some information about Astrid. How could such a pretty, quite likeable woman be friends with Tim, the mean policeman? Was her life in danger? Or did she herself participate in illicit wildlife trafficking and drug deals? Both she and Tim drove expensive cars. Was Astrid wealthy? Where did she live?

Lizzie decided to take good care of her children and to prevent them from getting involved in dangerous events. But how? She could neither lock them up at home nor watch them constantly. And what was going on with her neighbours? Maybe she should invite them to dinner one day.

Andy agreed with Lizzie's suggestion to invite Melissa and Gabriel. 'How about tomorrow evening?' he asked. 'I'm a bit puzzled, though, because you said you'd intend to keep the kids away from anything that is related to crimes! After all, Gabriel has admitted to stealing cars.'

Lizzie replied, 'Yes, he did! But I feel sorry for Melissa and Gabriel. It seems they have been through a rough time. Maybe we can somehow help them and prevent Melissa from suicidal thoughts.'

'Or prevent her from throwing heavy vases around!' Andy joked.

'I'll go over now and see if they'll be able to come tomorrow,' Lizzie said, ignoring Andy's remark. She quickly combed her unruly curls and went over to the neighbours. She knocked and shouted, 'Hello!' A bird chirped in the front garden, but nothing moved in the house. 'Hello there!' she shouted louder and knocked more vigorously. 'It's me, your neighbour Lizzie!' And now she heard approaching footsteps.

Melissa opened the door. 'Oh, hello! Um, Gabriel's not home.'

'Is he still in hospital?' Lizzie asked, startled.

'No, he's just gone out for a while. He'll be right back.'

'Oh, good! I don't want to bother you for long. I had the idea to invite you both for dinner tomorrow.'

'That's nice!' Melissa was pale and had dark rings under her eyes. She was barefoot, but wore long trousers and a warm jumper that was much too big for her and probably belonged to her husband.

'Tomorrow evening at about half past five? And are you allergic to anything? Are you vegetarian or vegan?'

'No, we can actually eat anything,' Melissa said. 'However, I don't like shrimps. They remind me of cockroaches or other disgusting insects, although Gabriel is always amused when I say so.'

Lizzie smiled. 'Don't worry, shrimps or prawns aren't really my thing, either.'

'Fine, see you tomorrow, then!'

'Great, I'm looking forward to it!'

Lizzie turned and almost cried out in horror at the sight of a tall man standing before her. He had long blonde hair, wore a floppy hat, a light brown jacket over a sand-coloured T-shirt, and black work boots. His dark blue jeans looked brand new.

'Alfred, what are you doing here again?' Melissa asked, instinctively taking a step back.

'Hi, Melissa! Hello, unknown lady!' the man greeted the two women with a slightly ironic smile.

'This is my neighbour,' Melissa explained.

Lizzie hesitated. Should she leave? But apparently Melissa was afraid of this man. Lizzie found him frightening too. He was very handsome, and his thick, long hair shone golden in the sunlight, but his blue eyes looked cold and calculating.

'Gabriel isn't in.' Melissa was backing away further.

A steep crease formed above Alfred's root of the nose and he growled gruffly: 'He never seems to be here. When is he coming home?'

'Who knows? Why don't you call him?' And Melissa quickly ran into the house, slamming the door behind her with a bang.

'Well, goodbye!' Lizzie said quickly, trying to get away.

But Alfred unexpectedly grabbed her arm. 'Wait! Have you seen Gabriel lately? I can never reach him, and he rarely answers his mobile anyway. Yesterday, I was here for nothing and I'm getting tired of it.'

Lizzie tore herself away in indignation and rubbed her arm. What a monster! she thought inwardly. Just then, she noticed a car slowing down and stopping at the side of the street. She said aloud, 'Here he comes!'

Gabriel was walking towards them. Lizzie detected a distraught look on his face, and with his ruff and a thick plaster on his head he looked quite pathetic.

'What's the matter with you?' asked Alfred. 'Have you been in another fight?'

Gabriel nodded briefly at Lizzie and then turned to Alfred.

'Nah, that was just a little accident. But why are you standing around here? Didn't Melissa let you in?'

'You know her!' Alfred said. 'She's suspicious as ever.'

No wonder, Lizzie thought.

'Anyway, I just want to talk to you about something, Gabriel! Come with me, we're going for a ride.' Putting his hand on Gabriel's shoulder, Alfred pushed him to his truck that was parked a bit further away under a large melaleuca tree.

'Goodbye!' Lizzie said and walked away. But she stopped in her own front yard, pretending to pluck some withered flowers from a shrub. As the truck drove by, she quickly read the number plate. At home she scribbled it down on a notepad before she'd forget it again.

'Are you writing a shopping list?' Andy asked. 'Will the neighbours come for dinner tomorrow?'

'Yes, I think so! But I only talked to Melissa about the invitation, because their friend was here again, wanting to discuss something with Gabriel. They have just left. The guy's name is Alfred, by the way, and I've written down his license number just in case.'

Andy laughed. 'Lizzie the detective!'

'After all, he could be the truck driver Alison had been watching,' Lizzie defended herself. 'And Alfred is a scary person. Melissa seems to be afraid of him, too.'

'There really are some nasty people in the world,' Andy said. 'Like Tim, for example, who keeps popping up in our lives. I wonder what Astrid sees in him? I hope she's not in any danger!

Because, um, if Tim were not only a smuggler of drugs or exotic animals, but also a mean murderer ...'

'Well, well, you are worrying about another woman,' Lizzie teased her husband.

'Yeah, she was actually very nice when I met her at Tim's house,' Andy said, somewhat embarrassed.

'Let's hope you're right about her! I'd already imagined that Astrid secretly tampered with the meter box to get rid of Tim. Because it's quite possible that she's the dangerous smuggler!'

Andy stared at her, aghast. 'What makes you think that? Are you crazy?' The next moment he laughed. 'Now I know why Anna and Sebastian always have such wild ideas – they must have inherited their tendency to vivid fantasies from you! But no, Astrid was sincerely concerned about her 'Timmy', as she affectionately called him.'

Lizzie smiled and wanted to reply, but was interrupted by the ringing of the telephone.

'I'll get it!' Andy grabbed the cordless phone. 'Hello? Oh, nice of you to call me back so quickly! I just spoke to the vet a few minutes ago and told him that I have an important message for you.' He whispered to Lizzie, 'It's Alison!'

He sat down in the living room, speaking with her for half an hour, even though he didn't know the woman. Finally, he said:

'I'm glad that Puck is well again! Yes, dogs really are the most loyal friends! And thanks so much! If you inform the police, it will take a load off my wife's mind! She believes that your testimony could be a step towards the arrest of the perpetrators. ... Yes, I think so, too, exactly! Goodbye!'

Lizzie wagged her finger at Andy. 'Do you always have to use me as an excuse for something?'

Andy smiled cheekily. 'After all, what is a wife for?'

'And what did you find out? Will Alison tell the police now what she'd observed? Is she even sure it was the same night Thomas was strangled?'

'Yes, one hundred percent! And she also spoke about another interesting incident. A woman got terribly upset because someone had allegedly poisoned her old trees. Claire – that is this woman's name – and her husband Geoff had a dense, evergreen hedge of tall trees along one side of a low fence. All of a sudden, these plants turned brown at the same time and then died. Claire and Geoff almost cried.'

'That's sad! But why did Alison tell you this story? Do these people live in her street?'

'No, but their back garden is adjoining to the one of Daniel's parents,' Andy said.

Lizzie's eyes widened. 'Wow! And what did their other neighbours say, the ones next to the tall hedge?'

'Only a single man lived there. Claire and Geoff suspected him, assuming that he wanted more sunlight for his new solar panels on the roof and therefore secretly poisoned their trees. But he vehemently denied it, saying that he was not even at home during that time, but sailing with a friend.' Andy pursed his lips. 'And you know what? Yesterday afternoon, Claire and Geoff told her that this neighbour had been killed on his own yacht! It was Martin!'

Lizzie was horrified. 'I don't believe it!'

'The tree story is interesting, isn't it? I wonder whether Thomas left Daniel's house at night because he heard something in the back garden and wanted to find out what was going on.'

'But he allegedly had headphones on, watching a movie.'

'Um, yeah! Besides, it wasn't his own house. Why should he even care about Daniel's neighbours?'

'Well, if I saw someone fiddling around with a poison spray in the middle of the night, or jumping over a fence, I would be suspicious too,' Lizzie said. 'And who knows, maybe Thomas had already switched off the movie by then.'

'It still is a great mystery to me. Who poisoned the trees of Claire and Geoff? Martin must have been innocent, as he was sailing back then.'

'No idea! Anyway, I'm glad we have our dogs! I'm sure they'd make a lot of noise if anyone were to enter our garden.'

'I'm not so sure!' Andy said with a grin.

'By the way, we might not keep our Lilly much longer. A young couple with a child has expressed interest in her. They'd like to visit us next week to get to know her.'

'Oh!' A shadow flew across Andy's face.

Lizzie smiled sadly. 'Partings are always so hard! But on the phone, the woman made a very nice impression to me. And they already have another young dog. I've asked them to bring it along to see if it could be a good playmate for Lilly. Because our dear protégé shall find a happy permanent new home!'

# 53 FITNESS PARK

Sebastian and his girlfriend were sitting on a bench in the fitness park near the campsite, waiting for Arielle and Jack. Susi and Lilly were sniffing around while Kirsty watched a scrub-turkey. It ran quickly across the lawn and then into the bushland at the dunes. Kirsty was looking quite somber. Sebastian had already noticed her bad mood at school this morning, but now he was feeling way too uncomfortable to cheer her up. He touched his stomach and moaned.

'What's wrong?' Kirsty asked. 'Do you have a sore tummy?'

'Yes, silly me! I ate far too much last night. Whenever we have guests over, my mother serves lots of delicious food. And yesterday Melissa and Gabriel had dinner with us.'

'How did it go?'

'In the beginning, everybody seemed a bit shy, but later we actually had a nice chat. Indeed, Gabriel was really funny.'

'I thought you and Anna regarded him as being creepy?'

'Yes, we did at first. And he can be a bit hot-headed at times – just like you,' he teased Kirsty, who promptly looked even grumpier than before. 'He did a few crooked things in the past, and currently he's facing criminal proceedings for car theft, but overall, he doesn't seem so bad. And even though Gabriel and Melissa have some nasty disputes every now and then, they seem to be very fond of each other.' Sebastian patted the dogs. 'It's possible that Lilly will go into a new home. On Wednesday someone will come to see her. I guess that's another reason for my stomachaches.'

'Really? How sad for you!' Kirsty also bent over to Lilly now, gently scratching her ears. Immediately, Susi squeezed herself between the two of them, and Kirsty's face brightened. Smiling, she said, 'Susi, you are and always will be the number one in the Kuhlmann family, so you shouldn't be jealous at all!'

'Yeah, we'll never give away our Susi,' Sebastian caressed the dog's chest, 'but we'll have to wait and see about Lilly. We are going to check out the family that wants to adopt her!'

'Oh, here they come!' Kirsty said. 'Hello!' she shouted from afar. She and Sebastian watched their friends strolling towards them. Arielle and Jack were holding hands, obviously being very amused about something.

'Where's Arielle's dog?' Sebastian wondered.

'Max got an injured paw and has to take it easy for a while,' Kirsty explained.

'Hi! What's so funny?' Sebastian asked as the couple arrived.

Arielle giggled. 'Oh, Jack has just made up a joke about two teachers. Actually, it was pretty stupid, and I only laughed because of Jack's funny way of talking.'

Jack pretended to be indignant. 'My joke was great! So, listen carefully!' Interrupted by several bouts of laughter, he repeated the rather long joke for Sebastian and Kirsty. But they only managed a strained smile.

Jack sighed. 'What's the matter with you guys?'

'Kirsty's in a bad mood all day, and I've got a stomachache,' Sebastian replied.

Arielle looked at her friends with concern, but Jack said boldly, 'Pull-ups could be a remedy! Let's go! Wanna bet I'll win?' He briskly walked to the station in the park, where you could do gymnastics on rings that were attached to thick chains hanging down from a bar. A scrub-turkey that had been sitting on top flew away in fright, and now even Kirsty had to laugh.

'Jack the scarecrow!' she shouted.

Sebastian struggled to calm down Susi and Lilly, as they wanted to chase after the scrub-turkey. He firmly commanded, 'Sit! Stay! No hunting!'

'Ten, eleven, twelve ...' Jack counted his pull-ups on the rings.

Kirsty joined in, grabbing the lower hanging rings next to him.

'Go, get him, Kirsty!' Arielle cheered her on.

'No!' Sebastian cried so loudly that Arielle froze and Jack almost fell off the rings. Kirsty, on the other hand, continued her exercises, stubborn and grim. Sebastian had let go of the leashes as soon as the dogs had sat down obediently beside him, and now they were suddenly taking off. Not after the scrub-turkey towards the dunes, though, but towards David Low Way.

'Come back!' Sebastian shouted and followed them, downright sick with fear they might run onto the main road. There was heavy traffic at this time of day!

'Susi! Lilly! Come here!'

Then, to his great relief, he spotted Annette, an elegantly dressed lady his mother's age, with her snow-white dog on the footpath. Daisy, a beautiful terrier mix, was Susi's best friend. No wonder Susi was so excited and eager to meet her! Daisy tugged wildly on the leash, and now the two dogs jumped around each other joyfully, while Lilly curiously sniffed at Daisy's butt.

Sebastian scolded, 'Naughty dogs, how dare you run away like that!' He apologised to Annette and quickly grabbed the dog leads that had got tangled up with Daisy's leash. When he saw Susi's shining eyes, his anger disappeared and he grinned.

'Susi and Daisy really love each other, hey?'

'Yes, they are best mates! And how are your parents and your sister doing? I haven't seen them for ages. You must all visit me sometime!' Looking at Lilly, she added, 'Together with Susi and your new dog, of course!'

The thought that Lilly might not stay with them for much longer stung Sebastian. 'Do my parents have your address?'

'No, my husband and I have just moved. Wait, I'll give you my new contact details right away.' Annette opened her fancy handbag, searching for a pen and some paper. After writing down her name, she suddenly paused. 'It's a bit scary because the previous owner of our house was murdered, but – um, well – we're not superstitious after all.' She scribbled on and handed Sebastian the piece of paper. 'Fortunately, he was not killed in his home.' She blushed like a young girl. 'Oh, well, I mean, lucky for us, because ...'

Sebastian cut in, 'Was Martin the previous owner? The man who was shot in Mooloolaba?'

Annette was puzzled. 'Yes, exactly! Did you know him?'

'No, but my sister was there.'

'What?'

'Well, not on the yacht, but in the harbour.' Sebastian told her the whole story, embellishing in every detail how bravely and selflessly Anna had acted. For now, he completely forgot his friends in the park and his stomachache as well.

Annette listened to him spellbound. It was only when Daisy growled at Lilly that her attention was distracted. 'Look, I have to go. But I can tell you this: Martin's house had been thoroughly investigated by the police and forensic experts before they approved of the real estate listing. And allegedly they'd found several kilos of drugs and some exotic animals in his house! Even now, Daisy is always snooping around with particular interest in a room where he'd kept the cages.'

'Really? What kind of animals were they?'

Annette shook with disgust.

'Mostly lizards and snakes, as far as I know. In the beginning, I hardly dared to open a door because I was afraid that a snake might have escaped and be lying in wait!'

She laughed.

'But by now Daisy should have found all animals on the property for sure. Unfortunately, she is a cruel hunter. Once she'd killed several chickens on a farm before I could stop her. Hard to believe, as she is such a cute little dog otherwise!'

Looking tenderly at Daisy, she stroked her fuzzy fur.

'But now I must go. See you! Come on, Daisy!'

Susi was visibly sad to leave her friend. Several times she turned around with a longing expression when Sebastian led her and Lilly back to the park. Meanwhile, his friends were exercising at another station. Arielle was already red in the face from all the effort she'd put in.

'So, here I am again,' Sebastian said good-naturedly. 'Who's won the chin-ups?'

'Jack!' Arielle replied.

'Other people seem to be more important to you than us!' Kirsty hissed at him. 'We've been waiting for you for ages! We were going to play Frisbee by the sea instead of hanging around in this park for hours!'

Sebastian got furious. 'You'd better stayed at home today! I can't stand your bad mood anymore, it's terrible!'

'Then go to hell!' Kirsty shouted angrily.

'Hey hey, don't growl at each other, you're no snappy dogs,' Jack tried to placate his friends.

Arielle looked from one to the other and didn't know what to say. She hated arguments.

'Who was that snazzy lady?' Jack asked, balancing on a wooden beam.

'An old friend of ours. We met her during a walk because her Daisy and our Susi loved each other at first sight.' Sebastian scratched his head thoughtfully, paused for a moment and then blurted out:

'Annette has told me the most interesting news! She and her husband moved into Martin's house, even though they knew he had been killed. And he really was a smuggler!'

On the way to the sea, he reported what he'd just learned from Annette. Kirsty trudged along in gloom and silence, but Jack and Arielle asked countless questions. As soon as they reached the beach, Sebastian let the dogs off the leash and they raced around, enjoying their freedom. The waves roared loudly and menacingly, the sky was cloudy, and a strong wind made the four friends realise that playing Frisbee would make little sense that afternoon. Sebastian wasn't sure if the gale or Kirsty's anger were responsible for the tears in her eyes. His stomach pains had gone away, but he suddenly felt completely drained and tired. A short time later everyone was on their way home.

# 54 THE GREENHOUSE

A few days later, the wind blew even stronger. But it had puffed away all the gloomy clouds and conjured up a bright blue sky. In the late morning, Lizzie decided to take Susi for a walk to Annette's house. Playing with Daisy, Susi would certainly forget her grief about Lilly's absence. Lizzie had to admit to herself that she was also curious to see Martin's former house. She wondered why the police had found drugs and exotic animals there only after his death. Had Martin used a different hiding place in the past? Or had he received a tip-off prior to the first search of his house that allowed him to remove all traces just in time? And what had been his connection to Malcolm and Tim? Who had shot Martin, and why? She was horror-struck thinking of her daughter and Bruce, having been so close to the scene of the crime. She fervently hoped that someone would finally shed light upon the matter so that she and her family would be able to put an end to their grueling deliberations, once and for all.

Directly after school, Anna visited Bruce who had the afternoon off. They hugged and kissed each other lovingly and then sat down in the living room. Soft music emitted from Lucy's room, the coffee machine in the kitchen made hissing and gurgling sounds, and the washing machine was humming in the background. A hint of lavender mingled with the aromatic smell of freshly brewed coffee.

'Our Lilly is no longer with us. She was adopted yesterday,' Anna said after a while.

'Oh no, that's sad for you, isn't it?'

'Yes, of course, we miss her very much! But the family that adopted her was super nice, and Lilly, strangely enough, jumped into their car without a second thought. She also got on very well with their other dog, a young Yorkshire Terrier. After all, that's the main thing for us, to know that our foster dogs are in good hands.' Despite these words Anna looked distressed.

'And Susi? How did she react?' Bruce asked.

'Well, she seemed partly sad and partly glad.' Anna was smiling now. 'She was always a little jealous, and now she has – at least temporarily – our undivided attention again.'

Bruce laughed. 'Knowing you, you'll soon have a new foster dog!'

'I think so, too! Usually it never takes long, because there are so many dogs that end up with the rescue organisation. I'm already curious to see what kind of doggie we'll get next. Hopefully a nice one that Susi likes, too!'

'I'll keep my fingers crossed. By the way, things are going to change here as well. Lucy will move to her new boyfriend next week and Oliver will take over her room.'

'Oh, that's good for you and Oliver!' Anna said.

'Yes, we are looking forward to it! But I don't want the Hot Ears playing music here in the house, that would be too loud.'

'I can understand that! Where do they normally meet for rehearsals?'

'So far, they've been playing in a double garage on a huge plot of land. It was perfect! But now the owner wants to divide his property and build two new houses on it. Soon he'll tear down his old house and the garage. Therefore, Oliver and his friends are looking for another place. One that's cheap enough and won't upset anyone in the area.'

There was a loud rumble coming from the laundry and Bruce jumped up. 'I have to hold on to the washing machine, the old thing sometimes jumps around wildly when it's spinning. Lucy must have overloaded it.'

While Bruce was busy, Anna looked around the room. Some of the pictures had already disappeared from the walls, leaving behind light traces. To her surprise, the picture of the cute monkey on the giant turtle, painted by Lucy herself, was still hanging in the same place where she had often admired it.

Lucy showed up at the door. 'Would you like a cup of coffee or tea?'

'Do you have mint tea?'

'I'm sure we do.'

Anna followed her into the kitchen and chuckled.

'The coffee machine sounds as if someone's sucking on a straw with all his might to get the last drop of his milkshake.'

Lucy grinned. 'You're right!'

She filled the kettle, handed Anna a mug with a tea bag and poured herself a cup of the fresh coffee.

'Too bad coffee never tastes as good as it smells,' Anna said.

'Leave some for me!' Bruce called out from the laundry.

Lucy and Anna sat down with their drinks in the living room, and Bruce joined them with a tiny cup of coffee.

Lucy said, 'You are so brave, Anna! Bruce told me how you threw yourself into the cold, black water to help a stranger. You should get a medal for that!'

'Nonsense!' Anna mumbled and blushed.

Once again, a racket echoed from the laundry, and this time Lucy hurried to stabilise the wandering, rumbling washing machine. Bruce went quietly whistling into the kitchen to refill his cup and look for something to eat, when Oliver came into the house. He waved to Anna, groaned loudly, took a large rucksack from his back and put it on the floor.

Anna smiled at him. 'Hello! I thought you weren't moving in till next week!'

'Yeah, but I've already started packing as I won't have much time in the next few days.'

He plopped himself down in an armchair.

'You can't imagine the enormous amount of junk Oliver has accumulated!' Bruce returned with a bag of chips, sat down next to Anna and chuckled. 'I'm a bit worried about how much stuff he'll bring here. Well, at least we'll soon have a better washing machine, a new radio and a popcorn machine.'

'I see! So, my puny possessions were the real reason for inviting me to be your flat-mate?' Oliver sneered. 'Lucky for you, I'll also bring my giant TV.'

'Are you still looking for a rehearsal room?' Anna asked him.

'We've just found one. But it's a bit weird!' Oliver was noisily munching some chips, and Anna had to grin. With his chubby face, big round eyes and fuzzy head, he looked more like a little boy than a rock star at the moment.

Bruce looked at him curiously. 'Why's that?'

'Recently, I spotted an ad on the Internet. Someone wants to rent out a building near Valdora. And so, yesterday Angus and I went there to check it out and to meet Greg, the owner. He apologised for the poor condition of the building that he offers for rent, saying that it was totally neglected for some time. Originally it was his parents' greenhouse, but they moved to a retirement home a few months ago. And now Greg is living on this property. However, he is not interested in plants at all, and the greenhouse is quite far away from his house.' Oliver laughed. 'It was indeed a wild jungle! The narrow path leading there was almost overgrown. Angus even hit his nose once when he stumbled over a thick tree root. But when we saw the greenhouse, we were both thrilled. It was actually more like a wintergarden, with glass facades on two sides and a large glass dome on the roof. The windows were filthy, everything was full of weeds and cobwebs, and it stank badly decomposed. But we think we could easily turn it into an awesome place.' Oliver beamed. 'Luckily, there is water supply and an outhouse. And above all, we wouldn't disturb a soul with our music. Greg said he'd clean everything up, install new electrical wiring, tear down the rotten raised garden beds, and lay new pavers. And we could even build a stage if we were to supply the timber and sign a year's contract.'

'I don't know!' Bruce said with a frown. 'It seems rather impractical if you have to bush-bash your way through this jungle every time. Especially at night when it's pitch-black.'

'Exactly what Angus said. But Greg intends to construct a new path from a side road, where we could also park the cars. That way, we wouldn't have to walk past his house, and so we'd hardly bother him. And he doesn't charge much rent and seems to be a very nice and honest man.'

'Well, it sounds super to me! Even if it's a bit of a pity not to use the old nursery for plant cultivation anymore. But what did you mean by your remark that it was weird?' Anna asked.

Oliver rubbed his nose. 'As I said, the stench in that greenhouse was pretty bad. Do you know the smell of stale water in a flower vase? That's what it smelled like, really nasty. And what we discovered then was disgusting! Angus got really pasty!'

'Come on, tell us!' Bruce said impatiently.

'In one corner, there was a huge old cupboard with a padlock. Greg had no idea where the key would be, but the smell definitely came from there. He looked for a suitable tool, finally found one and cleverly picked the lock with it.'

'And what was in the cupboard?' Anna asked excitedly.

'I hope it wasn't a half-rotten corpse,' Bruce joked.

Lucy had hung the washing out to dry and was returning to the living room when she heard Bruce's last words. She was so shocked that she forgot to greet Oliver and asked, 'Oh no, there was another dead body?'

Bruce kept grinning until Oliver said, 'More than one, actually!'

'What?' Anna and Lucy shouted.

'Yeah, there were seven or eight.'

Bruce's grin vanished. But then he noticed a sparkle in Oliver's eyes. 'You're pulling our legs,' he said indignantly.

Oliver laughed. 'You've got me all figured out! Unfortunately, I'm not a very good actor. We did discover some corpses, though. However, they weren't humans, but rats.'

'In a locked cupboard?' Anna asked incredulously.

'Yes, I guess they'd bitten their way through the thin back wall, which was made of plywood and pretty damp and rotten anyway.'

'What were rats doing in the cupboard? And why did they die?' Lucy wondered.

'Greg suspected that his parents had stored rat poison in it. And the poor rats died after their last meal,' Oliver explained.

'That's impossible! Normally rat poison doesn't work that fast, does it?' Anna asked.

'I don't know! Anyway, it wasn't a pretty sight. And then Greg found another body in the room.'

'Bullshit!' Bruce said.

'No, it's a fact! Greg is an electrician and tried to find out why the electricity in the greenhouse had been cut off. After some tests, he checked a socket in the wall and ... Bingo! ... he found a broken cable. And there was this rat! With eyes wide open and limbs outstretched, it was staring at us, and its hair was standing on end. Really scary! The poor rat looked like a crazy caricature, and seemed almost alive. But it had been electrocuted and was dead as a doornail.'

Lucy squealed. 'That sounds scary.'

'Poor animal!' Anna said. 'I'm not afraid of rats, but I have screamed loudly once when I opened our compost bin and discovered a fat rat in it, eating the vegetable leftovers with relish. And another time I found a snake in there.'

'Hopefully nobody will nibble on our cables or hide inside my guitar,' Oliver said.

'Isn't such a greenhouse too humid for you?' Bruce asked, grinning. 'And in summer it might get too hot for the Hot Ears!'

Oliver replied, 'We'll see. If necessary, we'll install some kind of sun protection, like shade cloth or curtains. And the glass dome could be sprayed with washable white lime paint. We simply have to test how everything works and whether the acoustics are reasonably good. The rest of our band wants to take a closer look next weekend, and I'm sure they'll like it. Angus already got all sorts of ideas! For example, he suggested to beautify the garden around the house and have an open-air concert sometime. Just for a small group, of course, and if Greg agrees.'

'Super!' Lucy was impressed.

Anna said, 'You know what? After we'd moved to Coolum Beach, my father started his own business with another electrician, also named Greg. I wonder if it's the same guy.'

'What does he look like?' Oliver asked.

Anna described Andy's partner, and Oliver nodded. 'Yep, that must be him. He's a very nice guy. So, keep your fingers crossed that everything will work out for the Hot Ears! You might as well visit our future rehearsal room yourselves. And you should meet Celina, our new lead singer. Did I tell you that she's from Ireland originally? Her voice is absolutely stunning!'

'Sounds great!' Bruce said. 'I'll help you set up the stage if you want.'

'That would be awesome!' Oliver was pleased.

'Anna, before I forget …' Lucy got up, went to her painting of the monkey on the turtle, took it off the hook and handed it to Anna. 'This is for you because you like it so much.'

'Wow, thank you, that's so nice!' Now Anna was also beaming with joy.

# 55 THE WIG

Annette had been very pleased about Lizzie's unexpected visit, and her dog Daisy had been absolutely delighted to see Susi again. The women planned to let their pets play together more often in the future, as these two dogs just loved each other. They would even eat peacefully from the same bowl. Watching them, nobody could deny that love at first sight and true friendship did exist among animals. On the way home, Lizzie found it somewhat strange to be alone with Susi. Although it was easier to take care of just one dog, she missed the droll Lilly with her bushy eyebrows and protruding teeth. Hopefully she would get along well with her new family!

'We'll get you a little playmate again soon, okay?' she assured Susi, patting her head briefly. Susi looked up, alarmed. Was there another monster swooping down on them? In panic, she pulled the leash to get herself and Lizzie out of the danger zone. Lizzie almost fell but had to grin when she spotted several skydivers and heard a distant whoop. Unfortunately, Susi could not be calmed down and Lizzie unintentionally started to jog to keep up with her speed.

'Who is leading whom for a walk?' someone shouted to her in a mocking voice from a car.

'Andy! What are you doing here?' Lizzie was surprised to see her husband.

'I have just finished a job. Get in quickly, then I'll drive you home and I'll have my lunch break there.'

Relieved, Susi jumped into the back seat. The danger was over, because in the car they were safe from the monsters! Weren't they? Just in case, she squeezed herself into the narrow gap on the floor behind Lizzie's seat.

'Now, tell me! Did you find anything special in the former home of the murder victim?' Andy asked his wife.

Lizzie smiled. 'You really know me too well. Yep, that was one of my reasons for visiting Annette. I was curious. But of course, there was nothing extraordinary to see.'

'Nothing at all?'

'Annette showed me the room where Martin allegedly kept the smuggled wildlife. And Susi and Daisy were quite excited. I guess there are still some special smells lingering.' Lizzie smiled. 'The doggies played like crazy and then cuddled up lovingly afterwards, just cute. Annette and I intend to meet more often and also help each other whenever we need a dog sitter.'

'Good idea!'

Andy parked the car in their driveway. Having a quick lunch, he told his wife, 'Later on today, Greg and I are going to install new power cables on his own property. It's a bigger job as he wants to replace the lines to his old greenhouse.'

'I didn't know he likes gardening.'

'He doesn't. But he moved into his parents' house after they had to go to a retirement home for health reasons. His parents were passionate hobby gardeners, but in the end, they could no longer cope with the work, and the once very beautiful garden has turned into a jungle. Greg has already torn down two foil houses. He just has too little time to take care of everything besides his job. That's why he's now thinking about repairing his greenhouse. He intends to rent it out to people who could use it as an art studio or a men's shed or whatever.'

'A men's shed or a men's pub?' Lizzie asked.

Andy laughed. 'I hardly think Greg would like any tenants getting senselessly drunk on his property. But it sounds nice to let them do their hobbies.'

'And what do the neighbours say?'

'They're all far enough away.'

'Not like our place!' Lizzie said. 'At any rate, I wouldn't like to have loud craftsmen or sculptors right next door. I'd rather have a painter in his studio.' In that very instant, she heard a moaning, and Susie also pricked up her ears. 'What was that?' Lizzie asked anxiously.

'It's probably Melissa!' Andy called out and jumped up. 'I'm going over there.'

'I'll go with you.'

The couple feared the worst. After her unsuccessful suicide attempt, Melissa had to take certain drugs prescribed by her doctor. But she was suffering from severe withdrawal symptoms since she'd stopped consuming the terrible drug 'FUN'. Both Andy and Lizzie wanted to keep an eye on her, without being too intrusive. At the same time, they were a bit scared of her. After all, she had recently attacked her own husband, hitting him on the head!

Andy knocked loudly at the door of the neighbours' house. 'Hello, is anyone home?' Lizzie shouted.

Again, they heard a pitiful noise, this time very close, and Susi, who had stayed in her own front yard, whimpered softly. Andy and Lizzie looked at each other indecisively. What should they do? Then the door opened with an unexpected swing, and Alfred fell straight into their arms.

'Help!' he gurgled hoarsely. His eyes rolled and he slumped to the floor.

Andy bent over to him in genuine concern, and now Melissa rushed towards them. Her face was angry and distorted.

'You snoopers!' she cried. 'Why do you always interfere in my life? Get out of here!' She uttered nasty insults until her voice broke and turned into a hysterical howl.

Lizzie was paralysed with shock as Andy carefully turned Alfred to his side and felt his pulse beat. Was he still alive? What was wrong with him?

'He got what he deserved!' Melissa yelled.

Hateful, she spat on Alfred. 'Today you had a chance to test your own medicine. Did you like it? You can't threaten us anymore, you bastard! Never again!'

The next moment she turned back to Andy and Lizzie.

'Get out of here, you snitches! Get out!'

Her lunatic gaze wandered around, then fell on the coat rack in the hallway, and in a rage, she grabbed a wooden hanger and hit Andy on the head with it.

'Stop!' Lizzie cried in indignation. 'Leave my Andy alone!'

She now sprang into action, clutching Melissa's arm, horrified to see how strong the thin and seemingly fragile woman was. Andy came to her aid, but Melissa was a fury gone wild. Again and again, she tore loose and flailed around, and at the same time she shouted obscene insults at them.

There was an angry, deep barking, and Susi came running with tremendous leaps and grabbed Melissa's hand that was just about to reach out for Lizzie again. Melissa let out a shrill cry of pain and tried to kick the dog, but hit Andy's leg instead. Andy cursed and now threw himself with all his weight on the woman, falling with her to the floor. Susi leapt nimbly to the side, bared her teeth and growled as threateningly as never before, just a few millimetres from Melissa's face. Lizzie and Andy were amazed. What had become of their normally so timid dog?

'Well done, Susi, you're a loyal friend!' Lizzie praised her in a gentle tone to calm her down.

Slowly, she stood up and reached out her hand to help Andy up. A thin trail of blood ran from his left ear to his chin and his right cheek was bluish and swollen. Melissa remained motionless on the carpet runner. Her demonic grimace suddenly turned into the tearful face of a vulnerable young woman, and Lizzie instantly took pity on her.

'We just wanted to help you,' she said softly.

Melissa stared at her in silence as tears rolled down her cheeks. Alfred didn't move.

'What's going on here?' asked a man in a commanding voice.

'Mr. Little!' Andy was so relieved that he almost hugged Ivory's father and completely forgot that he was supposed to call him Barry. 'We need a doctor! I have no idea if this man is still alive. I could not find any pulse at all.'

'An ambulance is on its way. Somebody in your street has called the police and the ambulance, too,' Mr. Little replied.

'I have poisoned Alfred,' Melissa now confessed. 'With his own drugs called 'FUN' which are anything but fun.'

Mr. Little crouched down next to Alfred, checking if he needed to use first aid for resuscitation. Melissa ran her shaking fingers through her hair and her wig slipped off. She hastily moved it back into position with both hands, and Lizzie noticed that her right hand had slight traces of Susi's teeth, but no blood.

In a strangely flat voice, Melissa told the others, without being asked, what had driven her to her deed:

'Alfred has been harassing us for a long time. At the beginning he didn't seem so bad, and my husband was glad to get a job. He helped him with deliveries from time to time; mostly they transported furniture and other stuff in Alfred's car. About half a year ago, there was a terrible accident in which Alfred knocked out a young woman on her moped. It wasn't his fault at all, but he had drunk a few bottles of beer beforehand, and therefore, he didn't want to have anything to do with the police. He was afraid of losing his driving license, and so, he just took off and let her die! Gabriel was sitting next to him when it happened. He was completely shocked and could hardly believe that Alfred continued driving as if nothing had happened.'

She swallowed audibly and raised her hand to wipe her eyes. Immediately, Susi growled threateningly.

'When my husband came home that day, I knew right away that something terrible must have happened. Gabriel was completely distraught. And Alfred put so much pressure on him that he didn't dare tell a soul but me about the incident. But Gabriel could never forget the gruesome scene, day and night it went on in his mind, again and again he heard the impact and saw the woman flying through the air, without being able to help her. He suffered from nightmares and began to drink booze and smoke like crazy. We fought all the time, and of course it didn't help that neither of us could find a permanent job. And I freaked out whenever Gabriel drove his car after he had a few beers. One night, he almost hit somebody, too. And I blamed him, even though that stupid woman didn't have any lights on her bicycle and was riding in the middle of the street.'

Melissa put her hand across her face with a nervous movement, and Susi continued to keep a watchful eye on her, ready to assist Andy and Lizzie if necessary. Melissa glanced briefly at the dog, and a sad smile played on her pale lips.

'Very often, I was so depressed that I took all kinds of sedatives to numb myself. Sometimes I even thought of suicide. And one day, I actually wanted to drown myself in the sea when Alfred happened to notice me and sat down next to me.'

She gave Andy, who already knew a part of this story, a fleeting glance.

'Alfred always pretended he'd come to my rescue back then. Ha, my ass! He just made me a user of that 'FUN', a terrible and far too expensive stuff. After that, everything only got worse. I could sleep better, but the 'FUN' made me puke, and my whole body started to itch like crazy. I also lost my beautiful hair!' she suddenly screamed in a new rage, ripping the wig off her head and throwing it away.

Everyone stared at her bald skull, on which only a few single tufts of hair were growing. The pale scalp was covered with flaming red, inflamed spots and brown scars.

'Yes, just stare at me! I know how ugly I am!' she screamed.

Lizzie feared another attack of frenzy and retreated in fear. 'Watch out, Andy!' she warned her husband.

'Mr. Little, can you ...' Andy began, but was distracted by his dog.

Susi had raced after the wig, grabbed it, dropped it in front of Melissa and looked at her expectantly. Melissa giggled and then snorted loudly. She writhed with laughter, rolled around on the floor and laughed and cried at the same time. Barry Little had seen a lot in his career as a policeman, but never anything like this! With a puzzled and helpless expression, he watched the woman he should have arrested on the spot.

In the meantime, a group of curious neighbours had joined them, and a fat man was already taking photos. Fortunately, an ambulance appeared now.

Barry pulled himself together, briefly told the paramedics the most important facts and ordered the onlookers to leave them alone. He then called for police reinforcements by mobile phone.

A paramedic hurried to Alfred. 'He is still alive,' she said. 'But we must get him to hospital as soon as possible.'

'He's alive?' Melissa asked stunned, only to laugh hysterically the next moment.

'We better look after this woman, too,' said an older paramedic.

'I'm going with you,' Barry decided. 'She is very dangerous, not only to others, but to herself.'

He pulled her up gently, spoke to her and handcuffed her. Addressing Lizzie and Andy, he said: 'I'll send one of my colleagues to take your statement. I'll be in touch with you later, okay?' Worried, he eyed the couple who was looking pretty upset.

Lizzie nodded.

Andy said, 'Yes, all right! I got to get to work, though.'

'Can't it wait?' Barry asked. 'You better take it easy and cool your cheek. And tend to your ear, it got a bad scratch!'

Andy carefully touched the bump on his cheek.

'My head is not too bad, but my knee hurts like hell. Well, I could try and postpone the job.'

'Come on, Susi!' Lizzie ordered. 'Let's go home!'

She shooed away a neighbour who wanted to ask her questions. 'Later!' she said, harsher than she meant to.

# 56 RIDING A HIGH WAVE

Sebastian and Kirsty had reconciled and were in a cheerful mood. After school, they cycled with Arielle and Jack to Sebastian's house, intending to practise for an upcoming math exam. Susi rushed to the door to greet Sebastian and Kirsty, but timidly backed away from Arielle and Jack.

'Now don't be such a coward,' Sebastian scolded her. 'You've known my friends for a long time.'

'When it comes down to it, Susi is really brave,' his father defended the dog.

'Hi, Daddy, you are at home already? But what happened to you? You look awful!' Sebastian gazed at his father with a startled expression.

By now Andy's right cheek was even more swollen and turned dark purple, and a plaster was stuck to his left ear.

'Did you play rugby league?' Jack asked bluntly.

Arielle nudged him in the side, but Andy replied friendly, 'I sure look like it, don't I? But no, I never played rugby in my life. Unfortunately, there an incident with a neighbour who'd gone wild ...'

'Hello kids, come into the living room for a while! Would you like some apple juice?' Lizzie cut in.

'Yes, I'd love to!' said everyone except Arielle who preferred a glass of water. Lizzie prepared tea for Andy and herself, and then everyone gathered in the living room. Andy sat down in a comfortable reclining chair where he could stretch out his sore leg. Sebastian put a bowl of coconut biscuits on the table. The students were quite happy to postpone their math studies, all listening eagerly to the interesting report from Sebastian's parents.

'Is Melissa going to jail now?' Sebastian asked, stroking Susi who was lying at his feet, now quite relaxed.

'I suppose so! She really is a dangerous person!' Lizzie sighed. 'Still, I do feel sorry for her. Perhaps some professional therapy will help her to get back on track in the future.'

'Nah, I have little sympathy for her. She's one coldblooded woman, trying to kill Alfred! She must have really hated him, to give him that gruesome drug!' Jack shivered at the thought.

Lizzie nodded. 'No wonder, after what she said about Alfred. The guy literally stepped over dead bodies! But when he kept coming to their house, trying to collect his money and intimidating them, I guess she finally had enough and she took the offensive. Whether she'd planned it beforehand or whether it was a spontaneous idea to poison him remains to be clarified. I don't want to judge Melissa hastily, and a judge must decide whether she will be held responsible for attempted manslaughter or murder.' She carefully sipped her hot tea.

'In any case, it was frightening how hysterical Melissa reacted, getting herself into a rage. Even with our combined forces, Andy and I could hardly fend her off, although she is actually a petite woman. You can see how badly she mauled poor Andy. Good that Susi came to our help!'

Gratefully, she looked at her dog.

'I could hardly believe how threatening our dear, shy Susi growled and snarled. She was completely transformed. But then she suddenly rediscovered her usual eagerness to play – and with Melissa's wig of all things.'

Andy tried to laugh, but it was too painful with the swollen cheek.

'Susi must have sensed when the danger was over and Melissa was no longer posing a threat,' Lizzie said. 'Animals have excellent instincts.'

Taking a biscuit, Jack asked: 'What exactly did Melissa's husband do for a living? He worked for both Martin and Alfred?'

'Yes, he even stole cars for Martin back then,' Sebastian said, gallantly handing the bowl with the biscuits to Kirsty and Arielle before serving himself. 'Somehow he hooked up with the wrong crowd.'

Kirsty took a bite and lost a crumb that Susi quickly gulped down. Lizzie said, 'And then Martin was murdered, still owing Gabriel about a thousand dollars for some work.'

'This exacerbated Gabriel's problems to pay for the expensive drugs,' Andy added thoughtfully. 'In any case, it looks as if Alfred was a mean drug dealer. And he made Melissa addicted to the terrible drug.'

'I wonder if Alfred sold the 'FUN' to many customers,' Arielle said.

'I would never touch that stuff,' Lizzie replied. 'Even if you were to feel a positive effect, for maybe half an hour or so, I can't understand why anyone would put up with the side effects such as nausea, itching and hair loss. Or who'd even risk a premature death! It's absolutely foolish! I prefer to spend my money on other things. And Melissa's skin looked so raw and inflamed, just nasty!'

'But why was Gabriel so very much afraid of Alfred? If he'd reported the tragic accident of that woman on the moped, she might have been saved.' Kirsty's eyes glittered.

Sebastian could sense how outraged she was and took her hand lovingly. 'Alfred must have known something about a dark secret of Gabriel and Melissa and blackmailed them. But what could that have been?'

Everyone looked at each other, at their wit's ends, until Lizzie said, 'Perhaps Gabriel had committed some other crime that Alfred knew about ...'

'That's it!' Jack shouted excitedly. 'Alfred must have found out that Gabriel was stealing cars. And that's why he was able to pressure him.' His triumphant grin made everyone smile.

'Some people are good at intimidating people anyway,' Kirsty said. 'Like our former English teacher, Mrs. Jane!'

'Oh yes, she always made me feel like a rabbit in front of a snake. And Alfred is like that. At first, I didn't like Gabriel either, but later he seemed quite nice,' Sebastian said. 'He is, um, well, like a man with a rough exterior and a soft heart.'

Andy smiled amusedly, although he inwardly agreed with his son.

'And what now? Will Gabriel have to go to jail?' Arielle asked.

'If he is lucky, he'll get away with a fine and his relatives can help him to pay off his debts,' Andy said. 'And yesterday I came up with an idea that I will propose to him. He might be able to start his own business as a mechanic offering mobile services. Then he wouldn't need a proper workshop but just a mobile phone, a car and his tools. In any case, I will ask him to repair our Toyota; that is, if he doesn't ask too much money for it. Of course, he should give me a fee proposal first.'

Lizzie was sceptical. 'You think so? Working independently is not for everyone. And it can take a while to build up a good clientele. Plus, he'll have to advertise his services, take out professional insurance and ...'

'You're right,' Andy interrupted his wife. 'It's not easy, we all know that. But it might be worth a try.'

Again, his smile was a little distorted and Sebastian looked compassionately at his father. He had never seen him in such a pitiful state before, and he was glad that Melissa hadn't hurt his mother, too. It was hard to fathom that his friendly, peaceful parents had got into a fight! What would Anna say to that? He released his hand from Kirsty's, smoothed his tousled hair thoughtfully and then said:

'It's frightening how quickly some people freak out! Do you remember the photos of Gabriel and Steven, the two surfers, fighting on the beach? Thomas had written about it on his Facebook page: 'RIDING A HIGH WAVE CAN LEAD TO WAVES OF VIOLENCE'. What did he mean by that?'

'Riding a high wave – um, it makes me think of a person who strives for something better in life. Someone who wants to get more power, fame or money,' Jack pondered. 'And if he lies and cheats, steals from others, or even kills a person just to achieve his goal, then further waves of violence might follow suit.'

'High waves sound like danger to me,' Kirsty said.

'But a surfer is happy about high waves,' Lizzie objected. 'If you can ride them, it's a positive experience and certainly an exciting thrill. You just shouldn't fall off the surfboard, drown or break your neck on an unexpected sandbank.'

'And you should beware of sharks,' Andy said.

Arielle was fed up! 'Stop talking about my cousin and what he might have meant at the time! The men probably just got in each other's way when they were surfing, something like that often happens,' she said snottily, frowning morosely.

'Thomas also showed a second picture of the surfers,' Sebastian mused, unmoved by Arielle's remark. 'But I've forgotten the text that went with it. You know what, I'll get my laptop.' And off he went and returned quickly.

'I made screen-shots of the relevant Facebook pages back then,' he said somewhat embarrassed. 'Because they could be important.'

He put the laptop on the table and turned it so that everyone could see the screen.

'Look here: The second photo is similar to the first, but it shows more of the background. You can also see other people on their surfboards and someone on a 'Stand Up Paddle'. And further in the distance, there are two boats.'

'What are you looking at?' Anna came home, surprised to see the assembled crew in the living room, gathering around a laptop.

'Sebastian reminded us of my cousin's Facebook page where he'd showed pictures of the fighting surfers,' Arielle explained in a choked voice. 'One of them is Gabriel, and the other one is dead by now. Just like Thomas.' She wiped her eyes.

Jack comfortingly put his arm around his girlfriend's shoulder, annoyed with Sebastian. Why did he bring up this subject again? He knew how emotional Arielle was and how much she still suffered from the murder of Thomas.

Anna squinted her eyes and asked Sebastian to zoom in to different parts of the photos. And then she shouted, 'Look at the two figures on the dark blue motorboat with the yellow inscription! One of them could be Malcolm! The guy who had a fight with Tim.'

'Really?' Lizzie asked.

Sebastian zoomed in more, and with some effort they could decipher the painted words STORM BIRD on the side of the boat. But the faces of the two men were quite blurred.

Kirsty now read aloud the words Thomas had posted with this picture: 'HOT ANGER IN THE COOL WET'.

'Well, it seems Gabriel had to deal with other violent people besides his hot-tempered wife,' Andy said.

'And this Steven Owen, whom I met twice myself, was later killed with a King Hit. But why, we never found out, even though they arrested that man. Jim was his name, I think.' Sebastian ran his fingers over his mop of hair again, making his hair standing on end.

'What a cruel, senseless act!' Kirsty said. At the same time, she was feeling disgusted by the way Steven had brutally kicked a frightened dog.

'According to the news, Jim came from a family with a criminal past. They reported about problems with alcohol, theft and violence. A sad case!' Lizzie sighed.

Andy suddenly clapped his hands. 'Well, that's enough talk about murder and manslaughter for today. You wanted to practise mathematics, didn't you?'

It was only now that Anna looked at her father and shouted horrified, 'What happened to you, Daddy?'

She was shocked to learn of Melissa's assassination attempt on Alfred and her malicious attack on her parents. But she felt no sympathy whatsoever for Alfred, the selfish drug dealer. He didn't seem to care about the devastating effects of the 'FUN' with regards to the health – and also the wallets – of his victims. And how mean to leave the young woman to her fate after the car accident! That must have been Olivia, the young singer. At least this mystery was solved now, but what a tragic story! Should she tell Oliver about it? Should she really open up old wounds?

Later in the evening, she thought about her own experience with Malcolm and Tim again, and she had difficulty falling asleep. Then she dreamed that she was sitting in a wildly swaying blue boat, together with a horde of frightened rats, struggling with nausea, while a storm bird emitted loud, monotonous cries from a ship's mast in the distance.

*   *   *

Andy had cooled his knee with an ice pack immediately after Melissa's attack and felt better the very next day. However, the wounds on his head caused many strangers to cast pitying glances at him for quite a while, and he was not spared from silly comments. Some acquaintances jokingly asked if his own wife had hit him, which he didn't find amusing at all. Fortunately, Greg had not held it against him when he postponed the planned work on his property to another date.

# 57 MELISSA

The Kuhlmann family learned that Melissa was in custody and that Alfred had survived the poison attack. However, he had to stay in intensive care for a while, and it was possible that he would suffer permanent damage to his brain, liver and kidneys. Later, he would certainly have to face further investigations as several bags of 'FUN' and various other illegal drugs in tablet form were found in his house. In addition, several wooden boxes were detected in a musty smelling shed on his property, full of exotic wildlife. Most of the animals had been squeezed close together and were in a pitiful state. Some lizards were dead, and an Indian star turtle was terminally ill and had to be euthanized by a vet. Anna and Sebastian felt sick when they heard about it. Because of Alfred, both humans and animals had suffered! Andy and Lizzie were horrified, too, but also glad that Alfred's crimes had finally been exposed.

Gabriel visited the Kuhlmann family to inform them about the current state of affairs. He was visibly upset and looked miserable. During his speech, he sometimes faltered, and once he sobbed loudly. He had very quickly become aware of Melissa's drug addiction. He had tried to dissuade his wife from this diabolical 'FUN' powder, but without success. They had argued violently over and over again, and once he had flushed the drugs down the toilet. But she had gone completely mad, and at the first opportunity, she'd got a new supply from Alfred, threatening to kill herself if Gabriel were to take the 'FUN' away from her ever again. He had found out about the secret compartment in the doll at some point, but hadn't dared to destroy the drugs. After a particularly heated argument with Melissa, he had plunged into deep despair. Both her mental and physical condition had worsened, and he couldn't bear it any longer to see her ruining her life. When his gaze fell on the naked doll with its staring eyes that evening, he was overcome by icy horror, and he made a decision.

In a low voice Gabriel now said to the Kuhlmann family:

'This ugly doll suddenly reminded me of a corpse, and in my mind's eye I saw my young wife, once so beautiful, lying in front of me, lifeless, cold, and bald. It was such a horrible and yet so realistic imagination! As you know, Melissa did indeed try to take her own life with an overdose of sleeping pills, and since then I've taken her threat of suicide more seriously than ever before. Still, I had to get rid of this destructive 'FUN' before it was too late. Somehow, I had to help Melissa overcome her addiction and start a new life.'

Gabriel cleared his throat and took a sip of water.

'And so, I waited until she was fast asleep. I put the doll into an old bag and hid it in the boot of the car overnight. As a precaution, I even removed all fingerprints on the doll and the bag. The next morning, I threw it into the bushes in a park. After that, I felt better at first, but soon I was overcome with fear again. What would Melissa do when she'd discover the loss of the doll?' Gabriel laughed bitterly. 'Well, you witnessed that moment yourself. She raved like a savage and hit me with a vase. It's only good that I'm a tough guy,' he tried to joke, smiling at Anna and Sebastian. Just like their parents, the siblings listened to Gabriel's monologue spellbound.

'However, it was all useless. Only now do I know that she followed a spontaneous intuition one day. After washing the doll's dusty clothes, she took a portion of the powder from the doll and put it into an empty baking powder container. So, even after I'd chucked out the doll, she continued consuming the 'FUN' without my knowledge. How often? No idea! I noticed that she was sometimes dazed and sometimes very euphoric, but I attributed this to the new pills that a doctor had prescribed for her depression. And in a way, I'd already got used to seeing her tired and listless at some times, happy and excited at other times, and then again ill-tempered and aggressive. But I can hardly believe that she tried to poison Alfred!'

Again, he put the glass to his lips and Lizzie noticed that his hand was trembling. Gabriel apologised and went out into the garden to smoke a cigarette, and when he returned to the living room his eyes were red, as if he had been crying.

*   *   *

The defense lawyer and a detective received more detailed information on the course of events. During her interrogation, Melissa made the following statement:

'Alfred simply wouldn't leave me alone, even though my husband was not at home. I felt so helpless! Actually, I was so scared I almost wet my pants, because we still didn't have enough money to pay our debts to him. Only recently he kicked Gabriel so hard that he had to limp for a few days. What would he do to him this time? I had to get rid of Alfred right away before Gabriel would come home! But how?

And that's when I had a clever idea! I asked Alfred to wait for Gabriel in the living room and offered him a cuppa. I knew that he liked his coffee with lots of milk and sugar, so I hoped he wouldn't notice the somewhat unusual taste if I added three spoonfuls of the 'FUN'. And it worked! He drank almost the whole cup without hesitation. But then he touched his neck and began to grunt and groan pathetically. His eyes almost came out of their sockets. He first turned red like a tomato and then all cheesy, and he made a grimace that was really devilish!'

Melissa burst into laughter, but quickly pulled herself together.

'I was sitting there, frozen, thinking of the horrible stomach-aches I'd often had from half a teaspoon of 'FUN'. Would three teaspoons be enough to put him out of action? Or would he even die? Actually, it would serve him right! After all, it was Alfred's own fault! Why did he sell me that disgusting stuff? Oh, I wish I'd never met this man and had never touched his drugs! However, I must admit that I was grateful to him at first, because the 'FUN' seemed to work wonders. It put me – unfortunately only for a very short time – in a relaxed state, making me feel like I was finally back on top, enjoying my life again.

So, when I was in a bad mood, I took a small amount of this new drug to either calm me down or cheer me up, although I always felt very sick afterwards. After a few weeks, my skin changed in a strange way, it became scaly and sore, I got pimples everywhere and it itched like hell, as if a swarm of fleas had attacked me. Finally, this 'FUN' gave me a terrible headache and hair loss. I hardly dared to leave the house anymore, I was so ashamed that I didn't want to see anybody.'

Now Melissa cried. It was only after quite a while, and after recovering from a massive hiccup, that she could continue.

'My husband quickly discovered that I'd become a drug addict, and reluctantly I confessed who'd given me the 'FUN'. He was as angry as I'd never seen him before! He wanted to fight with Alfred and take the powder away from me immediately. And a bit later he did flush it down the toilet. I was furious! But I bought more drugs, even though this time I couldn't give Alfred the full amount of money. When Gabriel detected my new drugs, I threatened to kill myself if he'd destroyed them again, and after many arguments, we agreed to hide the powder in an old doll. I promised to gradually reduce the intake of 'FUN' and never to buy illegal drugs again.'

Melissa scoffed, then wrung her hands in despair, looking directly at her audience for the first time.

'I couldn't afford the insane price anyway! We had no idea how we could pay off the debts to Alfred without begging my parents. I wanted to listen to Gabriel, who tried to get me off the drug, but for some reason I couldn't. You know, it's the same like with alcohol: during a bad hangover you're determined never to take a single drop again. But then, at some point, you start drinking again, just to relax, or to forget your frustration. Gabriel could roar and rage, or plead and cry, but I remained a user.'

She sighed. 'Of course, I was still afraid that he'd eventually take the 'FUN' away from me. So, I hid a part of it in an old baking powder tin where he'd never find it. Because Gabriel is an excellent cook, but he has never baked anything in his life.'

A tiny smile played around Melissa's lips.

'Gabriel was surprisingly patient with me, even though I constantly called him names and behaved like a furious bitch. I'm so sorry! And I didn't want to hurt my neighbours and their cute dog, either. It is such a nice family!'

For a while she stared broodingly into space. Then the detective asked her a few questions, and Melissa answered willingly:

'Alfred pretended to be an understanding friend, and when he found out about my depression, he said he would help me. Shortly afterwards, he secretly slipped me the first, rather small portion of this 'FUN' without asking for money. For the second, larger portion, however, I almost used up all my savings, and for the third one, I could pay Alfred only a small proportion of the total sum. Since then, he has been calling us all the time, literally terrorising us. But how am I supposed to come up with two thousand five hundred dollars in a flash? After all, we have to pay our rent and all that, we're already short of money anyway. And now Gabriel's other employer, Martin, is dead. He has been shot! It's unbelievable! Gabriel suggested to Alfred that he could slowly work off our debts, but Alfred didn't agree. He did not want to wait any longer and showed no mercy.'

Her expression darkened again.

'Alfred was not a friend! He had only money and power on his mind, and he could be terribly brutal. As time went by, I became more and more afraid of him. So, I had to get rid of him before he could hurt my Gabriel, you see? I was paralysed with fear when Alfred sat in my living room, putting the cup to his mouth. What would happen? When he actually drank the coffee, I held my breath until he looked at me in horror and began to shake. As I said, he first turned bright red and then pale, almost greenish around the nose. Suddenly he jumped up and tried to strangle me! I almost died of fright! At the same moment there was a knock on the door. He let go of me, touched his own neck, groaning and wheezing, staggered into the hall and fell over like a log, right into the arms of my neighbours. And then he stopped moving.'

Melissa took a deep breath, remaining silent for a while. And then she screamed in renewed rage:

'I thought Alfred was dead, but he's alive, and I hate him! He didn't care one bit that his drugs made me miserable, and he probably talked other people into it as well. I hope he will get sick and itchy all over the body! It serves him right if his own medicine doesn't do him any good!'

She scratched her arms bloody, laughed hysterically and finally cried. Only later did she whisper very softly:

'I'm really sorry about the way I treated Andy and Lizzie. It was such a shock to see them at the door and I was so ashamed! I didn't know what to do anymore, feeling nauseous and dizzy. And then I completely lost it and hit Andy. But he and Lizzie probably saved my life! Because without them, Alfred might have managed to strangle me.'

Melissa was medically examined and admitted to a psychiatric clinic. Her husband was not sure whether such a place would help her mental health or make it worse. Nevertheless, he was relieved that Melissa's parents were very understanding. They promised to help as much as possible. And besides, Melissa would finally undergo rehab therapy.

# 58 TIME HEALS ALL WOUNDS

Arielle stared at the computer screen until she could see nothing through her tears anymore. Since the conversation with her friends and Sebastian's family, she couldn't push the memories of her cousin Thomas out of her mind. Just now she'd again looked at old photos and e-mails of him, desperately seeking answers to the arising questions. Why had he taken photos of the fighting men back then? Who had killed him? Thomas had been a nice, sociable and fun-loving person, and she could hardly imagine that anyone could have hated him so much to plan such a horrific, violent deed. Had the killer been acting under the influence of drugs? How was he feeling now? Was he at least suffering from fear and remorse, or was he completely unmoved by this homicide? She nervously chewed her fingernails. And then a shiver ran down her spine. It must have been an intentional murder! After all, Thomas had been hoisted onto the giant horse sculpture, which indicated the involvement of more than one person.

Had Thomas indeed detected a smuggling ring without informing the police? Arielle's head was spinning, it was unnerving! Several months had passed since then, and yet nothing was pointing to the killers. She wondered whether the homicide detectives were even still working on the case. Perhaps they'd already abandoned the investigation, filed away as an unsolved murder mystery. And she felt so sorry for Aunt Heidi and Uncle Wayne! She was sobbing loudly when Max walked in and limped over to her. His injured paw hadn't healed completely yet, but it looked much better. 'TIME HEALS ALL WOUNDS' was a well-known saying.

'It's not true!' Arielle cried. Some wounds of the soul, such as the sharp pain of the loss of a beloved person or animal, would certainly never disappear. At the most, it might get easier to bear the grief with the passage of time. Tenderly, she patted her dog. 'Hello, my sweetheart! You'd also come to my rescue, hey? Just like Susi helped Sebastian's parents the other day, wouldn't you? I wish you could have saved Thomas!'

Max looked at her attentively, and his ears twitched. He gave a little fart while Arielle's stomach growled softly. Smiling, she now dried her eyes, cleaned her nose and stood up.

'Shall we take a quick walk around the garden? And then we'll see if we can find something tasty in the kitchen!'

Arielle handed Max a piece of banana after he'd sat down giving her his healthy paw. 'At least you didn't break your leg, because that's not much fun!' She stroked him, thinking back to her stay in the hospital and the women with whom she'd shared a room. Hopefully she would recover well! How nasty of the driver to do a hit and run! Had he been in a drunken state?

Arielle couldn't help but think of her Uncle Wayne and his earlier atrocities while drunk. But recently Aunt Heidi had told her mother that he would hardly touch alcohol anymore. And that they would treat each other as lovingly as they had at the beginning of their relationship. The common grief for their son had obviously brought them together again. However, they still felt numb, and they avoided meetings with other people as much as possible. Would they ever be able to laugh out loud and heartily again? Arielle sighed. And then her mobile rang.

'Oh, hi, Sebastian! What's up?'

'Hi! I have a question. Um, sorry, it's about Thomas again. I'd like to know if he had his mobile phone or his camera with him when he ...' he cleared his throat.

'When he was killed?' Arielle asked. 'Nah, he'd left his mobile with Daniel, and later it was seized by the police. It seems they didn't find anything unusual on it.' She swallowed loudly. 'But today I discovered some other interesting photos that also show a man who looks like Malcolm. I'll forward them to you so that your sister can check them out.'

They kept on chatting for a while and then ended the call. Arielle looked sadly into the bright blue sky, where only a single snow-white feather cloud appeared. Thomas had taken those photos in December and January, during the very last summer holidays that he had experienced. Never again would he look forward to new adventures and wonderful events, never again would he be able to enjoy love, happiness and success. Had his blatant curiosity become his undoing? Arielle's eyes filled with fresh tears, dripping hotly onto her clenched fists. However, her deep sorrow was now mixed with an unrestrained anger. Max sighed and lay down on the cold tiles at her feet, although he actually preferred his mattress or at least a warm carpet.

Jack stared disgruntled at an old poster with a torn corner. He had tried several times to call Arielle and Sebastian, but their phones were constantly busy. With whom were they chattering so endlessly? Annoyed, he tore the poster from the wall and crumpled it up.

# 59 A LOST BALL

Anna opened the glass door to let Susi have a pee in the garden and quickly closed it again as icy air blew in her face. After a sunny and clear day, it was going to be a cold night. Shivering, she went back to Sebastian's room. Her parents were visiting their friends Rosie and Bob, having hinted that they might come home late. Anna and Sebastian found it very pleasant to spend a whole evening without their parents. For a while they had been singing along to the music of the Hot Ears, having a great time and dancing around the house. And now they were looking at the photos from Arielle's last e-mail to Sebastian.

Anna recognised Malcolm immediately in them, as this time they were of high quality. The first photo showed Malcolm with a fisherman in the blue boat, in the second photo he was sitting at the wheel of a white car with a mobile phone at his ear, and in the third photo he was coming out of a house with a large suitcase. His face was thinner than Anna remembered. He was tanned by sun and wind, had a narrow nose and grey-blue eyes, a dimple on his chin and thinning, light brown, short hair. In the car he wore an elegant light grey jacket, outside the house he was casually dressed in shorts, T-shirt and sandals. On the sea he appeared as a tiny figure in the background, wearing a brown windbreaker and a blue cap. The other man in the boat had his blonde hair tied back to a ponytail, and his face was almost hidden by his large sunglasses. He was trying to pull a big fish into the boat.

'How old do you think Malcolm is?' Anna asked. 'I guess about mid-thirties.'

'Maybe,' Sebastian mumbled. 'Look, this car is a white Ford Falcon! And you can even read the number plate.'

'So what?'

'The same kind of car was involved in the hit-and-run.'

Since Anna obviously didn't understand what Sebastian was getting at, he explained: 'Gabriel was pretty amused that a car had been stolen from a car thief, namely from his former employer Martin. And he believes that Martin had nothing to do with an illegal wildlife trade. So, how did the remains of the Borneo earless monitor egg get into his Ford?' Sebastian's eyes were shining with excitement. 'Could it be that Malcolm had retrieved his own car from Martin? But then he was chased by Tim, put it in the ditch and escaped by foot.'

'You have crazy ideas!' Anna said. 'There are plenty of cars just like that! And I don't know if Gabriel is right about Martin. According to Annette, both exotic animals and illegal drugs were discovered in Martin's house.'

'Yes, but only after his death! Perhaps the real culprit tried to put the blame on him! And with success! Because of these unusual lizard shells in his car, Martin became a suspect. However, at first the police couldn't find any clues to criminal activities, neither in his house nor on the yacht.'

Gradually getting infected by Sebastian's zeal, Anna said, 'Well, Martin could've hidden his goods in another place. Or he'd already sold them at that time.' Anna raised her eyebrows. 'Hum, why did the other guy, Malcolm or whoever it was, attempt to get away from Tim, driving much too fast? Tim wasn't in a police car then. So, maybe Malcolm recognised Tim on the motorway, and he was afraid of him for whatever reason.'

'We should find out who owned this car that ended up in the ditch. I bet Mr. Little can help us! I could ask Ivory about the number plate. Then we'll see if it's the same car as the one in Thomas's photo.' Sebastian also intended to ask Gabriel if Martin could have stolen this Ford Falcon. Observing the photo, he had spotted a flaw in the windscreen. Perhaps Gabriel would remember it? In general, Sebastian would like to know how Martin had managed to sell his stolen cars. He must have changed all sorts of identification marks. How mean what people did to enrich themselves!

Sebastian and Anna were silent for a while, immersed in their thoughts.

'Tim and Malcolm knew each other, and both of them were on Martin's yacht. But who shot Martin?' Anna was getting a headache from all the question marks in her brain. Maybe she and her brother should listen to their mother's advice and give up their detective work. However, how could they just switch off and twiddle their thumbs after all the events? Impossible! Anna sighed and massaged her temples with her fingertips.

'Do you think I should show Gabriel the photo of Malcolm sitting in the car?' Sebastian asked, nibbling lightly on his lower lip.

'Um, I don't know! If our parents find out, they'll freak out.' At that moment she heard a soft noise at the door. She jumped up to let Susi back in, and an idea popped into her mind.

* * *

Gabriel was sitting in an old armchair watching the news on television. But his thoughts were with his wife. Despite Melissa's unpredictable alternation between fits of raving madness and apathy, he still loved her, and he found it terrible to be all alone in the house. He feared for her future which was now largely in the hands of strangers. His parents-in-law had promised to get a good defense lawyer for Melissa, but as yet nobody knew how long she would have to stay in the psychiatric hospital. Would she soon end up in prison? He could only wait helplessly and try to find a decent job. However, right now he felt much too dazed to even think straight. For days he had hardly eaten anything. His head and stomach hurt, and his heart seemed to be surrounded by an iron ring that made it difficult for him to breathe. A convulsive sob suddenly rose in his chest and his eyes filled with tears he no longer wanted to suppress. Finally, he could cry unrestrainedly, he was alone anyway ...

There was a knock. Someone came to visit. Embarrassed, he rubbed his eyes, quickly brushed his nose and stood up clumsily to open the door. To his surprise, he was facing the kids from next door.

Anna noticed straight away that Gabriel had been crying. Looking up into his ashen and distraught face, she was speechless. Fortunately, Sebastian came to her aid.

Seemingly impassive, he said, 'Hello, Gabriel! Sorry for the trouble, but we were playing with Susi and her ball flew over the fence. Could we get it back? It's her favourite ball!'

'Sure, no problem,' Gabriel replied friendly. 'So, you even play ball in the darkness? Susi must have eyes like a lynx!'

'Um, we have outdoor lighting everywhere, and my dad installed solar lamps in the garden,' Anna murmured.

'Well, it's pretty dark in my backyard, but let's have a look.' Gabriel went ahead of the siblings. 'Do you know roughly where the ball might have landed? Hopefully not on the roof of the shed? Because then I'd have to get a ladder out of the garage.'

A musty smell got into Anna's nose as she peered under a bush. Something rushed away, and in the distance a dog was barking.

'There it is!' Sebastian called out triumphantly and picked up the yellow rubber ball that had rolled under a white flowering shrub. On the way back into the house he chattered away. 'Our father told us that you are going to repair our Toyota. Great that you know so much about cars! Dad always likes to tinker around, trying to fix all sorts of problems by himself, but there are some things he doesn't dare to touch.'

'Well, that's my profession after all. That is to say, it was my profession, as unfortunately I no longer have a proper job as a mechanic.' Gabriel hesitated, scratching his neck, and then asked, 'Would you like some lemonade?'

Anna wiped a grin off her face. Sebastian had skilfully directed the conversation to where they wanted it.

'I'd love some,' she said quickly. 'Our parents are not home tonight, so we won't be missed right away.'

'And we'd like to ask you a question anyway!' Sebastian blurted out.

Anna rolled her eyes. Her little brother was always so direct! Diplomacy was certainly not his strong point.

Gabriel smiled amusedly. 'What is it? I can't wait!'

They went into the kitchen, where he handed them both a glass of lemonade and took a bottle of beer from the fridge for himself. Then they sat down in the living room and Gabriel turned off the TV. Anna looked around, surprised how clean and tidy it was, almost too sterile for her taste. Somehow, she had expected a rather messy house. But she had completely misjudged Gabriel anyway. Meanwhile, she hardly understood why she had found him so frightening. Sure, he seemed sinister at first sight, but that was probably because his eyes were a bit too narrow and his nose crooked as if it had been broken in a fistfight. Or was it due to his thick dark beard and a missing incisor? She didn't like his tattoos either, and when they'd first met, she had assumed he was a friend of Alfred whose disgusting remarks had immediately repulsed her. But Gabriel had kind eyes ...

'Well, go ahead, I am curious!' Gabriel said to Sebastian.

'Uh, well, it's quite a long story ...,' Sebastian suddenly felt awkward. Only when Anna nodded her head encouragingly, did he continue, 'A friend of mine was related to Thomas, the young man who was found dead in the 'Garden of the Seven Senses' and who ...'

Gabriel stared at him in shock. 'What? Your pretty girlfriend, the one I'd met before? That's so sad!'

'Um, no, it's Arielle, a friend of Kirsty and me. Thomas was her cousin and was very close to her, almost like a big brother. And now we'd all like to find out why Thomas had taken certain photos before he was murdered. On one of them, we noticed a car that you might recognise. Well, it's just a wild guess ...'

Anna took out her mobile phone as if on command and showed Gabriel the photo of Malcolm in the Ford.

'Look here, the windscreen has been hit by a stone or something.'

Gabriel viewed the picture, discovering the rounded damage from which slight cracks branched off in various directions.

Sebastian said, 'Some time ago, Arielle met a woman in the hospital who had been injured by a white Ford Falcon. It was a case of a hit- and-run. The owner of the car was Martin, your boss. But allegedly he had an alibi for the time of the accident. Um, and then I came up with the idea that this man in the photo might have been the rightful owner and that he ...'

'I recognise the car!' Gabriel shouted in surprise. 'Martin had stolen this Ford before he hired me as a casual labourer. I remember this stone chip damage very well! I had a hard time convincing Martin at the time that repair was out of the question because the damage was too close to the edge of the glass. We then considered replacing the windscreen and selling the car, but for some reason Martin decided to keep it. So, all we did was give it a little makeover and put on a new number plate.'

Ashamed, he paused and twirled nervously at his beard.

'I did terrible things in the past and my lack of money is no excuse for any of them. But from now on I will change my life! And in a way I am glad that I already confessed everything to the police, to you and your parents and also to Melissa's parents.'

Anna nodded at him friendly, searching in vain for a suitable answer.

'So, it's possible that Malcolm was the driver who hit the woman on the David Low Way!' Sebastian exclaimed.

'What makes you think so?' Gabriel asked, confused. 'I don't understand! It could have been who knows who.' He took a sip of beer and reached for a packet of cigarettes. 'You'll have to explain this better to me. How do you actually know the man in the photo? And what does this picture mean? How was Thomas involved?'

Anna and Sebastian told Gabriel in detail what they had learned about Malcolm and Tim, the exotic animals and the drugs on Martin's yacht and in his house. However, they avoided telling him about the existence of the two photos showing the fight between him and Steven on January 11th.

Smoking, Gabriel listened attentively. He only interrupted them occasionally to ask questions or to make stunned exclamations. Only at the very end did he admit that he knew Malcolm very briefly. He carefully squeezed the cigarette out in an ashtray and said,

'Slowly everything becomes a little clearer to me. Martin had stolen this car in New South Wales. I guess he never expected that anyone in our area could identify it. Otherwise, he would have replaced the windscreen, before publicly driving around in this car. And perhaps you are on the right track, Sebastian! If it was indeed Malcolm who took his car back at some point, then it seems that I had something to do with it – without my knowledge, though.'

He smiled when he noticed Anna and Sebastian's bewildered faces. 'Unfortunately, one day, during one of Melissa's happy, effervescent phases, she made a silly, revealing comment to Alfred. Therefore, he found out a lot more about my various jobs for Martin than I would have liked.' He laughed bitterly.

'Alfred promised us not to tell anyone about our illegal business. He even patted me on the shoulder and winked conspiratorially at Melissa. But I did not trust him! In reality, he's a nasty crook and involved in all kinds of criminal activities. Well, at some point Alfred told me enthusiastically about his old friend Malcolm. For a while, he'd lived in Mullumbimby, a town in New South Wales, and had now moved back to Queensland. A bit later, I helped Alfred to deliver a couch to a unit in Noosaville, and that's where I saw Malcolm and his friend Conny.'

Gabriel drank the rest from his beer thirstily and suppressed a burp.

'All right, so let's assume you're right and it really was Malcolm's car. Why else would he sit behind the wheel? Because I've never seen Martin lend his cars to anybody, he was very particular! No, I rather think it was just a crazy coincidence, a kind of a chain reaction: Malcolm told his mate Alfred about his stolen Ford Falcon. I bet Alfred then blabbed that he knew of two car thieves in Coolum, without suspecting that Martin had also stolen Malcolm's Ford. But Malcolm was curious, started investigating, found his sorely missed car, and reappropriated it at the first opportunity.'

Gabriel's face, cynically contorted for a brief moment, brightened up. It seemed to Anna that he approached the whole thing with a zeal that matched her own and her brother's. His eyes, previously swollen from crying, were now glowing with excitement.

'But why did Thomas take that photo?' Anna asked.

'Can I see it again?' Gabriel asked, and Anna passed him her smartphone.

'I see the number plate is not the original one, but the one I had screwed on,' Gabriel remarked. 'Um, Martin had never mentioned that he'd lost this Ford. And I didn't notice anything at all, because he usually went to his workshop earlier than me and always parked the car in the garage. He also had a double garage at home – so it can't have been easy for Malcolm to get his car.' He coughed. 'However, Martin was often away on business, and maybe Malcolm took advantage of that.'

'What a happy coincidence for someone to find his stolen car in a completely different place! Hard to believe!' Sebastian frowned.

'Well, his luck didn't last long, because he put the car in the ditch and had to flee on foot with his girlfriend,' Anna replied. 'And thus, the police discovered the suspicious remains of the lizard shells.'

'Oh yes! I'd almost forgotten about that part of your story! I wonder if Malcolm really is a smuggler? And what do you know about this young guy, Thomas? Had he tailed Malcolm, secretly taking photos?' Gabriel fiddled around with the cigarette box.

Anna hoped he wouldn't light another cigarette because she already had a slight headache. As if Gabriel sensed her thoughts, he stood up to open a window. Then he sat back down on his armchair, gazing at the siblings sitting next to each other on the sofa. Only now did he notice that they resembled each other in some way, although Sebastian was relatively small, brown-eyed and dark-haired and Anna was tall, blue-eyed and blonde. He admired their determination to clarify events that were apparently very dangerous. Suddenly he was ashamed of the fact that for a long time he had only thought about Melissa and himself, completely losing sight of his surroundings. When he had heard about the poor boy on the horse sculpture and later about the fatal blow to Steven, an acquaintance of his, he had been shocked but quickly erased the events from his consciousness. Even the news of Martin's murder had hardly shaken him, but only the recent attacks of his wife on himself, Alfred, Andy and Lizzie.

Nevertheless, he felt full of energy and drive, and he decided to become more involved with other people from now on, instead of lethargically sinking into self-pity.

When Anna cleared her throat, Gabriel apologised for the smoke in the room. He said,

'It's really a quaint story we're making up here! However, I still believe that Martin was not dealing with animals or drugs. Business of this kind just didn't suit him! He had his well-running workshop in Maroochydore, and occasionally he filled his already very fat wallet with the profits from stolen cars. I think he stole two expensive boats once and sold them to customers who didn't ask too many questions. He also owned a yacht, a house in Coolum and another one further north in Queensland. He was certainly not poor!'

'But Malcolm and Martin knew each other,' Sebastian said, running his fingers through his hair. 'Anyway, they were together with Tim on Martin's yacht before it went up in flames. Anna and I assumed that these three men were partners in smuggling but got into some arguments. And Martin was shot, either by Tim or by Malcolm!'

'And now we know that Malcolm was a friend of Alfred,' Anna pointed out, not daring to mention the 'FUN', which had already caused Gabriel enough grief.

To Anna's resentment, Gabriel lit up another cigarette, saying: 'There is another possibility. Malcolm may have found his car on Martin's property, confronted him directly and ordered him to hand it over immediately. Instead of turning him in, Malcolm demanded money from Martin. This is how the two men met. And Martin was so embarrassed by all this that he kept the whole affair from me.'

'That sounds plausible,' Anna said.

'By the way, would you like to have another drink? Or something to eat, peanuts or something?' Gabriel already got up to go to the kitchen.

'No thanks, we'd rather go home,' Anna replied.

Looking at her watch, she shouted, 'Poor Susi will be very worried! Because in the evening she is almost never alone!'

'Why don't you bring her along on your next visit?' Gabriel offered with a smile.

'Great idea, we'll do that!' Anna said. 'Bye!'

'Thanks for everything!' Sebastian extended his hand.

Gabriel shook it, grinning boyishly. 'You're welcome! Let me know if I can be of further assistance! And also, if you find out more, okay? As I've become very curious myself.'

'Okay!' However, Sebastian later regretted that he had mentioned Arielle's name and her connection with Thomas. Could they really trust Gabriel one hundred per cent?

# 60 COLD SMOKE

Returning home late at night, Lizzie giggled as Andy carried her over the threshold just for fun. She was a bit tipsy after a few drinks with Rosie and Bob, while he'd only had a small glass of white wine with his dinner. In the hallway, Andy sniffed and frowned, detecting an unpleasant smell. Like cold cigarette smoke! Had their children had a secret party, perhaps with Anna's boyfriend and the Hot Ears? Suspiciously, he went into the kitchen. However, everything was in good order, and the living and dining room were neat and tidy too. Susi rushed towards him, and he stroked her tenderly. Since Lilly had left, Susi was certainly getting pampered much more than before, but she deserved it. She was such a sweet dog! Lizzie also petted her, whispering all kinds of nice words into her ear. Then she laughed softly.

'We don't really implement our resolution, hey? Remember that we'd intended to ignore Susi briefly every time we come home?'

Andy smiled. 'Well, it doesn't matter so much in Susi's case. Luckily, she never barks when we go away or come back, doesn't do anything stupid in the house, and is usually a good dog anyway.'

Anna woke up when she heard the muted voices of her parents. But she didn't want to get up in the middle of the night. Also, her head was now hurting even worse than before. Had she caught another cold? Or was it the result from all the pointless rumination? Well, at least they had gotten some useful news from Gabriel today. Malcolm was an old friend of Alfred!

Then it occurred to her in a flash that the blonde man in one of the photos, sitting with Malcolm in the blue boat, could be Alfred! Perhaps Thomas hadn't been interested in the two fighters in the foreground at all, but rather in the people in the background? And what was Malcolm carrying in the suitcase in the other photo?

The next morning, Anna still had a headache and also abdominal pains. When she got up, her parents were having breakfast while Sebastian was already out on a walk with Susi.

'Good morning!' she said quietly and plopped down on a chair like a wet sack.

'Hi, Anna!' Lizzie greeted her daughter, observing her. 'Are you not feeling well? You're all pasty!'

'Hello, my girl!' Andy said good-naturedly. 'I almost thought you had a wild party here yesterday, because our house reeked of cigarette smoke. But Sebastian told me earlier that you'd been to Gabriel's place, and apparently his heavy smoking caused your clothes to stink.'

'You have a good nose, almost like Susi!' Anna smiled briefly, but the next moment she moaned as a violent cramp gave her new pain that radiated down to her legs. 'I've got my period,' she explained, embarrassed. 'And I've got a headache, too.'

Lizzie replied pitifully, 'You do look miserable! Quite often, I also felt terrible on days like this, and I wished I were a boy. Once I even fainted!'

She asked Anna if she wanted to go back to bed, offering her a cup of herbal tea and a hot water bottle.

'Thanks, Mum, a water bottle might help. And I'm going to lie down on the couch for a while,' she said gratefully.

Susi plonked down on the floor next to Anna, and both soon dozed off.

\* \* \*

Gabriel smiled as he spotted Susi's yellow ball on the kitchen table where Anna and Sebastian had forgotten it the night before. He had known straight away that the ball had only served as an excuse to question him. After talking to the siblings, he had been sitting in the living room for many hours, racking his brains. And he had slept far too little. Nevertheless, this morning he was filled with a refreshing energy. In a good mood, he whistled to himself in the kitchen while frying some eggs. Now that he had got rid of both Martin and Alfred, he would be able to take charge of his life again. Martin had been a good boss, but Gabriel hadn't liked to get involved in car theft. And he'd not been happy with Alfred's way of doing jobs, like secretly dumping all sorts of stuff, used oil and building rubble in the forest – just to save the fees and journeys to the local rubbish tips, even though his customers had already paid him for the legal disposal. It had been bad timing that Anna and her friend had caught Alfred and him chucking out a mattress in the local industrial estate. No wonder Anna had looked at him so suspiciously in the beginning! He grinned and ate with a good appetite for the first time in a long while.

With his second cup of instant coffee, he decided to plan his next steps and to write them down on a writing pad. First, he would phone Melissa and her parents and then drive to Centrelink in Maroochydore to discuss his options for a new job. He also had to do some shopping and make an appointment with

Andy or Lizzie to repair their Toyota. His last points to note were:

*Help Anna and Sebastian with their investigations!*
*What did Thomas have to do with Malcolm?*

On the way to Maroochydore his good mood disappeared as he was seized by a horrifying thought. What would Alfred do after his release from hospital? Would he seek revenge for what Melissa had done to him? How could he protect her and himself from Alfred? He became hot and cold, his hands began to tremble and sweat, and only with difficulty did he suppress the urge to light a cigarette. He had to resist, for that morning he had firmly resolved to give up smoking – forever! He opened the window, breathing deeply in and out. Then he turned the radio up to distract himself from his fear.

# 61 THE ESKY

Greg put the hoe aside and used the sleeve of his shirt to wipe off the drops of sweat from his forehead. He almost regretted having made so many promises to the young rock group, like the one to create a new path for them. He was simply too good-natured! For hours, he had eradicated thorny Lantana bushes, a bamboo thicket and other weeds, and he had also removed a thick tree root. The heavy rainfall of the last three days had loosened the soil that had previously been hard as a rock, making it easier to work. On the other hand, the humidity had now risen enormously. Well, his trailer was already fully loaded, and he would soon finish the work for today. Sighing, he took his spade to replant a young tree in a new location. Digging a hole in the chosen spot, his spade came across something hard. Damn, what could it be, a root or a rock? He kept digging until he unexpectedly saw something white in front of him. Was it rubbish? Near the road, he had already discovered two old car tyres in the bushes.

'Bastards!' Greg scolded and continued to work until he finally uncovered a large blue Esky. He could hardly believe his eyes! As a child, he had always dreamed of finding a treasure, and now his curiosity grew immeasurably. Nevertheless, he hesitated to open the whitish, dirty lid of this portable cooler. Why had anyone bothered to bury an Esky here? Suddenly he remembered the dead rats in the cupboard and Andy's reports about exotic snakes and lizards. With shivers he also thought of a movie in which a ruthless blackmailer had sent a bloody ring finger to his victim's wife. What would he discover?

But then he grinned self-mockingly. He had turned into a pathetic scaredy-cat! He jerked the lid open. What he saw took his breath away. He had indeed found a treasure! No gold bars, coins or sparkling jewels, but many bundles of Australian notes were stored in plastic bags. He laughed and cheered, danced exuberantly around the Esky, forgetting his exhaustion and the little tree he had dug up. He had to tell Andy immediately and celebrate with him and Lizzie! Even though he knew that he probably wouldn't be allowed to keep the money, it was an awesome experience! And maybe he would get a finder's fee!

His parents would be stunned too! Or had one of them buried the money here and then completely forgotten about it? Both of them suffered from dementia. Or could it be the money of a bank robber? Pensively, he stared at his find. It would certainly be wise to transport it carefully and only with gloves on – just in case the police wanted to look for fingerprints. At that thought, he heard a faint crackling sound, and the next moment he felt a sharp pain in the back of his head. His eyes rolled back and he fell helplessly to the ground.

* * *

Anna was feeling better again, looking forward to seeing the future music room of the Hot Ears. In the afternoon, Oliver picked her up with his little car, a bright red Hyundai Getz. She sat down between Bruce and Angus in the back seat behind Oliver and Celina, the new lead singer of the band.

'Does Greg know that we are coming?' Bruce asked.

'Yep! I spoke to him on the phone yesterday. He said he would do some landscaping and we should go to the back entrance. We'd certainly see him somewhere on the way to the greenhouse,' Angus replied.

Oliver and Celina started a song that Anna didn't know yet. Oliver's deep voice harmonized wonderfully with the crystal-clear, almost unearthly voice of Celina. She was a beautiful, delicate woman with silky, light blonde long hair. Angus hummed along, tapping his fingers to the beat, while Anna and Bruce held hands and listened. At the end they applauded and Celina smiled mischievously at them.

'Almost there!' Oliver said, turning into a smaller road, surrounded by thick vegetation on both sides. Only a few mailboxes and narrow access roads to properties indicated that this area was inhabited.

Anna had been curious about Celina. And also a little jealous because Bruce and his friends had raved about her so enthusiastically. Luckily, she instantly liked the young woman and was fascinated both by her musical talent and her gentle nature. The singer made a calm and almost shy impression on her, and Anna was startled when Celina suddenly opened the window, shouting with an energetic and now much darker voice: 'Stop!' Celina had been the first to spot a man jogging with a stick in one hand and an Esky in the other. From the way he ran, she immediately assumed something fishy.

'That's Tim!' Anna was puzzled.

Tim was running to an Audi that was parked on the hard shoulder. Oliver stepped on the gas and shortly afterwards stopped with screeching tyres. Even before Oliver's car skidded to a complete stop, Bruce jumped out and positioned himself in front of Tim, blocking the way to his car.

'What have you done?' he snarled at him, looking suspiciously at the stick.

Tim tried to kick and hit Bruce, but Angus and Celina came to his aid. Like a monkey, petite Celina hopped on Tim's back and covered his eyes while Angus reached for his arms. Instead of defending himself with both hands, Tim continued to clasp the cooler's handle doggedly. Frightened by Celina's unexpected attack, he had let go of the stick, though. By the time Anna managed to unbuckle and climb out of the Getz, her friends had already overpowered Tim. Oliver had fallen into a deep puddle on his way out and was now standing up, cursing. As he rubbed his mud-stained hands on the grass, peering through a gap in the bushes by the side of the road, he saw a lifeless man lying nearby.

'There's a dead body!' he called out in horror.

'What?' Anna gasped. Without thinking, she ran to the person on the ground. 'It's Greg!' she called the next moment. She bent down worriedly to her father's colleague, fervently hoping that he was not dead. Oliver followed her and also crouched down next to the man who now opened his eyes. Greg stared confusedly into space for a few seconds and then recognised Anna.

'Hello, what's happened?' he asked, sitting up laboriously. He touched his head with a groan and was perplexed to see the blood on his hand.

Anna stroked his arm reassuringly. 'Don't worry, we'll help you! Oliver, can you call the emergency number? I'll quickly ring my father, because he should be close by right now!'

Greg murmured something.

'What?' Oliver asked uncomprehendingly.

'Easy come easy go!' Greg repeated and grinned crookedly. 'The money is gone!'

'Excuse me?' Oliver asked, but this time he spoke into his mobile. He took a few steps to the side to answer the questions of a woman. He could hardly understand her because Anna was talking on the phone with her father, almost screaming with excitement. Oliver pressed his mobile phone to his ear.

'Yes, exactly! Um, I don't know how badly he is hurt, but I think ... pardon? Yeah, okay! Where? We're here in Valdora ...'

While Oliver gave the exact address, Anna ended her conversation and tended to Greg who still looked rather dazed.

'My father will be here soon. He's with Rosie and Bob right now, so he's not far away. My mother had left her reading glasses there the other day.'

Anna chatted away nervously until Bruce appeared at her side, saying: 'Celina is really smart! She put Tim's own handcuffs on Tim and chained him to the steering wheel! She and Angus are watching him so that he can't get away, because in movies some people manage to get themselves out of handcuffs somehow.' His happy, sparkling eyes darkened as soon as they turned towards Greg. 'Oh my, that looks like a bad laceration! Oliver, do you have any bandages in the car?'

'Yeah, there are some in my glove compartment. I'll get them.' He hurried off and came back with a first aid kit that he gave to Bruce. 'I think you'd better do it as my hands are full of dirt.'

'Okay!' Bruce put on thin gloves, removed the protective plastic cover of a bandage roll and gently wrapped the bandage around Greg's head.

Anna looked admiringly at his deft fingers and explained to Greg: 'This is my friend Bruce. You already know Oliver and Angus, and over there is Celina, the singer from the Hot Ears.'

'And Tim, the policeman,' Bruce added.

'A policeman?' Greg asked, looking at Oliver in astonishment. 'You just called the police a few minutes ago. How can they be here so quickly? That's impossible!'

'Tim is a police officer, but it seems he has knocked you down!' Anna said grimly. 'Anyway, he had a big stick in his hand and tried to escape when we arrived.'

'Really? But why?' And then it dawned on him. 'He must have seen me digging up the treasure!'

'What treasure?' Anna wanted to know, wondering whether the poor man had suffered a brain damage from the blow.

Despite his injury, Greg smiled. 'Did you happen to see a blue Esky? It's full of money!'

'Yes, Tim had it in his hand and refused to let it go,' Bruce confirmed.

'An Esky full of money was buried here on the property? Incredible! And what a coincidence that Tim came by just now!' Oliver marvelled.

'Maybe it was no coincidence at all,' Anna said.

'That's right, I've seen a spade in Tim's car! He must have known about the money and was planning to dig it out himself. But then he probably watched you from a distance, Greg, and so he sneaked up on you, grabbed a branch and knocked you out! That mean bastard!' Bruce shouted.

Greg grunted, rose to his feet and staggered a little.

'Whew! Careful, nice and slow!' Bruce rushed to his aid, and Oliver also linked arms with Greg to provide support.

'Thanks, I'm a little dizzy. How good that you came to my rescue, but strange that I didn't hear the man at all! Well, I was probably cheering much too loudly.'

Leaning on the two young men and followed by Anna, Greg slowly went to the street. He could hardly fathom that he had been attacked by a policeman of all people. More curious than angry, he gazed at Tim who was sitting in his Audi, fuming mad but powerless. Then Greg's eyes fell on the blue Esky next to the front wheel of the car. 'Is this yours?' He asked the prisoner. Tim remained silent. 'Well, let's see if the money's still in there.' Greg lifted the lid and everyone could see that the Esky was stuffed with notes. Anna gasped for breath, Oliver yelled something, Celina whistled, and Angus and Bruce said in unison: 'Wow!' Tim looked grim.

'And what shall we do now?' Celina asked, bewildered.

'I've already called the police,' Oliver explained. 'But we'll probably have to wait a while.'

At that moment Anna's mobile phone rang. Her father was having problems with his Toyota that wouldn't start. He sounded very upset. Anna quickly reassured him that there was no need for him to drive to them, and Andy reluctantly decided to let Bob tow him home. Anna was quite relieved, as in the meantime she regretted having called her dad for help, thinking that it had been childish. She looked at Oliver, and only now did she notice how muddy he was. And he had all these little twigs in his hair. She broke out into loud laughter. Bruce had to chuckle, too, and in the end, everyone laughed –- except Tim. Greg sat down on the back seat of the Audi, exhausted, without asking Tim for permission.

When two uniformed police officers appeared about half an hour later, they found a predominantly cheerful group of people. Next to two pretty ladies stood a small chubby guy with a shock of black hair, completely soaked and dirty. He had hung a plaid wool blanket around his shoulders that had seen better days. In the front seat of an Audi sat a big man in handcuffs, who turned out to be a colleague and wasn't happy at all. In the back seat there was a man in slightly soiled work clothes who seemed in good spirits despite a bandaged head injury. A slim blond man with an extravagant haircut pointed to the Esky and told them about its unusual contents, and now the two policemen were even more amazed. Anna and Oliver told them why they were in this location in the first place and how they had found Greg. Bruce then pointed to a branch about seventy centimetres long and five centimetres thick, which had presumably been used as a weapon by Tim. Nobody else had touched it. Celina confessed that she had found Tim's handcuffs in his glove compartment. And finally, Greg gave a detailed account of the relevant incidents from his point of view. Tim still didn't say a peep. By now, he seemed very meek, though.

* * *

'Awesome! So, you caught Tim red-handed,' Sebastian said in admiration, after Anna and Bruce had told him and his parents about the events in Valdora.

'How much money was actually in that Esky?' Lizzie asked.

'Thirty thousand dollars!' Anna replied. 'The fifty-dollar notes had all been bundled together and put in plastic bags. Tim was stubbornly silent, but I hope we'll hear more about this story at some point.'

'Who knows, maybe the other policemen are corrupt and will keep the money,' Sebastian mumbled and got a stern look from his mother. His father ignored his remark and asked worriedly,

'How is Greg? Have you taken him to the doctor?'

'Yes, but only after he led the police to the spot where he'd found his 'treasure chest'. And he proudly showed us all his landscaping works,' Bruce said, smiling at Andy. 'Your colleague is so nice, and it's great what he has already done for the Hot Ears!'

'It's terrible I couldn't come to your help! That bloody, unreliable car! I'll make an appointment for a repair a.s.a.p.,' Andy said. 'Oh, how's Greg gonna get home now, in a taxi?'

'Don't worry! Oliver will drive him back after the doctor's visit and then pick up Angus and Celina. We didn't all fit into Oliver's little car, so they stayed there. Celina was eager to have a good look at the property anyway,' Bruce replied.

Anna giggled. 'Greg asked Celina and Angus to plant a small tree, water it thoroughly and put his tools away. And he insisted that Oliver should clean up himself. He even cheekily threatened to spray him with a garden hose! He was quite lively and cheerful in the end, and I don't think his head wound was that bad. But Bruce had done a great first aid job on him!'

Lizzie had to smile at Anna's admiring look. It was obvious that her daughter was heavenly in love with Bruce. And it seemed to be the same the other way round. She was glad that Andy had fewer reservations about Bruce now. He also gradually accepted his somewhat wild looking friends Angus and Oliver.

'And what happened to Tim?' Sebastian wanted to know.

'The policemen freed him from his steering wheel, locked the Audi and then took Tim away in their own car. Tim was so ashamed that his face was bright red,' Anna explained and patted Susi who was sitting between her and Bruce.

'Or he was red because of his anger!' Bruce said, also stroking Susi.

The dog looked quite enraptured. After a while, though, Susi became restless, lifting her nose into the air.

'Something smells funny!' Sebastian said. 'Like smoke!'

'Oh dear!' Lizzie shouted and ran into the kitchen to turn off the oven. Luckily, their dinner wasn't burnt yet, but crispy and yummy.

# 62 TEST DRIVE

Gabriel was lying under Andy's car on his own driveway when he heard some noise. Spotting a pair of big work boots, he was immediately seized with icy horror. Was that Alfred? His bad premonition was confirmed as two strong hands grabbed his ankles, pulling him away from the Toyota.

'Hello, Gabriel!' Alfred said with a smiling mouth but cold glistening eyes. 'Are you doing dirty work again? And how is your Melissa?'

Gabriel wiped his oily fingers on his coverall and leaned against the front door for support because his knees were shaking. A thick drop of sweat ran from his forehead into his eye, and he blinked vehemently.

'Hi, Alfred! I'm ... I'm so sorry ... um, you know how Melissa was, she was completely dazed from all the drugs, and that day she had taken the 'FUN' and ...'

'Oh, nonsense, don't fool me!' Alfred growled. 'I'm sure you're just sorry that I didn't die!'

'Nah, bullshit, on the contrary! Do you think I want to be married to a murderess? I'm very glad you recovered.'

Gabriel tried to be friendly, but inwardly he was wondering why Alfred had already been discharged from the hospital. In any case, he still looked very unhealthy and terribly pale.

Alfred laughed maliciously and tucked his long hair behind his ears.

'So, Melissa has ended up in a mental ward. Your wife is a crazy, dangerous chick! You should be happy to be rid of her, right?'

He moved uncomfortably close to Gabriel who instinctively recoiled but couldn't move away because he was leaning against Andy's car. Only now did Gabriel notice that Alfred's skin was covered with tiny pustules and his eyes had a yellowish tint. And wasn't his hair much thinner than before? Would it possibly fall out in clumps, like Melissa's? But why was he at large and not in prison? While all these thoughts flashed through his mind, Alfred put his face even closer to him, and his bad breath almost made him sick.

'You won't get rid of me so easily, my dear friend,' Alfred hissed. He eyeballed him threateningly, but turned around the next moment because he heard approaching footsteps from behind.

'Hello!' someone shouted and patted Gabriel on the shoulder. 'Well, how is it going? Can you fix my Toyota?'

'Hi, Andy!' Gabriel said with relief. 'Yes, it's almost finished. Everything is already done in the engine compartment, and I've also fitted a new exhaust pipe. But I still have to check a few things, and then I should take a little test drive. Would you like to come along for a ride?'

Despite his greasy fingers he scratched his head briefly.

'By the way, this is Alfred. Alfred, this is my neighbour, Andy, the owner of this oldie.'

'Hello!' the men greeted each other with a fleeting smile.

'Gabriel is a good mechanic,' Alfred stated.

'I hope so!' Andy joked.

'See you later!' Alfred said to Gabriel, nodded at Andy and went to his car.

'Phew, you were my salvation, Andy!' Gabriel said gratefully as soon as Alfred was out of earshot. 'That guy scared me again! But now I better get going before it gets dark. Shall we take the test drive tonight or tomorrow?'

'I'd prefer tonight. Around seven p.m.?'

'Yes, okay, see you then!'

Gabriel crawled under the car, cursing quietly about a lost screw and whistling happily when he found it.

\* \* \*

Andy was thrilled. His car started immediately and the engine sounded much better than before.

'What did Alfred want from you, Gabriel? Did he come to collect debts?' Andy asked.

'No, but he certainly didn't forget them. But luckily my parents-in-law have lent me enough money in the meantime so that I can finally pay off Alfred. Once that's done, I never want to see him again.'

'Well, my Toyota seems to be running smoothly again, even without the new engine oil that you recommended. I'll transfer your well-deserved money into your account straight away,' Andy offered. 'By the way, a friend of mine is very interested in your quote for fixing his car.' He frowned. 'Um, but you'd probably need a proper garage and a hydraulic lift for that; it might be tricky otherwise.'

'Well, maybe I can do it without it. I'd be happy to take a look.' Gabriel glanced at Andy. 'However, I've decided not to set up my own business, at least not at this stage, because I'm going to work again in the same workshop that Martin had owned. Isn't that great?'

'Wow, that's good news!'

'Yes, a Greek has bought the workshop. I will start there next month and then I'm also supposed to look after a young apprentice. I'm sure it will be fun, as long as he's not too rebellious.'

Andy smiled. 'The boss or the apprentice?'

Gabriel laughed. 'Both! But the boss actually seems to be very nice and good-natured.'

He remained silent for a while, and then he sighed sadly.

'Sometimes I regret moving here. If Melissa and I had stayed in Brisbane and hadn't met Alfred ...'

'No, the past is irreversible and nobody knows if you were better off somewhere else. As you've told us, Melissa already had problems with suicidal thoughts and other drugs before.'

'That's true, but that horrible powder from Alfred made it worse!' Gabriel's voice sounded bitter.

Andy didn't reply, concentrating on the drive and the soft humming car sounds. A bird that had been nibbling on the flesh of a dead little animal on the road fluttered away.

'It's strange that the 'FUN' supposedly attracts and kills certain animals, reptiles and cats,' Andy said thoughtfully. 'And who knows what other effects it might have. You've probably also heard about the unusual bird extinction in the north of Queensland, haven't you?'

'Yes, Sebastian mentioned this when I came to visit you.'

Guiltily, Gabriel remembered how he had hurled Melissa's doll into the bushes, with the drugs hidden inside, without thinking of any danger to the environment. He was not much better than Alfred!

He was completely perplexed when Andy told him now that Lizzie had found this doll during a Bocce game in the park.

Gabriel shouted, 'I can't believe it!'

Andy smiled self-consciously, somewhat embarrassed. Melissa had already called him and Lizzie 'stupid snoopers' and 'informers', but he was still eager to ask Gabriel a few more questions.

'Um, did you and Melissa know that Alfred was not only a drug dealer but also an animal smuggler?' he asked after a moment's hesitation.

'No, I had no idea! However, his van did smell pretty bad at times. One day, when it stank really horribly of rotten eggs or something like that, I pointed it out to him, and he immediately snapped at me and accused me of farting.'

Andy chuckled. 'We usually blame Susi if there's a suspicious smell in the car or at home!'

Gabriel also smiled.

'Melissa and I always liked animals, and if it weren't so difficult to find landlords who'd allow us to have a pet, we would get a little dog. After Melissa had to quit her job for health reasons, she was even more depressed than before, and a loyal companion would certainly be good for her.'

'What a pity you couldn't get a dog! I really love our Susi! She is such a dear friend and gives us so much joy! Besides, I could almost write a novel about all the experiences with our foster dogs. And isn't it amazing what dogs can do? There are, for example, companion dogs for disabled people, and specially trained dogs that help former soldiers with post-traumatic stress disorders.'

'Yeah, it's awesome! Recently I watched a report on TV where prisoners were allowed to train dogs,' Gabriel said in a low voice, and he suddenly sobbed: 'I never thought Melissa would end up in prison. And I myself only got away by a hair's breadth.'

Andy tried to comfort him. 'Maybe Melissa won't have to go to prison after all, and you've found a new job, so just look on the bright side!'

He now drove onto the motorway, accelerating to a hundred kilometres per hour. There were only a few cars on the road because the rush hour was over. Gabriel sniffed, swallowed audibly and was ashamed of his weakness. He had already lost it once before, crying like a baby in front of the whole Kuhlmann family. When else had he ever cried openly? During his fight with Steven, tears had come to his eyes in pain and anger, but otherwise he had always tried to pull himself together.

'Excuse me!' he murmured and exhaled deeply. 'I think it's great that dogs – or cats and rabbits – can help prisoners to behave in a more responsible and social way. And truly wonderful if the offenders reintegrate better into society after their release from prison. But I do wonder if the animals are always treated well by them.'

'As far as I know, this kind of therapy is very successful and often melts, so to speak, the hardest hearts of the criminals.'

'That sounds reassuring! I always get furious when an animal is mistreated. Once, on the beach, I saw a surfer beating a cute dog just because it had tried to give him a friendly welcome. The poor dog ran away howling! And when I confronted Steven, he immediately punched me on the nose, the nasty guy!'

Andy listened up. 'Steven?'

'Yes, we had met before while surfing, but after our argument I tried to keep my distance. Fortunately, I rarely saw him anyway, and later he was killed.'

'We've heard about that, too, by a brutal King Hit, right?'

'Yes, so cruel! Hard to imagine that he died from a single blow! And I think the culprit was a complete stranger who just went crazy.' Gabriel suddenly shivered, thinking of his wife and her unpredictable tantrums.

Andy considered briefly whether he should tell him that Thomas had secretly taken photos of Gabriel and Steven during their brawl back then, but he refrained from doing so. Instead, he asked: 'Would you like to drive for a while? In my opinion, everything's fine, but after all, you are the expert.'

Gabriel agreed. After Andy had got off the motorway and parked the Toyota, Gabriel drove off.

'By the way, I'll do the oil change for you for free if you buy the oil,' Gabriel offered generously.

'No way! Of course I'll pay you! I've always hated doing this kind of dirty work, and Lizzie certainly doesn't like it, either.'

'You really are a great family! And I want to thank you all for helping Melissa and me! Also, for ... um, well, for letting me cry my heart out in front of you the other day,' Gabriel said quietly, pulling nervously on a piece of skin near his right thumbnail. His mouth felt uncomfortably dry and he was longing for a cold beer and a cigarette. Nah, no more cigarettes, he admonished himself inwardly.

'Come on, neighbours should always support each other!' Andy said and blushed, because the remark seemed quite hackneyed to him, although it was meant honestly.

'Well, neighbours can make each other's lives hell. Martin, for example, constantly had trouble with an older couple. The man, whose name is Geoff, was not that bad, but his wife Clara – oh no, Claire – was always grumbling about something. One day they accused Martin of poisoning their trees along the common property line. But Martin had been in holidays at the time. Anyway, he was stunned when he came home from a sailing trip, still in good spirits, and they immediately started calling him names. Only later it turned out that Geoff himself had been to blame. He had intended to kill a few weeds under the trees and had stupidly messed up both the chemical and the amount of spray.'

'Really?' Andy marvelled. 'Well, well!'

'Yes, Geoff confessed this to Martin at some point. But he begged him not to tell Claire at any cost, as she could be a real bitch.' Gabriel smiled.

Andy remained serious. It was terrible how often people got wrongly accused and how quickly false rumours were spread – throughout world history. Like Lizzie, he sometimes worried about his children, sticking their noses into affairs that were none of their business. And Gabriel's report about Martin and his neighbours reminded him not only of Alison and her observations, but also of the murdered seventeen-year-old Thomas. He became cold.

Meanwhile, the moon was shining brightly over the sugar cane fields, and in the distance Mount Coolum stood out as a gloomy but impressive silhouette. They quickly approached the entrance to Coolum Beach, and both men were looking forward to a cosy, relaxed evening. Just as Gabriel turned into a large roundabout, the centre of which was covered with dense vegetation and palm trees, a mobile phone rang.

Andy grunted, reluctant to take the call, and said to Gabriel: 'Hopefully it's not an urgent job!' However, he answered the phone politely, listening attentively to the person on the other end of the line, finally promising, 'Okay, I'll be there in about fifteen minutes and see what I can do.' Addressing Gabriel, he said, 'Bummer, I have to go back to work. But first, I get you home and let Lizzie know about the new job.' Then he added, smiling, 'That's one of the disadvantages of being a self-employed electrician. You keep getting calls outside normal working hours and still have to be friendly.

# 63 NASTY COMMENTS

On a sunny Saturday morning, Kirsty and Sebastian went for a long walk with Susi and then spontaneously visited their friend Ivory. As soon as they had taken a seat in the cosy living room, Ivory showed them four photos of Kate's young Labrador that Fiona had posted on her Facebook page the previous evening. Patrick, usually a very handsome dog, was portrayed in an ugly way: the first image was a photo of his extremely drooling head, with spit flying in all directions, a second image showed the Labrador making a poop, a third one depicted him eating some poop, and then there was a close-up of his stained mouth. Fiona had written about it:

*Look who's kissing Kate! No wonder she and her boyfriend stink. Anyway, I'm staying away from them!*

'Yuck!' Sebastian called out.

'That's horrible!' Kirsty shook herself in disgust, and Susi paused to drink from a water bowl, looked at her in amazement, continued drinking and then shook herself as well, spraying fine drops in the air.

Ivory grinned crookedly and explained, 'Well, now and then Patrick eats other dogs' excrements and even his own faeces. Kate and her parents haven't been able to stop his bad manners completely yet, although they already tried all sorts of things. It is repulsive, hey? Fortunately, little Abby, their other dog, doesn't eat shit.'

'Better don't kiss any dogs,' Sebastian said to Kirsty with a smile and patted his dog. 'Luckily Susi doesn't eat faeces, either. However, she enjoyed sniffing at some horse droppings recently, and another time she rolled around in the slimy crap of a bird quite enthusiastically.'

'Although Fiona's photos might show the truth, her snide comments about you and Kate are downright mean!' Kirsty said indignantly, gazing at Ivory. 'How did Kate react?'

'She was clever!' said Ivory. 'She not only took this nasty affair with humour but even stole Fiona's thunder, because she gave a short, scientific-sounding text about coprophagy as feedback and finally ...'

'Copro...what?' Sebastian interrupted him.

'Coprophagy is the technical term used to describe this animal behaviour, the eating of faeces, which can have a variety of causes,' Ivory explained. 'Well, and then Kate wrote:

*Nasty comments stink to high heaven and can destroy friendships.*

'Fiona has always been a horrible person, and I could never understand why Kate and Arielle used to hang around with her,' Kirsty said, frowning.

'Actually, one can almost feel sorry for Fiona. But good that Kate is not so squeamish. Arielle, on the other hand, would have been completely crushed,' Sebastian pondered.

'Um, Fiona also posted something mean about Arielle and her bottom,' Ivory said.

He nimbly scrolled to another picture on his smartphone and showed it to his friends. This time they saw a wet, slightly dirty backside in light-coloured jeans and the text:

*Did she pee her pants? Is she still a bedwetter?*

'How do you know it's Arielle's bum?' Sebastian asked, searching in vain for a clue.

'Because I was there! She and Jack plopped down on a rain-soaked bench and immediately jumped up screaming. And apart from Arielle I don't know anyone else who wears such lime green jeans. But I wonder how Fiona managed to take this photo without our knowledge. She must have been close by.'

'Have Arielle and Jack already seen this?' Kirsty asked.

'I don't know! But they should just ignore it.'

'Jack has nothing to do with Facebook anyway,' Sebastian said. 'He doesn't like people constantly sending selfies and silly jokes.'

Ivory nodded his head. 'True, a lot of things are stupid. And it's nasty to publish something about other people without their consent. Worst of all are those posts that are fake, or downright vile. And they can cause so much despair, or even death! Did you hear about that twelve-year-old boy in Sydney who committed suicide last week? Just because he'd constantly been teased by his classmates. Absolutely terrible!'

Once again, his fingers scurried across the screen, and Sebastian inwardly feared Fiona's next image would depict a fat pimple on his own face, but to his relief he was spared.

'Shoot! I wanted to show you something else, but I can't find it anymore!' Ivory growled. 'Oh no, and now the battery is dead. Wait, I'd better get my laptop!'

Soon afterwards, they all watched a short video, filmed by Fiona, while Susi dozed off at their feet.

'That's Alfred's van!' Sebastian exclaimed. 'What's Fiona got to do with it?'

'I think she loves spying on other people,' Ivory replied. 'Well, Fiona isn't very clever to post stuff like this in public. If this gets into the wrong hands ...'

'Hello, kids!' Ivory's father shouted in a booming voice and stepped into the room, filling it with a whiff of various smells of sunscreen, fresh sweat and deodorant. Barry was dressed casually; his cheeks were slightly reddened and his hair was tousled.

Ivory smiled at him. Kirsty and Sebastian, sitting close together on the couch, said: 'Hi, Barry! Hello, Mr. Little!'

'Please call me Barry, Sebastian!' Mr. Little begged him. 'Otherwise, I feel so old. But why are you all sitting here in the dark on a day with bright sunshine? Do you really have to fiddle around with a mobile phone or laptop all the time? You need Vitamin D and fresh air! I've been riding my bike for an hour, it's so beautiful outside.'

Kirsty laughed out loud and her green eyes sparkled mischievously. 'Oh, Barry, you make us look like pale couch potatoes. We are not, look here, I'm all tanned!'

She extended her arms, and Sebastian was amazed at how unselfconsciously she talked to the policeman. But she and Ivory had known each other since kindergarten, and Barry and Kirsty's mother were also friends.

'We have to show you something,' Ivory said seriously to his father and came straight to the point. 'Look, Fiona's caught someone graffitiing a car!'

'Fiona?' Barry asked, thunderstruck. 'Your schoolmate, the one you never liked?'

'Yes, exactly!'

Ivory started the film again, in which a darkly dressed, youthful-looking person was spraying the word *MURDERER* in huge, bright red letters on the windscreen of a car.

Sebastian blurted out: 'That's Alfred's Isuzu. He'll be mad as hell!'

Ivory nodded. 'I think so too, especially if he can't wash off the paint easily. But who is this man with the hood, and why does he call Alfred a murderer?'

'Maybe he found out that Alfred had knocked down Olivia, the singer, on her moped back then,' Kirsty pondered, biting her lower lip thoughtfully.

'But that had been an accident,' Sebastian defended Alfred, although he couldn't stand the man.

'Nah! I think I know the real cause,' Barry murmured, staring indecisively into the air for a while, stepping from one foot to the other.

Finally, he collapsed ungracefully into an armchair and said softly, 'I didn't really want to tell you about this tragedy yet. Unfortunately, a woman has died from an overdose of the 'FUN' powder. She might be the very first victim of this still quite new drug. Her name is – or was – Maryann King. She was only eighteen years old.'

'What?' Sebastian cried so loudly that Ivory flinched.

Barry swallowed hard.

'Yes, she was found dead in her flat the night before last, in fact by her boyfriend Simon. She had apparently experimented with drugs on several occasions and also loved high-proof alcohol. Despite her youth, she was not a clean slate, as the police had already noticed her for causing public nuisance and various petty offences. For example, she'd done illegal graffiti spraying and even shoplifting.'

'Maryann and Simon have also stolen Kate's dogs,' Ivory said with disdain.

'Probably with Fiona's help!' Kirsty called.

Barry looked at her in surprise. 'Oh, I didn't know Fiona had been involved. So, she might have known Simon. Do you think he's the guy in that video? But why was she filming him?'

'Where is this taking place?' Kirsty asked.

They watched Fiona's video clip once again, and this time they paid less attention to the blood-red letters and the blue van parked at the side of the road and more attention to the background. In the distance, a woman pushed a pram, moving away from Alfred's car. Kirsty thought she could hear a baby's whining and fragments of singing, but the main thing she heard was just an unpleasant sounding hiss.

At that moment the phone rang. Barry picked up and listened for a while. The children and Susi curiously watched his changing facial expressions. First, he smiled almost lovingly, then his eyebrows rose, his eyes widened in horror, his lips trembled, and finally he blew a whistle. Surprised, Susi sat up straight, pricking up her ears. Sebastian patted her soothingly.

Barry finished the call, put the phone down gently, took another sip of water, coughed and said in a husky voice:

'That was a colleague of mine. This morning someone found Alfred in the gutter where he was lying stone dead next to his van. He'd probably suffered a heart attack.'

# 64 BITTERSWEET MEMORIES

Anna and her parents listened eagerly when Sebastian informed them about the sudden death of both Maryann and Alfred. Anna was so shocked that she almost forgot her date with Bruce. But now she was sitting in his room, giving him a full account of the story.

After some astonished exclamations Bruce mused, 'I wonder if Alfred died because he was so upset about the graffiti?'

'Maybe! Or he was still so weakened by Melissa's poison attack that the strain of washing the word *MURDERER* off his windscreen killed him,' Anna said.

In any case, Bruce felt little sympathy for that ruthless drug dealer and animal smuggler. However, a thick lump rose up in his throat as Anna falteringly told him about Maryann's fatal overdose. Embarrassed, he stood up and turned away from Anna to hide his tears. Standing at the door to the garden, he looked up into the clear blue sky, while dark clouds seemed to accumulate inside him.

Anna was irritated. 'Did you still love Maryann?' she finally asked him.

Bruce remained silent and avoided looking at her, and Anna became sad. Had Bruce been faking it the whole time? Sometimes she felt so young and inexperienced in his presence, and now she began to doubt their relationship. As she looked at his well-built body in the dark blue T-shirt, his strong, momentarily slightly trembling shoulders and his thick mop of hair, she was overcome with a mix of feelings. Jealousy, distrust and fear of loss alternated in rapid succession with hope, tenderness, and love. Her heart was beating so loudly that she almost feared to get a heart attack as well. Why did he not answer? Should she rather leave him alone? She played indecisively with a strand of hair and remained sitting on the sofa like a pile of misery.

Bruce continued to stare at the sky without really seeing it. Just as Anna was getting ready to leave, he went back to her and gave her an awkward hug. 'Excuse me, Anna!' he muttered into her ear. 'I thought I hated Maryann, but now I just feel terribly sorry for her. She was still so young, not even nineteen. And I had no idea she had started using drugs. This 'FUN' is such a terrible invention!' Suddenly he sobbed loudly. 'Please promise me you'll never touch any stuff like that!'

Relieved, Anna wrapped her arms around him. 'No problem! I am too afraid of the effects of any drugs.' She grinned mischievously. 'Sebastian called me a 'control freak' the other day, and in a way, he's right. I never want to lose control of myself. Just for that reason, I won't touch any drugs! Moreover, I've seen what the nasty 'FUN' stuff did to Melissa. Shocking!'

'I'd never regarded you as a 'control freak' before. Anyway, you're a beautiful, great friend!' Bruce pulled her up by the hands and hugged her passionately. Then they kissed.

For a while they forgot the world around them, until Oliver returned home, singing loudly, and they quickly parted as if caught doing something forbidden. Oliver noticed the blush in Anna's cheeks and grinned at them. However, he stopped laughing when he heard about Maryann's death. Although he had disliked her from the start, she had been Bruce's girlfriend for a while and had therefore been a member of his closest circle of friends. He was overcome by an inner coldness when he realised that she was the second dead friend after Olivia in that group where no one was more than twenty years old. To die so young, terrible! He still missed Olivia painfully, even though she had left him shortly after her seventeenth birthday. And he kept asking himself what he might have done wrong.

Now he wondered whether the relationship between Simon and Maryann had been harmonious. Unlike Bruce, he didn't believe that Simon had been under her thumb. He considered him more insidious and dangerous than he appeared at first glance. Had Simon brought Maryann into bad company and driven her into a criminal drug world? She had been arrogant and sometimes cool and calculating, but still a little naive.

Bruce too had gloomy thoughts. He wondered how Simon was feeling now, having lost his beloved friend in such a tragic way. And could it be possible that Maryann received the 'FUN' from Alfred? Had Simon known about it, blaming him for Maryann's overdose, and hatefully painted the word *MURDERER* on his windscreen? And if so, would he be happy that Alfred had collapsed while washing the car? Or would he now regret his spraying action and feel like a murderer himself? Anyway, Bruce was glad that Tim didn't die of over-excitement when he discovered the word IDIOT on his fence. And as fate would have it, Bruce had met Anna, Sebastian and their father, of all people, during this stupid, childish tagging, for which he was very ashamed afterwards. He was so very lucky that Anna hadn't despised him and had even become his girlfriend. Suddenly he rejoiced and looked tenderly at Anna.

Anna was in a strange mood. On the one hand, she was floating on cloud nine because Bruce was obviously besotted with her. He had swept away her doubts with his stormy embrace and a deep kiss. On the other hand, she felt nervous and uncomfortable, gripped by an undefined fear. Was it fear of dying? In her mind's eye she saw the murdered Thomas on the horse, then the pale Melissa, collapsed in her garden, the bleeding Tim at the harbour, her wounded father, her frightened, sobbing mother, and the agitated Gabriel in their living room, then Greg with his laceration in Valdora. And now two people she had known by sight had died ...

She became downright nauseous, and she was no longer aware of her surroundings. She had the impression that she was standing at a yawning abyss and that she could fall at any time, deeper and deeper ...

But then Bruce grasped her hand and asked anxiously:

'Anna, what's wrong?'

'I just... I thought of that woman who found Alfred as a lifeless bundle. A long time ago, Barbara and I saw the foot of a murder victim sticking out of the mud near a creek, and then Sebastian discovered the hand of the murdered Thomas in the park. But to see the whole body of a dead man right in front of you ...' Anna swallowed hard.

Bruce continued to hold her hand and squeezed it briefly, saying: 'Yeah, that must have been a shock! But I have little sympathy for Alfred. Even though he didn't cause the accident back then, he was totally mean to leave poor Olivia lying there, dying in the street. He should have called an ambulance immediately and tried to save her.'

At the same moment Bruce cursed himself for his words.

Oliver stared at him, croaking, 'What did you just say? What did Alfred have to do with Olivia?'

Bruce declared: 'You never wanted to talk about Olivia, so I asked Anna and Sebastian to keep the story from you. The Kuhlmanns recently learned from their neighbour that it was Alfred who had hit Olivia on the moped. He took off because he had already drunk a few beers. But Olivia herself had caused the accident.'

Oliver became very pale. After a while he said in a flat voice: 'At least now I know!'

That evening Oliver listened to the music of the group 'Oliver & Olivia' for the first time in a long while. The magnificent dark, smoky voice of his ex-girlfriend filled him with melancholy and tears welled up in his eyes. Nevertheless, he was grateful that he had learned the truth today. After her death he had desperately tried to erase all memories of her, but without success. Only now did he realise that his decision never to speak about her and never to hear her voice again had been completely wrong, only making his grief worse. He would never forget her, and the recorded melodies of them singing together and the sounds of the didgeridoo made him cry, but at the same time a heavy burden seemed to fall off him. It was time to start a new life.

* * *

Andy assumed that Gabriel would be relieved to learn of Alfred's death. After Sebastian's report and a phone call to Barry Little, he decided to visit his neighbour and to bring him the news, knowing how much he had feared Alfred. To his dismay, however, Gabriel turned chalk-white and looked as if he would faint at any moment. Then Gabriel stammered, 'His heart must have failed because Melissa had secretly given him the 'FUN'. Will the judge now convict her as a murderer?'

# 65 CONCERT IN THE PARK

On Sunday the sun was shining from a blue sky, and it was unusually hot and humid for this time of the year. Anna and Bruce were looking forward to the open-air concert in Peregian Beach, where the Hot Ears would perform besides numerous other local musicians. When Anna and Bruce arrived in the early afternoon, a large crowd had already gathered in the park that was located above the dunes, offering views to the sea in places. Anna looked around to find Audrey, Brenda, Barbara and David, but saw only unfamiliar faces far and wide. Many young people as well as older people and whole families with children and dogs enjoyed the relaxed atmosphere in the warm spring air. Some people sat cross-legged on colourful woollen blankets or grey tarpaulins, others had brought folding chairs and their own food.

Anna also carried a small Esky with water, juice and biscuits. Bruce spotted a vacant place in the shade of a tree, and they carefully moved through the crowd. The park smelled of sunscreen, mozzie spray, sausages and mustard, doughnuts and cinnamon, and a band was playing loud hip-hop music. A fluffy black dog raced to Anna and sniffed curiously at the Esky before being pulled back by its owner. Anna had left Susi at home, fearing that her dog might try to take off, panic-stricken, as it hated mass gatherings.

Close to a group of three ladies with two small, very young dogs, Bruce spread out a huge beach towel on the lawn and sat down on it. Immediately, the puppies crawled towards him and he stroked them tenderly, keeping his face away from their licking tongues. Anna smiled. All dogs seemed to love her boyfriend! The five young men on the stage finished their performance and Anna breathed a sigh of relief.

Bruce whispered, 'They sounded horrible, didn't they? But the Hot Ears will be next.'

'Awesome!' Anna said.

She was distracted for a while as the two dogs now demanded her attention and she and Bruce were greeted joyfully by Barbara and David. Soon after, Celina started singing. Her song was so wonderful and yet so sad that everyone fell silent, listening devoutly. Celina, the Irish singer, had an incredibly full voice despite her graceful figure.

She began with a poignant solo, to which Oliver's soothing deep voice and gradually the various instruments of the other group members mixed in. And then their music, at first slowly and then faster and faster, developed into a stirring rock melody that made many people jump up and dance. Anna's feet also automatically bounced along with the dynamic rhythms, and she was completely thrilled. Although she had already heard many songs of the Hot Ears, this performance was particularly impressive and emotional. Oliver whirled around the stage, his mane of long hair waving. Dressed in glittering clothes, he sang at the top of his voice. Celina was now smiling happily too. During her former solo, she had looked heartwarmingly melancholic, lonely and lost, almost like a professional actress, her appearance matching the dramatic text of the song.

Anna was wondering whether Oliver and Celina could become lovers when she caught sight of Angus, playing his drums ecstatically. He seemed to be enlivened by the music and his eyes were shining like Anna had never seen before. She realised that he had fallen in love with the beautiful Celina, obviously adoring her. A little later, during a groovy funk-rock number, Anna finally discovered Audrey and Brenda who were dancing near the stage in hippie-like, airy dresses, swinging their heads with the long hair vehemently. At the end there was a short performance by the two guitarists whom Anna only knew briefly. One of these Hot Ears members seemed to have hot ears indeed, because they were deep red. Apparently, he was a bit shy, although he could play the guitar very well and looked extremely good. Did he suffer from stage fright at all his public appearances? Anna felt sorry for him. Poor guy! Or was it just a sunburn on his ears?

'That's Simon!' Bruce whispered to her.

'What?' Anna was startled, thinking for a moment that Bruce was talking about the same boy she had just watched. But no, Bruce was looking in a completely different direction, towards the sea. At first Anna didn't know who he meant until she saw a man with long blonde hair who reminded her a bit of Alfred. Simon was standing on the sandy path leading from the sea to the park, apparently waiting for someone. Bruce had told her that he was a surfer, so she was not surprised that he was quite tanned. His shorts and a light T-shirt sat loosely on his muscular yet slender body, and he was quite tall.

'Don't stare at him like that!' Bruce cautioned her.

Anna blushed and noticed that Barbara had already followed her gaze. Hastily she turned away and had to smile about David who was just being assailed and licked all over by the cute little dogs.

'Who is that?' Barbara asked quietly.

'The boyfriend of Maryann,' Anna explained, louder than intended, arising David's attention.

'I know that guy,' he said to their surprise. 'He used to work in our neighbours' garden, and recently my mother offered him an ice-cold drink on a hot day.'

'Yes, Simon is a landscape gardener,' Bruce said. 'I think he set up his own business a year ago, mainly doing maintenance work, like mowing, pruning, weeding and stuff like that.'

'Oh, that must not have been very good for his girlfriend Maryann who suffered from hay fever,' Anna remarked, at once annoyed with herself for reminding Bruce of his ex. Besides, she didn't want to think about the dead again on such a cheerful and relaxed afternoon.

Bruce took a hearty bite from one of the biscuits Anna had brought along, and his face contorted in a grimace of pain. 'Damn, there's a piece of a nutshell in there!'

Outraged, he inspected the rest of the biscuit and carefully touched a tooth with his tongue.

'Hope you didn't lose a filling!' Barbara said.

'But the biscuits are really delicious!' David mumbled with a full mouth.

Bruce grinned good-naturedly and was going to reply when a mighty thunder sounded. Only now did they notice that the sky had taken on an eerily bright yet somber yellow-grey colour and that it had become even muggier. It was the calm before the storm! Just as the next band was about to start their concert, another clap of thunder echoed. The trees bent in a sudden gust of wind, tarpaulins rattled, napkins flew through the air, and a heavy downpour of rain set in. The spectators shrieked, quickly packing their belongings and hurrying off in all directions to find refuge under a roof or hurrying to their cars. Anna, her friends and many others gathered close to the wall of the Surf Life Saving Club to remain at least reasonably dry.

After a short break, the group on the stage started again, playing unperturbed and doing their best to drown out the ongoing thunder. The remaining spectators rewarded them with fierce applause until the concert unfortunately had to be ended prematurely for safety reasons.

On the way to the car park Anna saw Simon again. Now he was standing under the eaves of a small shop – next to Malcolm. A particularly bright lightning flashed up, and she shivered involuntarily. What was the connection between Simon and Malcolm? Or was it not Malcolm at all? He looked different, with much darker and longer hair than she remembered, and he had a thick full beard and a bushy moustache.

# 66 NEW HOPE

After talking to Melissa's parents and a lawyer, Gabriel was filled with new hope that his wife would not be charged with murder. Moreover, Melissa's therapy seemed to be quite successful, as she was already significantly better. And he was very happy with his new job. For a week, he had been working full-time as a mechanic in the workshop in Maroochydore that used to belong to Martin. His current boss was generous and fair, and Richard, the apprentice, seemed a bit slow-witted, sometimes testing his patience, but was otherwise a pleasant and not at all rebellious colleague.

Gabriel was infinitely grateful to the Kuhlmanns who had treated him so kindly. And he had not forgotten his resolution to care more for others instead of constantly thinking of his own problems. But how could he help Anna and Sebastian with their secret investigations? Wouldn't it be better for them to stay out of these dangerous affairs and to leave them to the police? Andy had told him about Alfred's sudden death and Maryann's fatal overdose, and although he had never known this woman, he felt sorry for her. Like his own wife, she had been a victim of the terrible 'FUN' powder. At the same time, fresh hatred for Alfred and other drug dealers was stirring in him, and countless questions were buzzing around in his head. Was Alfred's friend

Malcolm also involved in illegal drug and wildlife trades? For what reason had Thomas observed and photographed Malcolm? Who had strangled the poor boy and put him on a fake horse of all things? And who had shot Martin on his own yacht? Thoughtfully, he was reading his handwritten notes on his pinboard: *Help Anna and Sebastian with their investigations! What did Thomas have to do with Malcolm?*

\* \* \*

That same evening, after an uneventful Sunday shift, Barry Little returned home more satisfied than he had been in a long time. He liked his new colleague. She was cold as ice, very determined and tough when it mattered, but usually cheerful, warm-hearted, and smart. And finally, he was rid of Tim! As Barry had already guessed, Tim had been a corrupt policeman who had accepted bribes. While preparing dinner he told his son what he had learned so far: 'Tim had indeed been on the trail of an illegal trade in drugs and exotic wildlife. Initially, he was only shadowing Alfred but later Martin and Malcolm as well. Moreover, he suspected they had partners in Thailand and Indonesia. But he kept it a secret as he intended to uncover the entire smuggling ring all by himself. Then, however, everything went wrong. One day he was careless, spying around, and walked straight into Alfred's trap. Fearing for his life, Tim quickly agreed not to report the smugglers. Since Alfred didn't quite trust him, he offered him regular payments in return for his ongoing silence. And thus, my dear colleague gladly turned a blind eye to this nasty business.' Barry scoffed.

'I am not sure if Tim felt pity for the victims of drug trafficking, and I almost believe that he likes animals more than people. At one point, he took courage and demanded that Alfred stop the animal trade.'

Ivory said, astounded, 'So, you were right about him being fond of turtles.'

'Yes, and he managed to steal two turtles from Malcolm's car that he believed to be Martin's car at the time. He kept one turtle for himself and gave an Indian star turtle to Claudia, the daughter of his girlfriend Astrid, as a birthday present. And for a while, Tim also kept a Green Python in his house that escaped.'

'Sebastian has seen that one!' Ivory called excitedly. 'But how did the smugglers transport all these animals to Australia, by plane? And the drugs as well?'

'Until recently, Tim had mistakenly assumed that Martin had been in cahoots with Alfred and Malcolm and that he'd transported the goods on his yacht. And Martin did, but without his knowledge.'

Ivory raised his eyebrows, not understanding.

Barry narrated: 'Occasionally, mainly on longer sailing trips, Malcolm had worked for Martin as a cook. Taking advantage of this opportunity, Malcolm had smuggled crates of various exotic animals, all miserably crammed together, and boxes of lizard and bird eggs on board, probably bringing them from abroad to our Sunshine Coast, perhaps with the help of some middlemen. The packets of 'FUN' came from the north of Queensland.'

'From the island with the secret laboratory? Where a mysterious bird death took place?'

'Yeah, that's right.'

'How did the drug dealers know each other?' Ivory almost cut his finger in excitement and momentarily stopped cutting the cucumber.

'Alfred and Malcolm had already known each other for a long time, and another friend of them was a chemist who made the drugs in that laboratory,' Barry replied. 'That woman and Alfred worked out everything with regards to the drugs and Malcolm was in charge of the wildlife trade.'

'And what about Martin? Why was he shot?' Ivory asked.

'Well, Martin was also a crook who occasionally stole cars and boats. As we already know, he also incited Gabriel, the Kuhlmanns' neighbour, to steal cars, but otherwise he was innocent. Tim was quite surprised when he figured this out.'

Barry was frying two juicy steaks in the pan and briefly checked whether they were done. The onions were already browned and smelled appetizing. Finally, Barry continued:

'Tim received an anonymous tip that someone was expecting a delivery of exotic snakes in Mooloolaba – please don't ask me for details. Outraged, Tim drove to the harbour, paddled in an inflatable dinghy under cover of darkness to Martin's yacht and climbed aboard. He confronted Martin who was totally off his rocker to face Tim. The two of them had first met each other during a holiday in Thailand. But Martin hardly knew Tim, and he certainly hadn't invited him. Anyway, Tim now accused him of animal smuggling. When he pulled out a pistol, Martin turned pale with fear. He stammered that he didn't know a thing about any snakes, but Tim still accused him, becoming increasingly agitated. However, Tim hadn't suspected that Malcolm might be on board, so he was taken by surprise when that guy jumped at him from behind, trying to snatch the gun from him. In the scuffle a shot went off – and hit Martin, who was killed instantly.'

Ivory widened his eyes in horror. 'Poor man! And then?'

'Tim and Malcolm fought wildly, and Malcolm managed to throw first Tim's gun and then Tim himself overboard. He also threw a box with five snakes into the sea and set the yacht on fire to remove all traces. Tim believes that, apart from the snakes, Malcolm had also hidden some drugs that he was supposed to hand over to Alfred for distribution. Unfortunately, Malcolm has gone into hiding.' Looking grim, Barry turned the steaks so vigorously that some fat splashed out of the pan, hitting him on the arm. He cursed and then apologised to Ivory.

'Well, it's time to eat. How's your Greek salad?'

Ivory gazed at the kitchen knife in his hand and only now realised that he had unconsciously cut the cucumber into tiny pieces while the tomatoes and feta cheese were still lying on the table, completely untouched. He grinned sheepishly and hurried to prepare the salad. Over dinner, he said, 'Anna was really brave to help Tim fend off Malcolm's knife attacks.'

'She was lucky! It could have turned out badly for her,' Barry murmured, spearing an olive with his fork.

'She'll be glad to know she helped the right man, as we all kept wondering whether Tim or Malcolm had killed Martin.'

Barry put on a serious face. 'Ivory, I told you this whole story only in confidence. Keep it to yourself while this Malcolm is still on the loose. Promise?'

'Promise!' Ivory said solemnly. Finishing off his salad, he remembered something else. 'What was actually going on with that Esky in Valdora?'

'That was an unusual treasure chest, wasn't it? Well, Tim never would have guessed that Greg would find it on the very day he was going to dig it up.'

'But it was Greg's place,' Ivory cut in.

'That's true, but his property was uninhabited for a while, and especially in the back part there was quite a wilderness anyway. One day, some people were brazenly throwing a wild party in the old greenhouse, smashing some glass panels, trampling a flowerbed and leaving behind rubbish and empty bottles. Tim and another policeman inspected the damage afterwards. No one ever found out who the vandals had been, but Tim got to know the lonely garden this way. When he himself was suspected of wildlife trafficking, he buried his illegally acquired banknotes there. As a precaution, he tucked them away in plastic foil in an Esky, somewhere behind a dense Lantana bush. Above all, he chose a place where the neighbours lived far away and nobody would suddenly look over the fence to have a chat.'

Barry now smiled. 'Tim didn't know that Greg had moved into his parents' house in the meantime. And he had no idea that Greg would rent the greenhouse to the Hot Ears, make a new path for them and discover his Esky while planting trees. You already know the rest of the story. It was great that Anna and her friends came to Greg's rescue and overpowered Tim.'

'So many coincidences!' Ivory shouted. 'It's just too bad Greg couldn't keep the money! And horrible that he got knocked down by Tim!'

'At least Greg's injury wasn't too serious, and there may be a finder's fee someday. But the police investigation is still ongoing. I wouldn't be surprised if Tim had also accepted gifts and bribes from other gangsters. He's always been very greedy. In any case, Tim's career in the police force is now over for good,' Barry said.

As the rain clapped against the windows and drummed loudly onto the roof, he felt a huge stone fall from his heart. At last, he was rid of the hated Tim, and on top of that he now had an honest, likeable and pretty female colleague.

The following night, Ivory had nightmares, dreaming first of treasure chests, pirates and parrots, and then of tongue-flicking snakes and a drooling dog. In another dream, he was sitting tied and gagged in front of a cook in a white apron, who grinned gloatingly while he sharpened a huge knife. The next morning Ivory felt exhausted and didn't feel like going to school at all.

# 67 OLLIE

Susi was in an extremely exuberant mood this Monday because the thunderstorm was over and she could play fearlessly outdoors again. Happily, she rushed through the shallow puddles on the lawn and finally wallowed blissfully in a small mud hole. Lizzie cried out in shock at the sight of her filthy dog but then had to grin.

'Susi, you're a piggy!' she cursed affectionately.

'Mum!' Sebastian shouted. 'Telephone for you! Some Petra!'

'So early in the morning?' Lizzie wondered, taking the phone.

Sebastian turned around quickly when the muddy Susi raced towards him. 'Don't jump!' he warned her but couldn't prevent her from sprinting past him into the room.

'Out!' Lizzie screamed. She motioned her hand wildly and made threatening faces, and Sebastian understood her gestures and quickly dragged Susi back outside.

'Oh, sorry, I meant my dog. ... What? That's terrible!' Lizzie spoke into the phone.

Sebastian pricked up his ears but only heard: ' the poor little animal! Um, no, but we can... yes, good idea! I'll definitely be at home. See you!'

'What happened?' Sebastian asked his mother.

'That was Petra, a member of the Moist Noses Rescue. She's on her way to bring us a new foster dog.'

'Hooray!' Sebastian yelled and ran straight to Susi in the garden to tell her about the new playmate. He would have stepped on a small brownish snake in the grass by a hair's breadth. He uttered a horrified scream, but the snake seemed to be just as scared and took flight.

'What's the matter?' Lizzie looked out the door, sincerely concerned.

'There was a snake!'

'Come into the house quickly! Susi, come!' Lizzie ordered.

Fortunately, Susi obeyed immediately and followed Sebastian. In the dining room Lizzie intercepted her and tried to clean her with a towel. 'Was it a tree snake?' she asked her son, rubbing Susi dry.

'I don't know, it was more brown than green, and quite small. It was probably very young,' Sebastian replied. 'Still, it's a good thing Susi didn't want to play with it, or attack it.'

'Yes, I'm glad too. Some dogs instinctively keep a respectful distance to snakes, but I'm not so sure about Susi.'

'So, what kind of foster dog will we get today?'

'It's a terrier mix named Ollie. Unfortunately, he has a problem with his legs, although he is only three years old, and has to take some medicine all the time. This probably became too expensive for his owner who turned him in to the animal welfare organisation.'

'How mean!' Sebastian protested.

'Well, if someone doesn't earn a lot of money, it could be difficult to pay for such expensive treatment, because the cost of living is getting higher and higher anyway. Maybe there were other reasons apart from the financial difficulties,' Lizzie said thoughtfully. 'And now Petra will bring the little one to us. I hope he will get on well with Susi.'

'I'd save a lot of money and only eat half of my food if I could keep my dog,' Sebastian said, petting Susi lovingly.

Lizzie grinned. 'Well, luckily we've got enough money to feed you and the dogs so far.'

'Good morning!' Anna said, entering the room. 'Yuck, you're all wet, Susi! Don't jump!' Laughing, she fought off Susi's stormy proofs of love.

'We're getting a new dog,' Sebastian told his sister excitedly when Andy came to them, yawning loudly, with tousled hair. He was also greeted exuberantly by Susi, but he ignored her, walked straight past her into the kitchen and switched on the electric kettle.

'Hello, Andy!' Lizzie said, sneering, 'Don't you pay any attention to us to prove you're the man of the house?'

Surprised, her husband turned around. 'Oh, sorry, I must have been half asleep! All I could think about was a cup of coffee. Good morning, everybody!'

He made an excessively polite bow, and Anna giggled.

'So shaggy and in crumpled pyjamas, you look like a little boy and not like the head of the family,' she said cheekily.

'You'll see!' Andy went to her and rubbed his cheek against hers.

'Bah, you're all scratchy!' Anna called, pushing him away.

'A little boy wouldn't have stubble yet,' Andy said and laughed as Lizzie rolled her eyes.

'Actually, Mum's the boss!' Sebastian winked conspiratorially at his mother, and Andy went into the bathroom to shave and comb his hair.

They had just finished their breakfast when a bell rang out, immediately followed by a shrill bark. Susi rushed to the entrance gate ahead of Andy, Anna and Sebastian.

'Oh dear, I hope we don't get a yapper,' Lizzie mumbled and followed her family outside. Aghast, she watched how a white, fuzzy dog snapped at Susi on their driveway. Susi retreated, looking puzzled but not afraid. Petra, a young, overweight lady with wavy dark hair, held Ollie firmly on a leash, saying apologetically: 'Sorry! I think Ollie is a bit shy and probably confused about the many changes in his life. He already had several owners. The last one, a nice pensioner, actually only intended to care for him temporarily, as Ollie's mistress had to look after her sick father in England. She was terribly sad to leave her dog, but she didn't want him to endure the long flight, let alone the hardships of quarantine that would be required on his return to Australia. But now she's going to stay in England much longer than planned, perhaps for years. So, the pensioner has now delivered Ollie to the animal rescue organisation on her behalf. He's very concerned about his welfare but doesn't want to keep him, as Ollie had some nasty brawls with his beloved cat.'

After this torrent of words, Petra took a deep breath and pouted her salmon-pink made-up lips.

'And so, the poor little fellow ended up here.'

'Does he get along with other dogs?' Andy suspiciously glanced at the terrier who didn't seem very friendly right now.

'Maybe he's just a bit aggressive on the leash. Attack instead of flight is the motto for some dogs.' Petra frowned.

'Well, let him run around the back garden and see what happens,' Lizzie suggested. Her uneasy feeling had disappeared as Susi raced around the group excitedly, obviously keen to play with Ollie, although he was once again barring his teeth.

'Susi doesn't take his threat seriously at all,' Sebastian said with a smile. 'She seems to like him anyway. No wonder, because he looks totally like Daisy.'

'That's right, they could be siblings!' Anna called.

'Who is Daisy?' Petra asked.

'Susi's best friend,' Sebastian replied.

Soon enough, Susi and Ollie frolicked around on the wet lawn, and it didn't take long before Ollie's snow-white fur was coloured green-brown. Petra said goodbye as she was on her way to work. She handed Andy several cans of dog food, a fleece blanket, two dog bowls, and a leash. When she shook hands with him, he noticed her pleasant-smelling perfume. At that moment Andy thought of Astrid for the first time in a long while.

Despite the initial mistrust, Ollie got on very well with Susi. It had probably been wrong to confront him with the whole family on arrival, Lizzie mused, a bit contrite. Next time she would greet a new foster dog on its own and let it sniff around the house and garden peacefully, and without Susi's presence. It surely would be intimidating for many dogs to be crowded by unknown people and a bigger dog.

The little creature with the beautiful round eyes had a few quirks, but in general it turned out to be an easy-care protégé. He was cheeky but extremely cute, and all four Kuhlmanns and Susi quickly took him to their hearts.

# 68 A PINK WALLET

Ollie tugged like crazy on the leash. Andy pulled him back gruffly, inwardly cursing not only the dog but also himself, as he hated it when he lost his patience too quickly. But all sorts of things had already gone wrong that day, and he had been terribly annoyed by the malicious behaviour of a customer. In order to cool off a bit, he had decided to take the evening walk with the dogs. But now his frustration was only increasing. Ollie was getting on his last nerve as he yelped and tried to run towards a cyclist he had spotted from a distance.

'Stop it!' Andy commanded.

Ollie ignored him completely and continued to bark, while Susi was startled by Andy's unusually grumpy tone, looking up at him anxiously. The chubby cyclist approached quickly and, swerving to avoid a plastic bottle on the road, came dangerously close to Ollie. The little dog jumped off furiously – and to its great surprise found itself in mid- air and then on the ground.

Andy had grabbed Ollie in a flash and now laid him gently on his back, holding him down for a few seconds. Ollie was completely confused and hardly dared to fidget. Nothing like this had ever happened to him before!

Strangely enough, the lady on the bicycle came to his aid. Stopping with screeching brakes, she hissed at Andy, 'What are you doing? This is cruelty to animals!'

'Hello, Astrid!' Andy replied. 'I just want to teach Ollie a little lesson. Somehow, he must learn that he must not jump on a bicycle.'

'Oh, hello, Andy!' Astrid's voice softened when she recognised the electrician whom she had met in Tim's house. Nevertheless, she observed Ollie critically and was relieved when he stood up and sniffed at her with confidence.

'What a cutie!' she called out and stroked him.

Andy smiled and told her that her new foster dog always tried to scare off all people on bicycles, skateboards and mopeds, and especially the postman.

Astrid replied, 'Postmen often get in trouble with aggressive dogs who think they'd have to defend their territory. But would Ollie really bite anybody? One would hardly expect that from this cute little doggie.'

'I don't know! I hope not! In any case, I'll try to get him out of hunting and yapping. Luckily, Susi hardly ever barks,' Andy said and patted Susi. She had kept herself in the background and only now timidly sniffed at Astrid's outstretched hand.

'You're both so pretty!' Astrid now also patted Susi.

'Tim wanted to give my daughter a dog, too, but I talked him out of it. Claudia will soon start her studies and won't have much time for a pet. I'll probably even have to look after her turtle Louise. Well, thank goodness Louise is lovely! I heard that some turtles can be really mean, biting your fingers! Once I heard of a notorious turtle in Germany called Schnappi that had bitten a boy.' She smiled, and with her chubby, red cheeks and tight shorts she almost resembled a schoolgirl. She took off her helmet, rubbed her forehead and shook her curls.

'I don't like these things much,' she admitted.

'What, the turtles?'

'Nah, my helmet!'

'Your friend Tim gave my son a hefty fine for riding a bicycle without a helmet,' Andy said more sharply than he intended.

'Yes, Tim can be quite strict. He's always taken the laws very seriously, especially those concerning road safety. Unfortunately, he's in big trouble right now. He wanted to be a hero but got involved with the wrong people,' Astrid sighed.

She looked around briefly and whispered: 'Tim has recently been arrested because he'd accepted hush money from a crook, and actually it's all my fault.'

Andy was speechless. How could she blame herself and defend the corrupt policeman?

Astrid explained: 'I inherited some money. Tim knew nothing about it until I gave him a brand-new car, an Audi. I shouldn't have done that, because Tim was embarrassed. Anyway, since then he gave me more expensive gifts than he could afford. I guess he tried to prove to me that he is not a poor church mouse either. Really silly, as I never cared if I got more money than he did, and we had so much fun together! You know, Tim had rescued me from the black hole I had fallen into after the unexpected death of my poor husband.' She blew her nose. 'Actually, Timmy and I were supposed to go on a holiday soon, but now our wonderful plans for the future have fallen through.'

Then she smiled sheepishly. 'Excuse me, I shouldn't burden you with all my sorrows! I'd better get back on the road before it gets pitch black.'

'Do you have far to go?' Andy worried, seeing that she didn't have any bicycle lamps at all. Spontaneously, he suggested, 'Why don't you come in for a drink or a cup of tea and then I'll take you home by car. Somehow, we'll manage to get the bicycle into my old car.' Noticing her somewhat shocked expression, he quickly added: 'Don't worry, I am happily married and have no nasty intentions!'

Astrid hung her helmet on the handlebars, grinning.

'Oh, then I gladly accept! I'm pretty exhausted anyway.'

She pushed her bicycle, walking beside him, and Ollie kept looking at the tyres but left them alone.

Hiding her astonishment at the unexpected visitor, Lizzie welcomed Astrid and gave her a large glass of beer and a bowl of peanuts. Astrid drank up her glass in no time and leaned back on the comfortable couch.

'Your home is very cosy! Pooh, my bicycle tour has done me in. I fear I'm not very sporty, and I don't cycle much at all.'

'I also had sore muscles from cycling recently,' Lizzie said and poured herself a glass of wine. Unlike Andy, she detested beer. She found it astonishing that many Australians always spoke of the famous Oktoberfest in Munich as soon as they heard about their home country, automatically assuming that all Germans were fans of the bitter brew.

Astrid's eyes fell on the nuts and she sighed.

'My husband was allergic to peanuts. When we went out, we always had to watch out like hell and ask for the exact ingredients of each meal. However, things went badly for him in a restaurant once because his dinner had a small amount of peanut butter in it without our knowledge.'

'Did he die of it?' Andy asked, entering the living room. He had given the dogs fresh water and now sat down in a recliner.

'No, my poor Billy was just having a severe allergic reaction. He rushed to the toilet, and fortunately, he only had diarrhoea and vomiting and didn't get an anaphylactic shock. We had an emergency kit with us as usual, but we didn't have to use it. Still, Billy looked miserable.' She faltered briefly.

'The manager and the cook were completely shaken, and both of them apologised to us personally. It turned out that the cook had used the same spoon for two different dishes. And it seems a tiny dollop of peanut butter had accidentally ended up in the sauce. After that event, we avoided going to restaurants for a long time.' Astrid's eyes became moist. 'We were always so worried about Billy's health when we were eating, but in the end, he drowned on a snorkelling trip.'

'Oh no!' Andy called out. 'How did that happen?'

Lizzie looked at Astrid with pity. So, this woman had also lost a husband at an early age, just like her friend Jessica, and the mother of Kirsty and Ellen, too.

Astrid wiped her eyes.

'Billy loved the sea, and he often went snorkelling. On his last holiday in Indonesia, he went on a tour with some others. And then he never ...' She sobbed up, struggling for composure.

'How awful!' Lizzie breathed.

'He never turned up again! They declared him missing as he didn't return to the boat. And they never found him ...'

Ollie ran to her and began to lick her calf.

'Stop it, Ollie!' Andy admonished him.

Astrid smiled through tears. Stroking the dog, she said, 'Ollie's certainly trying to comfort me. But I'd better get going before I annoy you even longer with my whole life story!'

Andy jumped up immediately. 'I'll drive you home.'

Astrid wanted to decline his offer, but Lizzie insisted as well, as it was already completely dark by now. Furthermore, Astrid had drunk two large glasses of beer in no time at all. With a little effort and with Astrid's help, Andy put the bicycle into the boot of his car. He didn't notice that a man in a car parked nearby was watching them.

\* \* \*

After visiting his former flat-mate Lucy in her new unit, Bruce accompanied Anna home on foot. They hugged and kissed each other goodbye at the garden gate, and both were startled when Gabriel suddenly appeared before them in the darkness. 'Hello, Anna and Bruce! I just wanted to let you know that Melissa had to go to the hospital.'

'What? Oh no!'

'Yeah, this afternoon. The doctors say her kidneys failed unexpectedly. She'd probably been taking that wacky 'FUN' for too long. Anyway, she had a horrible colic and now she's in a coma. My poor Melissa!'

His eyes seemed to glow madly in the cold street light and Anna shuddered. Bruce was about to say something to Gabriel when his eyes fell on a grey car in which he had noticed a movement. At that moment it drove away.

'Come on, let's go into the house first,' Anna now said to her boyfriend and to Gabriel.

When Andy returned, he found his family and Bruce in an unusually sad mood, and even Susi and Ollie seemed a bit subdued. Instantly fearing the worst, he was almost relieved to find out that it was about Melissa.

Gabriel had meanwhile gone home. He couldn't believe that his wife was fighting for her life, even though her therapy had seemed so successful and she had joked with him only the day before. And she had made all sorts of new plans for her future. For example, she wanted to take a course to learn how to cut dogs' hair. They had been so happy! But now all their dreams had burst like soap bubbles because there was little hope.

Bruce was feeling uncomfortable. He too felt sorry for Gabriel's wife, but since her attacks on Alfred and Anna's parents, he was concerned about the whole Kuhlmann family. He leaned back, moved a thick cushion to the side and called in surprise, 'Oh, someone has lost his wallet!'

'Let me see, that must be Astrid's!' Lizzie said.

Bruce handed her the pink wallet, and Lizzie opened it. 'Yes, here's a credit card with her name on it, and also her driving license and a wad of money. Oh dear, we'd best call her directly and let her know before she misses it and starts worrying!'

Looking over her mum's shoulder, Anna noticed a passport photo of a man's face underneath a transparent cover in the wallet. It didn't show Tim, but another man who looked quite young despite his snow-white hair. He smiled a bit cynically, had grey-blue eyes and a dimple on his chin. Somehow, he looked familiar to her. 'Who could that be?' she asked.

Lizzie replied: 'That must be Astrid's late husband.'

'Or it's her beloved little brother,' Sebastian grinned mischievously at his sister. He could hardly imagine that Anna would ever carry a photo of him around.

'That's Malcolm!' Anna blurted out.

Bruce frowned. 'You think so? Nah, he has brown hair!'

'Nonsense! Astrid's husband is no longer alive and his name was Billy,' Andy growled disapprovingly. 'Anna, you shouldn't stick your nose into other people's business all the time!'

Lizzie glanced at the clock. 'It's not too late, can't you just go back to Astrid's house and bring her the wallet, Andy?'

'Good idea! Bruce, do you need a ride home?'

'I'm coming along!' Anna called out before Bruce could reply. When everyone got up at the same time, the dogs jumped up excitedly.

'Okay, you can come, too,' Anna said.

# 69 DEAD-END STREET

Bruce shared the back seat of the car with Susi and Ollie, and Anna got in the front. She would have loved to sit next to her boyfriend, snuggling up to him, but she felt inhibited in the presence of her father anyway. Although he seemed to accept Bruce now, he was still quite reserved towards him.

She suggested: 'Let's see Astrid first, okay?'

Andy nodded and winked at Bruce in the rear-view mirror, saying amusedly: 'I bet the dogs would be happy to have more cuddle time with you, Bruce!'

Ollie had made himself comfortable on Bruce's lap, while Susi took up most of the back seat, delighted to be stroked on her belly. After only a short drive they reached the town centre, which seemed to be deserted at this time, and a little later Andy turned into a cul-de-sac near Mount Emu and parked the car under a tall palm.

Anna handed him Astrid's wallet. 'We'll wait in the car.'

'Yeah, sure, I won't stay long,' Andy replied.

He went to a two-storey house that looked modern and spacious, as far as he could tell in the dark. As soon as he stepped on the driveway, several sensor-lights came on at the double garage, helping him to find the front door. He rang the bell and waited, wondering if Astrid had already noticed the loss of her purse. He smiled as he imagined her joyfully surprised face, but the next moment, he heard a deep male voice asking, rather unfriendly: 'What do you want?'

'Can I speak to Astrid, please?'

'Who's there?' Astrid shouted, pushing her way past the man in the doorway.

'Oh, hello, Andy!' She looked at him questioningly, without making any effort to invite him into the house. Her girlish, chubby face looked frightened and confused, and Andy's inner alarm bell rang out. Nevertheless, he smiled at her kindly.

'Hello! You lost your wallet in our living room and Lizzie suggested to bring it to you straight away. Um, actually, we should've called you first ...'

'Oh, thank you so much! That's so sweet of you! I hadn't missed it yet.'

'No problem. Well, good night!'

The bearded man muttered, 'Bye!', and Astrid said with a forced smile, 'Goodbye, Andy!'

Andy went back to the car feeling queasy. Something was wrong! Was Astrid in danger? He laughed at himself, trying to shake off his gloomy thoughts. Somehow, Astrid seemed to evoke his protective instinct! Strange!

But then he heard the man screaming, 'Where are you always hanging around? And how could you be flirting with Tim?'

'I thought you were dead,' Astrid sobbed. 'And I was so desperate! Why didn't you tell me, Billy?'

'I just told you, you stupid cow. Oh, I'm fed up!'

Opening his car door, Andy was surprised when the light from the motion sensors flashed up behind him. Astrid's visitor marched past him with a pinched expression on his face. He stumbled on the uneven lawn and then jogged away in the middle of the road.

'Ollie, stop!' Bruce called.

The little dog had hopped onto the front seat at a breakneck speed and then out of the car, racing after the man. Prudently, Bruce held onto Susi to stop her from following her friend.

'Ollie, come back!' Anna yelled.

'That little bastard!' Andy cursed and went after him.

Ollie rejoiced and barked happily. Being chased was almost as great as chasing someone!

Astrid now also rushed out of the house and shouted:

'Billy, come back! Where are you going, and where's your car?'

Despite her pleading voice, Billy just ran faster without looking back.

'What's the matter with him?' Anna asked, getting out of the car, worriedly watching her dog and Andy. Ollie was already close to the man's heels. Would the cheeky rascal bite Billy's calf? Astrid stood there, stiff as a board, and ignored Anna's question.

Bruce patted Susi who restlessly pressed her nose against the window. 'Stay here, sweetie!'

But then he saw in horror that Billy suddenly stopped, turned around and kicked at Ollie. Bruce pushed Susi aside and jumped out of the car.

'Leave him alone!' he yelled.

Billy's kick missed Ollie, and the dog still thought it was all a fun game. It barked excitedly, whizzed around Billy, backed away, ran to Andy and jumped up at Billy.

The man cursed. He kicked again and hit Andy's right shin, causing him to cry out in shock. But instead of apologising, Billy went wild. His eyes full of hatred, he attacked Andy again, now hitting him with his fists. Bruce threw himself with momentum on Billy, who lost his balance, and all three men fell hard on the asphalt. A sharp pain shot through Andy's left side, but he held Billy tightly, and Bruce didn't let go either, although he had scraped his knee bloody on impact. Billy defended himself vehemently against his two attackers. He almost managed to break free when a larger dog grabbed his trouser leg. It was Susi! She had leaped through the half-open car window to help her friends.

'Susi, what are you doing here?' Bruce gasped and groaned as Billy punched him in the nose. Ollie yapped shrilly.

'No!' Anna cried in panic as she saw the flash of a bright knife in the pale light of the streetlamp.

'You bitch, I'll make dog food out of you!' the man threatened and stabbed at Susi. At that moment Ollie caught his right arm and Susi managed to jump aside, just in time to avoid the sharp blade. She growled frighteningly, making deep, rumbling sounds. Ollie whimpered as Billy forcefully hurled him away from him, and he landed rudely on the ground. Bruce was still trying desperately to steal the knife from Billy when Astrid came to his help unexpectedly. Unaware of the danger she was putting herself in, she grabbed her husband angrily by the elbow.

'Billy, how dare you! Stop it!'

'Stay out of it!' He tried to shake off his wife and to kick, punch and stab at the others, until he finally surrendered to the stronger force of his opponents and dropped the knife. Bruce quickly pushed it aside with his foot and smiled triumphantly. But his nose was bleeding heavily.

Anna bent over to the small dog in fear and lifted him up. He immediately licked her cheek with a rough tongue and began fidgeting in her arms.

'You naughty boy!' she scolded affectionately, holding him tight.

Andy relentlessly twisted one of Billy's arms on his back, while Bruce held onto his other arm. Susi whimpered softly, and Anna suddenly discovered the blood oozing from her father's left side. It had already discoloured half the shirt.

'Daddy, you're hurt!' Anna was petrified for a moment.

But then she noticed a group of curious neighbours standing around watching. She rushed to them, asking them to call for an ambulance and the police immediately.

'We've already done that, my dear child!' an old man replied in a shaky voice.

Anna thanked him and turned to Billy who was grinning at her cynically. Those cold eyes looked so familiar to her!

Outraged, she shouted: 'Malcolm!' And an icy horror seized her.

'Malcolm?' Bruce choked and held a tissue to his nose. His hand was also bleeding from a deep cut.

Anna was feeling sick. What should she do? First, she had to help her father, but how? Thank goodness a strong looking man from another house approached them now. He resolutely pressed a huge torch into Astrid's hand and asked her to point it at Andy. And then he expertly bandaged him. Anna was relieved. Thick tears rolled down her cheeks and Ollie licked them away gently. Fearing that Billy might escape after all, Bruce strengthened his iron grip around his wrist.

Then a red car stopped next to them. A young woman with long, curly hair leaned out of the window, asking, 'What's going on here?'

Astrid shouted, 'Claudia, good that you are here! Your dad isn't dead at all! But Andy is badly injured!'

'What?' Astrid's daughter didn't understand a thing, and she and her boyfriend Daniel quickly got out of the car, without bothering to park it properly or turn off the engine. Claudia stared at Billy in astonishment.

'Daddy, is that really you?'

Billy's gaze softened and a hint of shame and regret flickered in his eyes. 'Claudia, please forgive me! I'll explain everything! Your mum has...'

With a tremendous jerk he broke free, jumped into the car and drove away! Andy cursed, Astrid gasped for breath and Daniel ran after his Honda, waving his arms wildly. However, Billy didn't get very far anyway, as it was a cul-de-sac, and while he was turning, a police car arrived.

'Stop the car!' Bruce yelled at the cops at the top of his lungs.

'Daniel, watch out!' Claudia cried.

And then everything seemed to happen very fast and yet as if in slow motion. Sirens howled; brakes screeched. Daniel dived to the side, but was still grazed by the Honda and fell down. Ollie freed himself from Anna's arms and ran directly in front of the oncoming car. Bruce threw himself protectively over the dog, and Billy drove right past them and the police car. And crashed head-on into an ambulance car! Astrid screamed. She staggered and the torch flew out of her hand. Claudia ran to Daniel and kissed him, sobbing. Anna and Susi ran to Bruce and Ollie, and Anna uttered an inner prayer of thanks that they were still alive. Andy fainted.

# 70 COOK AND CROOK

At the last moment, Andy was caught by the strong man who had patched him up. A paramedic hurried to him, while another one inspected the front of the ambulance. Billy had suffered a laceration to his head on impact and offered no resistance. Two police officers pulled him out of the slightly damaged Honda and handcuffed him. Astrid stared at him accusingly, but he looked away, embarrassed.

He murmured softly: 'Excuse me, Astrid! I was just so jealous of Tim!'

Bruce tried to lift himself up into a sitting position, still in a dazed state, and smiled encouragingly at his girlfriend, even though all his limbs hurt like hell and his nose was throbbing.

Anna knelt down beside him. 'You're so brave! You saved my father and Ollie!'

Bruce hugged her and pushed Ollie away who was about to stick his tongue in his ear. 'Bah, stop that!' Then he grinned a little crookedly. 'Oh nonsense, I'm certainly no hero! I was really scared when this idiot waved his knife around wildly! How's your dad?'

Only now did Anna see that her father was lying motionless on the floor and one of the paramedics was bending over him.

'Papa!' she called out in horror, using the German word for 'Dad' involuntarily, and ran to him.

'He's lost a lot of blood and has to go to hospital,' the paramedic said seriously. 'But don't worry, the wound looks worse than it is.' Then he turned to Bruce. 'Hey, what's wrong with you?'

He inspected his nose and injured hand, shouted something to a colleague, and then said to Bruce: 'We'll take you straight to the hospital, too, because your cut needs to be cleaned and sutured.'

'May I come along?' Anna asked, anxiously watching her unconscious father. 'Oh no, I have to look after the dogs. But how ... but ... I can't even drive a car ...' she stammered, feeling terribly helpless.

Astrid pulled herself together. 'You know what? I'll take you and your dogs home in your car, and Daniel and Claudia can drive their Honda behind us and take me home afterwards. Luckily, Daniel's car only got a little scratch.'

'Thank you!' Anna mumbled.

After the ambulance had left and they had answered all the police questions, they drove off. On the way, Anna asked, 'Is this really your husband? I thought his name was Malcolm!'

Astrid bit her lips. Then she said in a soft voice:

'It's a long story, and I only just found out that he's still alive!' She suppressed a sob. 'I hardly recognised Billy myself, because with his dyed hair and that beard, he looks completely different. Normally, his hair is snow-white, and he used to have it cut short. He turned up out of the blue, explaining that he'd been in trouble. That he had to go into hiding back then, because some smugglers were after his life. And he didn't want to endanger Claudia and me. So, he faked his death, lived somewhere in New South Wales for a while and called himself Malcolm. I can hardly believe it! It sounds like a bad thriller!'

She swallowed hard. 'At first, I was so happy to see him again! After all those years! But soon we started arguing. He accused me of not waiting for him and of cheating on him with Tim. But how could I have known? I thought Billy was dead all along!'

'I don't understand! Didn't Tim tell you about Malcolm, uh, Billy? They knew each other! And they fought at the harbour, and besides ...' Anna paused. There was a terrible jumble of questions in her head. Had Malcolm really killed Martin on the yacht? Why hadn't he been arrested? How had he managed to create a whole new identity? So, Claudia was his daughter and Astrid his wife?

'What?' Astrid asked.

'Well, I ...' Anna faltered.

Astrid frowned. 'How do you know Billy?'

'That's a long story too. Maybe we can talk it all over at home. My mother will of course be totally shocked to hear about the attack on my father and Bruce!'

Tears came to Anna's eyes.

Astrid whimpered: 'How could Billy do that?'

Lizzie was watching a movie on TV in the living room when she heard voices. Cheerfully, she called, 'Hello! You've been away for a long time! Have you taken the dogs for a walk?'

Susi and Ollie rushed to her and made her smile. But then she saw her visibly agitated daughter with the three unexpected guests, and she froze.

Anxiously, she asked, 'Where's Daddy? Has there been an accident?'

Astrid embraced her. 'I'm so sorry! My husband went crazy! He injured your husband and Bruce, and they both had to go to hospital. But there is no danger to their lives.'

Now Sebastian burst into the room. 'What happened?'

Lizzie brusquely pushed Astrid away and turned off the TV.

'Your husband? I thought he'd died!'

'That's what I thought!' Astrid croaked and began to sob without restraint, and Claudia started to cry, too.

Daniel seemed insecure and shy when he put his arm around his girlfriend's shoulder. Lizzie's stomach felt queasy. She would have liked to rush to the hospital but forced herself to remain calm, asking the visitors to sit down. Anna told her and Sebastian about the events at Mount Emu, starting with Ollie's chase after Billy. Daniel was holding hands with Claudia now. She looked very much like her mother and still quite childlike with her sky-blue eyes and round, red-cheeked face.

Later, Astrid took over, narrating what she had learned about her husband.

'How could Billy disappear without a trace in Indonesia back then?' Sebastian asked.

Astrid blew her nose. 'He'd planned it well. He went snorkelling with a group of tourists, and he quickly swam far away from the others. And then a friend picked him up with another boat, or perhaps a small ship, and so he managed to get away.'

'Was that Alfred?' Anna wanted to know.

'I don't know!' Astrid replied, perplexed. 'Who is Alfred?'

Daniel let go of Claudia's hand, moved restlessly around the sofa, and his narrow face turned red. Sebastian and Anna gazed at him curiously. Daniel noticed their looks, blushed even more deeply and said, 'No! It was Simon, his son, who helped him disappear!'

'What?' Astrid and Claudia screamed simultaneously.

'Yes, Billy had a child with a former girlfriend, and that was Simon. Some time ago, Maryann told me this. She also knew about Billy's new identity and his drug dealing.'

Now everyone was stunned.

'Why did you keep this to yourself?' Claudia snapped at him.

Daniel let his head hang down. After a while, he said hoarsely: 'I didn't want you to find out what a mean guy your father is. I thought it would be better for you and your mother, and ...'

'Billy is a drug dealer? And he has a son?' Astrid asked incredulously.

Daniel nodded unhappily.

Lizzie only listened half-heartedly because she was terribly concerned about Andy. 'I'm going to call the hospital now,' she said. Just that moment, the phone rang.

'Hi, Lizzie!'

'Oh, hello, Bruce! How are you and Andy?'

'Much better! The hospital staff was great, and we both got treated quickly. Andy's fast asleep right now, and he'll have to spend the night here, but I am allowed to go home. Oliver will pick me up in a minute.'

'Thank God!' Lizzie sighed.

She asked him a few more questions, nodded to the others and put her thumb up in the air. Finally, she handed the phone to Anna so she could talk to her boyfriend.

Sebastian was hugely relieved as well, as Anna's description of the blood-stained shirt and the chalky white face of her motionless father had scared him. Claudia and Astrid sat cowering on the couch, feeling overwhelmed. Daniel twirled nervously on the sleeves of his dark blue jumper.

Only with difficulty did Astrid manage to suppress her sobs, and she said softly to Lizzie, 'I am grateful that my husband didn't hurt Andy and Bruce even worse! But I wish I could take it back!'

Lizzie squeezed her hand briefly. 'It's not your fault.'

Claudia asked in a squeaky voice: 'Daniel, did my father and Simon talk Maryann into taking the 'FUN'? Did they kill her?'

Daniel swallowed hard. 'I don't know!'

Something occurred to Sebastian, and he shivered.

'Maybe Thomas knew who Malcolm really was.'

'Thomas?' Daniel asked, startled. 'What makes you think so?'

Claudia turned pale. 'Thomas?' she also asked.

Astrid touched her face with agitated movements, smearing her make-up, already dissolved from crying, even more. Sebastian looked to his sister for help, but she was still on the phone with Bruce. Then he gave himself a jolt, saying:

'A classmate of mine, Arielle, is a cousin of Thomas. After his death, his parents gave her his computer as a gift. And because of that, she found out that Thomas had been spying on Malcolm. She detected some photos of this man that she forwarded to Anna and me.'

Anna heard her name and quickly finished her phone call. Sebastian continued, 'And Thomas had also been spying on Tim. Since your birthday, Claudia, he suspected Tim of selling exotic animals.'

'What?' Astrid asked.

'Tim?' Claudia's eyes widened.

'Yes, Arielle found a diary of Thomas, in which he'd written that Tim had given you an Indian star turtle as a present. He found it odd as turtles like that wouldn't usually be sold in a pet shop. And just by coincidence, he'd noticed Tim once before at the Brisbane airport where he'd behaved in a rather suspicious way.'

'This can't be true!' Astrid moaned. 'My Timmy?'

In Astrid's and Claudia's presence Sebastian refused to admit how much he detested the corrupt policeman, and Anna and her mother also wondered about Astrid's taste once again. Anna got goose bumps just thinking about Tim's googly eyes.

'Well, in the meantime we heard that Tim loves animals and was innocent with regards to the wildlife trafficking. And Martin had nothing to do with it, either,' Sebastian said.

Daniel ran his fingers through his dark brown hair. 'I don't understand anything anymore! Who is Martin?'

'Your neighbour! The man who lived behind your back garden who was shot dead on his own yacht in Mooloolaba.' Anna looked at him unintentionally grim, her mind focused on her terrible experience at the harbour. Only after a while did she take in what Sebastian had just said.

'How do you know that Martin was no smuggler?' she asked her brother excitedly. 'Just because Gabriel always claimed that?'

'Well, it was supposed to remain a secret for now, but... um, yesterday a friend told me that Malcolm – or shall we call him Billy – worked as Martin's cook. And he was the one who smuggled drugs and also wildlife and lizard eggs and so on, using Martin's yacht for that. And he...'

'This is all wrong! Billy wasn't a cook; he was a real estate agent!' Astrid shouted, confused and upset.

Claudia could hardly follow the conversation. The shocking reports about her father who'd been believed dead, and all the crying had exhausted her, and her head was throbbing. Daniel noticed her discomfort and comfortingly took her hand again, which caught Lizzie's attention.

'Are you all right, Claudia?' she asked pitifully.

'My head feels like it's going to burst,' Claudia said.

'Oh, sorry, I didn't offer you anything to drink. I'll get you something.'

In no time, she returned from the kitchen with a large water carafe and glasses for everybody. She also gave Claudia a headache tablet, which she gratefully swallowed. Ollie immediately sat down in front of her, looking up expectantly.

Claudia smiled at him. 'Nah, that's no food for you!'

Astrid also had to smile involuntarily and patted Ollie.

'The little rascal is really cute, although earlier I've cursed him for running after Billy and causing this whole mess.'

Then her mouth distorted, making her smudged face look like a grotesque mask. 'Billy always was a bit hot-headed, but I never imagined that he could stab someone so brutally!'

Lizzie feared that her two female guests would cry again and quickly asked, 'So, your husband never worked as a chef?'

'No! He always liked to cook, but professionally he was a real estate agent. At first in Sydney and later in Maroochydore. Billy had quite wealthy parents who owned various properties, and I think that's how he got into this business. And he was very successful!'

Sniffing, Astrid took a fresh tissue from the box Lizzie had put on the table.

'Are his parents still alive?' Sebastian asked.

'No, they passed away a long time ago. Billy and I moved here to the Sunshine Coast shortly after his father's death. That is, Billy was in Vanuatu and in North Queensland for a while, taking care of the sale of two plots of land.'

She faltered and cleaned her nose again.

'We've never been short of money and I find it hard to believe that Billy would do such things behind my back. He's supposed to be a smuggler? And he actually has a son he never mentioned to me? And then he disappears for years on end, turns up out of the blue and accuses me of cheating on him with Tim!'

Claudia replied angrily, 'Dad must explain everything to us! By the way, why didn't he drive his own car when he came to see you today?'

'No idea, I was surprised too!' Astrid said. 'Well, let's go! We can't sit around moping forever.'

The three guests said goodbye and Lizzie accompanied them to their Honda. She noticed the light from Gabriel's living room. He was obviously still awake, probably worrying about his wife. Lizzie felt heartfelt empathy for her neighbours and also for Astrid and Claudia whose world had completely fallen apart that evening. But then her thoughts turned to her husband. Poor Andy! She would visit him the next morning. And hopefully she'd be allowed to take him home.

Anna thought of Malcolm's, oh no, Billy's girlfriend in Noosaville. Under what name did she know him? Was she aware of Astrid's and Claudia's existence, and of Billy's illegal activities? Was she perhaps Simon's mother?

Sebastian had a guilty conscience about having revealed Ivory's secret. But after all, Billy had now been arrested and could no longer be dangerous to anyone. Or could he?

# 71 BLABBERMOUTH

Bruce had been on sick leave for a few days. The bandage on his right hand was interfering with many everyday activities, and his nose was still hurting a bit. Still, he was in a good mood, humming a tune to himself as he clumsily spread honey on a piece of toast with his left hand. Somewhere in the garden, a bird was chirping and then Bruce noticed a movement behind him.

'Hi, Bruce! Have you read the paper today?' Oliver asked.

Without waiting for an answer, he held an article right in front of his nose. Bruce pushed the newspaper a little further away from him and read the headline:

*FAMILY FATHER BELIEVED LOST TURNS OUT TO BE A DRUG DEALER AND WILDLIFE TRAFFICKER*

'Give me that!' Bruce grabbed the paper, took his toast and sat down at the dining table to read the article. Oliver poured a cup of coffee for his friend and himself, sat down with him and beamed. 'Finally, they caught the creep, whatever his name is. Well, I guess we should call him Billy and not Malcolm!'

Bruce frowned, and a splash of honey dripped on the newspaper. 'That's weird, there's no mentioning of Simon in the article.'

'Which Simon? Do you mean Maryann's boyfriend?'

Oliver ran his fingers through his mane of black hair that was still damp from the shower and smelled of shampoo. Bruce finished his toast and told him what he had learned from Anna.

Oliver was stunned. 'The guy who attacked you and Andy is Simon's father? Wow!'

'Yes, it's quaint. By the way, Anna and I saw Simon and Billy together at the rainy festival in Peregian Beach, and we wondered how they knew each other. Of course, we'd never suspected that they're related. This whole story must be such a shock for Billy's wife and daughter!'

'And who is Simon's mother?'

'No idea! Anyway, I'm glad that Andy is better again. Phew, the poor man looked awful when they took us to the hospital, almost like a corpse, and when I squeezed his hand, it was freezing cold,' Bruce said, and a shiver ran down his spine.

Oliver chuckled. 'Who would have thought that you of all people would be holding hands with Anna's father?'

Bruce laughed. 'Certainly not me! But Andy's all right, and actually, I understand what makes him tick. He just wants to prevent his beloved daughter from getting into bad company, and it bothers him that I'm already of age.'

'Well, and now you two got attacked by that evil man, and Anna could have been killed by Billy when she helped Tim! You can always bump into the wrong guys!' Oliver pointed out.

He peered out through the open window into the garden and watched the noisy bird that was now sitting on the fence. A lone white cloud hovered over the pink sky. He liked Anna a lot and was glad that nothing had happened to her. And although he had never cared for Bruce's ex-girlfriend, he was suddenly very sad. Maryann would never see another sunrise; never hear a birdsong; never listen to music again, all because of an overdose of the terrible 'FUN'. Had Simon introduced this drug to her? Was he a user too? Would there be more deaths of people known to him?

He sighed softly, looked at the clock and shouted: 'Oh boy, I have to go! Can you manage on your own?'

'Yes, I'll be fine! Go and take care of your troupe!'

'I will! And tonight, I'll bring something delicious for dinner!'

Bruce smiled. Oliver had become even more caring since he got a new job as a social worker looking after disabled people. His work had also inspired him to write a song about an autistic boy and his wonderful friendship with an ugly dog. Bruce was eager to listen to Celina and Oliver singing it together.

*   *   *

Andy looked pale and miserable after he'd got discharged from hospital. Billy had inflicted a deep flesh wound on his left side, fortunately missing his vital organs, and a few superficial scratches on his hands. Andy was still visibly suffering from the shock about this vicious knife attack. Back at home, Anna had to tell him everything about the fight in detail, as he could only vaguely remember some nasty fisticuffs, hoarse screams, Susi's threatening growl, and finally an icy coldness. Listening to Anna, his eyes fell on Ollie, and he grinned as he suddenly recalled a strange dream from last night: Anna and Bruce were married under a tall palm tree, while Susi dropped a black wig at their feet, making them all laugh. Then the newlyweds and the Hot Ears sang happily and loudly in the middle of the street, and Ollie ran around them all, barking along to the rock song. Anna was glad to see her father smile again. And she was relieved that Bruce was doing well.

Sebastian was genuinely remorseful, afraid that Ivory would be mad at him. Why was he such a blabbermouth? The next day, he confessed to Ivory that he'd talked about Martin's cook and the smuggling business. As he had feared, Ivory became angry, threatening to never confide in him again. But then he said,

'Well, I am not much better than you, as I broke the promise to my dad to be quiet about that whole story!'

Sebastian smiled crookedly. 'For a while, Anna and I had the idea to become private detectives, but I don't think that's for me. Somehow, I can't keep secrets.'

A little later, Sebastian told his other friends about Billy's attack on his father and Bruce, and also the news about Simon being the son of Billy alias Malcolm. None of them noticed that Fiona was listening intently. She had a talent for spying on others. However, she had once been caught by Maryann. As a kind of compensation, she had readily promised her to help steal Kate's dogs. Fiona had both feared and admired Maryann, almost regarding her as an older sister, and her unexpected death had deeply upset her. Now she decided to take a closer look at Simon. Had he given his girlfriend the drugs? After all, his own father had been a drug dealer. Had the overdose been an accident, as everyone seemed to think, or could it possibly have been a murder? Why had Simon sprayed the word MURDERER on Alfred's car?

That same evening, Gabriel got wonderful news: Melissa had woken up from the coma. She was still very weak but would most likely survive! He was so relieved that he danced around the house for a while. And some other information took a burden off his shoulders. An autopsy had shown that Alfred hadn't died from the effects of the 'FUN' powder Melissa had mixed into his coffee. No, he had been bitten by a poisonous brown snake, and the shock alone had caused a fatal heart attack.

# 72 RELATIONSHIPS

Daniel woke up with a start and couldn't fall asleep again. The night was full of stars and the moon cast a faint glow on the pretty photo of Mount Coolum that had been hanging on the wall above his desk for many years. It had been a gift from Thomas. Ever since his friend's lifeless body had been found on the huge horse sculpture, Daniel suffered from nightmares. Both he and John sorely missed Thomas, with whom they had developed a very special, irreplaceable friendship. They had never ceased mulling over their mate's fate. Why had he left in the middle of the night? To meet somebody? Perhaps a new girlfriend? After his short relationship with Maryann, Thomas hadn't had a girlfriend anymore – or had he fallen in love again? But with whom?

Right now, Daniel fervently hoped that Claudia and her mother would forgive him for having kept Maryann's story about Simon and Billy to himself all this time. One evening, several months after Thomas' death, Daniel had met Maryann on the beach, staring at the sea. She had been in a tipsy and maudlin state. And then, completely unexpectedly, she'd poured her heart out to him. He had hardly known her, but nevertheless she had told him in confidence that Claudia's father was still alive and that he was also the father of Simon. And that Billy, now called

Malcolm, was a shrewd drug dealer. Daniel had taken pity on her and promised to keep everything secret. But now she was dead, too! Somehow, he felt guilty. Perhaps it had been an unconscious cry for help back then on the beach? Had Maryann felt threatened by Simon or Billy?

And Daniel felt a shiver thinking of his former neighbour Martin who'd been shot. Suddenly it occurred to Daniel that Simon had regularly kept Martin's garden in order. He absolutely had to find out more about that boyfriend of Maryann!

In the same night, Claudia was also lying wide awake in bed, turning restlessly from side to side. She could hardly believe what she had learned about her father. After her tears had dried up, she was feeling more anger than grief. She loathed all drug dealers and people who tortured animals, and her own father, of all people, had turned out to be such a bastard! Out of pure greed, he had been involved in all sorts of crooked deals. And as soon as he reappeared in her life, he became brutal, fighting with a knife and almost running over Daniel! How could he do this to them? Good that Daniel hadn't been hurt! He was such a reliable and loving friend! Or not? Out of the blue, Claudia was overcome with new rage. Why had Daniel concealed that her father was alive and that she had a stepbrother? Could she ever trust him again?

However, she had also concealed something from her boyfriend. Thomas hadn't been happy with Maryann and had fallen in love with her. Unfortunately, Claudia had flirted with him at a party once, and then he had confessed his feelings for her. Well, it had never come to more than that, but since that evening, she hadn't been able to behave as light-heartedly in his presence as she used to, always afraid that the deep friendship between Thomas, Daniel and John might suffer a crack because of her. Now all this seemed so childish to her! Poor Thomas! Who had murdered him? And why? He had been such a nice person!

And now Maryann was dead. Had she been killed too? Claudia didn't fall asleep until the kookaburras started their morning concert.

Astrid had a severe hangover when she woke up. No wonder, after she had gulped down several glasses of beer and, out of sheer frustration, also a few glasses of brandy. She cursed herself for being a pathetic boozer. She was really not a good role model for her seventeen-year-old daughter! Well, she was certainly better than Billy! That scoundrel! For almost three years she had believed him dead, drowned while snorkelling. And she had suffered like hell, especially in the first year after his mysterious disappearance. She had never found any indication that he might still be alive. Billy hadn't withdrawn any money from their joint account; obviously, he had been rich enough.

About two years after his presumed death, Astrid and Claudia had even held a small mourning ceremony for him, although it had still been too early to issue an official death certificate, for which one would have had to wait seven years. Astrid had missed her husband painfully for a long time, until the day she met Tim. And now he was in prison too! It seemed she had no luck with men! But instead of getting drunk again and sinking into melancholy, she decided to have a serious word with Billy and to find out more about Simon and his mother.

\* \* \*

Simon had no idea that so many people he barely even knew were thinking about him. He knew only one thing: he was furious with his father! For years, Billy had managed to rebuild his life with Alfred's help, making big bucks. He had been very successful as a smuggler and drug dealer, even though the nasty policeman Tim and Thomas, that young snooper, had been on to him. But now Billy, the bloody fool, had run to his wife, gone completely crazy and been arrested. That loser!

Once again, Simon skimmed over yesterday's newspaper article that described his father as an impostor, drug dealer, and arsonist. He had only found out about it this morning, from Conny, an old school friend of his father with whom Billy had lived in Noosaville for a while. Would the police also search her unit? Would they look for him? In any case, he had to go into hiding as soon as possible. But how? Alfred, who had helped his father to obtain the false papers and his new identity as Malcolm Millar, was no longer alive.

Simon ran his fingers through his hair, feeling downright sick. If only Billy had stayed in Mullumbimby! No one there had known him from his past, and it would have been much safer for all of them. But no, he wanted to return to the Sunshine Coast to be closer to Astrid and Claudia. For so long, he had remained hidden, only watching the two women from a safe distance, but then he had obviously become weak and had visited Astrid in her house. Simon cursed, and his former hatred for his father flared up again.

Simon's mum had raised him as a single mother in a tiny flat in Sydney, as Billy had already left her during her pregnancy. Before Simon's fifteenth birthday, his mother became terminally ill with cancer. She had little money and was terribly afraid for her beloved son, and therefore she finally told him who his father was. With some effort, Simon managed to find him. In that time, Billy had not changed his name yet.

And Simon contacted him, although he hated him deeply. Billy had been leading a cheerful, carefree life with another family, namely with Astrid and Claudia who hadn't got a clue about Simon. Billy, a successful real estate agent, had never given a single cent to his son. Unfortunately, Simon's mother had been either too proud or too scared to ask Billy for the financial help she would have been legally entitled to.

As a result, Simon's first meeting with his biological father hadn't been very harmonious. However, Billy had offered to take care of him, and over time, Simon had begun to trust him. Later on, he even admired him as a bold and cunning man. He couldn't bring himself to call him 'Dad', but gratefully accepted his support. Among other things, Billy helped him to set up his garden maintenance company, and Simon enjoyed being his own boss and working outdoors.

Nevertheless, he had higher aims, wishing to get rich in an easier way, just like his dad. Since Billy had faked his death and had changed both his name and his appearance, he didn't work as a real estate agent any longer but got more and more involved in criminal activities. He was a man without scruples. And Simon assisted him.

While mowing lawns Simon kept dreaming of a life in luxury. He and Maryann had imagined countless trips overseas and all sorts of glorious things. And yet, he had never thought of her as a partner for life. Had he ever really loved her? At the beginning of their relationship, they'd had a wonderful time together. Good-naturedly, he had joined in her childish acts like graffiti spraying and silly bets. The dog thefts had also been Maryann's idea. He had found her entertaining and amusing, pretty and sexy. But her high alcohol consumption and her constant flirting with other men had increasingly disturbed him. To his dismay, she had also been flirting with Alfred. Simon had only kept his mouth shut because the rather attractive guy had been a good mate of his father. And Simon was already too deeply involved in their illegal business, happy to replenish his wallet doing easy work for them.

When Simon found his girlfriend dead in her flat, he was stunned, too numb for any emotions. Only gradually was he overcome by ambivalent feelings that completely confused him. Grief and anger alternated with feelings of relief and shame. How had she got hold of the horrible 'FUN' powder? Had it been his fault? He didn't think so! However, he had temporarily hidden several bags for his father's customers in his wardrobe, and once he had curiously taken a tiny amount for himself. After a disappointingly short period of euphoria, he had felt mortally ill for two days and vowed never to touch the stuff again. To be on the safe side, he had never let his girlfriend into his business with Billy and Alfred, having kept both cash and drugs away from her. But who had mixed the deadly cocktail for Maryann? Maybe Alfred?

That messy bitch, Simon now thought involuntarily as his eyes fell on Maryann's elegant handbag that he had given to her on her last birthday. Seeing that she had carelessly thrown it into a corner, Simon was filled with new anger. Maryann had been extremely untidy and lazy; she had hardly ever lifted a finger to help with the housework. She had often complained about his landscaping business as she'd suffered from hay fever, and she'd constantly mocked him about his dirty fingernails and his grass-stained work clothes. Nah, she hadn't been the right woman for him!

In the end he was even annoyed by the way she meticulously polished her fingernails or brushed her nose with a pitiful expression. It was actually understandable that her previous boyfriends Bruce and Thomas hadn't stayed together with her for very long. And yet, he missed her!

The hum of a helicopter tore him from his thoughts. Were the police already on his trail? Had Billy confessed everything, naming him as a partner in crime? Simon was terrified! In no time at all he packed a rucksack with clothes, washing utensils, a thick wad of cash, some important documents, and the charger for his smartphone. Then he grabbed his iPad and ran to his truck. The fresh, sticky droppings of a bat were hiding the first *S* from his advertisement: *Simon's Landscaping Services*, and even the raised green thumb next to it had got an unsightly brown blob. But he didn't care about that anymore. He only wanted to drive away fast. He would go to the railway station in Nambour and take a train somewhere where he could start a new life. He would certainly do it smarter than his father and never show his face around here again.

# 73 HIDDEN IN A LEAFY TREE

The night before, Sebastian and Anna had got into a bitter dispute over nothing, and Sebastian felt bad when he woke up. He liked his sister very much and regretted his stupid behaviour now. To make up for it, he offered to accompany her on her morning walk. Anna was surprised but didn't mind, and the two dogs were happy. By now, Ollie had already learned a lot. He no longer pulled on the leash like crazy, and in general he didn't chase cyclists or joggers anymore. However, he still barked excitedly at people on their skateboards whenever they came too close to him.

That morning, they were on the road quite early. The sky was changing its colour with the first sunshine and the lawns were still wet. Sebastian remained unusually silent for almost ten minutes, and Anna, too, hung on to her thoughts as they wandered side by side. Then Sebastian said, 'Phew, what have you been eating, Ollie? It smells awful!' He wrinkled his nose as he picked up Ollie's poop and closed the bag with a knot.

Ollie scraped at the ground with his hind legs, throwing blades of grass and dirt right into his face. 'Stop!' Sebastian shouted indignantly, and Anna laughed amusedly. 'Ollie really is a pig!'

Susi sniffed at a shrub and peed, and immediately Ollie did a mighty jump to lift his leg on the same bush. At that moment a mobile phone rang. It was Ivory calling.

'Hi, Sebastian! I have thrilling news! My dad told me that Billy had a total break-down down after his arrest and confessed all sorts of things. And you know what? At the very end he claimed that Simon had murdered Thomas!'

'What?'

'Yes, but don't tell anyone, hey?' His excited voice turned into a whisper. 'Um, my father just called me, I have to go. Talk to you later!'

Anna asked curiously, 'What's up?'

Sebastian didn't know what to do. On the one hand, he didn't want to upset Ivory again by blurting out a secret. On the other hand, he wanted to reconcile with his sister. After yesterday's argument, their relationship still seemed a bit tense.

He bit his lips and said, 'Billy has testified that it was Simon, his own son, who killed Thomas!'

'I knew it: the gardener is always the murderer! Oh no, the other way round, I mean the murderer is always the gardener,' Anna said and began to laugh out loud.

Sebastian looked at her, appalled. 'It's not funny at all! And you mustn't tell anyone about this, you have to promise me!'

Anna snorted: 'You look like a scared rabbit!'

Sebastian got angry. 'Stop that nonsense and your silly giggling! Or I'll never tell you a secret again!'

'You'll never manage that anyway!' Anna teased him. 'You are and always will be a blabbermouth!'

'And you're a hysterical, silly goose!' Sebastian hissed.

Susi pinched her tail between her legs, mustering him worriedly, while Ollie nibbled at a tuft of grass with relish. Anna's amused face gave way to an angry expression. Unlike Sebastian, she hadn't taken their former argument so seriously, but now she was offended.

'You're a miserable gossip who can't be trusted! I'm going on without you,' she said angrily and turned around. 'Susi, come on!'

Susi was visibly confused and didn't want to leave her friends Sebastian and Ollie, and Anna had to drag her behind her. Sebastian stood there, petrified. His own sister did not trust him anymore? He had to pull himself together not to burst out in tears due to his anger and disappointment, and he slowly walked on, following the little dog without really looking at the path. Although the sun was now bright orange, his mood was dark. Anna jogged back home with Susi, and already on the way she regretted her harsh words.

* * *

Simon could have wept with rage. Someone had slit the rear tyres of his truck, and he couldn't drive away! Who had done this? He only had one spare tyre and didn't want to waste any time. Damn it! Even if he ordered a taxi or took a bus, he would definitely miss the train to Brisbane. His gaze fell on the old red car of a neighbour. It might be relatively easy to open and start it, and he would only borrow it to drive to the Nambour railway station. The road seemed deserted. And so, he quickly walked over to the rather rusty Subaru with the tinted windows. To his delight, the window on the driver's side was half open, and he cheered happily when he discovered that the key was in the ignition. He threw his luggage onto the next seat, sat down and was just about to drive off when he saw a gaunt, pale face in the rear-view mirror staring at him with fear-dilated eyes. Scared to death, he screamed out loud, jumped out of the car and ran away. He could no longer hear the hoarse croaking of the old woman on the back seat.

Fiona smiled and climbed down from the broad, densely foliaged tree where she had been patiently waiting for almost forty minutes. By the first light of dawn, she had slashed two tyres of Simon's car with a knife. She was glad that the first part of her plan had succeeded. Now, the man who might have been responsible for Maryann's death would not escape so easily. Although her limbs ached from sitting for so long on the branch of the huge Tuckeroo, she ran after Simon nimbly.

*   *   *

Sebastian had gone much further than he had intended and only now realised that he had unintentionally landed in the street where Arielle and Kate lived. Instinctively, he grabbed Ollie's leash tighter when he saw two joggers coming towards him, still not quite trusting his foster dog whose hunting zeal could be quickly awakened. The tall, muscular figure with the long hair was unknown to him, but the petite person, already close on his heels, was Fiona. Since when did Fiona go jogging? he wondered.

The young man suddenly stopped, shouting angrily, 'Oh no, my backpack!' He raised his arms in a dramatic gesture and turned around so abruptly that he collided with Fiona.

'Ow!' Fiona cried.

'What are you doing here?' the jogger asked.

'Hello, Simon! Um, I'm just, I'm just ...' Fiona stammered.

'Have you been spying on me?' Simon eyeballed her suspiciously.

Fiona thought desperately about the best answer. Her original idea had been to ask him if he could kindly give her the twenty dollars that Maryann still owed her, pretending that she had seen him just by coincidence. But when she faced Simon now, he appeared to her like a huge, grim Viking, and she got scared. So, she quickly changed her plan and said,

'You lost five bucks, and I wanted to give them back to you!'

She pulled a folded five-dollar note from her trouser pocket and handed it to him. Simon squinted his eyes. He had never been particularly fond of Fiona, but Maryann had taken the girl to her heart for some reason.

'Thanks! That's so nice of you!' Simon reached out his hand, but changed his mind, saying: 'Um, just keep the money and consider it a finder's fee!'

'Hey you! Are you trying to steal my dogs again?' a man snarled, stepping out of a front garden. He had a black Labrador on a leash and was accompanied by his daughter and a Jack Russell. It was Kate and her father with their dogs Abby and Patrick. Abby growled audibly while the Labrador wagged its tail in a friendly manner. Ollie yapped shrilly.

Simon moaned. Everything seemed to go wrong today! Now he had to meet the very people whose dogs he and Maryann had once stolen. And how could he be so stupid and forget his luggage with all his important papers and his money? Only because of an old, harmless woman he had taken off like a headless chicken! He needed his backpack! Hastily, he turned around, ignoring Kate's father.

Clinton was usually a gentle and calm person; but now the bile was rising in his throat. He would never forgive this man and his girlfriend for what they had done to his beloved dogs.

'Answer me, you lout!' he said curtly, reaching for Simon's shoulder.

Sebastian's blood seemed to stop in his veins. Due to Fiona's words, he understood that this young man was Simon, and without thinking, he cried out, 'Careful, he's a murderer!'

Clinton pulled his hand away as quickly as if he had burnt himself, and Kate gasped for air. Fiona turned pale. She had secretly suspected Simon of having killed Maryann and had been tailing him because of that, but now her knees were weak.

'Poor Maryann!' she murmured.

'Nah, he killed Thomas!' Sebastian said.

'What? Who are you?' Simon asked, perplexed.

Sebastian turned bright red. Anna was right, he really shouldn't be trusted with secrets, and he was an idiot! How would Simon react? The guy was huge and strong, and with his thoughtless exclamation he had put everyone in danger. Sebastian felt awkward. Most of all, he wanted the ground to swallow him up! Abby growled threateningly again, glaring at Fiona. Apparently, she remembered her abduction all too well. Simon was completely confused. But he decided not to waste any more time and to get the hell out of here. Again, he turned around and took off.

Both Sebastian and Fiona called out something like:

'We must not let him get away!' They smiled at each other, almost forgetting their former enmity.

'I better call Ivory and his dad!' Sebastian took his mobile phone and told Barry in brief about his chance encounter with Simon. Fiona then told the policeman the address of Simon's truck, also mentioning the slashed tyres but concealing the fact that she had been the assassin. Barry acted swiftly and informed his colleagues on duty straight away.

Clinton breathed a sigh of relief, glad to leave the matter in the hands of the police. He persuaded Fiona and Sebastian to have breakfast with them so that they could explain everything in more detail. Fiona quickly informed her parents, and Sebastian sent a text message to his sister: *I met Kate and have breakfast here. Her dad will drive Ollie and me home later. Please let our parents know! Best wishes from the stupid blabbermouth.*

Anna was happy to receive Sebastian's news because she had already been worried about him, constantly checking her watch. She wrote back: *Okay, enjoy! Hope you don't have to eat Vegemite or flabby sausages!*

Simon hurried on, fervently hoping to retrieve his backpack. The clothes in it weren't that important, but the money and his documents! He stopped abruptly, very close to the house in which he had lived for a while, renting the flat of a friend. No, he couldn't risk being caught. The old woman in the car had definitely informed others about his attempted theft. And his backpack in the car was proof enough. But what should he do? And why had this strange boy called him a murderer? He had no idea who he was! Simon broke out in a cold sweat, thinking, 'Billy must have tried to pin the murder of Thomas on me! What a bastard!'

Angrily, Simon clenched his fists and ran on, now heading for the next bus stop with a new plan. First, he would go to Maroochydore to visit a friend. He'd have his hair cut and dyed, and then he would travel by train in peace. He could live in Sydney for a while, or maybe in Melbourne. At least he had his wallet in his pocket! And luckily, he had instinctively seized the bag with his iPad in his hurried escape from the car. In addition, he had money hidden somewhere else, and somehow or other he would certainly succeed in establishing a new identity. Fortunately, he had no tattoos that could betray him.

He reached the bus stop with renewed confidence as a bus was approaching. He waved happily as a signal for the bus driver to stop. But at the same moment he received a push that made him stagger, and a policeman handcuffed him in no time at all. Simon was so surprised that he didn't even try to resist.

# 74 A SLY FOX

Sitting in the police car, Simon was sweating and freezing at the same time, alternately cursing his own stupidity and his father's rotten character. Despite his size and strength, Simon was enormously afraid of the prison and its inmates. He decided to come out with the whole truth, hoping his father should get the punishment he deserved! Simon was ready to admit all his deeds. Besides selling illegal drugs for his father and Alfred, he had occasionally hidden exotic animals in Martin's house. Martin had often been away on business or sailing trips and had never locked his back door. Since Simon had regularly maintained his garden, he hadn't aroused suspicion in the neighbourhood. He had no idea where the drugs and the animals came from, but he had been careful from the start not to ask too many questions. And he had always cleaned up Martin's house so that nobody would notice anything, like a bad odor from the wildlife. Luckily, Martin had lost his sense of smell, as Simon's father had noticed once when he'd almost burned a dish on Martin's yacht by accidence.

During his testimony, Simon became very agitated talking about his father.

'Because my dad had abandoned my mum when she'd got pregnant with me, I hated his guts. And it was very strange to finally meet him. I still despised him for a long time. And just when we started to get along better, he got scared of being exposed as a smuggler. Therefore, he faked his death in Indonesia and called himself Malcolm Millar ever since. But I still called him Billy when we were alone.'

Simon pulled a face.

'I guess he never even thought of my mother and me, after he'd left her, but it seems he loved his wife and daughter. As often as he could, he watched Astrid and Claudia from a distance, without daring to show his face even though he'd dyed his hair and looked quite different now. Unfortunately, at some point he ran into Thomas.'

He cleared his throat.

'Thomas was Maryann's boyfriend for a while. I didn't know him well, but he was a good-looking, likeable guy, and Maryann didn't take it too well when he broke up with her. However, he kept sticking his nose into things that were none of his business. He was friends with Claudia and her boyfriend Daniel. Somehow, Thomas noticed Billy often hanging around, watching Claudia. Thomas probably thought he was a pervert, and perhaps dangerous. He couldn't have known that he was her father and that he just longed for his family!'

Simon swallowed. 'I'd always wished for brothers and sisters, but of course I wasn't allowed to tell Claudia that her father hadn't drowned and that I was her half-brother!'

He rubbed his eyes, struggling to keep his composure. Then he went on, 'Thomas started to shadow not only Billy but also Tim, no idea why! And Billy panicked. There was no way he was going to let anybody mess up his good business. And he didn't want to end up in jail! And so ...' Simon was sobbing. 'And that's why he killed Thomas!'

\* \* \*

· 452 ·

Ivory had been angry as hell, both about himself and about Sebastian. He should have kept his mouth shut! How could Sebastian dare call Simon a murderer in public? Luckily, thanks to Fiona, they found out where Simon lived, and he was arrested near that address. Nevertheless, Ivory decided to be more careful in the future and not to reveal police secrets to anybody.

A few days after Simon's arrest, Mr. Little invited the Kuhlmann family, Bruce, Ivory's best friends and Fiona over to his house. It was a sunny, cloudless Saturday morning when the guests gathered in the living room. Because of Fiona, Kirsty almost stayed home sulking, but her curiosity won out in the end. She took a seat far away from her old enemy, though. Arielle looked pale and distraught, and Jack held her hand comfortingly. Kate had brought her Labrador Patrick along. It ran around the house for a while and then lay down on a runner. Ivory made sure everybody got a drink and Barry put some nibbles on the table.

'How did Billy manage to lure Thomas out of Daniel's house in the middle of the night?' Sebastian asked.

He was grateful that Ivory had forgiven him once again for being such a chatterbox.

Barry replied, 'Billy was a sly fox. He knew that Maryann would quickly become maudlin – and very talkative – whenever she drank too much alcohol. Over dinner with her and Simon, he grilled her about Thomas, her ex-boyfriend. Although she didn't say much good about him and was visibly in love with Simon, Billy got the impression that Thomas was soft-hearted. So, he came up with a diabolical plan. He stole Maryann's mobile phone, sent Thomas a text message in her name and ambushed him.'

'But how did he know where Thomas would stay that night?' Arielle asked in surprise.

'One day Billy overheard his daughter Claudia talking loudly on her phone. Thus, he found out that Thomas and his friend

John wanted to stay at Daniel's place that weekend. Since Martin's house is right behind it, Billy found the opportunity tempting. That same evening he visited Maryann and Simon, gave them heaps of booze and took her mobile phone, right after the young folks disappeared into the bedroom. He drove to Martin's house and waited there until Daniel's light was switched on. And then he wrote a text message to Thomas ...,' Barry hesitated.

'What did he write?' Kirsty asked curiously.

'I don't remember the exact words, but something like this: «Help! A man is following me! Don't call the police, it takes too long. I'm hiding in Daniel's front garden, come quickly! Be careful!» I think that's what Billy had told us.'

'What an evil man!' Jack said in indignation.

Barry went on, 'So, Thomas ran out of the house, worried, probably without thinking. Billy immediately threw a big bag over his head to prevent him from screaming and strangled him. He's a strong man.'

Arielle sobbed loudly and Patrick jumped up and licked her knee. Anna also got tears in her eyes.

'And then he dragged him to the park? How did he do that all by himself?' Lizzie felt nauseous remembering their discovery of the young dead man.

'Did Alfred help him?' asked Sebastian.

'No, he didn't. Well, long before that horrible deed, Alfred and Billy had been discussing how to deal with the snoopers, Tim and Thomas. In the end, Alfred paid bribes to my corrupt colleague so that Tim wouldn't interfere in their affairs any longer. And according to Billy, he suggested to give Thomas some hush money as well. But Billy was sick and tired of this boy spying on him. He had noticed him doing that several times, one day even brazenly taking photos of him, when he came out of a client's house with a suitcase full of cash.'

'We've seen that photo!' Sebastian called. 'And who was this customer? Had he bought illegal drugs?'

Fiona moaned softly. She, too, had often secretly taken photos of other people, and she had been shadowing Simon. She was glad that nothing had happened to her!

Andy frowned and said to his son, 'Don't interrupt Barry and let him finish!'

Barry smiled soothingly, took a sip of tea and continued:

'Anyway, Simon's father became more and more afraid of being exposed as a drug dealer and animal smuggler. Because he trusted Alfred completely, he told him about his plan to kill Thomas. However, Alfred was appalled by this idea. Alfred had no qualms about hurting, humiliating, or drugging other people, but murder? No, absolutely not! So, Billy turned to his old friend Conny. And she was willing to help him. Together they quickly loaded the body into her VW van, drove to the park and lifted Thomas over a fence and then onto the horse sculpture. The tools they used included a sturdy fishing line and a climbing rope. Conny is a sporty, strong woman who likes to swim and climb and who's ...'

'What? A woman helped him?' Lizzie shouted in outrage.

'Yes, unfortunately, women can be terribly brutal too! It was Conny's idea to put Thomas onto the sculpture, and also to dress him with a cap, a flipper and a glove, to give everyone a riddle. Apparently, Conny had found the cap and the flipper somewhere short before, and she added one of her own leather gloves.'

Kirsty said thoughtfully: 'I'd always wondered whether someone had done that to make it look like the act of a lunatic.'

'Or like a cruel prank by a youth or a drunk,' Kate said.

Barry nodded grimly. 'Yes, something like that must have been their reasoning. They must have thought it was funny!'

'Weren't they concerned about DNA and fingerprints?' Anna asked.

'I guess they didn't worry too much about that.'

'But why did Billy say that Simon had killed Thomas?' Arielle asked in a tearful voice.

'And why did he even mention Thomas at all? After all, he wasn't arrested for murder!' Jack wanted to know and lovingly squeezed the hand of his girlfriend.

'I think Billy lost his nerve when he was in custody. You're right, Jack, the police hadn't connected him with this murder case until then! Anyway, Billy suddenly thought he could blame his son, as Simon had often been in Martin's house and garden and as he'd been Maryann's boyfriend. So, he accused Simon of murder, saying he was jealous because Maryann still loved Thomas.'

'How mean to falsely accuse your own son!' Andy said indignantly.

'This is all nonsense! I read on my cousin's computer how much the two of them, Thomas and Maryann, hated each other in the end,' Arielle cried.

'Well, unfortunately, Thomas still had enough empathy left for his ex to help her in need!' Barry looked at her sadly. 'And he fell into the trap, the poor boy!'

'Did Billy throw away Maryann's phone afterwards?' Ivory asked. 'And how come the police didn't find this text message on Thomas' mobile phone although they checked it out?'

'Yes, that still mystifies me,' Barry admitted.

Arielle now shouted excitedly: 'I know the solution! Thomas still often had his old mobile with him because his new smartphone was losing its power so quickly. Gee, why didn't I think of that earlier? Billy must have found his old number when he sent that text. And Thomas took this phone with him just in case when he stormed out of the house to help Maryann. And Billy sure as hell destroyed it afterwards.'

Barry was impressed. 'That could explain everything if Thomas' old phone wasn't registered in his name.'

'What about Maryann's mobile phone?' Jack asked curiously.

'Of course, Billy immediately deleted his SMS to Thomas from her smartphone. And afterwards, he secretly put it in her handbag the next time he met Maryann and Simon. That's what Billy told the police. Meanwhile, that phone has disappeared without a trace.'

'A horrible story!' Lizzie sighed. 'Poor Thomas! And now Maryann is dead, too.'

Fiona murmured: 'Well, I suspected that Simon might have given Maryann an overdose of the 'FUN' for whatever reason. But perhaps it was Billy? Maybe she had found out about his drug dealing and the wildlife trafficking? Or even about the murder of Thomas, and he wanted to prevent her from dobbing him in?'

Fiona had been very surprised when Ivory invited her, and she felt a little uneasy and out of place. After all, she had regarded him and Kirsty as enemies since kindergarten, and she had noticed Kirsty's grim looks at her. Nevertheless, she was pleased to be able to take part in the conversation.

Bruce, who had been silent until now, looked at her in shock. 'You think so?'

'Well, Maryann certainly knew a few things,' Anna said. 'For example, at some point she told Daniel that Billy, now called Malcolm, was in fact Claudia's father who'd been believed to be missing, and that he was a rotten drug dealer.'

At the same moment she was annoyed with herself. Oh no, now she had blabbed something in the presence of Mr. Little, the policeman, which could get Daniel into trouble! She turned bright red and Sebastian had to grin.

'You're a blabbermouth too!' he whispered into her ear.

Barry looked at the siblings sharply for a moment, and then he said, 'Somehow, you all became more or less involved in these dramas. And that is why Ivory and I have asked you to come to this meeting. Most of all, however, I'd like to warn you: please learn from Thomas' tragic fate and never spy on criminals! And stop making any accusations prematurely! So, from now on, leave all investigations to the police, okay?'

'Okay!' Kirsty and Jack said, and everyone else nodded.

'Has Conny been arrested, too?' Sebastian asked.

Ivory smiled broadly. Even his father's stern look hadn't really intimidated Sebastian.

'Yes, luckily she was caught just in time when she was about to take off on her bicycle,' Barry explained.

Jack suddenly laughed out loud.

'In movies, gangsters are always chased in adventurous car races, but this woman was arrested on a bicycle and Simon was arrested on foot at the bus stop!'

Even Arielle now had to smile, and she patted Patrick who had put his head on her knee.

Bruce replied, 'That reminds me of the wild car chase in our town! Were the drivers Billy and Conny back then? Did they hit the woman on David Low Way and just took off?'

'Yes, it was them! Billy recognised Tim on the highway and got scared. He was very stupid to drive in that speed! But he was determined to prevent Tim from discovering his relationship with Conny. She was an old school friend of his and still a blank slate with the police. Billy lived with her for a while after his return from New South Wales, even though they never had a love affair.' Barry shook his head, adding grimly: 'It seems she's a horrible person, having no remorse whatsoever!'

'And Simon?' Fiona asked. 'Was he involved in the murders of Thomas and Maryann?'

This time, Ivory replied. 'Simon initially blamed Alfred for Maryann's death. She'd sometimes flirted shamelessly with Alfred, and so he suspected that they'd had a date and that Alfred had given her the 'FUN' powder in a drink, either without her knowledge or with her consent. Although Simon thought it was more likely to be an accident, he was very upset. In his rage, he sprayed the word 'MURDERER' on his Isuzu.'

He looked briefly at Fiona who had secretly filmed Simon during that spraying action. Fiona lowered her head in embarrassment and Kirsty suddenly felt admiration for the girl. Despite their years of quarrelling, she had the courage to meet with them today.

Barry took over again. 'But Alfred had been innocent in this regard, as by now we know that Billy killed Maryann! He had increasingly seen her as a threat and wanted to make sure she couldn't talk. Simon is still in shock. He hardly believes that his father, of all people, gave Maryann an overdose with malicious intent. He wishes he'd never met him. And he says he is sorry for his involvement in the drug business and would never deal with drugs again!' Barry growled gruffly. 'But we'll see! Maybe he just regrets that he hadn't been smarter and that he'd been arrested. And also ...'

'What did Simon know about Thomas?' Kate interrupted him. Hearing her voice, Patrick ran back to her, looking at his best friend with faithful eyes, and Kate lovingly stroked him.

'When Simon heard the news that the dead man in the AIRY TOES theme park was Thomas, he was aghast. At first, he suspected Maryann, as she seemed to hate her ex after he'd broken up with her. Furthermore, she had some truly intimidating acquaintances. But then he thought that his father and Alfred might have murdered Thomas, getting rid of the young man who'd kept spying on Billy. But Simon didn't really want to believe that either, so he simply suppressed the terrible story from his mind.' Barry sighed briefly and then turned to Sebastian.

'You were very careless to call Simon the murderer of Thomas! I know you intended to warn Kate's father, but it was dangerous and could have caused big trouble. Simon was completely confused by your exclamation, until he suddenly realised that his father must really have been the murderer. Because who else would try to blame him for everything? And once again, Simon's old hatred for his father was rekindled. Billy had not only killed Thomas and then tried to pin the blame on him but had also killed Maryann.'

'And what will the punishment for Simon be?' Anna asked.

'Well, that remains to be seen. In any case, he was involved in many crooked deals. And probably some other people will be arrested who have either bought illegal drugs or exotic animals from this evil group.'

# 75 FATE

Aunt Heidi and Uncle Wayne still cried very often. The violent death of their beloved son had left gaping psychological wounds that would never heal one hundred percent. But they were grateful that the murderer and his ghastly female accomplice had finally been caught. Arielle also missed her cousin dreadfully. Luckily, Jack, her dog Max and her cat Sniff made her laugh often, and she was happy to be friends with Kate, Kirsty, Ivory and Sebastian.

Fiona mourned for Maryann whom she had almost regarded as a sister. She still couldn't make friends with her classmates, but from now on she left them alone, and the others treated her kindly since their meeting with Mr. Little.

Billy was in prison pondering about his fate. The only thing he really regretted, though, was his behaviour towards Astrid and Claudia and that he had left them for his own safety. He had missed them so much! And yet, only his strong wish to see them again, at least from a distance, had raised the suspicion of Thomas and caused the fatal consequences.

To Simon's great surprise and delight, Astrid and Claudia visited him in prison. They treated him like a long-lost relative, even though they had never known him before. Astrid and her daughter also visited Tim, and they forgave him but not Billy.

They didn't want to have anything to do with a vicious murderer and drug dealer! And they were appalled that he had faked his own death, leaving them to mourn him. Moreover, being very fond of animals, they were horrified at how little compassion he had shown for the animals he had sold. They assumed many creatures had perished miserably in captivity.

Daniel voluntarily went to the local police station. He contritely confessed that he had learned a little about Malcolm alias Billy from Maryann, but had remained silent in fear for the lives of Maryann, himself and also Claudia and her mother. To his relief he got off with a warning. And he stayed together with Claudia.

The Kuhlmanns remembered that they had seen Billy's accomplice once, namely at the cliffs of Mount Coolum where they had admired her climbing skills. Now Conny had to serve her sentence and would hopefully never be able to climb any prison walls to escape.

And another case was solved. It turned out that Steven Owen had also worked for Billy and Conny, selling drugs on the Sunshine Coast. The young man named Jim who had attacked him and had been arrested, finally spoke out, revealing the reason for his King Hit. At some point in the past, Jim had discovered that his father had become a user of the dreadful 'FUN', delivered to him by Steven. For many months, Jim was very upset to see the suffering of his dad. But he never intended to kill Steven. By pure chance, he spotted him on his way to a pub one evening. Suddenly he was so furious that he lost his head and hit him. Meanwhile, his father had died, so Jim was no longer afraid to testify about his dad's former illegal drug possession. And now just the memory of his brutal King Hit filled Jim with remorse and the deepest horror. With a single blow, he had not only ended Steven's life but also ruined his own, and he would have to stay in prison for a long time.

\*    \*    \*

Lizzie watched Susi and Ollie play, feeling content. Finally, the murders of Thomas and Maryann were solved. And also the other sinister events that had shaken up their daily lives. She hoped that the 'FUN' powder had been completely destroyed and would never be distributed again. Her neighbour Melissa was serving a prison term, but she was in good spirits and full of plans for the future. Her husband Gabriel turned out to be a fine, helpful man, and he was confident that Melissa would be able to cope better with her life.

Lizzie had to smile when she heard the loud laughter of Andy, Anna and Bruce. Andy had overcome his aversion to Anna's boyfriend, and they actually got on very well. Currently, her husband was teaching them 'Skat', a three-person card game that he had often played in Germany.

Sebastian put his crime novel aside, asking rather himself than his mother, 'Why do people like me enjoy reading about such creepy things?'

When he thought of the leather glove on the back of the horse sculpture, he still felt freezing cold. Nevertheless, he would really like to visit the 'AIRY TOES' theme park again!

At that moment the phone rang and Kirsty gushed out happily: 'Hi, Sebastian! Mum's boyfriend has invited us to go to the climbing forest. Would you and Susan like to come along? And Ellen absolutely wants you to bring Anna!'

# NOTES BY THE AUTHOR

Most of the places described in the book (for example, the 'Tickle Park') are real, but the plot is fictitious, and the 'AIRY TOES theme park' with the barefoot path, a climbing forest, the 'Garden of the Seven Senses' and the unusual sculptures only exists in my imagination.

Coolum Beach, often just called 'Coolum', is a town in South East Queensland. Very interesting information about its history and the first settlers of this area can be found in the historical books of Frances and John Windolf in the libraries of the Sunshine Coast, such as 'An Island Surrounded by Land'.

I invented the 'Moist Nose Rescue Organisation' for my novel. However, some of the dog stories in this book are based on similar events that I experienced with my own dogs and various foster dogs. Some time ago I was a volunteer for the '4 Paws Animal Rescue', taking care of foster dogs until they could be rehomed. But I have changed the names and descriptions of all dogs and their owners.

If I have used any wrong English words or odd sounding phrases, I do apologise! I also ask for your indulgence, as I have taken literary liberties in this novel. Some parts of the text, such as comments on police work, investigations and arrests at the scene, punishments and first aid procedures, may not correspond to the facts. The powder and its terrible effects on people and animals in my story are pure imagination.

# ABOUT THE AUTHOR

*Marion Birkenbeil* was born in Wuppertal, Germany in 1963. After working as a horticulturist and landscape gardener for many years, she studied landscape architecture. She immigrated to Australia in 1997 and lived in Brisbane for some time. Later, she and her husband (and their dog) moved to the Sunshine Coast. Marion is a self-employed landscape architect and became a registered member of the Australian Institute of Landscape Architects in 2007. Her novels reflect her love of nature and dogs. And although her books are fictional, she likes to include some real places and events. She hopes that her readers will enjoy her stories!

# OTHER BOOKS BY MARION BIRKENBEIL

**Scheherazades Finger Food**
Books on Demand. Language: German

**Unser Schweigen schützte die Täter**
Books on Demand. Language: German

**Der Mann mit den gelben Turnschuhen**
Books on Demand. Language: German

**Bake a Cake – Backe einen Kuchen**
Books on Demand. Language: Bilingual, German and English

**BH über dem Pulli**
Books on Demand. Language: German　.

**Bra over Jumper – My Mum has Alzheimer's**
IngramSpark. Language: English

**Deadly Datura**
IngramSpark. Language: English

## Marion's website:

https://m-birkenbeil-autorin.jimdofree.com

# Deadly Datura

The Kuhlmanns, a German family of four, have immigrated to Australia. They are thrilled with the beautiful Sunshine Coast, the friendly and helpful people and the fascinating wildlife. So many animals are unique to Australia! A dream comes true for Anna and Sebastian when their parents adopt a dog. Taking Susi for long walks on the dog-friendly beaches, they feel as though they were living in paradise. But one day, two teenagers discover a woman's body in dense bushland along Stumers Creek. Everyone is shaken! A murder in their own town? What was the motive? Nobody seems to have a clue. Lizzie Kuhlmann is worried about her children who are constantly playing detective. Why won't they stop talking about the grisly crime?

## Bra over Jumper – My Mum has Alzheimer's

Michael, 47 years of age, is living on the Sunshine Coast in Queensland, in a beautiful part of Australia. However, his life is not always cheerful. After fifteen years of marriage, his wife Tina wants to split up and stay in their house. Fortunately, he finds a small rental property and keeps the company of his beloved dog. But he becomes increasingly worried about his mother in Brisbane, since she suffers from Alzheimer's disease. One day she almost starts a kitchen fire by accident. What should he do? He and his brother have to find a solution, and fast! Just when Michael thinks he has everything under control, a mysterious murder happens nearby. Someone finds a half-naked, lifeless woman in a park in Coolum Beach. Who killed her, and why? Michael is horrified, as Tina is living in this normally peaceful seaside town. It turns out that the murdered woman was a nurse named Maureen. But many months pass by without any hints about the culprit and his motive. Maureen's sister and her parents are inconsolable. Michael and Tina can't forget the gruesome deed either, and Tina is more anxious than ever before. And then an acquaintance of them disappears without a trace. Meanwhile, Michael's mother no longer recognises her own sons ...

www.ingramcontent.com/pod-product-compliance
Lightning Source LLC
Chambersburg PA
CBHW020241120726
47904CB00001B/56